Praise f

SMALL ACTS O

"In *Small Acts of Defiance*, Michelle Wright paints
a beautifully intimate portrait that celebrates the
courage and resilience of the human spirit."

Jane Harper, author of *The Survivors*

"Wright has engaged in meticulous research, creating an authentic
and gripping tale. *Small Acts of Defiance* is historical fiction of
the highest order. Lucie's involvement with the French Resistance
and the sacrifices she makes to protect the lives of those she loves
is riveting and authentic, laced with fascinating detail. Myriad
twists and turns keep the reader guessing until the very last page.
Wright's prose is elegant, taut, and masterfully controlled . . .
An engrossing, deeply satisfying read, one of the year's
outstanding, not-to-be-missed debuts."

Melissa Ashley, author of *The Birdman's Wife*

"A powerful and elegantly wrought story of women's
resistance. This is required reading for our times."

Myfanwy Jones, author of *Leap*

"*Small Acts of Defiance* is a gripping, meticulously researched
novel and a nuanced, poetic, and deeply serious exploration of the
difference that individual choices can make in a society crumbling
physically and morally. Wright re-creates occupied Paris with
immediacy and with melancholy tenderness, and asks questions
about personal responsibility that are just as relevant today as
they were eighty years ago. This is a book to savor and treasure."

Lee Kofman, author of *Imperfect*

SMALL
ACTS
OF
DEFIANCE

MICHELLE
WRIGHT

WILLIAM MORROW
An Imprint of HarperCollins*Publishers*

HarperCollins books may be purchased for educational, business, or sales promotional use. For information, please email the Special Markets Department at SPsales@harpercollins.com.

Originally published as *Small Acts of Defiance* in Australia in 2021 by Allen & Unwin.

FIRST U.S. EDITION

Library of Congress Cataloging-in-Publication Data has been applied for.

ISBN 978-0-06-322390-5

22 23 24 25 26 LSC 10 9 8 7 6 5 4 3 2 1

For my mother, "Yvonne" Claudette Wright

1940

1

THE PRE-DAWN CHILL of the pavement leached through the soles of Lucie's feet as she stood in her cotton nightie and gazed at the empty space where her family's house had been. Though her toes and fingers were numb, there was a heavy throbbing in both her palms. She looked down and saw the blood dripping from her fingertips, splashing on the tops of her bare feet, running down between her toes. She pushed her palms against her thighs, clenching wads of fabric in her fists, and searched among her shattered thoughts. Gradually the images took shape—the breaking glass, the jagged shards, crawling through the window of her burning bedroom.

On the footpath a few yards away, her mother, Yvonne, stood wrapped in a blanket, mumbling softly to herself, repeating over and over in French, "*Mon Dieu*, Alfred. *Mon Dieu*." Lucie went to her side and put an arm around her waist. Yvonne shuddered, then was quiet.

Lucie gazed back at the fragmented outline of the place she'd called home for the past sixteen years. It looked like a pen-and-ink sketch—just a few straight lines with shades of charcoal gray. A breeze blew through the blackened frame, lifting tiny flakes of ash that fluttered into the street. They settled on her hair and skin, powdery like snow.

All was strangely still now after the cacophony of the fight to extinguish the blaze: water, shouts, bells. And then the silence that came with the stretcher bearers—like those she'd seen in her father's sketches from the Great War, white sheets draped over frozen bodies, stiff arms grasping at the air. Lucie shut her eyes tight against the image of her father's body being carried down the gravel path.

From the gathered crowd, she'd heard the muffled question: "How could this have happened?"

But when Lucie pictured her father's face that day last September, she knew the real question was: How could it have not? And though she tried not to hear it, there was another question ringing in her head . . . Had he meant to kill her and Yvonne as well?

* * *

When Lucie searched her memories of their life together in Kilcunda, she could count on one hand the conversations with her father. She remembered the last one all too well. It was the fourth of September the previous year—her sixteenth birthday. The day before, they'd learned of Hitler's invasion of Poland, and Great Britain's declaration of war against Germany. Lucie and her parents had listened to Prime Minister Menzies' speech late that evening, informing the nation that, as a result, Australia too was now at war.

The next evening, after Lucie had blown out the candles on her cake, Alfred opened a drawer in the buffet and took out a small rectangular package wrapped in crumpled tissue paper.

"Happy birthday," he said, laying it on the table in front of her.

She unwrapped the parcel to reveal a sketchpad bound in leather and a set of pencils. It was a surprising gift, not one she'd have expected from her father. She'd always loved to draw, but this was the first time he'd acknowledged her interest.

When Alfred spoke again, it was as he always did—in short, unadorned phrases; like telegrams sent without expectation of a response.

"You're a young woman now. Living in the adult world," he said. "It's a brutal place. You'll need art to make sense of it."

Yvonne laughed nervously. "That's a bit somber for a birthday wish, isn't it, Alfred?"

Her husband frowned at a wine stain on the tablecloth. "There are somber times ahead."

Yvonne pulled on a piece of skin next to her thumbnail. "Well, it's lovely that you're encouraging Lucie to draw," she said brightly. "I think she's inherited your talent."

Lucie looked at her father. His head was still bowed.

"I didn't know you drew, Dad," she said.

Alfred didn't respond.

"He was very talented," said Yvonne. "When we first met in Paris, he showed me his sketches from the Western Front." She turned to her husband. "Your drawings were so tragic, so powerful. Perhaps you could show Lucie your sketchbook? I think it might still be down in the basement."

"No, I don't think so," said Alfred, rubbing at the wine stain, smudging its edges into the cloth. "I'm sure I threw it away."

After her parents had gone to bed, Lucie crept downstairs to the basement, determined to see if her father's sketchbook was there. After a few minutes of searching, she found it in the bottom of a dusty crate. As she pulled it out, she glimpsed a movement in her peripheral vision and turned to see her father standing in the doorway.

"I'm sorry, Dad," she said. "I should have asked your permission."

Alfred slowly came down the stairs and sat on the bottom step.

"Go ahead," he said. "Take a look. You might as well know what's coming."

Lucie hesitated, then knelt, the sketchbook on the floor in front of her. She opened the stiff, leather cover and leaned forward to study the drawings. They weren't the quick field sketches she'd expected. The pen-and-ink illustrations had been worked and reworked over time; precisely, meticulously, unflinching in their detail. Wounded soldiers crying out in agony. A man with only half a face. Corpses decomposing in the mud. Lucie took a deep breath in—the dank, earthy scent of the basement settling like silt in her throat. She tried to imagine her father's eyes moving back and forth between the paper and the scene before him, only his pen to translate the indescribable. She wondered if these were the images that visited him while he slept. His screams had punctuated Lucie's nights for as long as she could remember.

She closed the sketchbook and looked up at him.

"So now you know why," he said.

Lucie wasn't sure what he meant, but she knew it was useless to press him for an explanation. She'd seen other men like her father, with scars both visible and not; some veterans of the war, some who'd fought the devastating Black Friday bushfires back in January that year. That was why people around these parts knew not to ask too many questions. Everyone had suffered. Everyone was tired of remembering.

Alfred brought his hand to his forehead and pulled on a strand of greasy hair. "And now there's going to be another horror like the last one," he said. "Well, I did my duty once, and I saw the result." He nodded towards the sketchbook.

"But you're not a soldier anymore, Dad," Lucie reminded him. "You won't have to do anything this time."

"There's no such thing as doing nothing," her father replied. "Doing nothing is still a choice. A choice to stand aside and let it happen."

Lucie didn't know what to say; she'd never heard her father speak this way. In his eyes she saw something she hadn't seen before: a look of utter desolation.

When she went back up to her bedroom, Lucie sat at her desk and took a pencil from the drawer. Opening the sketchbook Alfred had given her to the first page, she started to draw her father's face. She examined his features one by one, pulling each into focus. She had always been told she looked nothing like him, that she was the spitting image of Yvonne. It was true that she had her mother's rounded cheeks, the same small chin, the same straight auburn hair. But Lucie had always thought she had her father's eyes—dark and slightly melancholy. As she continued the portrait, she tried hard to capture the expression she'd seen in those eyes just minutes before, tried to understand the thoughts that lay behind.

* * *

Four months later, standing barefoot on the pavement with the odor of destruction in her nostrils, Lucie knew she should be grieving the loss of her father. Instead, what she felt was grief for the father she'd never known. She recalled the look in his eyes that night in the basement. She hadn't understood it then, and she still didn't now. She wondered if she ever would.

2

FOR THE NEXT month, Yvonne and Lucie lived in a cottage that the headmistress of Lucie's school, Miss Freeman, let them use for free. She was exceptionally kind to them. She was also very discreet, telling the students and their parents that the fire had been caused by a frayed electrical wire. No one questioned her explanation—except, of course, the Catholic Church and Empire Assurance Company, both experts in the uncovering of "willful self-destruction." The Church denied Alfred a funeral and Empire refused to pay out on either the house or life insurance policy.

When they informed her, Yvonne didn't dispute the findings. She'd guessed what was coming. That evening as she washed the dishes with Lucie, she told her daughter of the decision she had made.

"I've written to my brother in France to ask for his assistance." She spoke in French, as she always did when the two of them were alone.

Lucie put down the plates she was carrying. "I didn't even know you had a brother. Why have you never mentioned him?"

"We haven't had any contact in a long time."

"Why not?" asked Lucie.

Yvonne paused and pushed a strand of hair from her cheek with the back of her hand.

"Gérard wasn't happy about my decision to marry your father and move to Australia. He thought I should stay and help rebuild our country after the war."

Lucie paused, struggling to imagine how someone could make such a demand.

"Were you close before that?"

Yvonne nodded. "When I was young, yes. We were quite close, actually. He is ten years older, but I adored him and he doted on me. He was very protective." She ran her fingers across the surface of the water. "I was fourteen when he went off to the war. He was away for three and a half years. After he was wounded he was captured by the Germans. They sent him to a prison camp. When he returned, he was a different person."

Lucie handed her more dishes.

"Is he married?"

"He was," said Yvonne, pushing the plates below the surface of the water, "but his wife died in childbirth a year after your father and I left for Australia."

"That's so sad," said Lucie. "Was the baby all right?"

"It was a little girl. Gérard wanted me to go back to France to help look after her, but I couldn't—you were just a newborn yourself, and we were so far away." She rinsed a plate and handed it to Lucie. "He was living in Paris; the apartment we grew up in. It was big, so he would have had room for us. That wasn't the problem. But things were difficult in France after the war. Food was still being rationed, there was terrible unemployment, and so many people dying of the Spanish flu. I didn't want to take a little baby back to such a situation."

"He must have understood that," said Lucie.

"I don't know. We never discussed it. And his little one died of pneumonia when she was three." Yvonne pulled another plate from the sink, but held it dripping in her hand. "He took it very hard."

Gérard had written her long, rambling letters at the time, she explained, cursing the Germans for the death of his wife and daughter. He blamed them for the misery the war had brought to France, for the lack of coal to banish the winter cold from his home, for the malnourishment they'd endured for so many years.

"Anything he could blame them for, he did," she said. "Even when things improved, and he was doing well enough to buy a country house in Normandy, he was still bitter. And then, about ten years ago, he stopped writing."

"Do you think he'll be willing to help you after so long?"

Yvonne pulled the plug from the sink and watched the water drain away.

"Hopefully," she said. "I don't think money is a concern for him nowadays. If he could just lend me enough to buy a small house, that's all we'd need. I don't think he'll deny me that."

* * *

One February evening a month or so later, Lucie went down to the beach. She waded out to her knees and unwound the bandages from her hands for the last time, trailing them through the waves. The cuts had been deep but had healed well. She was left with a series of scars; fine white lines that crossed and followed the deep creases of her palms and wrapped themselves around her hands.

The sun had just set, but the air was still warm when Lucie arrived back at the cottage. Yvonne was standing in the kitchen holding a letter, the skin of her cheeks blotched red and white.

"It's from Gérard," she said. She spoke quickly, hardly pausing to take a breath. "He's only sent a small sum of money. Nowhere near enough for a house. He says that's all he can afford."

"What are we going to do?" asked Lucie.

Yvonne pulled out a chair at the table and sat down.

"He says we should come and stay with him in Paris. He's already booked tickets for us."

Lucie took the letter from Yvonne's hands and scanned the tightly scrawled words. "But how can we go to France when there's a war?"

Yvonne brought a hand up to her throat and wiped the sweat away. "It's just a phony war for the moment. There's been no real fighting."

"But no one knows when it might begin," replied Lucie.

"Gérard doesn't seem concerned," said Yvonne. "He's confident it'll be over in a short time. France and Germany have always fought over territory. The Germans probably just want to win back the Alsace and Lorraine regions they lost in the last war."

Lucie sat down next to her mother. "It's so far away, though. I won't know anyone there."

"I know, *ma chérie*. But I don't think we have a choice." She squeezed Lucie's wrist, a smile pulled tight across her lips. "We'll make a new home in France. You'll see. We'll start a whole new life."

* * *

A week later, Lucie was wiping down the kitchen counter when Miss Freeman appeared at the open front door.

"Oh, good, you're still here," she said. "I was afraid I might have missed you. When are you leaving?"

"We're taking the train to Melbourne at eleven. Our ship sails tomorrow morning."

"Well, I'm glad I caught you. I found this in your desk at school."

She held out the sketchbook that Lucie's father had given her for her birthday. "I thought you might want it."

Lucie had taken it to school the day after her birthday and hidden it in her desk. She hadn't drawn anything in it since the portrait of her father.

"Did you do this?" asked Miss Freeman, opening the book to the first page.

"I'm sorry," said Lucie. "I shouldn't have had it at school."

Miss Freeman cut her off. "No, don't apologize. It's very good. A beautiful portrait." She handed Lucie the sketchbook. "You have a talent for art," she said. "I hope you'll use it one day."

After Miss Freeman left, Lucie studied the sketch of her father, trying to make sense of who he'd been and of his final actions. She thought she might have begun to understand, but he was still no more than a shadow. She tore out the page, folded it in four, and put it in her pocket. She left the house and walked towards the beach, following the damp sand beside the creek. As she passed under the trestle railway bridge, she stopped and slid the paper from her pocket, then reached up and wedged it tight between the thick round upright and one of the diagonal beams. She hoped that someone would find it there one day. Perhaps they would be able to make sense of it.

***

The next morning, Lucie stood at the railing of the RMS *Orontes*, her home for the next four weeks. She'd looked at the route they'd be taking. Fremantle, Colombo, Port Aden, Port Said, the Suez Canal, Marseille, London, and finally a ferry across the English Channel to France. She struggled to define what she was feeling as they prepared to leave. Anticipation at discovering the land of her mother's birth, and the majesty and beauty of Paris was undercut by a growing uncertainty about what awaited them there. She would be living with an uncle she'd never met, in a strange and crowded city. And despite Yvonne's assurances that they'd be safe in France, she worried about what it would mean to live in a country officially at war with its powerful neighbor.

As the last mooring lines were cast off and the ship began to pull away from the dock, Lucie looked at Yvonne standing a few yards further along the railing. She tried to imagine how her mother must be feeling about returning to Paris after all these years. She was barely twenty when she left; she was now a woman of forty-one. Lucie took her sketchbook from her handbag and started drawing the outline of Yvonne's face. It wasn't turned to the crowds down on the pier but up towards the overcast sky, limp strands of auburn hair escaping from a carelessly fastened bun. Lucie drew her in profile, her eyes half closed, the mist of the cool March morning condensing on the warm skin of her cheeks. When she'd finished, she tore the page from the book and folded it in four. She leaned over the railing and let the paper fall. It fluttered and spun in the upward draughts and eddies, and then was lost among the paper streamers that stretched from the ship to the pier below. Lucie felt like she was floating too—between the past she was leaving and the future that awaited.

3

WHEN THEIR FERRY from Portsmouth docked in Le Havre, Lucie and Yvonne disembarked and waited with their luggage on the quay. Once the crowd had cleared, Yvonne put her hand on Lucie's shoulder and pointed out a tall, thin man advancing towards them. He walked with a slight limp, a lopsided roll of his hips.

As he stopped in front of them, he removed his faded blue workman's cap to reveal light brown hair, plastered down, with strands of gray that sprang up from his scalp. The skin of his cheeks was tight and red, as if he'd scrubbed his face with steel wool. A tobacco-stained moustache curled down over his upper lip. He leaned towards Yvonne and kissed her on each cheek.

Lucie smiled at him. "*Bonjour*, Oncle Gérard," she said.

He glanced over and cleared his throat. "Just Gérard will do," he said. "It feels odd to have a stranger call me *uncle*."

Lucie hesitated before responding, taken aback by the coolness of his tone. "Of course," she replied.

Gérard fiddled with the set of keys he was holding, then looked at Yvonne. "I'm sorry about Alfred," he muttered.

Yvonne took a deep breath and turned her head, her eyes searching left and right. "We should get going. Where did you park?"

Gérard found a trolley and piled their luggage onto it. As he strode along the quay, Yvonne and Lucie hurried to keep up with him. On the street outside, he loaded their cases into the back of a van emblazoned with the words *Déménagement Hébert*—Hébert Removalists—and the three of them climbed into the front seat.

As they drove out of Le Havre, Lucie gazed out the window, eager to see the French countryside, but the fatigue of the journey caught up with her and within minutes she was asleep.

When she woke, it was almost four o'clock and they were already in Paris, practically at the foot of the Eiffel Tower. She craned her neck to see the top.

"I can't believe it," she said.

Yvonne squeezed her hand and smiled.

Continuing along the river, they crossed a majestic bridge adorned with gilded sculptures, then rounded a vast open space with a huge Egyptian obelisk at its center. They cut across to a long, wide street, one side lined with stone arcades. Through metal railings high on the right, Lucie caught glimpses of vast, formal gardens filled with people sitting, walking, children running, riding ponies. Looming ahead was an ornate building that she recognized as the Louvre. It was so much bigger than she'd imagined. Its sculpture-studded walls seemed to go on forever. They continued until they saw the Cathedral of Notre-Dame, standing strong and solemn on its island in the very heart of the city. Gérard turned left down a street that led away from the river and into a residential area. He told Lucie that their apartment was in the fourth arrondissement. The area was called Le Marais as it had once been swampland. The streets they drove along were narrow and filled with people, most of the buildings ancient and dilapidated. Some, though, were elegant, with wide *porte-cochères* and large courtyards or gardens.

"Here we are," said Gérard as they pulled up outside a building on the rue de Sévigné. Lucie noticed that the facade was quite ornate compared to most of the other apartment buildings in the area, although the details were encrusted with soot and grime.

Gérard got out and opened the heavy wooden doors leading into the courtyard. "I'll unload your belongings and then take the van back to the garage," he said.

As they drove in, a small woman who looked to be in her fifties appeared from behind a narrow door.

"Ah, Monsieur Hébert. You're back."

Gérard nodded. "*Bonjour*, Madame Maurel." He laid his hand on Yvonne's shoulder. "Do you remember my sister?"

"*Bonjour*, Madame," said Yvonne. "You haven't changed at all."

"Oh well, a few more wrinkles, perhaps. But I would have recognized you anywhere, Mademoiselle Hébert." She pressed both hands against her cheeks. "But I should say Madame Blackburn. Your brother told me about the tragic loss of your husband. I'm so sorry."

Yvonne nodded. "*Merci*, Madame."

"And this must be your daughter," continued Madame Maurel. "Welcome, Mademoiselle. I'm the building's concierge. If you need anything, don't hesitate to ask—I'm almost always in my lodge. And if I'm out, I won't be far, just cleaning or doing the daily mail delivery. In any case, my son will be here keeping an eye on the comings and goings."

"Thank you, Madame," said Yvonne. "We're very happy to be here, aren't we, Lucie?"

Lucie smiled and nodded. She glanced towards the door of the lodge, but saw no sign of Madame Maurel's son.

Sharing the luggage between them, they climbed the wide wooden stairs to the fourth floor. Gérard opened the door of the apartment and stood aside to let Lucie and Yvonne in. Yvonne put her bag down and took a few steps from the entrance hall into the living room.

"It looks different from how I remember it," she said.

"I had to divide it in two and sell off the other half a few years ago to keep my business going," said Gérard. "There have been so many people arriving, migrants from the east. They came in their thousands, moved in, set up shop, created competition. As if it wasn't hard enough already." He hung his jacket and cap on a hook behind the door and ran his hand across his scalp, smoothing down his hair. "They've completely taken over the quarter. Did you see how it's changed since we were children? Our grandparents wouldn't recognize the area."

Lucie could tell the apartment had once been quite elegant. In the living room, floor-to-ceiling windows overlooked the street and there was a fireplace with a pink marble mantelpiece. Above it hung a large mirror, the gilt of its frame peeling and worn, black stains seeping from the edges of the silver-backed glass. In addition to a couch and armchair, a dining table, chairs, and buffet were crowded against a wall. Lucie realized the original dining room must now be on the other side, part of another apartment. There were only two of the original bedrooms. Gérard had moved his things into the smaller one and given his to Yvonne. Lucie stood in the doorway as he dragged his sister's trunk in and pushed it against the foot of the bed. The room was dark and masculine, the walls adorned with the heads of deer and wild boar.

After he'd carried all their luggage in, her uncle showed Lucie to where she'd be sleeping, a small room next to the kitchen that looked as though it had once been a storeroom. He'd added a narrow bed, pushed tight against the wall with a wooden shelf fixed above it, as well as a small desk and chair.

"There's a maid's room on the top floor, but I'm renting it to a couple from Alsace for extra money. Otherwise I'd have put you in there."

"This is more than adequate," said Yvonne, squeezing Lucie's forearm as they stood together in the doorway. Lucie nodded at Gérard. Although he turned away almost immediately, she noticed the expression of shame that swept across his face.

After they'd unpacked their cases, they joined Gérard in the living room. Yvonne presented her brother with a merino wool cap in a mustard-and-black check.

"A small gift from Australia," she said.

Gérard took the cap from her and turned it around in his hands, running an index finger along the leather trimmed edge, his thumbs pressed into the satin lining underneath.

"A bit fancy for a laborer," he said.

Lucie saw the disappointment in her mother's eyes. She didn't know whether Gérard saw it too, but he paused before clearing his throat. "Thank you, Yvonne," he added. "It'll be very useful."

The three of them sat together at the oilcloth-covered dining table and Gérard poured them each a glass of deep red cordial.

"Made with cherries from my property in Normandy," said Gérard. "I had to sell the house in thirty-one, but I managed to keep a shed and a bit of land with fruit trees. I go there from time to time, spend a night or two when I can. It's good to get out of the city. There's a folding bed in the shed and a wood stove. That's all I need."

Yvonne gazed out the window at the stone facades and rows of windows and wrought-iron balconies on the opposite side of the street.

"It's strange to be back," she said. "I didn't think I'd ever see Paris again."

Gérard drank a mouthful of cordial. "It was the end of one war that separated us and the start of another that reunites us."

Yvonne took a small sip of her drink. "Let's hope this one won't last as long."

"There's no need to hope," said Gérard, wiping the condensation from his glass with the side of his thumb. "We're well prepared. Germany stands no chance against our troops."

Yvonne took another sip. "I don't know if Herr Hitler would agree," she remarked, setting her glass back down. "He seems quite confident in the might of his armed forces."

"Herr Hitler can believe what he likes," said Gérard. "There's no greater fighting force in Europe than the French army. We'll show the English how it's done." He wiped his palms together, as if washing his hands of the argument.

Lucie's mother raised her glass to her lips again, but this time she didn't drink. She stared into the bright rose-colored liquid. The light hanging low over the table reflected off its surface and turned the whites of her eyes a watery pink.

"I'm tired," she said, putting the glass down. "If you'll excuse me, I think I'll have a lie-down before dinner."

Gérard watched as she left the table and closed the bedroom door behind her, then took a small sheet of paper from the pocket of his trousers and laid it flat on the table. He ran his finger along the lines of words and figures, chewing on his moustache as he read. Outside, the sky had begun to cloud over, but a thin ray of afternoon sun shone through the tall windows. In the slanted light, Lucie had her first good look at Gérard. His features were hard and precise, as if painted on. The curve of his nose and the arcs of his nostrils were outlined in thin, dark strokes. His eyes were paler than Yvonne's, almost colorless, like a winter's sky on a day of low gray clouds. They looked alert, on edge, as if waiting for an accusation. Two vertical lines like quotation marks were etched between his gray-flecked brows.

He finished his drink and cleared his throat.

"I'll take the van back to the garage now," he said, folding the sheet and slipping it back into his pocket. "I have to finish the paperwork I should have done today. Don't wait for me for dinner. There's beef and potatoes in the kitchen."

He got up from the table, took his cap and jacket from the hook behind the front door, and left without saying anything more.

Lucie went to her room and took the sketchpad from her bag. She sat at the small desk and started drawing Gérard's face. She wanted to understand this new person who was suddenly at the center of her life, on whom she and Yvonne were totally dependent. He was taking them into his home, providing for them, keeping them safe. Although she hardly knew him, she felt a tinge of pity for her uncle. She imagined he too was still carrying the pain of the war that had so damaged her father. She softened the lines of his nose and eyes, and drew him with his mouth half open, as if he was slowly breathing out, getting ready for a difficult task. When she finished, she tore the drawing from the pad and folded it tight. In the kitchen she opened a small window and dropped the paper, watching as it fluttered down four stories and landed in the tiny enclosed courtyard below.

***

When Gérard came home late that evening, Lucie was already in her room seated on the edge of the narrow bed. Through the thin wall, she heard him come into the kitchen and take the plate of food Yvonne had left in the oven. She listened as he set it down on the dining table and ate his dinner in silence. The scraping of his knife and fork against the china plate was the only sound he made. After a few minutes, she heard him push his chair back from the table. She followed the shadows of his feet through the gap at the bottom of the door separating her makeshift bedroom from the kitchen. He moved slowly along the floorboards carrying the empty dishes to the sink.

Lucie pictured his stiff, lopsided gait and his thin, lonely face. From the living room, the ticking of the clock on the mantelpiece accompanied his footsteps, perfectly in time.

Once she'd heard him close his bedroom door, she got into bed and pushed her feet down under the sheet. It was pulled across and folded into the corners so tightly that she had to point her toes to slide them down. The thick white cotton pulled heavy on her chest. Each time she twisted her shoulders to loosen its grip, an odor of camphor squeezed out and pressed itself against her lips. She wondered how long it had been since anyone had slept in these sheets, since the heat of a living body had softened the stiffness of the fibers. She realized this might have been Gérard's young daughter's bed. Perhaps she'd slept here in her final fading days. Lucie shifted her weight against the springs of the thin mattress, shivering at the thought of her infant cousin lying between these same sheets all those years ago. If she'd lived, they'd be nearly the same age.

4

THE NEXT MORNING, after a breakfast of stewed apples and coffee, Yvonne took Lucie out to do the grocery shopping and show her around the neighborhood. They took a round wicker basket from the corner of the kitchen and the money that Gérard had left on the bench.

There were almost no cars in the narrow streets of the Marais, but they churned with pedestrians. Lucie was overwhelmed by the strangeness, the newness of everything around her, so different from what she'd known back home, so different from what she'd imagined it would be. Stores lined the street—pastry shops with beautifully decorated cakes, bars, cafes, and restaurants, some little more than holes in the wall while others took up a whole block, enormous awnings stretching over tables and chairs arranged on the footpath. As they turned from the rue Pavée onto the rue des Rosiers, Lucie saw that many of the shop windows contained signs in Hebraic lettering. There were things that Lucie had never heard of—"kosher butchers," and bakeries selling "matzo bread." As they headed south towards the rue Saint-Antoine, there were clock-makers, shoemakers, tailors, stalls selling leather goods, chinaware; more shops than she'd ever seen. On a corner, a man leaned on a handcart piled high with vegetables, and a woman selling chickens in wooden crates called out at the top of her voice. People sold their wares right there on the footpath—secondhand crockery, pots and pans, clothes. Lucie breathed in the sticky-sweet smell of candied peanuts bubbling away in a copper pan at a street stall.

She followed Yvonne as they wove through narrow side streets, taking note of their names, trying to build a mental map of the area she could use to find her way. Finally, they emerged with the Seine in front of them. Down below, right by the river's edge, women were seated at large wooden frames with striped mattresses strung between them, piles of fluff laid out on large sheets in the sun.

"We used to have the stuffing of our mattresses cleaned every spring and new covers sewn," said Yvonne. The smell of fatty, earthy dust rose up as the women combed the yellowed, flattened wool.

Further along the riverbank, they passed lines of houseboats and barges tied up on the water. They crossed an old stone bridge onto the Île Saint-Louis, and walked along the edge of the small island, looking out across its mossy stone walls, then entering the maze of narrow shaded streets and ancient buildings.

As they emerged into the sun on the other side of the island and crossed the river to the Left Bank, people were seated on kitchen chairs on the pavements, soaking up the warmth and chatting to neighbors, and the river's edge was lined with fishermen. Lucie noticed there were many more women than men in the streets, and that the men she did see were mostly older. She knew that all males between twenty and forty-nine had been mobilized to defend France, millions of them, but she hadn't thought that their absence would be so visible.

Yvonne led Lucie through the Latin Quarter, showing her the famous Sorbonne University. She commented on the number of young women entering and leaving the building.

"There weren't as many girls admitted before I left as there are now. If it had been like that when I was young, I might have tried to enroll."

"What would you have studied?" asked Lucie.

"I don't know really. Anything. Just to prove I was smart enough, I guess."

"Prove it to whom?"

"My parents, Gérard." She paused. "Myself maybe." She pushed her hair behind her ear and gazed up at the heavy, ornate doors. "But then I met your father and life took a different path."

Lucie wondered whether Yvonne regretted leaving France to follow her new husband to the other side of the world. How different would her mother's life have been if she'd stayed in Paris? How different would her own have been?

From the Place de la Sorbonne they took the long narrow rue Champollion back towards the rue des Écoles. On the corner, Yvonne stopped and looked up at the curved white facade of a small cinema.

"This is new," she said. "There used to be a bookshop here." She ran her fingers across her throat. "Your father and I used to meet there. He was staying in a hotel a little further along the street while he waited to be sent home to Australia."

Lucie looked at her mother, trying to understand what she might be feeling, remembering those days when her husband had been a different person from the man Lucie had grown up with. She wished she could have known him then.

As they turned the corner onto the rue des Écoles, Lucie's eye was caught by a display in the window of an art supplies store next to the cinema.

"Oh, they have Winsor and Newton Series Seven paintbrushes," she said.

"Are they good?" asked Yvonne.

"The best," said Lucie. "Queen Victoria had them made especially. But they're so expensive."

"Shame," said Yvonne. "Maybe one day." She pointed to a notice in the window. "Did you see this? They're looking for an artist to draw postcards of Paris. Maybe you should apply."

Lucie shook her head. "I'm not good enough."

"Why would you say that? You're an excellent artist."

"Maman, I drew in high school in Australia. It's not the same as someone who's studied in Paris."

Yvonne shrugged. "Well, you should at least think about it."

As Lucie followed her mother along the crowded pavements, conversation seemed to surge from doorways. The people she saw were more animated than back home. They reminded her of actors in a melodrama—gesticulating, speaking intensely, urgently. A group of men seated at a cafe terrace openly argued about politics. Two women standing in a doorway glared at each other angrily, then threw back their heads and laughed. Girls her own age strode about in pairs, arm in arm, talking loudly. They showed no sign of the self-consciousness Lucie felt as she walked the streets. She was sure that everyone could see how out of place she was. She tried to imagine one day possessing their confidence, speaking out like they did, holding her head as high. For the moment, though, she felt utterly incapable of being anything like these people.

She glanced at Yvonne walking half a step ahead. She seemed hardly any more at ease, despite being back in her home country. Lucie struggled to picture her mother as a young woman here in Paris twenty years earlier. Had she been like these young Parisian women? Had she looked as self-assured, laughed out loud, flirted with the young Australian soldier who would become her husband? Where had she found the courage to leave her home to start a new life on the other side of the world? Lucie wished she could ask Yvonne these questions, but she feared they'd evoke painful memories. If she could, the answers might help her face her strange new life with more assurance.

***

Over the next weeks, Lucie ventured out on her own, each day exploring new neighborhoods. She was mesmerized by the vibrancy; the
chaotic, loud, gritty life that she encountered on every street. From
time to time, she sought relief from the noise and constant presence
of other people by taking refuge in parks and gardens: the Jardin du
Luxembourg, the Place des Vosges, and the Jardin des Plantes. She
also discovered the smaller, hidden patches of green dotted around
the city where she could sit on a bench in the sun and listen to the
birds in the trees overhead.

She especially loved exploring the wide tree-lined boulevards and
the ancient narrow streets of the Latin Quarter. She often lingered by
the Sorbonne and watched the students coming and going. They always seemed to have something important to say; frowning, gesturing,
then laughing and continuing on their way. The weather was warm
and Lucie was starting to feel less of an outsider, less overwhelmed,
more relaxed. She'd started to fall in love with this city, to admire its
determination to get on with life as if everything was normal. Perhaps
Yvonne was right to be optimistic. Perhaps the "phony war" would
turn out to be not a war at all.

***

One Sunday in late May, Gérard took Yvonne and Lucie to visit the Arc
de Triomphe and the majestic avenues, like twelve spokes of a wheel,
that converged at the Place de l'Étoile. As they drove around the area,
Lucie was surprised to see the wide roads lined with large numbers
of people on bicycles and on foot, laden with bags and large bundles.
Gérard explained that they were refugees from Belgium and Holland
who'd started arriving a few days earlier. Lucie had heard reports of
the German onslaught in the north and the news of advancing troops.
First Denmark fell, then Norway, the Low Countries, and Belgium. In

the previous days, radio bulletins were still full of positive tales and the patriotic posturing she'd been hearing for weeks. But, when the news of the destruction of Rotterdam came through, it put an end to the illusion that the war would spare civilians. The city was in ruins. Reports spoke of hundreds killed, thousands of homes destroyed. And now Lucie saw with her own eyes the despair of the survivors, pushing slowly south, hoping that here they'd finally be safe.

As Gérard drove through the wealthy western areas of Paris, the streets were almost empty, many of the windows of the grand apartment buildings shuttered. Lucie gazed out the windshield at the expensive cars loaded with suitcases and monogrammed trunks. Gérard mocked the residents who were leaving, heading south towards the Loire Valley.

"They're nothing more than panic merchants," he declared. "Running scared. They should be ashamed."

"Perhaps they know something we don't," said Yvonne.

"Nonsense," her brother replied. "The government has promised that Paris won't fall. Remember Verdun. They didn't pass then, and they won't pass now."

Although Yvonne looked concerned, she didn't contradict her brother.

As they returned towards the center of the city, the familiar streets were as crowded as ever and the terraces of the many cafes overflowed with people. These Parisians didn't seem at all worried by the threat of German advances in the north. The predominant mood was one of carefree defiance. They seemed to share Gérard's confidence that the French army would once again triumph over their traditional foes.

By the start of June, however, Lucie found it more and more difficult to ignore the relentless westward progression of the German troops. At eight one evening, Gérard tuned the wireless to the nightly radio bulletin and the three of them moved their chairs from the dining table and drew close around the sideboard. The tall windows of the living room were shut tight and draped in black, but the glow of the long midsummer evening seeped through the gaps and gleamed like gold dust on the polished parquet floor.

Lucie sat close to Yvonne, her knees pressed against the glass-paneled doors of the sideboard, listening in silence to the broadcast. Like the rest of France, she wanted to believe the reassuring and patriotic news from the front, desperately hoping that the fabled Maginot Line would hold, not daring to think of what would happen if it didn't.

5

ONE THURSDAY MORNING towards the middle of June, Lucie went out to buy bread as she did each day. This morning, though, everything was different. The pavements were filled with people heading for the train stations or cramming luggage and possessions into cars. The streets echoed with the clattering of iron shutters being pulled down over shopfronts, sending pigeons swirling from the footpaths. As she lifted her eyes, Lucie saw the sun just above the rooftops. It was dull and gray, dimmed by a heavy shroud of smoke. In the streets, she overheard people saying that the fuel reserves had been set alight and the consulates and ministries were burning documents before the German troops arrived. There was a sense of confusion and disquiet that Lucie hadn't felt before. No one had been told whether Parisians were expected to stay and fight.

"Should we hide? Should we flee?" they asked one another, knowing very well that nobody had the answer.

Lucie rushed home to tell Yvonne what she'd heard and seen. "I'm scared, Maman," she said, sinking onto the couch. "I don't know what's happening."

Yvonne sat beside her, her arm around her daughter's shoulders.

"It'll be all right," she said. "The government will tell us what to do."

Gérard came home from work late morning. He strode into the kitchen where Lucie and Yvonne were making lunch.

"We have to leave now," he said, his voice flat, his face expressionless. "Pack your clothes, food, cooking utensils. Take only essential items. We need to keep room for the mattresses."

"Where are we going?" asked Lucie.

"South," he replied. "German troops will be here soon. They're approaching the northern suburbs. Paris is gone."

"No!" cried Lucie. She couldn't believe that the city she'd grown to love was about to fall to the Germans, that it would be annihilated like so many other cities before it.

"They can't let them destroy Paris," she begged. "They have to keep them out."

"It won't be destroyed," said Gérard. "Paris has been declared an open city."

"I don't understand," said Yvonne. "What does that mean?"

"It means we're not defending it; there'll be no battle. The Germans can enter unopposed and take it over."

Yvonne shook her head. "What are the authorities doing? Surely they can't have given up."

"The government has fled to Bordeaux." Gérard wiped the sleeve of his shirt across his chin. "We don't have time to discuss it. We have to leave before they get here."

"Where will we go?" asked Yvonne.

"Toulouse? Maybe Bayonne?" he replied. "As far away as possible."

***

Gérard filled metal cans with petrol and water and secured them in the back of the van. Lucie and Yvonne helped strap mattresses to the roof and load up the inside with as much as they could fit. As they prepared to drive out of the courtyard thirty minutes later, Madame Maurel came to bid them farewell. She was staying behind in Paris. Traveling with her invalid husband would be too difficult, she said.

"Will you be all right, Madame?" asked Yvonne.

"My son is staying with us. He'll protect us if needs be."

Lucie had seen Madame Maurel's son a few times in the last month. He looked to be just a few years older than her, but with something jaded in his attitude that made him seem middle-aged. Although she'd passed him on the stairs several times, he'd never introduced himself.

Yvonne gave Madame Maurel some apples and bottled beans they had no room for, and left the key to the apartment with her.

"I hope you'll be back before too long," the concierge said.

"Of course," said Yvonne. "This will all be over soon and life will return to normal."

Lucie wondered if her mother really believed that, or if she was lying for her daughter's sake. There was no way to tell, but for the moment it was a comforting illusion they all needed to hold on to.

As they drove towards the rue Saint-Antoine, Lucie noticed the eerie silence in the streets. It took her a minute to work out what it was. No fluttering, no chirping, no cooing. The complete absence of birds. She looked up at the blackened sky and wondered if they had been poisoned by the smoke.

***

As they drove out of Paris, the whole city felt like a giant ship foundering in the middle of the ocean. On the roads that led south, cars like overloaded lifeboats desperately tried to pull away. Lucie stared blankly at the slow procession of trucks, cars, bicycles. There were thousands on foot as well: men pulling handcarts loaded high with household goods, sometimes with a grandmother perched on top, slumped and sweating in a thick black dress; women pushing prams with red and crying babies squirming between bundles of clothes and blankets; the glowing faces of early summer tinged with gray, heads bent low, advancing in total silence. Despite the heat, some people wore several shirts and jackets, three hats one on top of another, anything to avoid leaving them behind.

"Madame Maurel said some people killed their pets rather than be burdened with them on the road," whispered Yvonne.

Lucie had heard the same thing in the streets that morning. She'd also heard of elderly relatives being left behind. She couldn't imagine the despair that would drive people to such a decision—and she didn't want to imagine what horror might pursue them as they fled.

***

As they joined the exodus south, the creeping tide of those fleeing swelled by the hour; the traffic so heavy that those on foot advanced more quickly than the vehicles.

Occasionally they encountered French soldiers in army trucks, their faces hidden under caps and helmets, the weary slope of their necks and shoulders betraying a mix of shame and disbelief as they fled the advancing German troops.

Each evening for those first chaotic days, Gérard pulled the van over by the side of the road or in a field. They ate the food they'd managed to bring, and when that ran out they bought produce from the farmers on whose land they camped. Around them, Lucie heard the panicked conversations of their fellow refugees. It was clear that the memories of the last war were still very present—the brutality, the atrocities towards civilians. Rumors of what would happen when the German troops caught up with them flowed from group to group; supposed firsthand tales of savage hordes that slit women's throats and chopped off children's hands.

On the third day, they stopped to eat lunch in a field. Lucie was lying on a blanket, her arm draped across her eyes to shade them from the midday sun, when suddenly Gérard yelled, "Run! Take shelter! Not in the van!"

Lucie sat up and heard the rumbling of Stukas, the German dive bombers, approaching low from the north. She grabbed Yvonne's hand and started to run, surrounded by hundreds of other frantic people, like swarms of mice, scrambling left and right, off the road and into ditches or under trees. She threw herself facedown next to Yvonne beneath a towering elm, her hands clamped over her ears. She bit down on her tongue as the planes screamed towards them, their sirens drilling through her skull. As they passed overhead, she felt a dull percussion in her stomach as bullets pierced the ground and ricocheted off trees. She lifted her head and watched in horror as some of those fleeing panicked and ran along the road, becoming moving targets for the planes as they swooped and fired on cars and carts and horses.

As the noise of the motors faded, she looked around. She saw Gérard not far away, sitting up unharmed. At first there was nothing but a terrifying silence. Then the wails and pleas for aid began. Yvonne took her daughter's arm and pulled her up.

"Come on," she said, her lips trembling. "We have to help." As they started towards the road, Lucie saw a horse convulsing in a ditch, its back leg torn and broken. Its unanswered pleading screams cut through her like a knife.

Fifty meters further, they found two children lying in the middle of the road next to an abandoned car. The older child, a girl of nine or ten, wore a mauve-and-black-checked dress. Her arm was draped across her little brother's chest. He couldn't have been more than three, with caramel hair and a sailor suit. Both were dead, a dotted line of bullet holes etched across their torsos.

"Where are their parents?" Lucie cried. "Why did they leave them alone?"

Yvonne took off her cardigan and laid it over the children, then put her arm around Lucie's shoulders and led her away. "Come," she said. "There's nothing we can do."

Lucie lifted her face and took a slow breath in. Above her the sky was brilliant blue without a single cloud. Somehow that made the attack seem even more horrific.

***

That evening they stopped for the night in a small village near the town of Tours. While Yvonne prepared dinner, Lucie went to the public washtub in the town square to rinse out her dirty clothes. As she was walking back along the main street, a woman came running from the town hall.

"Marshal Pétain has been made head of government," she yelled. "France has surrendered to Germany."

As Lucie hurried back to her mother, she saw people walking aimlessly, muttering, clasping their heads, grown men weeping in the street, not bothering to hide their sorrow.

When she reached Yvonne, she told her what she'd heard.

"What does it mean that we've surrendered? What's going to happen now?"

"I don't know, *ma chérie*. I guess it means the fighting's over."

"But will they take us prisoner?" asked Lucie, her eyes filling with tears. "What will they do with us?"

Yvonne cupped Lucie's cheek in her palm and pressed her lips to her daughter's forehead. "We'll be safe," she assured her. "They'll surely stop shooting civilians."

"But who is Marshal Pétain?" asked Lucie. "Why has he taken over?"

"He's a good man, a very old and respected soldier," replied Yvonne. "In the Great War, he led France to its grandest victory at Verdun. It lasted nine months and cost hundreds of thousands of lives. People call him the Lion of Verdun. He's a national hero."

"Then why has he surrendered?"

Yvonne shook her head slowly. "I don't know," she whispered. "Perhaps your uncle can explain it."

They found Gérard leaning against the van, talking to another man. His face was red but his demeanor was strangely calm. Lucie told him what she'd seen, the old men crying in the street.

"It was awful," she said. "Such a sad sight."

Gérard dismissed their shows of grief as hysteria. "They need to act like men," he said. "Not fall apart like women."

Lucie understood the need for strength, but she was surprised that Gérard seemed to accept the surrender so readily. She'd thought his hatred of Germany would drive his desire to continue the fight.

"What will happen now?" asked Yvonne. "It feels like the government has abandoned us."

"Marshal Pétain hasn't abandoned France," said Gérard, his tone firm and defensive. "He's setting her up to re-emerge even stronger than before. We have to put our trust in him. He's the cool head we need right now, a brilliant military strategist. We'll soon see what he has planned."

***

That evening, when they gathered to prepare their dinner in the school hall with dozens of others, the mood was mixed. Some showed their approval and expressed relief that the fighting would be over. Lucie was surprised. She'd expected more anger and regret. She sat quietly and listened as others talked about their fears of Germany, France's enemy in so many wars.

As the conversation continued, Lucie felt the mood become more solemn. Some people wept quietly in the dark. Some spoke of fleeing France, trying to make it down to Spain or even across to England. Gérard remained silent throughout the evening. When he'd finished eating and drunk his coffee, he stood up from the table and went to sit in the front seat of the van.

While the talk around them continued, Lucie leaned close to Yvonne. "What if we can't go back to Paris?" she whispered. "Where will we live? How will we survive?" She wrapped her fingers around Yvonne's wrist. "We have to leave France, Maman. We should go back to Australia before it's too late."

Yvonne didn't move. She kept her eyes on the untouched food on her plate. When she answered, her voice was somber. "Where would we get the money?" she asked. "And who could I ask for help? I don't know anyone here. Only Gérard. And he already spent most of his savings to bring us here."

***

When they stopped to spend the next night in another village further along the route, it was clear that something had changed. Lucie heard people speaking about an appeal that General de Gaulle had launched from London. He was refusing to accept defeat and was calling on the population to continue the fight. She thought that Gérard would be reassured that all was not lost. Instead, when she told him, he was livid.

"What we need now is unity, not division. A military man should know that. We need obedience and discipline, not a hothead going off on his own and undermining his superiors."

Lucie didn't think it wise to question Gérard any further. His views seemed set in stone. Instead, she waited until she was alone with her mother and asked her who she thought was right.

"I don't know," Yvonne said. "Your uncle understands the situation better than I do. I've been away so long." She looked around the church hall where several dozen of their fellow refugees had gathered to eat dinner. "He seems to trust Marshal Pétain. I assume he has good reason to."

Lucie too wanted to believe that Gérard was right. However, from the conversations she'd overheard, she could see that people were already divided in their loyalties.

***

When the armistice was signed a few days later, France was officially cut in two. The north and west formed the "occupied zone," under the control of the German forces. South of a newly drawn demarcation line was the "free zone," governed by Pétain's administration, based in the town of Vichy.

Over the next fortnight, the number of people escaping southwards continued to increase. Lucie watched in astonishment as thousands more individuals and families were absorbed into the throng of bodies. They were swept up by the flow and became part of a river that grew in width and strength every day. It felt like they were being pushed forward by a force of nature rather than by any human will. Radio reports told of millions of people on the roads. When the petrol ran out, Gérard bought a draught horse from a farmer to pull the van. Lucie spent most of the day walking beside the horse, holding onto its harness. Though it was exhausting, she preferred the fresh air to the stifling front seat of the van.

In the heavy heat of the long July days, the huge column of people settled into a silent stupor—out of shock or exhaustion, or a combination of the two. Many had decided to return north, but many more were too scared. Mothers breastfed babies and people urinated and defecated on the sides of the road, too exhausted to seek out privacy. Many days there was only enough water for drinking, so they slept with the odor of armpits, their whole bodies slick with sweat and gritty with the dust of thousands of shuffling feet.

In some places, the locals they met were kind and generous, offering them food and making up beds for them in a barn. But as the weeks went by, Lucie felt a growing hostility in the villages they passed through. Some of it was directed towards the refugees from Paris, but more towards those from Belgium and Holland. Most people, though, were too preoccupied with their own concerns to care about the plight of the masses passing through.

Walking in front of Gérard's van, Lucie gazed blankly ahead as they crept slowly south. Living in this strange new reality, it was almost startling to observe the natural rhythm of the day continue. The sun rising and passing from east to west, shadows shortening then growing long again, the sun disappearing and nighttime taking over.

Gérard still spoke with reassurance of Marshal Pétain and rejoiced when the news came of the parliamentary vote to give him full powers. He spent his evenings away from Lucie and Yvonne, in the company of an ever-growing group of men who talked loudly about the need to support Pétain. However, he refused to join the conversations around the roadside campfires or in the municipal halls where Yvonne talked to the strangers who'd become their fellow travelers. Lucie sat to the side with her sketchbook on her lap and drew their faces in the dim light, their tired eyes and worried mouths. Late into the evening, they continued their discussions, speculating on what was happening up north, exchanging news of the defeats they heard about—Dunkirk especially, a retreat immersed in blood. When Lucie heard the news of the British attack on the French fleet at Mers-el-Kébir, resulting in the death of more than a thousand French sailors, she couldn't help but feel that the whole country was now friendless, abandoned to its fate.

Though she never dared mention it to Gérard, like some of those she heard around her, she'd still held out hope that de Gaulle's appeal to continue the battle would mean all was not yet lost, and that others would be inspired to join him. Her timid optimism was squashed, however, when one hot evening at the start of August, Gérard came back from the town hall of the village they'd stopped in and announced that General de Gaulle had been sentenced to death in absentia by a military tribunal.

Lucie wondered why such an extreme measure was needed. "Isn't it a good thing that he's continuing the fight from England?"

Gérard shook his head, adamant. "We can't have division at a time like this. He's a traitor and a deserter. France has a leader and we need to unite behind him and his National Revolution."

He looked from Yvonne to Lucie, as if daring them to disagree. Yvonne said nothing. Lucie kept her head lowered over the skirt she was mending, grateful that her eyes were hidden in shadow.

The next morning, Gérard told them he'd heard that the Vichy government had established a plan for the return of those who'd fled, including providing coupons for fuel. As Lucie tipped the breadcrumbs from the breakfast dishes onto the ground, her uncle announced that he'd sold the horse and filled up the van with petrol. After almost two months on the road, it was time to return to Paris.

6

AS THE VAN rolled past the Champ de Mars, a single ray of sun broke through the heavy evening clouds. It shone like a searchlight on the flag fixed to the top of the Eiffel Tower. The fabric stretched itself out, a scarlet slap against the muted purple of the early autumn sky. At its center glowed a circle, white as death. Lucie squinted at the thick black symbol, deformed in the folds of flapping cloth. One moment they looked like eyes and a mouth narrowed in anger, the next like arms raised in stiff salute.

She'd first seen the huge black swastikas in newsreels of Hitler and his Nazi Party, his rallies at Nuremberg, the Olympic Games in Berlin. At the time, she'd found the symbols harsh and ugly. Here, the bloody redness of the flag was even more disturbing.

She peered through the van's dusty windshield as they crossed the Pont de l'Alma, drove along the avenue Montaigne, and advanced slowly down the long tree-lined avenue of the Champs-Élysées. Behind the wheel Gérard was silent, his jaw uncharacteristically slack. From the corner of her eye Lucie noticed the skin under his chin, loose and trembling with the jolting of the wheels on the cobblestones.

As they arrived at the Place de la Concorde, Lucie turned towards the National Assembly building on the other side of the Seine. A giant white *V* had been fixed to the ornate stone pediment. Below, a banner stretched across the row of massive columns. In huge black letters it declared: *Deutschland siegt an allen Fronten*—Germany Victorious on All Fronts.

As they rounded the empty square, more red flags came into view, huge and glaring, covering the delicate stonework of theaters and hotels. Along the rue de Rivoli, they hung one after another, aligned and spaced with military precision; thick branding irons stamped on the city's skin. Gothic-lettered street signs, black on white, pointed to new and fearful sounding landmarks—*Kommandant von Gross-Paris, Der Militärbefehlshaber.* Lucie pinched the inside of her forearm and twisted till it ached. *This isn't a nightmare,* a voice inside her head repeated. *This is real. This is real.*

Despite the warmth of the September evening, the avenues and boulevards were deserted. The streetlights had been painted blue as a precaution against air raids. They created an impression of a city submerged. The streets were silent, the only sound the creak of a handcart pulled by an old woman disappearing under the arches of the long arcades.

And then she heard it: the *click click click* of the boots of a German patrol echoing off the stone facades. Lucie craned her neck and peered along each side street as they drove past, but the source of the sound remained hidden from view. As the sun turned the sky from pink to orange, the van cut in front of the Louvre and crossed the Pont Royal. On the far side of the river, she noticed that the clock on the Orsay Railway Station was an hour fast. When she mentioned it, Gérard replied sullenly that it had been set to Berlin time.

In Paris there was no evidence of the bombings Lucie had seen so much of in the past two months. On the road that had brought them back up from the south, the carcasses of vehicles were still where they'd broken down or burned during the exodus in June, the craters made by the Stukas' bombs now filled with autumn rain. Only the decomposing bodies had been removed.

As they pulled into the courtyard of the apartment building on the rue de Sévigné, the engine choked and stalled. All around, the ground was covered in detritus—yellowed scraps of paper, oily rags, broken glass. A dripping tap had filled the hollows and cracks of the cobblestones with stagnant pools. The far end of the courtyard lay in shadow; smooth and silent, like a layer of thick black ash. Lucie got down from the front seat and staggered back against the door, her legs stiff, her head heavy from the drive.

While Yvonne fetched the key to the apartment from Madame Maurel, Gérard untied the ropes holding the mattresses on the roof of the van and slid them down onto his shoulders. As they climbed the stairs, Lucie stepped carefully over dropped and abandoned objects: a doll with open eyes and a painted smile, a saucepan minus its handle, one green high-heeled shoe. Several doors stood gaping, the insides of the apartments exposed for all to see. A table set for dinner patiently awaited its guests. On the next floor, curtains flapped in the evening breeze, startling pigeons as they picked stuffing from a sky-blue armchair. Lucie wondered why the occupants had chosen not to return to Paris. She asked herself if they were the ones who'd made the right decision.

While Gérard unpacked the rest of their belongings, Yvonne began to prepare their dinner. She asked Lucie to go down to the cellar to bring up some of the bottled preserves that Gérard had stored there when war was declared almost a year ago. Lucie took the wicker basket from the kitchen and went back down the four flights of stairs.

The access to the cellar was off the entrance hall. As she pushed the door open, it disturbed the chilled, sunken air, which swirled like cool water around her calves. She turned on the light and made her way into the stone-walled maze, past the padlocked doors of the storage rooms that belonged to each apartment in the building. She moved slowly in the growing darkness, her fingertips skimming the seeping stone walls. As she advanced along the corridor, the sweet heavy odor of rotting fruit seeped up and filled her nostrils. She worried that rats had tipped the glass jars from the shelves while they'd been away.

At the door to Gérard's storage room, the dim light from the bulb was no more than a yellow wash. While she fumbled with the key, she noticed a mass in the shadowed depths of the corridor, heavy and hard, like a sack of coal. As her eyes adjusted to the darkness, she realized it was a person. She took a few steps forward until she could clearly make out the small, thin frame of an old man. He was seated on the ground, his back against the wall. His thin legs lay at attention, stiff along the cool, dirt floor. The heels of his worn brown boots were together, the toes pointing awkwardly outwards. He wore an old, faded uniform, medals pinned to the right side of his soft blue jacket. Lucie gasped as she saw the rifle lying on his knees and the dark brown stain across his chest. She stumbled back, her hands reaching for the wall. She glanced down at his face and recognized him as a neighbor from the third floor. She'd met him once on the stairs just before they fled south. Gérard had told her that, like himself, the man was a veteran of the Great War.

The thought of her father's death rose to the surface. What suffering had driven both these men to such an act? She forced herself to look at the man's face. His bottom jaw hung open and his dentures had come loose from his gums. She imagined him alone down here in the darkness, the sad sound he must have made as his final breath leaked out.

Back in the apartment while Gérard spoke to Madame Maurel and they waited for the police to arrive, the sight of the old man played over in Lucie's mind. She remembered all the other deaths she'd witnessed: the women, old people, horses. She saw the faces of the two dead children on the road that day. She'd hoped that now they were back in Paris all that horror would be left behind. But it seemed the Paris she'd returned to was not the same city she'd known before.

***

Later that evening, while the undertakers removed the old man's body, Lucie waited with Yvonne in the apartment. They sat beside each other on the couch, staring through the window onto the trees below, their leaves just tinged in gold. Although the couch was large, they sat close, arms pressed together as if they were still in the front seat of the van. As the small glass-domed clock on the mantelpiece chimed eight times, Yvonne turned to Lucie. The color had gone from her face, shadows in the place of eyes, her mouth a straight gray line. Lucie remembered the first time she'd seen that expression. The day of the fire. It had taken weeks before the light had returned to her mother's eyes; now they'd retreated into darkness once more.

When Gérard came back upstairs, they didn't speak about the old man. They ate dried sausage and lentils for dinner and then Lucie asked to be excused. She went to her small room next to the kitchen and lay down on the narrow bed, but couldn't fall asleep. She waited till she heard Gérard and Yvonne retire and then she pulled her pencil and notepad from beneath her pillow and started to sketch the old man's face. When she'd finished, she looked around the tiny room for somewhere to hide it. Behind a warped section of skirting board was a gap where the plaster had crumbled away. She tore the drawing from the pad, folded it in four, and forced it in.

7

LUCIE SPENT THE next morning helping Yvonne wipe down the furniture to rid the dull surfaces of the fine coat of dust that had accumulated in the months they'd been away. Afterwards, they went out to buy groceries.

Despite the warmth and bright blue sky, the streets were much quieter than they'd been in May. Paris had been emptied of its people, and not all had returned. In the faces of those who had, Lucie saw the sorrow and humiliation at the loss of their country. When she'd first arrived in Paris, she'd felt as though she didn't belong, that this would never be her home. Now Parisians too seemed out of place in their altered, emptied city. Many shops were closed. There were still street vendors, but fewer than before. As they made their way along the rue des Francs-Bourgeois, a glazier walked past, a pane of glass strapped to a frame on his back. He rang his bell half-heartedly as he gazed up at the shuttered windows. Near the central market, horse-drawn wagons transported coal and huge pumpkins and men pulled handcarts piled high with leeks. Here more shops were open. Lucie noticed a new sign in several windows: *Hier spricht Man Deutsch*. We speak German here. In some, German soldiers bought chocolates, pastries, cheese.

"I won't be buying from those people," said Yvonne.

"Why not?" asked Lucie.

"They're only concerned with profiting from the occupation, lining their pockets."

Lucie understood Yvonne's attitude. At the same time, she wondered if some of the shopkeepers were struggling to get by in these new circumstances, maybe just trying to feed their children. If that was the case, could she really blame them?

Since the end of June, food rationing had been introduced in the occupied northern zone. They had been allocated cards of different colors, giving them the right to bread every day, meat, butter, and oil once a week, and fifty kilograms of coal for the winter.

Some of the shopkeepers they dealt with seemed to relish this newly granted authority over their fellow citizens. The woman at the grocery shop scrutinized the ration cards and peered over her glasses at Yvonne before snipping off the small individual squares of paper with scissors she kept on a string around her neck.

After buying the weekly ration of beef, oil, and sugar, Lucie and Yvonne waited in a long line to buy bread. Lucie listened to the rumors being passed between the mouths and ears of people who'd been complete strangers hours before. The forced intimacy of the queue reminded her of the exodus, all of them part of a serpent-like line which writhed and inched its way along the pavement. Some women sat on small folding stools. Others knitted or darned while they chatted with their neighbors. Lucie eavesdropped on the conversations.

"Did you hear about the bombing of the Channel Ports?"

"They say there'll be butter available tomorrow."

"No, I heard we'd only have margarine from now on."

"Or lard. All the butter is for the Krauts."

"Yes, and the potatoes too."

"We're left with swedes and Jerusalem artichokes."

"They give you enough gas to power a bus!"

The women broke off into laughter.

Lucie turned to Yvonne. "I'm glad we have our reserves in the cellar," she said in English.

A young woman in front of them turned to look at her.

Yvonne took Lucie's arm and pulled her to one side.

"Shhh!" she whispered.

"But no one understood."

"They understand you're an English speaker. That makes you the enemy in some people's eyes." She glanced around at the women near them. "Let's go. I'll come back after lunch."

"But Gérard will be furious if there's no bread."

"He can come and queue up himself if he's so desperate. There are more important things to worry about than a damn baguette."

Yvonne pulled her cardigan tight around her shoulders and strode off in the direction of the apartment.

Lucie hurried to catch up and walked beside her, their shoulders almost touching, not speaking, their steps perfectly matched. The clicking of their heels was like the rhythm of the German patrol that had echoed up through the kitchen window the night before as Lucie tried to sleep, the five pairs of boots striking the cobblestones in unison, as though they belonged to just one man.

As they turned the corner, Yvonne grasped Lucie's arm and they stopped abruptly, a German officer blocking their path. He was bent over a florist's display, examining the bunches of flowers in detail, taking up the entire width of the narrow pavement. He immediately straightened up and brought his heels together.

"*Excusez-moi, mesdames,*" he said in careful, clipped French.

Lucie lifted her face slightly, careful not to focus on his features, taking in just his presence, his height, the blondness of his hair, the thinness of his face.

"*En français? 'Coquelicot'?*" he asked, indicating a bunch of poppies.

Lucie shook her head and lowered her eyes. "*Je ne sais pas,*" she replied, her voice trembling. She'd never spoken to a soldier, hadn't imagined how intimidating it would feel.

"*Oui,*" said Yvonne a little too firmly, angling her body between Lucie and the officer. "*C'est ça. Des coquelicots.*"

"*Et ça?*" asked the German, indicating a small plant, its tiny purple flowers pressed tight together.

"*De la bruyère,*" replied Yvonne. Heather. She turned towards the road, hoping to put an end to the interaction.

"*Auf Deutsch . . . 'Heide,'*" he said, reverting to his mother tongue. "*Heide,*" he repeated and smiled.

Lucie glanced up at his eyes. They weren't blue as she'd expected, but a grayish green, the same shade as his uniform. She was shocked to see they held a sadness that made him look like something other than a soldier. She could almost imagine meeting him in a park or at the beach and finding him inoffensive, even pleasant.

He reached inside the jacket of his uniform and pulled out a leather billfold. From it he took a photo of a young blond woman.

"*Bitte,*" he said handing the photo to Yvonne. "*Meine Tochter.* My daughter. Her name is Heide."

Yvonne looked at the photo and nodded. "*Très jolie,*" she said, handing it back to him.

The officer slid the photo into the billfold, then held his hand up, his index finger raised.

"*Un moment, s'il vous plaît,*" he said and turned away.

Lucie waited beside Yvonne, her stomach tight with nerves. What did the man want with them? Her eyes followed the officer's right hand, the tip of one finger tapping the tight bud of a single yellow rose, then the next and the next, like a touch on the keys of a piano. He picked one from a tin bucket, holding it between his thumb and forefinger. He turned to face Yvonne, gave a slight nod of his head and held out the flower.

"*La rose jaune*," he said. "*Le symbole de l'amitié*." The symbol of friendship.

Yvonne extended her hand and took the flower from him, flinching almost imperceptibly as the outside of her little finger brushed against the German's thumb. In her peripheral vision, Lucie saw her mother's face, the skin of her throat mottled red, as if the contact had triggered an allergic reaction. Yvonne mouthed *merci*, but her vocal cords produced no sound. Lucie pushed her hand into the gap between Yvonne's arm and waist and pulled her towards the edge of the pavement. She tried to get past the officer, but a handcart blocked their way. Stiffening with embarrassment, he pulled himself tight against the flower display, leaning back, his chin pressed down against his chest. As Lucie pushed Yvonne forward, he slid further backwards, the heels of his boots knocking over the bucket of yellow roses and another of white carnations. The flowers fanned out on either side of his feet, the buckets on their sides clanging, rolling back and forth, water running like a miniature stream around the islands of his boots and cascading into the gutter. Lucie stepped past him and pulled Yvonne with her down the street.

As they turned the corner, Lucie glanced back over her shoulder. In the shadowed doorway of the florist's shop, the owner stood with her arms crossed, not moving, looking down at the soldier as he crouched and picked up the flowers one by one.

* * *

When they arrived at the apartment, Yvonne took a glass from the kitchen and filled it with water. She tried to stand the rose in it, but the stem was too long. She pulled it out and snapped off the bottom half.

"Who gave you that?" asked Gérard, emerging from his room.

"No one," said Yvonne, setting the glass down on the dining table. "I found it in the gutter."

Lucie looked at her mother's profile, but saw no hint of her dissimulation. She wondered why Yvonne hadn't simply thrown the rose away in the street. Surely that would have been easier than lying about it now. She thought back to the encounter with the German officer. She'd heard Parisians describing them as "correct"—proper, polite, courteous. Perhaps holding on to this image of them made it easier to accept their presence as an occupying force. She found the situation incredibly confusing. From afar, they were so threatening, so hostile; and yet, up close, this one had seemed so harmless.

* * *

The next day, Gérard left for work early. He told Yvonne he wouldn't have time to eat lunch at home. He handed her a metal thermos and said he'd drop by at twelve to pick up his soup. Lucie wondered if he really was busy or if he was trying to avoid eating two meals a day with them. He'd lived alone for so long. She imagined their constant presence was hard for him to adapt to.

After breakfast, Yvonne went to her room and came back with a box wrapped in blue tissue paper. "Happy birthday, *ma chérie.*"

"Oh!" said Lucie. "With everything that's happened, I'd forgotten."

"Your first French birthday," said Yvonne. "Seventeen years old."

Lucie set the box on the table in front of her and ran her fingers over the paper. "You didn't need to get me a present."

Yvonne smiled. "Just open it."

Inside the box were three Winsor and Newton sable-hair paintbrushes.

"I know you really wanted them," said Yvonne. "I bought them back in June."

"I can't believe you remembered," said Lucie. She got up from her chair and wrapped her arms around her mother. "But I feel bad. You deserve something nice too."

Yvonne kissed her daughter's cheek. "I have everything I need. We're here together and we're safe. That's all that counts. As long as you're happy and healthy, I need nothing else."

***

They were listening to a musical show on the wireless after dinner that evening when the program was cut off by a series of chimes, followed by the sound of an air-raid siren. Gérard joined them in the living room and turned up the volume. An announcer apologized for the interruption and stated that all residents of Paris should immediately put on the gasmasks that had been given out at the declaration of war and proceed quickly and calmly to their designated shelter.

Lucie gasped. "Why are the Germans bombing us? I thought the fighting was over."

"It's not the Germans," said Gérard. "It's the English."

"But why? Why are they trying to kill civilians? What have we done?"

"There's no need to panic," said Gérard. "They'll be bombing the factories out in the suburbs, not us." He took three gasmasks from a cupboard in the hallway. "We need to go down to the cellar. Monsieur Dorel from the third floor is our building's warden. Follow his directions. I'll turn off all the lights. You go on ahead."

Lucie and Yvonne made their way down the stairs with all the other residents. Once everyone was inside the cellar, the warden closed the door and several men helped to reinforce it with sandbags. Despite the bleach Madame Maurel had used to scrub the corridor, Lucie was sure she could still smell the old man's body.

The few chairs that had been brought down were reserved for the elderly. Lucie stood next to Gérard, their backs against the thick stone wall, listening in silence for the sound of falling bombs. The Germans had installed anti-aircraft guns around the city and their strident stuttering could be heard even in the sunken darkness of the shelter.

Lucie looked at Yvonne. She was standing against the opposite wall, her eyes fixed on the ceiling as if trying to see through the stone and the five floors above it. Lucie tried to read her expression, to detect a shadow of despair, or fear, or a silent sign of unsuspected strength. She saw nothing.

On a chair next to her, an old woman cradled a cage on her lap. Lucie had seen similar wood and chicken-wire constructions on several balconies. She thought the rabbits they contained were pets, but when she mentioned it to Gérard, he just laughed.

"They're being fattened up and bred for food. People learned the lessons of the last war. Parisians will do anything to avoid going hungry. During the siege of 1870, they ate dogs, cats, sewer rats. At Christmas they slaughtered the animals from the zoo at the Jardin des Plantes and ate them too. Wolves, bears, camels. Even the elephants." He rolled his eyes. "Parisians. The only thing we haven't tried yet is humans."

Lucie looked at the old woman and the two small rabbits in her cage. She was whispering to them, "*Petit, petit,*" while feeding them dandelion leaves. Lucie smiled at her and poked a finger through the wire to stroke one of the rabbit's ears, trying not to think about Gérard's story.

After the all clear was sounded, Lucie didn't go straight back up to the apartment. Instead, she went out to the entry of the building, opened the big wooden doors and gazed out into the street. Above her all the windows were smothered in blackout drapes or hidden behind closed shutters, their inhabitants invisible, the only signs of life the muffled sounds of radios and babies crying themselves to sleep. On the corner a group of boys huddled together. One of them cradled pieces of shrapnel in his palms. The others scuttled off, their eyes focused on the gutter, hunting for more of these trophies, remnants of the anti-aircraft fire that had fallen onto the streets.

Lucie closed the doors behind her and walked back into the court-yard. She sat on the step of a closed locksmith's workshop, her feet on a loose cobblestone, rocking it back and forth. In the strange, tense atmosphere of this newly occupied Paris, it suddenly felt safe to be alone. She took a small notepad and pencil from the pocket of her cardigan and drew Yvonne's face as she'd seen it in the cellar, eyes raised towards the ceiling. Once she finished the drawing, she folded it in four, pushed her heel against the edge of the cobblestone, and slipped it into the gap. When she took her foot away, the cobblestone, fell back into place, hiding the paper from view. Lucie put her hands over her eyes like when she was a child, making herself invisible, hidden from the war in the darkened solitude of the courtyard. She imagined sitting like this for months and months, waiting for it all to end; then, when it was over, taking her hands from her eyes and everything being as it had been, as if none of this had happened; seeing the Paris that had existed before the war, the one she'd discovered traces of in the few weeks she'd spent here before the exodus.

* * *

The following weekend, Gérard made a trip to his property in Normandy. He returned late Sunday evening with crates of peaches, plums, apricots, pears, and apples. He went down to the cellar and returned carrying a huge copper pot filled with empty glass jars.

"Perhaps you can teach your daughter to make jam and preserves like you and Maman used to do."

Yvonne smiled and nodded. "Yes. Good idea."

Lucie didn't say anything, but she wasn't sure she liked the way he said "your daughter" rather than addressing her directly.

All Monday afternoon, Lucie helped Yvonne to peel and cut fruit, her fingers sticking to the paring knife, her forearms running wet with juice. They waited till evening to light the stove in the small, airless kitchen and took turns to stir the boiling, bubbling mixture till it thickened. They filled the jars with jam and stewed fruit, then lined them up to cool in jewel-colored rows on all the windowsills. The next morning, Gérard carried them down to the cellar, keeping aside one large jar of peaches in syrup for his breakfast for the week. It was the daily indulgence he said he'd never give up, no matter what the Germans threw his way.

They were seeing little of Gérard these days as his moving business had started to pick up. He'd been granted one of the precious few hundred authorizations available to private citizens to use a motor vehicle in order to carry out essential work. With the petrol shortages, he'd converted the van to run on gas, like the public buses. Many of the Parisians who'd stayed down south were wanting to empty their apartments in order to rent them out, so there was plenty of demand for removalists. He'd even ordered new jackets with the name of his company embroidered on the pocket.

He could no longer do much heavy lifting, so he'd asked Madame Maurel's son to work for him. Lucie still didn't know the young Maurel's first name, but she saw him almost every time she left the apartment or came home. When he wasn't working, he seemed to spend most of his time sitting on a stool outside the lodge, smoking or cleaning his fingernails with a match. He was short and stocky, with arms covered in dark hairs. He reminded her of the gorilla she'd seen through the railings of the zoo in the Jardin des Plantes.

She finally learned his name later that week, when he came up to the apartment to return the keys to the van. Gérard introduced him as Émile. He nodded, but didn't shake Lucie's hand.

"Émile will be coming by the apartment to pick up my lunch from now on," said Gérard. "It'll need to be ready by twelve."

Lucie nodded. "Of course," she said. When Émile didn't say anything, she felt obliged to fill the silence. "It must be hard working with my uncle," she said. "Carrying all that furniture, I mean."

"It's all right," said Émile, squinting at her like someone was shining a light in his eyes.

Gérard slapped him on the back. "We need people who aren't afraid of a hard day's work."

"Of course," said Lucie. Until now, Gérard hadn't said anything about her getting a job, but she wondered if this was his way of saying she should. Because so many of the people who'd fled hadn't returned, there were lots of roles to be filled. Yvonne had found work earlier that week at the central post office of the fourth arrondissement. She'd be working three days a week in the mail sorting room. Lucie also wanted to contribute to the household expenses. She realized Gérard was far from wealthy, and supporting two more people was a big imposition on him. But what kind of work could she do? She remembered the notice Yvonne had pointed out in the art supplies store on the rue des Écoles. Although she hadn't felt confident enough to apply at the time, she decided now she would.

That evening after dinner, she went straight to her room and spent the whole night filling her sketchpad with drawings to show the owner of the store.

8

WHEN LUCIE PUSHED open the door, the art store was empty except for a woman sitting behind the counter, drinking a cup of tea. Her long face was partially hidden by a fringe of shiny light brown hair that fell down over her eyes, but Lucie guessed that she was in her mid-thirties. She wore a turquoise frock embroidered with sunflowers. She looked like a van Gogh painting.

"Would you like one?" asked the woman, looking up and offering Lucie a biscuit from a battered metal tin. "They're terribly unappetizing, but filling. A sort of failed currant bun." Her French was correct, but she had a strong English accent. "I call them Squashed Fly Biscuits." She took a bite of one and grimaced, exaggerating a shiver down her spine.

Lucie took a biscuit and thanked her in English.

"Ah, a fellow Anglophone. Lovely to meet you. I'm Margot."

"Lucie."

Margot took a piece of blotting paper from the counter and wiped the sweat from her forehead. "Can you believe this heat? In September? Too hot for this wilted English rose. I'm as pink as a baboon's bum."

"I thought you might be English," said Lucie, nibbling at the biscuit.

The woman groaned. "I've been here twenty years and I still can't disguise my God-awful accent when I speak French."

"I like it," said Lucie. "It makes me feel less foreign myself."

"Where are you from?"

"Australia. I only arrived a few months ago."

"Lordy. You're a long way from home." Margot pulled a second cup from under the counter. "Here. Have some tea. I have jam in mine." She stirred a spoon of dark red syrup into her cup. "This one's too runny. Not enough sugar. Would you like some in yours?"

"No thanks," said Lucie. "I'm trying to get used to doing without it."

"Wise course of action," said Margot, licking the back of the spoon. "So, Lucie. If you're Australian, how is it that you speak French?"

"My mother's French. She always insisted that I speak it with her. It means I don't sound too much like a foreigner here."

"You certainly don't. But why on earth did you decide to come over in the middle of a war?"

"We didn't have a choice." Lucie hesitated, not sure how much to reveal. "We lost our house in a fire. My father passed away."

"Oh, I'm so sorry."

Lucie took a bite of the biscuit. She pushed it up against her palate, letting it dissolve into a sweet paste before swallowing it, hoping the woman wouldn't probe any further.

"My mother's brother lives in Paris, so we've come to stay with him," she explained.

"How long had your mother been away?"

"Twenty years," said Lucie. "She left after the last war. She and my father went to live in Australia and that's where I was born. We'd never even visited France. That's why I feel like a foreigner here despite my French."

"You'll fit in fine. Look at my accent. It doesn't stop me from being a fully fledged Parisian. You'll be one too in no time."

"I hope so," said Lucie. She realized she hadn't decided how she felt about the idea of returning to Australia when all this was over. Despite the situation, or perhaps because of it, she was falling in love with Paris.

Margot sighed, brushing crumbs from her lap. "Here," she said, holding the biscuit tin out to Lucie. "Have another mouthful of squashed flies."

"Makes me feel right at home," said Lucie, laughing. "How long have you been running your store?"

"It's actually my parents'," said Margot. "I have an apartment above on the third floor."

"Are they here with you?"

"No, they left me in charge when they went back to England last year."

"Why didn't you go with them?" asked Lucie.

"I did consider it. For about a second. But I'm French. I made the decision to be naturalized when I turned twenty-one. Paris is my home. I need to be here for her."

"So you never considered not coming back to Paris after the exodus?"

"I never left," replied Margot. "I'm like Picasso. He's still in Paris. Not far from here. Making his 'degenerate art' under the nose of the occupiers. I actually have a few German customers coming in here to buy supplies. There are some talented artists among them. I keep them coming back by telling them Picasso pops in occasionally."

"Does he?" asked Lucie.

"No, but they don't know that. They're quite enthralled by him. Apparently he has a handwritten sign on the door of his studio that reads simply: *Here*. Some of the most passionate German officers discreetly drop by and ask to see his paintings."

"That's amazing," said Lucie. "I'd give anything to see his work."

"Are you an artist too?"

"No, not really," said Lucie. "I just draw a bit."

"Well, I'm looking for someone who *draws a bit* at the moment."

"I know," said Lucie. "That's actually why I'm here."

She pulled the sketchpad from her bag and passed it to Margot.

"Please don't feel obliged to say you like them."

Margot leaned back and smiled. "Don't worry about that," she said. "I never feel obliged to do anything."

She turned the pages slowly, examining the intricate details of the sketches through a small magnifying glass pendant she wore around her neck. She glanced over the top of the page at Lucie after each one, shaking her head and raising her eyebrows.

When she'd finished, she laid the sketchpad on the counter.

"*I just draw a bit*," she said, mocking Lucie's modest claim. "What an absolute load of bulldust." She pointed an index finger at Lucie. "Dear girl, whether you know it or not, you are an artist."

Margot explained that she sold hand-drawn postcards of famous views of Paris.

"Unfortunately, the artist who was making them left Paris earlier this year and it's not easy to find someone else who can do them as well. It's a job that requires an eye for detail, which you seem to have in spades."

"Thank you," said Lucie, not sure whether she was being offered the job.

"All right then," said Margot, smiling and sliding the sketchbook across the counter. "You can take the first lot of blank cards today. Will a week be sufficient to have the finished product back to me?"

Before Lucie could answer, Margot stood up.

"Excellent!" She disappeared into a storeroom on the far side of the shop and returned with a wooden case.

"There's everything you need in here," she said, handing it to Lucie. "I can't wait to see your creations. And I promise I'll have something more palatable to serve you next time."

***

When she got home, Lucie told Yvonne and Gérard about her new job.

"I'm so proud of you," said Yvonne. "I knew you were good enough."

Lucie turned to Gérard. "And I'll give you half of what I earn to help out with expenses."

Gérard nodded. "Thank you. That will be a welcome addition."

After dinner, Lucie examined the contents of the case. There were several photographs she was to use as models for her drawings; images she'd seen on postcards sold by street vendors and in front of newspaper kiosks: the fountains of the Trocadero Gardens with the Eiffel Tower in the background, the Place du Tertre and Sacré-Cœur Basilica, the Moulin Rouge and Notre-Dame. It was clear the photos had been taken before the war. The unconstrained joy of the people in them—the way they stood and looked at the beauty around them, insouciant and proud.

She set up the equipment on the dining room table. She held the first postcard in place on an inclined board, and laid out the selection of Bristol card, Indian inks, watercolors, nibs, and a set of round brushes. Margot had also provided a magnifying glass on a stand to make it easier to draw the fine details of the architecture.

She started with a drawing of the Eiffel Tower and Trocadero, sketching the outlines in pencil. Once she was happy with the result, she carefully went over the lines and added details in ink. After she'd finished, she added a fine wash of color to some of the elements—the sky, the water of the fountains, the long symmetrical lawns. The scene took on a vibrancy that made it seem more alive than Paris currently did. With each hue she applied, Lucie felt like she was giving the city back some of the light and color that had been dimmed since the start of the occupation.

***

She returned to Margot's shop the following Monday afternoon and showed her the postcards she'd drawn. Margot laid them out on the counter, then held them up to her face one by one.

"Magnificent," she said, beaming. "Picasso would be proud."

Lucie laughed. "Picasso would be horrified. It's one step up from painting by numbers."

"Don't tell the customers that," said Margot. "And don't sell yourself short. It takes a lot of skill."

"Skill, maybe," said Lucie. "But that's very different from talent."

"In any case, you've earned your dough." She took a wad of francs from a drawer and handed it to Lucie. "And some edible dough as well. Will you stay for afternoon tea? I'm expecting a friend and I'd like you to meet him."

Margot put the kettle on and took a teacake from her biscuit tin. As she was slicing it, the door opened. She dropped the knife and hurried to greet her visitor.

"Lucie, this is Samuel Hirsch," she said, her arm linked through her friend's.

"I'm so pleased to meet you, Monsieur Hirsch," said Lucie.

"*Enchanté*, Mademoiselle Lucie," he replied, smiling warmly. He was in his mid-sixties, short and bald, with soft, sad eyes. He spoke with a slight accent that sounded Eastern European. He took Lucie's hand in his, his fingers light and limp against her palm. "And please, I'm not one for French formality," he said. "You must call me Samuel."

They sat at the counter while Margot served her cake and put jam into a small bowl. Samuel spooned some onto his plate, then stirred a second spoonful into his tea. He licked the spoon and smiled.

"Delicious! Mirabelle. My favorite."

"I see Margot has taught you her bad habits," said Lucie.

"On the contrary," said Margot. "It was he who corrupted me. Samuel is a very old and gifted friend of mine."

"Margot is exaggerating, of course. I'm not so very gifted, and certainly not old." He chuckled at his own joke.

Lucie took a sip of her tea. "How did the two of you meet?"

"Samuel was our first customer back when we opened the store. Our only customer for a while. He'd drop by on the pretext of purchasing materials and hang around till I offered him a cup of tea."

"And a squashed fly biscuit," said Samuel, grimacing.

"I couldn't get rid of him after that." She winked at him and smiled. "Samuel created the most exquisite engravings."

"My family have been engravers for four generations."

"I remember the first time I saw your work," said Margot. "I cried at the beauty of it." She put her hand on his. "That was twenty years ago now."

Samuel laid his hand on top of Margot's. "Who would believe it? Unfortunately, those days are behind me." He made a clicking sound with his tongue and tossed a forlorn glance over his shoulder, as if bidding his past farewell. "My engravings have had to give way to less delicate works. These days I can hardly draw a straight line. But Margot tells me you're a fine illustrator."

"She certainly is," said Margot. "I'm sure her postcards will be popular with our guests in gray-green."

"Do you mean German soldiers?" asked Lucie.

"Yes, they can't get enough of Parisian memorabilia. Especially handmade."

Although Margot had mentioned her German customers, Lucie

hadn't really thought about the fact that they might be the ones buying her drawings.

"Is it hard to have to serve them?" she asked.

"Of course," said Margot. "It's excruciating being civil to them." She paused. "I have to admit, though, there are one or two regulars who, in different circumstances, might be decent chaps."

"I don't know if that's true," said Samuel. "But they clearly have a love of art."

"And they spend up big," said Margot. "Can't complain about that."

Lucie swallowed the last of her piece of cake and wiped the crumbs from her skirt.

She thought about the people she'd seen doing business with German soldiers near Les Halles and how Yvonne had condemned them. She couldn't dismiss the unease she felt at the thought of them buying something she'd produced.

"Do you feel bad . . ."

"Doing business with the occupier?" said Margot, anticipating Lucie's question. "No. I use the money I make from them for a good cause." She looked at Samuel and smiled. "So, no. I don't feel bad about taking their dirty money."

Lucie wondered if she'd been wrong to ask the question. She was grateful when Samuel changed the subject.

"So, Lucie, have you studied fine arts?"

"No, but my father used to draw. He was very talented. I guess I got it from him."

"I also inherited my passion for art from my father. He was a master engraver, the truly gifted one. My son has also followed in his grandfather's footsteps, though he's not here to run his workshop at the moment."

"Where is he?" asked Lucie.

"He was called up for military service when the war was declared.

He was sent east in May and taken prisoner like all the others during the debacle. We haven't had news other than an official postcard to say he's in a POW camp in Germany."

"I'm so sorry," said Lucie. "That must be terribly hard for you and your family."

"Mine and so many others," said Samuel. "We're all in the same boat. At least I can keep his workshop open while he's away. With my few hours of teaching, that keeps me busy."

"Samuel's much too modest to tell you, but he's a professor at the National School of Fine Arts," said Margot.

"Really? That's incredible." Lucie had heard of it, one of the most prestigious art schools in the world. "I can't imagine studying there. It'd be wonderful to be surrounded by so many other art lovers. I don't have anyone to share my passion with."

"I'd be happy to show you some of the engravings in the workshop, if you'd like. It's always a pleasure to meet a fellow artist and someone who appreciates fine art."

"I'd love that," said Lucie. She was flattered that Samuel considered her a fellow artist. She hadn't realized until now how much she craved this type of connection. She'd sometimes wondered if she could have had it with her father if he hadn't been so damaged by the war.

"Why don't you drop by around half past three on Saturday," Samuel suggested. "We can have afternoon tea together. I can't promise it'll be as good as Margot's squashed flies, but I'll do my best."

Samuel finished his cup of tea and stood up. "I must get going, my dear. I'll just take my supplies."

"Here you are," said Margot, reaching behind the counter and passing him a roll of canvas tied with string.

"It was lovely meeting you, Lucie. I look forward to next Saturday."

Margot accompanied Samuel to the door and watched him as he walked away down the street.

When she returned to the counter, Lucie decided to clear the air after her earlier comment.

"I'm sorry I was rude about you doing business with Germans," she said. "I didn't mean to sound like I was accusing you."

"I didn't think you were," said Margot. "There are lots of ways to resist and some of them require compromise. We're all just making this up as we go along. There's no rule book." She pushed her forefinger down onto a crumb of cake, brought it to her lips, and licked it off. "We just do whatever we can."

9

THE FOLLOWING SATURDAY Lucie went to meet Samuel at his workshop as arranged. It was on the ground floor in a small, shaded lane in the eleventh arrondissement, not far from the Place de la Bastille.

As she arrived, she saw a large yellow notice posted in the window. Big black letters in German read *Jüdisches Geschäft* and underneath in French were the words *Entreprise Juive*. Jewish business. Lucie had read about the new laws and had noticed many shops in her area displaying the same sign. She was surprised to see one on Samuel's workshop. Until then, she hadn't realized he was Jewish.

When Samuel saw her through the large windows, he smiled broadly and hurried to open the door.

"Welcome, dear Lucie," he said. Once they were inside, he closed the door behind them and pointed to the notice. "I see you've spotted my new window decoration."

"I didn't know that you were . . ."

"Jewish?" Samuel nodded. "Yes, I am. Though my family's not religious. We celebrate some of the holidays, but we don't go to synagogue. We've learned it's wiser to be discreet." He looked at the notice in his window. "Although the Germans seem to be making that a little difficult these days."

"I don't understand why they're doing this," she said. "It feels like they're trying to punish you. You've been in France for years."

"Lucie," he replied, "you're new here, but believe me, this country has a long history of anti-Semitism."

Lucie had never heard that term before, but she could guess what it meant. She remembered the priest in the Catholic church in Wonthaggi blaming the Jews for the death of Jesus.

Samuel told her about the Dreyfus affair and how it had exposed the anti-Jewish sentiment of a large proportion of the French population. But that was just one manifestation. It had always been there, festering below the surface. There were newspapers that were openly and proudly anti-Semitic, and when a Jew had become prime minister just a few years earlier, the hatred erupted once again. A far-right group had even tried to kill him.

Lucie was shocked to hear these stories.

"You shouldn't be," said Samuel. "In July the Vichy government started revoking the citizenship of thousands of people, many of us who were naturalized but are Jewish. Yesterday I received a letter saying my case is being examined."

"I had no idea they could do such a thing. At home we were taught that France was the country of freedom, of equality."

"Oh, my poor Lucie," he said. "I think there's a lot you still have to learn about human nature and about the French." He clapped his hands together. "But there is time for that. For the moment, let us address more pleasant matters. Come, I'll show you what we make here." He led Lucie into the light-filled workshop. On a workbench were several bundles wrapped in cloth. Samuel picked them up one by one and removed the covers to reveal three finely engraved silver objects: a large round pendant, a christening mug, and an octagonal jewelry box.

"They're stunning," said Lucie. "Are these all your work?"

"No. These were done by my son." He picked up the jewelry box and handed it to Lucie. She looked more closely at the image on the lid—an intricate design of blossoms and butterflies, composed of hundreds of fine lines.

"When I was younger, I produced many beautiful pieces," said Samuel. "Sadly, those days are over." He held out his hands and Lucie noticed the gentle tremor that started in his wrists and moved all the way to his fingertips. "Nowadays I paint, but just for my own pleasure. It's less expensive to make mistakes on canvas than on silver." He smiled. "I'd hoped that my oldest granddaughter might follow her father and me, but she has other ambitions. I'm not surprised. She has a brain for different types of details. In any case, there's not much demand for our work in these times." He gestured towards the objects. "Even these orders haven't been collected."

Lucie turned the jewelry box over and noticed a small symbol engraved on the base. It looked like two leafless tree branches.

"We always mark our work with this emblem," said Samuel. He traced the symbol in the air with his two index fingers. "The antlers of a stag. It represents our family name—Hirsch. It means *deer.*"

"That's lovely," said Lucie.

"It has special meaning for my family," he said. "Did you know a deer's antlers fall off and regrow many times during its lifetime?"

"No," said Lucie. "I didn't."

Samuel smiled. "I think it's a good symbol for our lives. A lot of loss, but also much regrowth."

He looked at his watch. "Four o'clock," he observed. "Teatime. It's my one indulgence. Every day, no matter what." He led Lucie from the workshop, locking the door behind them, and ushered her up the stairs to his apartment.

There he placed a kettle of water on a kerosene burner balanced precariously on a crooked wooden bench against the far wall. Returning to the small sitting area, he slowly lowered himself into a faded blue armchair opposite the small green sofa where Lucie was seated. On a lacquered table between them was a large silver teapot, an engraved stag stretching across its curved body. The animal's fur was made up of thousands of individual lines, as fine as hairs and layered one on top of another, the massive antlers seeming to emerge from the flat surface.

"Not bad, *n'est-ce pas*?" said Samuel.

"Extraordinary," said Lucie. "It's a stunning engraving."

"It's the work of my father, our family's tea set. It's much too big for just me, but I use it anyway. My parents gave it to me when I left Poland to come to France."

"When was that?" asked Lucie.

"When I was still a handsome young man," he replied, laughing. "This is where I met my dear late wife."

When the kettle had boiled, Samuel filled the teapot and carried it back to the table, returning for a tray on which sat two slices of apple tart, cups and saucers, and a jar of jam.

"And this is another habit I can't break," he said, stirring a teaspoon of jam into his tea. "You should try. It's good."

Lucie smiled and added a spoonful of the ruby-colored jam to her cup. "Do you still have family in Poland?"

Samuel nodded slowly and raised his eyes to meet Lucie's.

"My mother and two older sisters are still there. Very early I realized the danger of Hitler and his Nazi Party and tried to convince them to leave, but my mother is too old now and even my sisters are not so young anymore. They're set in their ways. All their friends are in Poland, so they stayed."

"Are they safe?"

Lucie saw Samuel's eyes moisten. They seemed to grow a little darker and more distant.

"Who can know?" he replied, his voice suddenly fainter. "They say very little in their letters. And what place is safe now anyway? Where can you flee? I prefer to hold onto the faint hope that here, of all places, in the land of liberty, equality, and fraternity, I will be safe."

"Do you think you'll be proved right in the end?"

"I'm not so sure. Coming back to Paris after the exodus was a difficult decision, especially when there are children to think about. We left my two young granddaughters with my nephew and his wife in Limoges. My daughter-in-law and my eldest granddaughter returned to Paris with me. Aline is at university; she's about your age."

He got up to refresh the teapot.

"How long have you been in France?" he asked, once he'd set it back down on the table.

"Just a few months. My mother and I came to live here after my father died."

"Oh yes. I'm so sorry. Margot told me that. It must be incredibly hard for you both. Not only losing your father, but now this terrible occupation."

"It's not easy," said Lucie, "but hopefully it won't be for too long."

"And you have your uncle here, is that right?"

"Yes," said Lucie. She was reluctant to say any more and was relieved when the door opened and a young woman entered the apartment. When Lucie looked up, the sun was directly behind the girl, so her features were hard to make out. Lucie could see that she was tall and slim, but broad-shouldered. Her hair was short and dark, and she brushed it back from her face before sliding her spectacles further up her nose. She wore loose beige slacks and a short-sleeved red shirt. Despite the warm weather, she carried a trench coat over her arm.

"Ah," said Samuel. "Here's my granddaughter I was telling you about, Lucie."

Lucie stood up and moved around until she could see the young woman's face more clearly. "I'm Lucie Blackburn," she said.

"Aline Hirsch." Behind the lenses of her glasses, Lucie noticed, she had the same sad eyes as Samuel's.

"I can't stay, Papy," said Aline, kissing her grandfather on both cheeks.

"That's fine, Lina," he said.

"I'll just take my books and get going." She crossed to a buffet against the far wall and opened the bottom drawer. She took out a package wrapped in brown paper and put it into her satchel.

"See you next week, Papy," she said, before turning to Lucie. "It was nice meeting you."

"You too," said Lucie.

After Aline left, Samuel rested his head against the back of the armchair and massaged his swollen knuckles.

Lucie was worried she'd overstayed her welcome. "I'd better get going," she said.

"So soon?" replied Samuel. "You wouldn't like another cup of tea?"

"That's very kind of you, but I really should get home. I'd love to visit again, though."

"I look forward to that," said Samuel.

As she walked back to the rue de Sévigné, Lucie reflected on what Samuel had told her about the French and their attitudes towards Jews. How naive her notions of France and its past had been, she realized, aware now of how little she understood her new compatriots. She wondered if it was possible to really know what was in their hearts and minds.

*＊＊

The following Tuesday afternoon, Lucie visited Margot's shop with another batch of illustrated postcards. She left home a little after three and took a small pot of plum jam from the cellar as a gift. When she arrived, she found the front of the store hidden behind the metal shutters that were normally closed only at night. The windows of Margot's apartment on the third floor were open, though, the lace curtains trembling with the air that rose up from the busy street below.

"Margot," she called.

Half a minute passed before her head appeared at the window.

"Lucie! What a lovely surprise. Please, come up."

As she climbed the stairs, Lucie heard the sound of muffled voices and music through the walls. When she reached the third floor, Margot was waiting at the door. She embraced Lucie, kissing her on each cheek.

"Sorry about all the noise," she said, gesturing down the stairs. "It's the cinema next to my store. It opened a couple of years ago and I've since discovered that the walls of this place are paper-thin. The sound from the films comes right up the stairwell." She shrugged. "At least I get to hear them all for free."

Lucie laughed. "I thought I'd find you in your shop," she said. "I brought you some jam for afternoon tea."

"Thank you, my dear," said Margot. "Come in. Samuel's here."

Lucie followed Margot into the living room. It was small, but bright, the walls lined with shelves that housed a large collection of teapots and china cups.

"Hello, Mademoiselle Lucie," said Samuel, standing to greet her. "You're just in time for Margot's latest creation."

Margot opened her biscuit tin to expose a dense, pale yellow cake. "Butter cake, made with genuine margarine and saccharine."

"Sounds delicious," said Lucie, helping herself to a piece and sitting down in a dusky pink armchair next to the window.

Margot poured them each a cup of tea, then sat on the floor at Samuel's feet.

"So, what's the occasion?" asked Lucie. "It must be something pretty important you're celebrating to warrant closing the shop."

"It is something important," said Margot, "but I'm afraid we're not celebrating."

"What do you mean?" asked Lucie.

"There are big changes happening, my dear," said Samuel. "Some things had already changed, but now they're getting worse."

"What things?"

"The government has brought in a new law," explained Samuel. "I'm no longer able to teach."

Lucie put her teacup down on the low table beside her. "Why not?" she asked, even though she feared she already knew the answer.

"Because I'm Jewish," said Samuel. "And it's not only teachers who are affected. There's a whole list of positions we're no longer permitted to hold."

"How can they do that?" asked Lucie. "How can you live?"

"Ha," said Samuel, raising one eyebrow. "That's our problem. Not theirs." He shrugged. "We'll have to find ways."

"Is there anything I can do to help?"

"That's very kind of you, Lucie, but I'll be all right. We're among the fortunate ones; my daughter-in-law is still working. But it'll be harder for some of our compatriots, and I'm not sure we can count on getting much help or pity. It's not only our precious value of liberty that's taken a beating in this new France. Equality and fraternity are also fading fast."

"It's bad enough that Pétain and his government are doing this," said Margot. "However, it's the support he has among the population that really worries me."

"I think my uncle's one of those supporters," said Lucie. "He trusts

Pétain. He thinks he's done the right thing by France, that he'll lead us out of this."

Margot shook her head. "Of course. Pétain loves to portray himself as the father of the nation, the protector of the people. Listen, Lucie, I don't want to tell you what to think, but personally I'm not counting on him to protect us. He doesn't understand who he's up against. This isn't the last war with its cavalry and bayonets. Pétain thinks he has the upper hand with Hitler, but he's just a doddering old fool. He's going to regret his decision to sign that armistice. I think we'll all see what a mistake it was."

"But there are lots of people who support de Gaulle's cause as well, aren't there?" asked Lucie. "People who want to fight for his Free France?"

"Some," said Margot. "But I get the impression there are many who are just waiting to see what happens."

"In any case," said Samuel, "you have to be careful what you say out loud. You never know who you're talking to and where their loyalties lie."

***

The next day, while Yvonne went out to try to buy butter, Lucie stayed in the apartment to clean. Gérard was in the dining room, but when she came in he left and went to his bedroom. He'd been reading an article in a magazine and had left it open on the table. He didn't mention it to Lucie or suggest that she read it, but she couldn't help but feel the intention behind his act. Over the months since the armistice was signed, his conversations were often peppered with mentions of the "new reality" in France and the need to accept it.

Lucie leaned over the table to read the article. It was written by Marshal Pétain. In it, he justified his decision to replace the official French motto—*Liberté, Egalité, Fraternité*. He was introducing new values for a new era, he said. A new France in a new Europe. The motto under which the French were now to live was spelled out in three short words. Six syllables sufficed, it seemed, to summarize the values of this new, efficient France. *Travail, Famille, Patrie.* Work, Family, Homeland.

As Lucie finished reading, she looked up and saw Gérard watching her from the shadow of the hallway. She closed the magazine and turned to face him.

"I'm glad your mother saw fit to bring you home to France," he said.

Lucie was surprised to hear him refer to France as her home. In her mind, home had always been Australia.

"I'm not sure Maman would have been so willing if she'd known we'd be living in an occupied country."

Gérard didn't shift his gaze from Lucie's face.

"It's important for you to know the land your mother grew up in, the country she loved."

"It's not really the same country it was, though," said Lucie. "I think she'd probably leave if she could."

Gérard wasn't ready to let the matter go.

"Your mother is a proud Frenchwoman. She won't desert her country again."

"But hasn't Pétain already sold it to the Germans?"

"He hasn't sold anything," said Gérard, his cheeks redder and more inflamed than usual. "What do you know about any of this? Politics and war are beyond your comprehension. Sometimes it's necessary to retreat, negotiate. Marshal Pétain is a great soldier, a great leader. He'll lead us out of this and back to our true united France, with values we can all be proud of."

"I don't understand why he needed to change the motto," said Lucie. "I thought the French were already proud of *Liberté, Egalité, Fraternité.*"

Gérard picked up the magazine and put it away on the bookshelf. Lucie stood by the table, waiting to see if he would respond. When it was clear he wasn't going to, she went to her room and closed the door behind her. Through the thin wall, she heard Gérard in the living room, his heavy footsteps crossing to the buffet, the neck of a bottle against a glass as he poured himself a drink. In the imposed intimacy of his small apartment, she was rarely more than a few feet from him, yet she could feel the emotional distance between them growing. Every day she saw more of his character and it became more and more difficult to accept the things he said. Even when she took refuge in her room, she heard his every movement. She closed her eyes, attempting to will herself away. She tried to picture life without the constriction of the space she was forced to share with him. She missed the freedom and expanses of her childhood, the beach at Kilcunda, the horizon at the edge of the sea.

When Yvonne came home, Lucie told her she had a headache and stayed in bed until dinnertime.

***

When Lucie arrived at Margot's store to deliver her postcards the following week, Samuel was there again. She saw straightaway from the look on his face that something was wrong.

"I have to lock up the workshop and I'm not to go there anymore," he said.

"Why? What's happened?" asked Lucie.

"Now they've decided that Jews can't own a business. We have to register and they appoint a temporary administrator to manage it."

"That's crazy," said Lucie. "It's stealing."

"They prefer to call it 'Aryanization,'" said Samuel.

"What are you going to do?"

"I'm not going to register it," he replied. "It's my son's business and

I promised I'd keep it safe until he returns. I've locked it up and taken his name down from above the door. I hope that will be enough."

***

Later, on her way home through the streets of the Marais, Lucie realized what she'd failed to notice on the way to Margot's store just an hour or so earlier: shop after shop with their metal shutters closed. Whole streets in the Jewish area deserted. On the rue des Rosiers, there was none of the usual activity in front of the grocers, the bakeries, the tailors, the butchers. As she turned onto her street, she saw a pen repair shop with a new notice in its window:

Under new management.
As of 18 October, the management as well as the personnel of this
establishment are Catholic and French.

10

AS THE WEEKS went by, more and more of Lucie's and Yvonne's time was spent lining up for food and ration tickets, never knowing whether what they needed would be available. They'd spend hours in a line for beef to discover there was only offal, and sometimes even that would run out. Then they'd join another queue for eggs or milk or vegetables. Lucie wondered if this was just what the Germans intended: to keep Parisians figuratively as well as literally "in line." Everything was controlled. Time, food, the way they spent their day, the company they kept, the conversations they listened to and who listened to theirs. Yvonne had told her about a rumor going around that women were paid sixty francs a day for denouncing anti-German comments overheard in queues.

Lucie had noticed their flags and swastikas proliferating too, not only on the Eiffel Tower and the rue de Rivoli, but everywhere; sinister, ugly stains on the beautiful City of Light. The vibrant spontaneity of Paris also felt more static and contained. Nights were controlled by curfews. She would set out to take the Métro and find the stations closed, requisitioned for storage or turned into air-raid shelters. Even riding a bicycle along certain boulevards was no longer possible. The magnificent Rex cinema that Margot had told her about, the largest cinema in Europe, was no longer open to the public, its beautiful facade now deformed by a huge sign, towering black capital letters proclaiming it to be a *Deutsches Soldatenkino*.

Lucie had hoped that the occupation would be short-lived, or that things might at least begin to loosen up, but as time went by it seemed just the opposite was happening. She tried to seek out her own space, going for long walks along the river, crossing back and forth over the bridges, focusing on the architecture, the changing light on the limestone facades, taking solace in their permanence, their quiet self-assurance. She carried her notebook with her everywhere and found quiet spots to sketch. She left the drawings where she drew them, folded up and tucked away for others to discover.

In the areas around many of the famous monuments, tour buses filled with German soldiers had become a common sight. Whenever Lucie saw one, she turned her head away, pretending to look at a store window or read a notice on a wall. If she encountered a group of soldiers, she found some tiny detail to fix her eyes on—a patch of moss on a damp wall, a pigeon taking flight. Anything to avoid an interaction. She was determined to deny them any sense of human contact. They might have conquered the city, but as long as she and her fellow Parisians ignored them, it would be a city without a face.

***

One Wednesday evening, Yvonne was late coming home from work. Lucie was in the kitchen chopping vegetables for dinner while Gérard listened to Radio Paris in the living room. When the speaker announced an important speech by Marshal Pétain, she heard Gérard pull his chair close to the wireless. She put down the knife and went to the doorway to listen. She wanted to hear the speech but didn't want to find herself alone with Gérard, having to hear his comments and face his questions. He must have sensed her presence, though, for he turned the volume up just as the Marshal's speech began. It was the first time she'd heard Pétain speak. His old man's voice was barely audible, the ends of his sentences frayed, the force gone from his lungs.

Citizens of France, last Thursday I met the chancellor of the German Reich. That meeting roused hopes and provoked concerns. I owe you some explanations regarding this. Such an interview was possible, four months after the defeat of our armed forces, only thanks to the dignity shown by the French in face of their trials, thanks to the huge effort of regeneration they have made, thanks also to the heroism of our sailors, the energy of our colonial leaders, and the loyalty of our Indigenous populations. France has picked itself up. This first meeting between the victor and the vanquished signals the first recovery of our country. I chose freely to accept the Führer's invitation. I was not subject to any diktat or pressure from him. A collaboration has been envisaged between our two countries. I have accepted it in principle. The ways and means will be discussed later. To all those who today await the salvation of France, I am anxious to say that that salvation lies first and foremost in our own hands. To all those who will be kept distant from our way of thinking by noble scruples, I am anxious to say that the first duty of every French citizen is to have trust. I will remind both those who doubt and those who dig their heels in that by being too rigid, the finest attitudes of reserve and pride are likely to lose their strength. The man who has taken charge of the destiny of France has a duty to create the most favorable atmosphere for safeguarding the country's interests. It is honorably and in order to maintain French unity—unity that has lasted ten centuries—in the context of an activity helping to build the new European order, that I enter today upon the path of collaboration. Thus, in the near future the weight of our country's sufferings can be lessened, the

*fate of our prisoners improved, the burden of the costs of occupation
mitigated. In this way the demarcation line could be relaxed and
the administration and supplying of our Territory facilitated. This
collaboration has to be sincere. It must exclude any thought of
aggression. It must involve patient, trusting effort. Moreover, the
armistice is not peace. France is bound by many obligations towards
the conqueror. At least it remains a sovereign state. That sovereignty
means it has to defend its soil, extinguish divergences of opinion,
reduce dissidence in its colonies. This policy is mine. Ministers are
responsible only to me. It is me alone whom History will judge. Up
to now I have spoken to you in the language of a father. Today I use
the language of a leader. Follow me. Keep your trust in everlasting
France.*

When the speech ended, Gérard switched the wireless off but
didn't turn around. From where she stood, Lucie could see just a thin
slice of his face. It was completely still. His chin rested on the tips of
his fingers, his thumb tapping against his jaw. She tried to imagine
what he could be thinking, feeling. Although she'd only been living
in this country for a few months, even she was alarmed to hear the
man who called himself the father of the nation now desperately trying to sell himself as the guardian of French pride in a time of such
national shame.

After a minute or more, Gérard turned in his chair to face her.

"*Bon!*" he said. "At least we have some certainty about the future.
Things will start to be less difficult from now on."

"Less difficult?" echoed Lucie. "Do you really believe that?"

"Yes. Absolutely," said Gérard. "If you'd listened more closely to
the message our leader gave us, you'd agree."

"Which leader?" replied Lucie. "Pétain or the Führer?"

As soon as the words left her mouth, she regretted her flippant, provocative comment. She didn't want to antagonize her uncle. She knew she had to learn to keep her thoughts to herself.

Gérard stood up, the chair legs juddering as they scraped across the floorboards.

"Our leader is a great man, a war hero, a true patriot," he said, his face growing red. "You're too young to know what he did for this country, what he means to us. You can't understand in the same way that we French do. And I for one have confidence in the Marshal. I agree wholeheartedly with his vision for our nation. And I fail to see what objection you could have to honoring work, family, and homeland."

"But this isn't my homeland, Gérard," said Lucie, her tone as conciliatory as she could make it.

"It is now," he replied. "And if you're going to live here, you'd do well to remember that, and show some loyalty and obedience."

"But is unconditional obedience always a good thing?"

"It is when the best interests of the nation are at stake."

"It's just hard to think of it as our nation when there are foreign troops on every corner and foreign flags flying from the rooftops."

"Of course it's our nation," said Gérard. "We're still here, aren't we? We still have a head of state. We haven't been annihilated."

He picked up his chair and pushed it back under the table, banging its legs down on the wooden floorboards, an emphatic full stop to the conversation.

***

After dinner, once Gérard had gone to his room, Yvonne asked Lucie about the discussion she'd had with him.

"What did he say?" asked Lucie.

"He's just concerned you might have formed some misguided opinions."

"I think he's the one whose opinions are misguided," said Lucie.

"I mean, he was a soldier. Doesn't he have a sense of duty to defend his country?"

Yvonne moved her chair closer to Lucie's.

"Your uncle's a good man," she said, "but he's been through a lot. The war was hard enough, but then he had to cope with the death of his wife and child. That's not an easy thing to live with."

Although Lucie knew that Gérard had suffered, she wasn't sure that explained his attitude now. But she did understand how difficult it must be for Yvonne to be caught between her daughter and her brother, trying to understand them both, support them both. Lucie decided she'd make more of an effort to get on with Gérard, to not challenge his opinions and beliefs.

***

The following Friday morning, she left home early and headed for the Jardin du Luxembourg. It had been drizzling for the last few days, but although it was cold, this day promised to be dry and she wanted to make the most of it. She crossed onto the Île de la Cité and cut through the small garden behind Notre-Dame to avoid the groups of German soldiers taking photos of themselves in front of the cathedral. She continued on to the Left Bank and wove her way through the deserted back streets to avoid the Boulevard Saint-Michel and its frequent military patrols. She found their constant presence intimidating—the way they roamed in packs, like gray wolves who'd emerged from the woods to take possession of the city.

As she turned onto the rue des Carmes, she saw Samuel's granddaughter, Aline, on the other side of the street. She wasn't sure the other girl would recognize her—they'd only met briefly and that was more than a month ago—but just as she made up her mind to keep walking, Aline called out to her.

"Hello, it's Lucie, isn't it? We met in my father's workshop."

She crossed the street and shook Lucie's hand. "Are you on your way to university?"

Lucie shook her head. "No, I wish I were. I've heard so much about it and I'd really like to see it. Unfortunately, I'm not a student."

"You can visit even if you're not a student," said Aline.

"Really?" asked Lucie. "I had no idea."

"I'm going there now. Why don't you come with me? Unless you've got something else you need to do."

"No, not at all," said Lucie. "I'd love to come."

As they crossed the rue des Écoles, it felt as though the whole Latin Quarter was under siege. German military vehicles rumbled through the streets and the French police were everywhere.

"Stay close to me," said Aline. "Just keep your head down and they won't bother you."

Lucie felt her heart start to race. She'd heard about the frequent and sometimes brutal searches and interrogations that had been happening in the Latin Quarter since members of a student communist group attacked a German soldier a week earlier, but this felt much more serious. She was afraid of what she might be heading into.

On the Place de la Sorbonne was a large crowd of students. As they started singing "La Marseillaise," the police advanced towards them, attempting to disperse them with blows from their batons. Lucie and Aline took shelter under the awning of a cafe, watching the students as they scuttled to hide behind trees, shielding their faces with their satchels. Lucie stayed where she was, not daring to move until the commotion subsided. When Aline saw that the entrance to the university was clear, she took Lucie by the arm and they rushed through the doors together. In the quadrangle, groups of students were conversing urgently, but the atmosphere was calmer. Lucie leaned against a wall to catch her breath.

"Are you all right?" asked Aline. "I'm sorry—this isn't the pleasant visit you were expecting."

"I've learned you can't know what to expect nowadays," said Lucie.

Aline smiled. "True." She turned and searched the faces in the courtyard.

"Can I leave you here for a few minutes?" she asked. "I need to check on something."

Before Lucie could answer, Aline hurried off to join a group of young men and women huddled on the curved stone steps that led down from the marble foyer of the main building. They leaned in close, their heads almost touching, bent over a sheet of paper.

Lucie found a space on a cold stone bench against the far wall. She laid her bag at her feet and looked around the quadrangle. The sky had been overcast early morning, but as the clock on the chapel facade struck nine, the sun shone through a slit in the clouds. Its rays hit the massive gilded sundial high on the wall at the opposite end of the courtyard. The glint of gold caught Lucie's eye and she noticed the Latin inscription curved around the inside of the arch above it. She read it aloud to herself.

"*Sicut Umbra Dies Nostri.*"

"I think you need to work on your pronunciation," said a voice to her left.

Lucie turned and saw a young man. Aline was standing next to him and he had his arm around her shoulders. He was tall and slim, with a gentle face and wavy brown hair.

"Like a shadow are our days," he said, squinting as the sun slanted into his eyes, the hazel irises glowing with yellow flecks.

"Pardon?" replied Lucie.

"That's what you were saying just now. In your faulty Latin. I'm Robert, by the way."

"Lucie."

Robert shook her hand. His skin was cool and dry against her palm.

Lucie looked away, fixing her gaze on the sundial, the reflection stinging her eyes.

"So are you a Latin tutor?" she asked him.

Aline laughed. "Hardly," she said. It was the first time Lucie had heard her laugh and she was surprised at how free it sounded. "Both Robert and I failed first-year Latin miserably. I was actually studying Ancient Greek as well before I came to my senses. I've given up dead languages this year. I'm going to be a journalist instead."

"That's a big change," said Lucie.

"Well, there have been other big changes," said Aline, suddenly serious.

Lucie could feel her pulse against her jaw. There was something she liked about Aline's directness.

"Lucie has just arrived from Australia. She wanted to see the Sorbonne."

"Well she certainly chose the right day," said Robert. "I have a feeling things are about to get interesting."

"Why? What's happening?" asked Lucie.

"I think we're starting to annoy the Germans," he replied. "Some of them have been coming into lecture theaters, and we just get up and leave. Wherever students show their defiance, they react. They've closed lots of cafes around here."

"They're starting to see we won't take the occupation lying down," said Aline. "That's why there are so many of us here today. Apparently the rector's about to make an announcement."

"About what?" asked Lucie.

"I'm not sure, but we have our suspicions." Aline took a sheet of paper from her coat pocket and unfolded it. It was a printed tract. She held it close, hiding it with her sleeve from the view of the students standing nearby. Lucie read the text.

Students of France!
11 November is still a day of national celebration for you.
Despite the order given by the oppressive authorities,
it will be a day of remembrance.
You will not attend any classes.
At 5:30 pm you will go and honor the Unknown Soldier.
11 November 1918 was the day of a great victory.
11 November 1940 will be the sign of an even greater one.
All students are united in saying: "Long live France."
Copy these words and distribute them.

"So, does that mean the authorities are canceling the commemoration of Armistice Day on Monday?" asked Lucie.

"They'll try," said Aline, "but we'll be there regardless."

As she folded the tract and put it back in her pocket, a sudden silence spread through the gathered students. On the steps leading up to the chapel, flanked by the statues of Victor Hugo and Louis Pasteur, the rector of the university had appeared. Just as Aline had predicted, he read a declaration, stating that the public holiday on the eleventh of November had been canceled, that classes would take place as usual, and that all commemorations were banned. As he turned and reentered the building, Lucie saw students forming new groups, whispering, thumping their fists against their palms.

"What are the authorities afraid of?" she asked.

"Us," said Robert. "They know we're not going to let them erase history, forget everything this country's suffered. We've always fought on regardless of the challenges."

"You're not fighting now," said Lucie, immediately realizing her statement sounded like an insult.

"The soldiers might not be fighting the Germans, but the rest of us haven't surrendered," replied Aline. "That's why it's so important to demonstrate—to defy the ban and go to the Arc de Triomphe. There'll be thousands of us, university and high school students, to send a message to the Boche."

"Exactly," said Robert. "That old traitor, Pétain, might have lain down like a beaten dog, but we, the youth, are willing to bare our teeth and show them we're not cowed."

"Do you think the Germans will just let it happen?" asked Lucie.

"There aren't many things they'll just let happen anymore," replied Aline. "But we can't let that stop us. We won't let them dictate what we can and can't do. Only we can decide that."

Lucie nodded, but didn't know how to respond. She'd never met people of her own age who were so passionate and politically active. Compared to them, she felt so young and naive.

"I really hope you succeed," she said.

"Why don't you join us?" asked Aline.

Although she was ashamed to admit it, Lucie was too scared to do anything so bold. She admired the students' determination, but felt she knew too little about the situation to get involved. Despite the months she'd spent in Paris, hearing Aline and Robert speak made her realize she was still an outsider, completely out of her depth.

"I don't want to do anything that would make life more difficult for my mother," she said. "It's been hard enough for her since my father died. And now we're stuck here in France."

"Like all of us," said Aline. She smiled and took a step away. "But that's all right. I understand." She turned and took Robert by the elbow. "I hope I'll see you again soon, Lucie."

Lucie stayed where she was, watching as they crossed the courtyard and joined their friends. She thought about Gérard and his exhortations for obedience and loyalty. She knew what he'd say about Aline, Robert, and those who shared their beliefs. But she was in awe of the courage it took to disobey a direct government order. She wished she were half as brave.

As she sat in the courtyard, Aline, Robert, and the other students left the steps and entered the building. The sun disappeared behind a cloud once more. Lucie looked up at the statues of Hugo and Pasteur gazing down on the quadrangle. The expressions on their faces were serious but not severe. They seemed contemplative, not judging the young people they watched over, perhaps waiting for time to hand down its own verdict. Lucie thought about the demonstration. Maybe she could show her support by going and just watching from the sidelines.

11

THE CHILLING RAIN that had fallen throughout the day had cleared by the time Lucie came up onto the street from the Georges V Métro station the following Monday afternoon. Several groups of students were already making their way towards the Arc de Triomphe. Some carried French flags marked with the two-barred Cross of Lorraine—the symbol of those who'd rallied with de Gaulle. Others sang "La Marseillaise" and yelled "*Vive de Gaulle! Vive la France!*"

Although Lucie was happy to be sharing in the atmosphere of the demonstration, she was also fearful of being caught up in something she didn't understand, so she kept her distance, standing by the entrance of an apartment building on the corner of the Champs-Elysées and the rue Balzac.

Suddenly a commotion arose further along the street; whistles, screams, and loud bangs that sounded to Lucie like gunshots. A minute later, another series of detonations bounced off the fronts of the buildings. Lucie screamed and jumped back. Retreating into the covered entry of the building, she pulled the iron gate closed, her back against the wall, not daring to look out. After a few minutes, there was still some noise, but it seemed to have receded. As she approached the gate, she saw small groups of students in the street, running away from the Arc de Triomphe. Several were injured, some limping and others being dragged along the footpath by classmates. From the cinema on the opposite corner a large group of German soldiers suddenly spilled onto the pavement, trying to catch the students as they ran past, then pulling out their pistols and taking aim at them.

Lucie sprang back behind the gate, hiding in the shadows against the wall once more, her hands over her mouth to stop from crying out. A patrol of soldiers approached along the avenue George V, firing into the crowd. A grenade exploded, and students were flung to the pavement. A group of young people ran past the gate, one of them with blood staining the side of his shirt, his arm around a woman's shoulder. Lucie recognized Aline among them, struggling to walk unaided. She called out, "Aline! Over here!"

Aline turned towards her.

"Lucie! Let me in!"

Lucie turned the heavy handle and the gate swung open. Aline stumbled in, falling against the wall of the entrance hall, her face white and clammy.

"I've been injured," she gasped, clutching her thigh. "It hurts like hell and it's bleeding a lot. I've got to get home."

"You need to go to hospital," said Lucie, gazing in horror at the blood seeping through the leg of Aline's trousers.

"It's too dangerous. They'll turn me in to the police. Robert was arrested. The Germans took him away." She gripped Lucie's forearm. "I just need to get home. My mother's there. She's a doctor."

"I'll help you," said Lucie. She took her scarf off and tied it tight around the wound on Aline's thigh.

"I can't walk that far," said Aline. "We'll have to take the Métro."

They waited until the crowds had cleared and the street was free of soldiers. When they emerged into the dark of the early evening,

Lucie saw the remnants of the violence that had taken place. Smears of blood stained the pavement and congealed along the joins between the cobblestones. Shoes and handbags lay in the gutter, and the street was strewn with trampled flags, floral wreaths, shards of glass from shopfronts. Aline pulled up the collar of her coat to conceal her pained face as Lucie took her arm and helped her to the stairs leading down into the Métro station.

On the platform, the ticket controller waved them through without punching their tickets. He tapped Aline gently on the back. "Bravo, Mademoiselle," he said.

When the train arrived, they got into the last carriage, knowing German soldiers usually rode in the first-class carriage at the front of the train. Lucie sat beside Aline on the fold-down seats next to the door, surveying the other passengers, watching for any signs they might betray them to the authorities.

As the train pulled into the next station, they saw a German soldier on the platform. He strode quickly towards their carriage and got in. He stood in front of the doors, looking around, taking in the passengers, an air of calm indifference on his face. As the train pulled out of the station, Lucie stole a glance at Aline's leg. The blood from her wound was seeping through the scarf. Luckily, the soldier had just turned his head away, his attention caught by a peculiar sight at the far end of the carriage. Lucie followed his gaze and saw an elderly man clinging to a pole with a pair of dead pigeons hanging from a string around his waist.

While the soldier was distracted, Lucie slid her satchel from her lap and gently placed it on Aline's thigh. She looked down and saw blood falling in drops, forming a small red rivulet between the wooden slats of the carriage floor. As they approached the next station and the train began to slow, the bead of blood inched along the tiny furrow towards the toe of the soldier's boot. Lucie lifted her eyes slowly from the floor and met the soldier's gaze. She knew she had to hold his attention, to stop him from looking down. She stood up, positioning herself in front of Aline, and smiled at him.

"*Bonsoir*," she said.

After a moment's hesitation he returned her smile and touched his finger to his cap. As the train came to a halt, he took a final look around the carriage and turned to open the door. Lucie didn't move; she stood smiling at him through the window until the train lurched again and moved forward along the platform. When she looked around the carriage, every pair of eyes was on Aline. Her face was pale and covered in beads of sweat. Lucie sat back down and wiped Aline's forehead with the sleeve of her coat, not daring to return the gaze of the other passengers. No one spoke until the yellow lights of the station had disappeared from view.

***

Aline's apartment was on the rue Pavée, just a few minutes from the rue de Sévigné. When they arrived, they saw Aline's mother on the third-floor landing, the front door open behind her. When she saw the two girls at the bottom of the stairs, she called into the apartment, "Samuel! Lina's back." Without waiting for a response, she rushed down to meet them and took hold of Aline's arm. She was a tall woman with thick, black hair pulled back from her face and fixed into a bun at the nape of her neck. Her face was broad and smooth.

"*Merci*, Mademoiselle," she said to Lucie. "Thank you for your help. I can look after her from here."

"Maman," said Aline, "this is Lucie—Papy's and Margot's friend. She saved me just now."

Samuel arrived to help Aline up the last flight of stairs. He smiled at Lucie and squeezed her arm.

"I'm very grateful," said Aline's mother, glancing at Lucie, "but I'd rather not have too many people involved in this." She lowered her voice and addressed her daughter directly. "We need to be especially careful, Lina."

"I know, Madame Hirsch," said Lucie as they arrived on the landing. "I understand."

The woman paused as if about to answer, but then turned and helped Aline into the apartment, signaling to Samuel to close the door.

"Come in, Lucie," Samuel said. "Simone's just worried because . . ." He sighed, but didn't finish his sentence. "She'll be fine once she gets to know you."

Lucie followed Samuel through the living room and along the hallway to the bathroom where Aline was seated on the edge of the tub. Her mother came in with a large pair of dressmaker's scissors in her hand.

"I hope you're not given to fainting at the sight of blood," she said over her shoulder to Lucie as she began to cut Aline's trousers away to expose her injured thigh.

"No," said Lucie. "I've got used to it."

Aline's mother paused and turned to consider Lucie, taking in her bloodstained satchel. "Thank you for helping my daughter," she said after a moment. Her voice was low and even, like a bow drawn slowly across a single cello string. "It was a brave thing to do."

Until now, Lucie hadn't considered the courage of her own actions. It was the students who were brave, she thought. She admired their decision to demonstrate; she just wasn't sure if it was worth the sacrifice. Aline had been lucky—her injury was not too serious—but Lucie had seen others on the street who were much more gravely wounded. And then there were the students who'd been taken away by the Germans. She couldn't stop thinking about what would happen to them. What price would they pay for their idealism?

Once she'd finished dressing her wound, Aline's mother helped her daughter to the living room. Aline sat on the couch, her leg resting on the coffee table. Lucie sat next to her, not sure whether she was intruding. Madame Hirsch sat opposite, her back straight, her hands crossed in her lap.

"Aline told me you're a doctor," said Lucie.

"An obstetrician," replied Madame Hirsch.

"That's a wonderful job. Bringing life into the world."

"It is," she said. "Though I'm not sure it's such a good thing anymore."

When she raised her chin, Lucie could see her eyes were filled with tears. Samuel moved to her side and laid his hand on her forearm.

"I'm sorry," said Lucie. "I didn't mean to upset you."

Madame Hirsch shook her head and took a sharp breath in. "It's not your fault." She laid her hand over Samuel's. "My two youngest daughters are in Limoges with relatives. We haven't seen them since July."

"I know," said Lucie. "That must be so hard."

"We thought it would be too dangerous to bring them back to Paris. I'm glad now that we didn't."

"Why didn't you stay down there with them?" asked Lucie. "Wouldn't it be safer for you too?"

"Probably," she said. "But I'm needed here. We've already lost so many doctors." She smiled sadly. "I miss them, though."

She rose and crossed the room. From a small table in the corner, she took a silver frame and brought it over to the couch. "They're twins. Ten years old. Rachel and Danielle. We had this portrait taken just before we left Paris."

Lucie looked at the photograph of two pretty young girls. They sat close together, gazing away from the camera, their eyes wide, hair pulled back in dark pigtails. Their faces were partly covered by a large brown stain.

"Unfortunately the photograph was damaged by rain while we were on the road," said Samuel.

Aline's mother stared at the image, her fingers tracing the outline of the stain.

"That's Danielle on the left. She's the taller of the two. Rachel's eyes are lighter. They're more green than hazel."

Lucie looked up at Madame Hirsch and smiled. "They look like you."

"The authorities are finally allowing mail to cross the demarcation line," said Aline. "Until recently, we couldn't even let our family in Limoges know we'd made it back to Paris safely."

"Even so, all we're allowed to send are pre-printed cards, not even real letters," said Madame Hirsch. "What harm could there be in sending letters? Why must they be so heartless?"

Lucie said nothing, knowing she had no answer to the question.

Aline's mother stared at the photograph without speaking for several seconds. She brought one finger up to her mouth and ran it across her bottom lip.

"I'm sorry," she said eventually, returning the silver frame to its position on the table. "If you'll excuse me, I need to finish preparing dinner."

Samuel accompanied her to the kitchen.

"Maman used to work in the Port Royal Maternity Hospital," said Aline once they were alone. "We were so proud when she was appointed." She pulled the cushion from behind her back and slid it under her thigh. "She had to leave her position recently. She's at the Rothschild now. It's a private hospital."

"Did she have to leave her job at Port Royal for the same reason that Samuel can no longer teach?" asked Lucie.

Aline nodded. "There was a decree in July. Jews are no longer allowed to work in the public service. We can't work in hospitals, schools, universities, ministries . . . nowhere."

"I had no idea," said Lucie, ashamed of her ignorance. "I remember Samuel mentioning a new law, but I didn't realize it was so restrictive."

Aline sat up straighter, wincing as she moved her leg. "I know you're new to all this, but believe me, it's been going on for years. Not only in France. Everywhere. You must have heard about all the Jews who've fled here from Eastern Europe. There are tens of thousands of them looking for safety. Maman has colleagues from Poland, Czechoslovakia, Russia."

Lucie remembered Gérard's complaints about migrants from the east.

"I feel terrible," she said, putting a hand on Aline's arm. "I haven't paid enough attention to everything that's been happening."

"Maman was naturalized years ago. She's a French citizen, so it's not so bad for her. But she's Jewish all the same. And that's enough these days."

Aline looked down at Lucie's hand and frowned. "It looks like you've been through a battle of your own," she said. "How did you get those scars?"

Lucie was taken aback by Aline's directness. Not sure how to respond, she slid her hands beneath her thighs.

"I'm sorry," said Aline. "I didn't mean to pry."

"It's all right," said Lucie. She hesitated, then brought her hands out for Aline to see.

"I cut them breaking a window to escape from my house." She felt a tightness across her chest, her breaths coming faster. "It caught fire one night. My father was killed."

"I'm so sorry," said Aline. "That must have been awful."

Lucie bit her lip. "It was," she said. "I don't really like to talk about it."

"Of course," said Aline. "I understand."

***

"Where have you been?" Yvonne asked when Lucie opened the front door. "You were gone for hours."

"I went to drop off postcards at the shop."

"Why did it take so long?"

Before she could answer, Yvonne spotted the bloodstains on her bag. She gasped. "What's this? Are you hurt?"

"It's not my blood," Lucie said. "It's a friend's."

"Which friend? What happened?"

"There was a student demonstration for Remembrance Day at the Tomb of the Unknown Soldier. The Germans attacked them. She was injured."

Yvonne put a hand to her chest. "Oh my God, Lucie. What were you thinking?"

"I wasn't at the demonstration. I just helped her get home."

"Lucie, you have to be careful. I understand you want to help, but you have no idea how dangerous the situation is."

Lucie took Yvonne's hand and squeezed it between her palms. "I'm fine. Don't worry. And please don't tell Gérard."

"Don't tell me what?"

Lucie turned her head to see Gérard standing in the doorway.

"It's nothing," said Yvonne, passing her arm around Lucie's waist. "There were some students demonstrating while Lucie was out today."

"I heard," said Gérard. "At the Arc de Triomphe."

"They just wanted to commemorate the eleventh of November," said Lucie.

"We'd all like to commemorate it," replied Gérard. "What do they imagine? That this is easy for the rest of us? For those who actually fought in that war? Well believe me, it isn't." He stared at Lucie, his cheeks pink with anger. "But that isn't a reason to stir the hornet's nest. Those young hotheads will make life more difficult for all of us. It'll give the Germans an excuse to really come down hard."

"They were just trying to place wreaths when the Germans fired on them."

"They were doing more than placing wreaths," Gérard said. "There are agitators among them—communists, Jews. Don't get involved with them. They're dangerous people."

Lucie had never heard Gérard say the word *Jew* before. She noticed how he spat it out as if it had a bitter taste.

"They're just university students," she said.

"That's where you're mistaken, young lady. There are others behind them, intent on bringing us down. They've been preparing this for years and now they're seizing their chance. You'll keep well away from them if you know what's good for you."

Lucie went to her room and closed the door behind her. She was shivering, so cold that she kept her coat and scarf on. She sat at her desk, took a sheet of paper and a pencil from her drawer, and started sketching. She drew Aline as she imagined she would have looked at the demonstration in the moments before she was wounded, her arm raised above her head, fist clenched around a pole from which fluttered a French flag emblazoned with the Cross of Lorraine. She'd just finished when there was a knock on the door.

"Can I come in?" asked Yvonne. "I've got some soup for you."

Lucie quickly slipped the sketch into the pocket of her coat.

Yvonne put the bowl down on the desk and sat on Lucie's bed. She waited several seconds before speaking.

"Lucie, I'm just as concerned by what is happening as you are, believe me. But I need to look after you. The situation is much more dangerous than you realize."

"I'm not a child," said Lucie, folding her arms. "I understand what's going on."

Yvonne looked at Lucie's face as if seeing her for the first time in years. Lucie thought about how few real conversations she'd had with her mother in her life. Yvonne had always been so caught up by her husband's crises that she'd never had the time to form a clear idea of who her daughter was. Lucie didn't blame her. After all, she wasn't even sure she knew herself.

* * *

The following afternoon, Lucie went to see Aline. When her friend answered the door, she was limping but looked a lot better than she had the previous evening. They sat on the couch together, and Lucie picked up the book Aline had put down on the side table: *The World as I See It* by Albert Einstein.

"What's it about?" she asked.

Aline lifted her arm and swept it in a wide arc. "Everything," she said. "Nature, humanity, religion, the forces of good and evil." She leaned closer to Lucie. "Einstein says that each of us exists for other people—not only those close to us, but also for those we don't know. Sympathy links us to every other human. We're bound to their destinies, their existence."

"Sounds interesting. I'd love to borrow it from you once you've finished."

"Of course," said Aline. "But you'll have to be careful where you read it. It's on the Otto List."

"What's that?"

"It's a list of books banned by the Germans," replied Aline. "You can get in serious trouble if you're caught with one."

"But why would they ban Albert Einstein? Because he believes in caring about other people?"

"Yes, because of what he believes, but mainly because of what he is."

"A physicist?" replied Lucie.

Aline laughed. She leaned closer and put her lips next to Lucie's ear. "A Jew," she whispered. Lucie thought about Samuel and Aline's mother. She was starting to see how each measure that the Germans put in place was designed to be part of something bigger, a gradual exclusion of Jews from society.

Aline stood up from the couch. "I was planning on going to the university to see if there's any news of Robert and the other students who were arrested yesterday."

"You haven't heard anything?"

"No, nothing at all," said Aline, "and I'm really worried about them."

"Are you sure you're well enough to go out?" Lucie asked. "Is your leg all right?"

"Yes, it's fine." Aline smiled. "But I wouldn't mind a shoulder to lean on."

***

When they rounded the corner of the rue Champollion, there was a crowd of students on the Place de la Sorbonne, talking loudly, visibly angry. As Lucie and Aline approached, they saw that the huge wooden doors of the university were locked and a notice was pasted on them. They pushed their way to the front and read the sign. By order of the occupying forces, it stated, all classes were canceled and the university closed until further notice. All students were required to sign in at their local police station daily.

"Can they just shut the university down like that?" asked Lucie.

Aline shrugged. "Who's going to stop them?"

Lucie realized how naive her question must have sounded.

"Do you want me to come with you when you report to the police station?"

"No," said Aline. She looked around at the gathered students, then back at Lucie. "I'm not going to do it."

Lucie wasn't surprised by her response, but she couldn't help asking, "Isn't it dangerous not to?"

"It's dangerous either way," said Aline. "I'd rather take the risk of disobeying." She glanced back at the sign on the door. "I'm not surprised they've closed the university. Not after what happened at the demonstration. They know it's the start of something. They want to shut it down before it has a chance to grow." She leaned against the wall, shifting her weight from her injured leg. "But they won't succeed. They can lock up buildings if they want, but they can't lock up thoughts." She pressed her palm against the stone facade. "They may not realize it, but they've given us a stronger will to fight."

Lucie pulled her coat tight around her waist. "I'm not sure I could be as brave as you. My mother says things are getting serious. She worries about me."

"She's right to," Aline said. She pointed to the side of Lucie's coat. "And this makes you a little more conspicuous than she'd want."

Lucie looked down and saw dried bloodstains.

"Give it to me," said Aline. "It can't be keeping you very warm anyway." She removed her own coat and gave it to Lucie. "Take mine for the moment. I'm warm enough."

"It's fine," said Lucie. "I'll find somewhere to have it cleaned."

"That's not a good idea," said Aline. "My mother can have it laundered at the hospital. The bloodstains will be less likely to raise eyebrows there."

Aline took Lucie's coat from her.

"And look," she continued, "I understand that you want to be careful. This isn't really your battle."

Lucie knew she was right. She didn't understand French politics or history, only what she'd learned in high school and from Yvonne. After just six months in France, she was still a relative newcomer.

"I'd like to be more involved," Lucie said to her. "I just feel like such an outsider."

"We all feel like outsiders in France nowadays," Aline commented.

"What do you think will happen now?" asked Lucie.

"I don't know," said Aline, pushing herself away from the wall. "But I'm going to be part of it." She looked straight into Lucie's eyes. "I can't not be."

***

In her room that evening, Lucie reflected on Aline's words. Ever since she'd seen the students fired on at the Arc de Triomphe and dragged away bleeding, she'd been thinking about what she was doing here in Paris. Despite her claim to be an outsider, she'd been starting to feel more and more like she belonged here, and she too felt an urge to defy the occupiers. And yet, she struggled to understand Aline's lack of fear. How could she commit to an action without knowing what the consequences might be? They still had no news of Robert or the other students who'd been arrested. Aline's friends had heard rumors that some of them had been executed by firing squad. How had it come to this? How had the world changed to one in which students were gunned down in the streets of Paris?

***

That Saturday, Lucie and Aline met up again. Lucie suggested they go to see a film, thinking it would be good for Aline to have a couple of hours of distraction, to take her mind off what was happening to her classmates.

As they cut in front of the Panthéon heading towards the cinema, they saw that the doors of the town hall of the fifth arrondissement, which were usually closed on a Saturday, were both wide open. Several laborers were coming down the front steps carrying marble busts of Marianne, the symbol of the French Republic. Aline pulled Lucie into a doorway to watch as they wrapped the sculptures in blankets and loaded them into the back of a small van. Other men carried large busts of Pétain into the building.

Lucie had seen bronze statues disappearing from parks and public squares, taken away by the Germans to be melted down and made into arms, but she didn't understand what they needed with the marble sculptures.

"It's not the Germans doing this," said Aline. "It's Pétain and his henchmen. You see it in all their newspapers and hear it on Radio Paris. Marianne is the symbol of all the French Republic stood for; to them she's everything they find most offensive. The only woman they're comfortable with is Joan of Arc. She's Catholic, anti-English, pure, a virgin. Marianne is emancipated, free—so in their eyes, a whore. They blame France's defeat on the low birth rate. They want us women to be docile wives and breeders, not freedom fighters." She paused. "That reminds me," she said, taking a piece of paper from her bag. "I found this in the pocket of your coat when I took it from you the other day." She unfolded it and Lucie recognized the drawing she'd done of Aline the night of the student demonstration.

"I hope you don't mind," said Lucie, blushing. "It was my way of trying to understand everything that happened that day."

"I don't mind at all," said Aline. "I'm flattered actually."

"I was pretty impressed. You're the only person I know who's been wounded in a demonstration against an occupying force," said Lucie. "I pictured you in a Delacroix painting. Liberty leading the people."

Aline laughed. "That's why Pétain's statements about women are so contemptuous. He refuses to see us for what we are."

"Should you care what he says?" asked Lucie. "Isn't it better to ignore it?"

"That's what I thought too," said Aline. "But Robert made me see that it's too easy to turn away, to let them say what they want. If we're going to defeat our enemy, we need to know them; we need to pay attention to every word they utter."

"Who's the enemy?" asked Lucie. "The Germans or Vichy?"

"Both," said Aline. "And that's why we need to fight them both."

* * *

Throughout the rest of November, the streets near the university crawled with even more soldiers than before. They patrolled the Latin Quarter, stopping any young people they saw, demanding their papers, searching their bags. As the weeks went by, rumors about the missing students continued to circulate. Each day, Lucie dropped the postcards she'd made at Margot's store, then joined Aline and her classmates in a small cafe near the university to hear the latest on what they knew or, more often, what they didn't know.

Almost three weeks after the demonstration, the news came through that the arrested students had been released. Aline and Lucie were in the cafe when Robert arrived and they hurried to join the group that gathered around him.

No one asked any questions, giving him time to be ready to speak. He took a breath in, as if waiting to be sure he could contain his tears, then told them how he'd been held in La Santé prison near Montparnasse, just a couple of kilometers from where they were now sitting. He described the beatings the Germans had inflicted on even the youngest students, some of them only fifteen.

"There was a game they liked to play," he said. "At dawn they took us out into the courtyard one by one and tied us to a wooden post, our arms behind our backs. They lined three soldiers up in front of us, rifles raised, then barked something in German. *Ready, aim, fire*, I guess. And then they pulled the triggers." He paused, took a deep breath in, then exhaled slowly. "It was just a joke, to teach us a lesson. A mock execution." He looked around the group, his eyes moist. "They untied us and stood around in a circle, laughing at our tears, making fun of those who'd pissed themselves or shat their pants. And when they'd had enough, they'd drag us into a cell on the other side of the courtyard and go to get the next victim."

Robert dropped his head, his hands flat on the table. No one spoke.

"And the worst thing," he said, his face flushed red with rage, "were the French police who watched from the sides and did nothing to stop it. They said nothing when they came to guard us in our cells. Not a single word of sympathy."

***

That evening at dinner, when Yvonne asked Lucie what she'd done that afternoon, she felt she had to speak up about what had happened to the students.

As she expected, Gérard reacted furiously.

"You realize that the actions of these rebellious traitors could compromise everything Marshal Pétain has put in place to protect us from the Germans," he said. "Our leader has agreed to certain conditions and we all have a responsibility to comply with them. His words were clear for all to hear. We have laid down our arms, promised to cease hostilities. That doesn't apply only to our soldiers; it applies to all of us. Whether these young imbeciles like it or not, they're French and bound by the Marshal's undertakings. They have a duty to act in the interests of the whole nation, not just pursue their own selfish goals or the goals of those who are pulling their strings."

"No one's pulling their strings," said Lucie. "They're motivated by a love of their country and its ideals. They say that this new regime isn't the real France, that Pétain is the one who's having his strings pulled; that he's Hitler's puppet."

Gérard slapped both hands down on the table. "This man they call a puppet saved our country from a massacre. Look at what's happening in England. Paris isn't burning like Coventry. Is that what your friends would rather? That we suffer Coventry's fate? Where do you think you'd be now if he hadn't complied with the Germans? You and your friends wouldn't be in cafes spending your days playing at being grown-ups. You'd be blown to pieces by German bombs or locked up like dogs in camps."

"Gérard, please don't talk like that," said Yvonne. "Have you forgotten that more than a million of your former brothers-in-arms are, as you put it, locked up like dogs at this very moment?" She pushed her plate away. "It's not right to speak of them that way."

Gérard picked up his fork and speared a piece of carrot. He didn't respond.

Yvonne reached out and laid her hand on Lucie's. She kept her eyes on Gérard's face as she addressed her daughter. "I'm sorry about what happened to the students. You're right to be upset."

Lucie turned her head to look at Yvonne's profile. Her eyes were still on her brother, her bottom lip trembling, her neck splotched with red. It was the first time Lucie had seen her mother stand up to Gérard.

* * *

When Gérard left after dinner to finish paperwork at the garage, Yvonne came into Lucie's bedroom and sat on the edge of her daughter's bed.

"I know it's difficult, *chérie*, but I think it's best to avoid talking to Gérard about things you don't agree on."

"He's the one who criticized me. He thinks he can tell me what I can and can't think, who I can associate with."

"I know," said Yvonne. She laid her hand on Lucie's leg and rubbed her thumb back and forth against her knee. "But he's only acting out of concern. He feels responsible for us now that we're on our own. He wants to protect us."

"There's a difference between protecting and controlling, Maman. We're capable of making our own decisions."

"I know that, Lucie. But this situation is complicated. Nothing's normal. And I was away from France for so long. I don't understand what's happened here. Gérard does. He understands politics. He knows how to get us through this." She ran her hand over her throat. "I'm not sure I trust my own judgment."

12

THE START OF winter dropped a veil of bleakness over the entire city. By the third week of December, the temperatures had fallen to near freezing. Two days before Christmas, Lucie woke early and went out with Yvonne to queue up for bread and vegetables. As they waited in line a light snow began to fall, the first snow Lucie had ever seen. She tipped her head back and let the flakes float down onto her face, sticking her tongue out to catch them. The streets were more beautiful than she'd ever seen them, every surface dusted white like icing sugar on a cake.

They returned home two hours later, just as the morning fog was clearing. The snow had already lost its whiteness. It was trampled, mashed like the potatoes that were so hard to find these days. As they prepared lunch together, the mist turned to a fine rain. It billowed back and forth against the kitchen window with each gust of wind.

"I can't believe it's Christmas in two days," said Lucie. "It doesn't feel right."

"Nothing feels right in Paris these days," said Yvonne.

"It's more than that," said Lucie. "Everything's so cold and gray.

Christmas should be hot. We should be having our lunch on the beach and then going for a swim."

"I'll miss that too," said Yvonne. "Though I won't miss the flies and the sand stuck to my slice of ham." She laughed. "For the moment, though, we'll have to make a new tradition. A family Christmas Eve dinner. We'll have mulled wine and decorate the chimney with candles. A wintry Christmas can be lovely too. You'll see."

That evening when Gérard came home, Yvonne told him about her plans.

"I'm sorry," he said. "I should have told you earlier. I have to go to Normandy tomorrow. There's a hole in the roof of the shed that needs fixing."

Lucie wasn't altogether surprised that her uncle would choose to not celebrate their first Christmas together. She imagined the festive season might be difficult for him. Maybe the roof was an excuse, a way to spend this time alone with the memories of his wife and child.

"That's all right," said Yvonne. "It won't be much of a feast anyway." Lucie wasn't sure if the tremble in her voice was disappointment or resentment. In any case, Lucie was happy to have this Christmas alone with Yvonne. She needed some time away from Gérard.

***

First light on Christmas Day revealed a Paris brittle with frost. The temperature was not expected to climb much above freezing all day. After breakfast, Yvonne shooed Lucie out of the kitchen, telling her she needed to prepare a surprise. She worked all morning and emerged just after midday with her market basket filled and covered with a teacloth.

"Take the blanket from my bed and rug up," she said to Lucie. "We're eating outside."

"What? It's freezing! We can't eat outside."

"Well, we can't have our traditional Christmas picnic on the beach inside."

"You're crazy," said Lucie as she put on a thick pair of socks and wrapped a scarf around her head.

Outside, she followed Yvonne as she headed in the direction of the river. The streets were empty, with everyone else warm inside eating Christmas lunch.

When they reached the riverbank below the town hall, Yvonne turned to Lucie. "Here we are," she said. "It's not quite the beach, but I love this place. I used to play here as a kid in summer. People would do their washing here, gather to chat. It was such a lively place."

She laid the rug on the cobblestones, set the basket down, and took out several tins.

"So, for our Christmas picnic, we'll be starting with rabbit pâté and bread, followed by cold chicken and mayonnaise, and then for dessert . . ." She paused and opened the largest tin. "Pavlova!"

"I can't believe you managed to put together such a feast!" said Lucie. "Where did you find chicken? And enough eggs for pavlova and mayonnaise?"

"One of my colleagues lives in Montmartre and has chickens in her garden. I traded her preserved peaches and pots of jam."

She pulled out Gérard's thermos, which was filled with hot mulled wine flavored with cloves and slices of dried apple. They sat in the freezing cold and ate their picnic lunch as quickly as they could. After she'd drunk a glass of mulled wine, Lucie stuffed the last of her piece of pavlova into her mouth and stood up.

"This is crazy," she said. "We're crazy." She started doing jumping jacks to try to keep warm.

Yvonne laughed. "All right, we'll go soon, but there's one more tradition we need to keep. Our Christmas Day swim."

"No, no, no," said Lucie. "That's where I draw the line."

"Just our toes, then," said Yvonne, pulling off her shoes and socks.

"You're even crazier than I thought." Lucie shook her head in disbelief, then removed her shoes and socks as well. They both ran down the cobblestoned ramp, dipped their feet in the freezing water, then ran back up screaming and laughing, hurrying to dry their feet with their scarves and put their socks and shoes back on.

As they started walking home, a misty rain began to fall. It quickly grew heavier and then turned to icy sleet. Soon their coats and scarves were soaked through and water seeped through a hole in the sole of one of Lucie's shoes.

Back in the apartment, Lucie wrapped her arms around Yvonne and kissed her neck.

"That was very special," she said. "Thank you."

"I know how hard it is for you to be spending Christmas here," said Yvonne. "I just wanted to bring back a few good memories."

***

Lucie was still feeling cold after changing out of her wet clothes. Yvonne prepared a hot-water bottle for her and she curled up in bed under two thick blankets.

It was seven in the evening when she woke sweating and shivering, with a fever of 104 degrees.

"Oh, *ma chérie*. I'm so sorry I've made you ill with my stupid idea."

"It wasn't stupid—it was lovely," said Lucie. "And I'll be fine."

"You should see a doctor," said Yvonne. "If I can find one at this hour on Christmas Day."

"My friend Aline's mother is a doctor," said Lucie. "If it'll make you feel better, you can ask her if she'll come see me. They don't live far away."

Yvonne telephoned the number that Lucie gave her and spoke to Simone who agreed to come at once.

"I'm so sorry to bother you, Dr. Hirsch," said Yvonne as she showed her into Lucie's bedroom fifteen minutes later.

"Not at all," Aline's mother replied. "And please call me Simone. Both of you." She smiled at Yvonne.

Lucie watched silently as Simone examined her throat, her face just inches away. She seemed different from the first time Lucie had met her, on the evening of the demonstration; calmer, of course, but gentler too. Her eyes were much darker than Aline's, almost black in the dim light. When she looked at Lucie, they were perfectly still. Lucie could imagine her on the hospital ward, her sureness, her quiet confidence.

When she'd finished examining her, she explained that Lucie's tonsils were infected, but that it wasn't serious. She applied an iodine solution to them and gave her a sachet of aspirin for her fever. She left more iodine and aspirin with Yvonne, along with a medical certificate.

"You can use this to request an extra ration of coal," she explained.

"I don't know how to thank you for your kindness," said Yvonne as Simone packed away her medical supplies. "You hardly know me and here I am imposing on you."

"We all have to help one another in times of need."

"But I feel so bad about bringing you out on such a cold night. And taking you away from your family on Christmas Day as well."

Simone glanced at Lucie, then back at Yvonne. "It's fine," she said. "Don't hesitate to call if you need anything else."

After Simone had left, Yvonne came and sat on the edge of her daughter's bed. Lucie closed her eyes as her mother rubbed her back through the damp nightgown, making tiny circles with her fingertips.

"Is Aline's family Jewish?" Yvonne asked.

"Yes," said Lucie, her eyes still closed.

Yvonne continued making circles on Lucie's back.

"I don't think it would be a good idea to mention that to Gérard," she said. "I'm not sure how he feels about—"

"I know," said Lucie before she could finish her sentence.

***

As the end of the year approached, the temperatures fell even further, struggling to reach freezing. Everything was coated in a dampness that never seemed to dry. Lucie had never been so cold. Although she'd recovered from her bout of tonsillitis, she wore her coat and scarf all the time even in the apartment. She struggled to draw, her fingers stiff and numb. Her toes grew red with chilblains and she spent the evenings soaking her feet in a tub of warm water, squeezing them to stop the itching.

The night before New Year's Eve, Yvonne sat silently at the dining table mending the hem of a dress while Lucie listened to the BBC's Radio Londres broadcast on the wireless in French. Yvonne knew it was forbidden by the Germans. She didn't stop Lucie from listening while Gérard was away, but she made sure the volume was turned down low so the neighbors wouldn't overhear and was careful to turn the dial back to its original position afterwards.

The program began by denouncing the collaborationist station, Radio Paris, run by the Vichy regime. After the news, de Gaulle gave his regular five-minute address. That evening, he included something new—an appeal to all loyal French citizens to take part in a coordinated protest. He asked his compatriots all over France to stay inside between three and four in the afternoon on the first of January. His vision was that every city, town, and village in France would appear empty, the occupier alone in the deserted streets. By this action, he said, the citizens of France would make a silent statement—a new year had begun and things would no longer be the same. The shock and confusion of the defeat were behind them. Now the French were coming together. They would be unified and show the Germans what they were capable of.

As soon as the broadcast ended, Lucie turned to Yvonne, her cheeks warm for the first time in days.

"Will you take part with me?"

Yvonne sighed and leaned back in her chair. "Lucie, I'm as horrified by what's happened as you are. But I don't think de Gaulle should be relying on us to act. He's in England, not here."

"He'd be here if he could, but there's a death sentence on his head."

"I know that," Yvonne said, putting down her sewing, "but that doesn't change the fact that he's not fully aware of the situation here. Things are too difficult. Nothing we do will make any difference."

"Yes, it will. It'll send a message to the Germans that we're unified, that we're going to fight."

"But we're not unified," said Yvonne. "Do you think Gérard would agree with anything de Gaulle has to say? And there are lots of people who think like your uncle."

"I don't care what Gérard thinks and neither should you. It's important to take a stand; even a small one like this."

"I don't think there's any point, Lucie. Even if the Germans notice, what impact will it have? When the clock strikes four, everyone will be back out on the streets, going about their lives, trying their best to ignore the situation. And the day after that will be a day like all the others. And a week later, this tiny protest will be forgotten and people will be so cold and so obsessed with finding coal and getting their hands on a slab of butter or an egg or two, they'll have forgotten that de Gaulle exists."

"That's not true," said Lucie. "This protest is needed precisely because people are cold and hungry. They need to be reminded of the importance of taking action, even if it feels insignificant." She licked her dry lips and took a breath before going on. "All these symbolic acts aren't just aimed at the Germans. They're to show all those people who think they're too cold and hungry to care that they must care all the same." She moved closer to Yvonne and took hold of her mother's hands. "And when the sun comes back out and those same people think that life isn't so bad when they're sitting on the terrace of a cafe, that's when we'll also need symbolic actions like this—to remind them that they still need to care, and they still need to act."

"I wish I had your sense of hope," said Yvonne, picking up her sewing again. "Perhaps I know my compatriots too well."

Although she didn't want to admit it, Lucie knew there was a chance Yvonne was right. Perhaps what de Gaulle was asking was of no significance at all. Or perhaps it was the start of something greater. It was too early to judge. But she knew she couldn't wait around to see which way the axe would fall. She understood that Yvonne, like so many others, was trapped between fear and hopelessness, and that the two were numbing her into inaction. One thing was becoming clear to Lucie, though: her father had been right. Choosing not to act was a choice in itself. She was still not certain whether she was up to it; she was well aware of her insignificance and the size of the task. She knew there was no guarantee that anything she did would make a difference—but nothing about the future was certain. She had to take the first step, however timid. Aline already had when she confronted German bullets on Remembrance Day. Lucie had chosen not to take that risk and she regretted it.

1941

13

THE NEW YEAR arrived with heavy falls of snow. It lay thick on the streets, making the cold less piercing and the air a little stiller. With electricity blackouts becoming ever more frequent, most Parisians retreated to their homes or sought out the warmth of crowded, smoke-filled cinemas and cafes. Lucie preferred the vacant silence of the streets.

On the first Sunday of the month, she got up early while Gérard and Yvonne were still asleep. In the bathroom a thin sheet of ice had formed on the basin of water she'd filled the previous evening to soak her chilblained fingers. She broke it with her knuckles, the fragments sharp against her swollen skin, and splashed handfuls of freezing water onto her face. She slipped a pencil and a notepad into the pocket of her coat and went outside.

The sky was just starting to lighten as she walked along the pavement above the Seine. The snow-covered surfaces glowed pale blue and the river below was silver, the moon floating on its surface like a lost balloon. The closed booksellers' stalls were coated in a smooth layer of pure white, like perfectly iced wedding cakes. Lucie held her hand up to her eye and peered through the circle formed by her curled forefinger and thumb. She isolated tiny details of the landscape, shutting out the rest of the street, the rest of Paris. On the lichen-coated trunks of the plane trees, she discovered hidden forms—human faces, old and young. Other trees on the riverbank reached leafless branches up above the low stone wall, stretching thin naked arms skywards to wave at the passing moonlit clouds. She took the pencil and pad from her pocket and quickly sketched the scene. In the bottom corner of the sheet, she inserted her own face, tilted up towards the darkened sky.

When she'd finished, she folded the sketch in four and pushed it into the metal grate at the base of the tree. As she stood back up, the snow began to fall again, but lightly, in big soft flakes that spiraled as they fell. A few feet away, a stray dog sniffed at the base of a lamppost, then limped off through the snow, its paws leaving a trail of dark blue dots. Lucie turned her head and stared along the street. Everything was silent, the dog and the trees the only living things in sight. She held her breath and listened to the city empty of its people, freed from the violent presence of humanity, a landscape momentarily at peace.

**

After the first day of fresh powdery whiteness, the streets became a grubby slush that stayed around for days. The freezing temperatures turned the waters of the Seine into a slow, churning slurry.

Lucie spent her days inside, wrapped in a blanket on the couch, retreating to her bedroom to draw her postcards when Gérard came home from work. One freezing Saturday afternoon in early February, she went to drop them off at Margot's shop.

"Ah," said Margot, once they'd had a cup of tea, "before I forget, there's something I wanted to show you." She opened a drawer behind the counter and took out a pen-and-ink drawing of the Arc de Triomphe.

"It's beautiful," said Lucie, studying the finely detailed illustration.

"You need to look at it with this to fully appreciate the detail," Margot said, holding her magnifying glass pendant over the drawing, waiting while Lucie scanned the finely rendered lines. Hidden in the details of the monumental winged sculpture of Liberty charging into battle, Lucie made out three words in tiny capital letters, imperceptible to the naked eye. *Vive de Gaulle!*

"Oh my God," she said. "Where did you get this?"

Margot leaned in closer and whispered, "An English pilot I hid for a few days last September gave it to me as a token of appreciation. He got it from a French soldier who'd made it to England to join de Gaulle."

Lucie was flattered by the trust Margot had shown by confiding in her. "It's wonderful," she said.

"I like to think of it as secretly subversive—a little like me," the older woman replied, grinning. "Every little way we can find to thumb our noses at the Germans is a small act of resistance."

***

As she started working on her next batch of postcards that evening, Lucie couldn't stop thinking about Margot's words and the hidden secret message. She took out the sketch of Notre-Dame she'd begun. She pulled the magnifying glass down over it and studied the facade, then picked up her pencil and drew the first timid lines of her own secret message. Though she'd already decided she wasn't going to show it to anyone but Margot, this one small gesture made her nervous all the same. She knew it was nothing compared to what Aline and her friends had committed to. Even so, she felt that with this one drawing she was in a tiny way emulating Margot's "secret subversiveness."

***

The following Thursday, Lucie went out after lunch to drop off the batch of postcards she'd finished.

"You're such a productive worker," said Margot. "How do you do it?"

"It's not easy, actually," said Lucie. "There's not much room in my uncle's apartment. I have to draw on the dining table, which means clearing everything away whenever we eat, or else working at my tiny desk."

"Why don't you draw here?" suggested Margot. "It's not like we're swarming with customers."

"That'd be great."

"Done," said Margot. She picked up the batch of postcards and looked through them one by one before putting them back down on the counter.

"Perfect as usual," she said, patting the back of Lucie's hand.

"Actually, I think this one might have a slight imperfection," said Lucie, taking the drawing of Notre-Dame from her bag.

Margot held her magnifying glass pendant over the drawing and bent her face closer. After a few seconds her eyes widened as she recognized Marianne and her Phrygian cap on one of the sculptures. She leaned back in her chair and clapped her hands together. "Just splendid!" she said. "Our Lady of Paris indeed!"

"I thought you'd appreciate it," said Lucie. "It's for you."

"I'll keep it here with my other little hidden treasure. My English soldier friend would be very proud." She stood up. "That reminds me, I wanted to ask a favor. I've got an urgent errand to run and I have to leave the shop for a few hours. I was hoping you could mind it while I'm away."

"I don't know how to run an art shop," said Lucie.

"There's nothing to it. I spend most of my time sitting here drinking tea. Samuel and Aline are coming at two. You just need to be here to let them in. They'll explain when they get here."

***

Lucie sat behind the counter, warming her hands in front of the small kerosene stove while she waited for Aline and Samuel.

"Good afternoon, Mademoiselle Storekeeper," said Samuel as he opened the door twenty minutes later. He kissed her on both cheeks.

"You look right at home," said Aline.

"Do you think so?" replied Lucie. "I actually have no idea what I'm supposed to be doing. Margot's only instructions were to sit and drink tea."

"Well, you seem to be doing that exceptionally well," said Aline.

"Actually, there's another new skill I've acquired recently." Lucie took her postcard from the drawer and a magnifying glass from the shelf behind her. "It's just a silly little thing, but I'm quite proud of it."

After they'd both examined the drawing, Samuel stood up and hugged her. "It's not silly at all," he said.

"Absolutely not," said Aline. "These small acts of defiance might not seem like much on their own, but they all add up. They remind us we're not alone in this."

Lucie was flattered that Aline considered her drawing an act of defiance, however small. In her words, she felt a burgeoning sense of purpose.

"I think you've found a useful way to spend your time here," said Samuel.

"Well, I've only done this one," said Lucie. "And I don't think it'd be wise to draw them here." She looked around the empty store. "Not that I've had any customers. I think people prefer to spend their time at the cinema nowadays. At least they can keep warm there."

"Well, the fewer customers the better, as far as we're concerned," said Samuel. "Did Margot explain why we're here?"

"No. She said you'd tell me," said Lucie. "It all sounds very secretive."

"It is," said Samuel. "Come. Let us show you."

Lucie followed Samuel and Aline to the storeroom at the back of the shop.

"The reason I come here once a week to pick up a roll of canvas isn't just for painting."

He pushed aside several large stretched canvases to reveal reams of paper stacked on the floor.

"We use it to make tracts," said Aline. "Anti-German. Pro de Gaulle. I give them out at university."

Lucie remembered the handwritten messages she'd seen at the Sorbonne. She hadn't thought about who made them and where they got the paper.

"The Germans have placed strict controls on anything that can be used for printing. Luckily we're able to use the ink that Margot has in her shop, but for paper we rely on what the English parachute in. Margot stores it here and hides it in rolls of canvas."

"And then I smuggle it out of the store," said Samuel. "We were making the tracts in my workshop. Lina would pick up small bundles of them to take to university."

Lucie thought back to the first time she'd seen Aline in Samuel's apartment and the package of books she'd taken from the buffet drawer.

"After they closed down the workshop, we were concerned that the comings and goings might raise suspicions."

"Whose suspicions?" asked Lucie.

"The neighbors, the concierge—even the police," said Samuel. "It's impossible to know. Perhaps I'm being overly cautious."

"I think you have good reason to be, Papy," said Aline. "We know what happened in Poland. Neighbors denouncing neighbors." She turned to Lucie. "We decided it was less risky to make the tracts here."

"Isn't it just as dangerous?" asked Lucie. "There are German soldiers who shop here."

"That's the best cover of all," said Samuel. "No one would think we'd be audacious enough to do anything subversive right under their noses."

Lucie smiled, but she couldn't hide her nervousness. "You don't think they might be watching this place, though? After all, Margot's English."

"They might be," said Samuel. "But I think they're more interested in keeping their eye on Jewish people at the moment." He reached inside his jacket and took out his identity card. "We all had to report to our local police station in October to get this." He held up the card for Lucie to see. Stamped inside in big red letters was the word *Juif*—Jew.

"We won't let that stop us, though," said Aline. "We're continuing to spread our messages and recruit new supporters." She looked at Lucie. "And we could do with your help, if you're willing."

"What help could I be? I don't know anyone. I'm not even a student."

"No, but you have skills that would be very useful," said Samuel. "I've seen the drawing you did of Aline, and now your postcard as well."

"Why my drawings?" asked Lucie. "They're just simple pen-and-ink sketches."

"Our tracts are powerful," said Samuel, "but at the moment they're just words. We need to show the strength and truth of our combat. Your drawings can do that."

Although she supported their actions, Lucie wasn't sure she was ready to be part of them. A hidden drawing on a postcard was one thing, but this felt riskier. And she wasn't sure her drawings would make as big a difference as Samuel seemed to think. Before she could explain her hesitation, Samuel laid his hand on her forearm. She felt the gentle tremor of his fingers through her skin. "When there is so little ink, we must concentrate on showing the essential."

Aline came and stood next to her grandfather. "You've seen with your own eyes how Vichy is trying to erase Marianne," she said. "We want to put her image wherever we can, alongside de Gaulle's words."

She opened her satchel, took out a sheet of paper, and showed it to Lucie. On it was a handwritten quote by de Gaulle: *Silence is the ultimate weapon of power*. Beneath it was a call to action: *Make your voices heard for a free France.*

"We need to spread de Gaulle's message," said Aline. "And Marianne will be the symbol of our resistance."

Lucie thought about Gérard and his unquestioning veneration of Pétain, his contempt for those who were heeding de Gaulle's appeal to continue the fight.

"And you want me to draw Marianne?"

"I'd do it myself," said Samuel, "but unfortunately my hands are no longer up to the task. Not for the quantities we need."

"Even for me it'd be a slow process," said Lucie. "We won't get many out there."

"True, but we may have found a mimeograph machine," said Aline. "I have a friend in the law faculty who can 'procure' one for us. With that, we'll be able to spread the word much further. We'll keep making them as long as we have paper and ink, and I'll distribute them through my student networks once the university reopens."

"You'll have to be careful, Lina," said Samuel. "They know how effective these tracts are. Those in power always have. It was François I who said that the lead of the printing press is more dangerous than the lead of the pistol. I think he was right."

"I know, Papy. I heard about some students who were denounced for producing a newspaper. There have been arrests." She looked at Lucie. "It's a big commitment to make. I'll understand if you prefer not to join us. There's no shame in being afraid." Lucie knew Aline was right. But she'd seen so many female students participating in the November demonstration, and she wanted to show her friend that she was willing to take a risk.

"I do want to help," she said. In the gloom of the storeroom Aline's face was hardly visible, the dim yellow light of the bulb overhead glinting from the metal rims of her glasses. "I have to admit, though, I'm frightened of what could happen."

"So am I," said Aline. "But we can't let them scare us into inaction."

"Is Robert going to help distribute the tracts?" asked Lucie. "You said he's keen to continue the fight."

Aline glanced at her grandfather, then back at Lucie. "I'm not sure this is how he'd choose to continue it," she said. "He's not a big believer in the power of words."

Samuel leaned forward, his face moving into the light. "Your friend is mistaken," he said. "Words have power exactly because their existence is under threat. Those who would try to control them know they have the ability to reveal what they wish to hide." He hesitated, taking the time to formulate his thoughts. "There is a quote I heard not long ago," he said slowly. *"In times of war, words are weapons."* He opened his eyes and looked from Aline to Lucie. "Do you know who wrote that?"

Aline shook her head.

Samuel paused, his face pale and solemn.

"Hitler," he said.

***

The next afternoon, Lucie met Samuel and Aline at Margot's shop. While Margot kept watch at the counter, they set themselves up in the storeroom. The three of them worked crowded around a small table, their elbows almost touching. Lucie sketched her portraits of Marianne, and Aline and Samuel added the quote and call to action. Samuel folded the sheets and tied them in bundles of ten, ready to be sent out with Aline the next day. As the piles of finished tracts grew, Lucie saw the excitement in Aline's eyes. When she looked at her friend, Lucie felt her own throat squeeze with determination.

At seven o'clock, Samuel stood up and stretched his arms above his head. "I think that's it for me," he said. "My poor back is broken."

He kissed both girls goodbye and headed home.

When they'd almost finished their final set of tracts, Margot came to the door to tell them she was going out to dinner and asked if they could close up the shop when they were done.

"I was going to head home anyway," said Aline. "I'm famished."

"Me too," said Lucie.

"You're welcome to stay and have something to eat upstairs. I've got leftovers from lunch that I won't be eating. And some cake as well."

"That'd be fabulous," said Lucie. "Thank you."

After Margot left, they packed everything away and went up to her apartment.

"It'll actually be nice to have an evening away from my uncle," said Lucie.

"I can imagine," said Aline. "It mustn't be easy living under someone else's roof."

"I hate it. His apartment is so small that even when I'm in my room it feels like he can hear my every movement."

"How does your mother feel about living with him?"

"I think she tolerates him, but that's about all. I know she doesn't agree with his politics—he's pro-Pétain—but she's reluctant to argue with him."

"Why?" asked Aline.

"I don't know," said Lucie. "It's complicated. He's the only family she has. That's important to her, I guess. Maybe she's afraid of losing that connection."

Once they were done eating, Aline tuned Margot's radio to the BBC. At the end of the news bulletin there was a pause, followed by the deep beat of a drum, *ba ba ba boom*, repeated several times. Lucie recognized the opening bars of Beethoven's Fifth Symphony.

The Belgian announcer explained that these notes—the Morse code for the letter *V*, three dots and a dash—would be broadcast every day. They were a new rallying cry. He called on the people of the occupied lands, Belgium, Holland, and France, to write the letter *V* on the walls of every town, to hum the four notes in public, to spread the *V* as a sign of victory.

"We need paint and brushes," said Aline as soon as the broadcast was over, her face flushed with excitement. "Do you think we can take some from downstairs?"

"You're not serious?" replied Lucie.

"Of course, I am." She didn't say anything more, but looked at Lucie, the corners of her lips raised in the slightest of smiles. Lucie felt the skin on her back crawl, with anxiety or excitement she wasn't sure. She stared at Aline, trying to return her look of quiet confidence.

"Chalk will be easier to hide in our pockets," she said.

"Perfect," said Aline, smiling.

Lucie returned her smile, the tightness in her back subsiding.

"Where do you think we should write them?" she asked.

"Wherever we can. On every single wall. A thousand small acts of defiance."

***

When Lucie arrived home around nine o'clock, Yvonne and Gérard were sitting in the living room reading. She slid her hands into her pockets, trying to wipe the chalk dust off against the lining. Her nose was red from the cold air, and the light drizzle had plastered her hair in feathers against her forehead and cheeks.

"It's late," said Yvonne. "I was worried."

"I'm sorry," said Lucie. "I had dinner at Aline's house after the movie."

"I was expecting you home earlier. You should have phoned."

"Aline asked me to help her with her studies. We didn't realize how late it was."

"I thought the university was still closed," said Gérard.

Lucie felt the blood draining from her cheeks. "I think it just re-opened."

"I see," replied Gérard. He folded the newspaper he was reading and placed it on the small table next to his armchair. "I'm going to bed," he said, standing up. "I have to get up early for work tomorrow."

"I might read a little longer," said Yvonne. "Lucie, go and get a towel to dry your hair. You'll catch a cold if you go to bed with it wet. I'll make us both a cup of tea."

Once Gérard had closed the door of his bedroom, Yvonne took Lucie by the hand and pulled her down beside her on the couch.

"Were you really at Aline's house all evening?" she whispered.

"I was with Aline, but we weren't at her house."

"Where were you?"

"Out," she said. "Doing what I said I would. Not sitting around doing nothing."

"And what does that mean exactly?" asked Yvonne.

"We were just planning a couple of little acts of defiance." She pulled her feet up onto the couch and wrapped her arms around her knees. "I don't think it's a good idea to talk about it."

"So you'd rather hide what you're doing from me?" asked Yvonne.

"It's not easy to talk to you when Gérard is here."

"He's not here now," she said.

"It's just better if you don't know too much. It's to protect you."

"It's not your job to protect me—it's my job to look after you."

"Maybe," said Lucie. "It's just that sometimes it doesn't feel that way."

Yvonne let her head drop. Lucie felt bad as she saw the red patches creeping up her mother's throat and spreading across her cheeks.

Yvonne took a deep breath, then spoke softly without lifting her head. "I'm sorry if I'm not as strong as you think I should be."

Lucie leaned forward and pressed her forehead against her mother's.

"No one's as strong as they should be," she whispered.

***

When the university reopened and Aline resumed her classes, Lucie spent her days at Margot's store working on the postcards of Paris, as well as her portraits of Marianne for the tracts. One afternoon, when she was sitting at the counter drawing, Margot asked her to mind the store again while she went out to pick up paper. She hadn't yet returned when Aline arrived on a bicycle just after five, pulling a small trailer covered with a plain gray blanket.

"It's the mimeograph machine," she whispered, untying the ropes that held the blanket in place. "Help me carry it in."

After they'd taken it into the storeroom, Lucie turned to Aline. "I can't believe you just brought it here with all the Germans in the area. What if they'd stopped you and asked what was under the blanket?"

"How else was I supposed to get it here?" asked Aline. "Anyway, sometimes looking like you've got nothing to hide is the best camouflage."

"Do you know how to work it?" asked Lucie.

"My friend showed me," said Aline. "It's not difficult."

"If you teach me, maybe I could run off copies while you're at university. I could do them when I close up at lunchtime."

"That'd be great," said Aline. "You'll need one of these too." She pulled a blank stencil from her satchel. "You draw the image the same way you've been doing, but with a stylus instead of a pen. Once you're done, I'll add the quote."

When the stencil was ready, Aline set up the machine, pouring ink into its drum and putting the stencil in place. She loaded blank sheets of paper into the tray. Lucie watched as she slowly turned the handle and the first printed sheets emerged.

For the next hour, Aline ran off tracts while Lucie stayed at the counter, keeping an eye out for anyone in the street who looked like they might be watching the store. When she was finished, Aline came out and placed five bundles on the counter. She'd put an advertising poster for a brand of paint on top of each pile to disguise them.

"First print run done and ready for distribution," she said. "This is all I can take today. The rest are in the storeroom."

"Isn't it dangerous to carry them on you like that?"

"Robert says they don't stop women as much as they do men. And even if they do, I doubt they'll make me unwrap them."

Lucie accompanied Aline to the door and watched as she rode away, pulling the trailer behind her. She couldn't help but feel slightly overwhelmed by the growing distance between her new life in Paris and the one she'd known in Australia. There, the only dangers to worry about were in the ocean or the bush. Here, the dangers followed you around—along the streets, down into the Métro, up stairways, and into shops. She remembered the account Robert had given of his treatment at the hands of the Germans after his arrest. Despite Aline's bravado and the thrill Lucie felt to be part of her clandestine activities, she knew full well that this was not a game, and certainly not one that they could afford to lose.

14

ONE DAY A few weeks later at lunchtime, Lucie locked the door and hid away in the storeroom to run off the finished tracts. Aline took them with her each day and gave them out at the university and in the cafes nearby. She visited public libraries too, and slipped them between the pages of books before putting them back on the shelves. She even visited clothing stores and hid them in the pockets of jackets and coats.

One mild afternoon in the first weeks of spring, Lucie arranged to meet Aline after her last class. The air was still and clear as they crossed the Pont de Sully at the tip of the Île Saint-Louis and took the steps down to the riverbank. As they neared the Jardin des Plantes, Lucie could hear the howling of the wolves from the zoo and, further along the river, the long, low blasts of boat horns in the Port de l'Arsenal. They sat on a bench in the weak March sun and watched the river flowing slowly past. Lucie told Aline about sitting by the Yarra River when she visited Melbourne. She described it as she'd seen it for the last time, muddy and languid, gum trees shading the paths along the banks.

"Melbourne doesn't sound much like Paris," said Aline.

"I suppose it's not," said Lucie. "At least, not like this Paris."

"My father always said he couldn't live in a city that didn't have a river running through it," said Aline. "He said rivers teach us to accept our place in history. They pass by, like time, like the lives of those who watch them. He said living in a city with a river running through it is like living with something you can't hold on to. It's always about departures."

"Do you miss him?" asked Lucie.

"Of course," said Aline. "Like you miss your father, I imagine."

Lucie realized she hadn't thought about her father in weeks. When she examined her feelings, she wasn't sure if she could honestly say she missed him. She wondered, though, what he'd think of her life now in Paris and how much she'd changed in just the last few months. She was beginning to understand why he'd decided to remove himself from the flow of history, afraid of what the river would bring.

Aline turned to face the Seine. "Will you go back to Australia as soon as all this is over?"

Lucie didn't know how to answer Aline's question. Instead, she asked her own. "What about you? Do you think you'll ever leave France?"

"I don't know," said Aline. "I didn't think I would, but now I'm not so sure."

***

The following Thursday, Lucie spent the day alone in the store while Margot left Paris to arrange paper supplies for the next few weeks. At lunchtime, she turned the sign on the door to *CLOSED* and went into the storeroom to run off tracts for Aline to pick up that afternoon; she wanted to distribute as many as possible before the university closed for Easter break. Lucie poured ink into the drum of the mimeograph machine, loaded the stencil, and turned the handle. Little by little she'd grown more confident at operating it. She knew the tension needed adjusting often and the stencil was only good for a few hundred copies. It was inconvenient and messy, but she was getting more proficient each time.

When she had run off enough copies, she stacked them in neat piles, each topped by an advertisement for drawing classes, then wrapped them in brown paper and tied the parcels with twine. Now that they were making so many tracts, Aline used the trailer behind her bike to transport them. Lucie thought it was risky, but so far Aline's ploy of looking like she had nothing to hide was working.

Once she'd hidden the tracts behind the canvases in the storeroom, Lucie came back into the shop and made herself a cup of tea. As she sat down behind the counter, cup in hand, she glimpsed a movement by the door. She looked up and saw a German soldier, his hands cupped around his eyes like binoculars and pressed against the glass, peering in at the darkened interior of the store. Even though she knew there were a few Germans who were regular customers, his presence still made her start. At the same moment, he caught sight of her. He stood up straight and knocked on the glass. Lucie pointed to the closed sign, but he kept his eyes on her and knocked again.

She went to unlock the door, then turned and walked back to her stool behind the counter, trying not to appear as if she were rushing.

The soldier took two steps in and closed the door behind him. He cleared his throat and waited till Lucie looked up.

"*Bonjour*, Mademoiselle," he said, smiling at her. "How do you do?"

"Well, thank you," said Lucie, feigning absorption in a sheet of blotting paper on the counter.

"The other lady isn't here?" he asked.

"No," said Lucie, searching for a reason to explain Margot's absence. "She's not well today. I'm helping out."

"I see," said the soldier.

"What can I do for you?"

The man hesitated. "I'm looking for a small watercolor sketchpad. Do you have any?"

Lucie stood, made her way to the front of the shop, and pulled a pad down from a shelf.

"This is the only type we have," she said, handing it to him.

He opened the cover and flipped through the blank pages as Lucie moved back to her stool. The soldier followed, setting the sketchpad down next to Lucie's teacup. She kept her eyes lowered, afraid that if she looked up, she would catch his eye. But when she glanced up at him, he was looking over her head at the display case of Winsor and Newton brushes.

"I see you have the Series Seven," he said.

Lucie nodded.

"Can you show me the double zero?" he asked.

Lucie turned and reached up to take the fine brush from the display. As she picked it up, she saw that the ink from the mimeograph machine had left stains on her nails and the pads of her fingers. She turned and quickly laid the brush on the counter, then slid her hand into the pocket of her dress. She glanced up at the soldier's face, looking for an indication that he'd spotted the stains. Luckily, he was focused on the brush.

"And can I see a triple zero also?"

Keeping her right hand in her pocket, Lucie reached up with her left hand to take the brush from the display. There were also small ink stains on her left forefinger and thumb, but she hoped they weren't as noticeable as those on her right hand.

As she placed the brush on the counter, the soldier reached out and took hold of her wrist. "Show me the other one," he said softly, almost in a whisper.

Lucie felt her cheeks begin to redden. She held her breath as she slowly removed her right hand from her pocket and placed it palm down on the counter. The soldier took her wrist between his fingers and turned her hand over. He examined her palm, then turned it again and looked at the ink stains on her nails.

"I've been drawing," said Lucie, hoping her explanation would prevent further questioning.

The soldier didn't respond, but looked her in the eye, his breathing slow and steady. In the silent shop, Lucie heard the ticking of his watch.

"Show me what you were drawing," he said, letting go of her wrist.

Lucie didn't know what to do. Since she'd stopped making the postcards, the only pen-and-ink drawings left in the shop were the one she'd drawn of Notre-Dame with Marianne's face and the one the English soldier had given Margot. Was it possible he knew about them? She knew it was dangerous showing either to the German, but it was the only way to explain the stains on her fingers. She opened the drawer of the counter and slid out the postcard of Notre-Dame.

The soldier picked it up and brought it close to his face. Lucie watched for any hint that he might have detected her hidden image, but his expression didn't change.

"It's good," he said. "Can I buy it?"

"No," said Lucie, a little too suddenly. "It's not for sale. It's for a friend. It's her birthday tomorrow." She knew she was saying too much, but couldn't stop.

The soldier put the card back on the counter and paused, still looking at her, then picked up the sketchpad and set it down on top of the drawing.

"I'll take this then," he said. "And the double zero brush."

After Lucie took the soldier's money, he picked up his purchases, slid them into a pocket on the inside of his jacket, and walked towards the door.

"Enjoy your tea, Mademoiselle," he said as he left.

When the door banged shut behind him, Lucie remained seated

behind the counter, too shaken to move. This was the first time she'd come face-to-face with a German soldier since the officer who'd given Yvonne the yellow rose in their first days back in Paris after the exodus. This one was different, though. She'd detected a more sinister, suspicious undercurrent.

She picked up the cup, her fingers trembling, and drank the rest of the tea, letting another minute pass before standing and walking to the door. With her cheek pressed against the glass, she peered along the street in the direction the soldier had taken. He was nowhere to be seen. She locked the door, then went up to Margot's apartment and telephoned Aline. Without explaining why—there were rumors that calls were being monitored—she asked her friend to come over to the store.

When Aline arrived, Lucie locked the door behind her and took her into the storeroom. She waited till Aline sat down before starting to speak.

"I had an unusual customer just now," she said, trying hard to suppress the tremble in her voice. "A German soldier."

"What?" replied Aline. "Why would a German soldier come here?"

"Margot told me there are a few who are regular customers. I guess some of them are artists. She said most of them seem quite decent chaps."

"And was this one of her 'decent chaps'?"

Lucie shook her head. "I'm not sure. He'd definitely been here before. He asked where Margot was." She chewed at a piece of skin on the side of her thumb. "He was polite enough. He had a look around. Bought a sketchpad and brush."

She hesitated, then showed Aline the ink stains on her fingernails. "He asked me about these. I told him I'd been drawing. I'm not sure he believed me."

"I don't think we should wait to find out," said Aline. "We need to move the mimeograph machine and all the paper out of the storeroom in case he comes back."

"Where should we take them?"

Aline thought for a moment. "Can we put them in Margot's apartment for now? When she gets back, we'll ask her what she thinks we should do."

After they'd made several trips to carry the machine and the paper up the three flights of stairs, they sat down on the floor in Margot's living room.

"Do you think he'll be back to search the shop?" asked Aline.

"Maybe," said Lucie. "I thought they had bigger fish to fry, but maybe they're worried about what the small fry are up to as well."

"I think you're right," said Aline. "Our little acts of defiance might be worrying them after all."

* * *

The next morning, they all met in Margot's apartment to discuss the situation. Samuel agreed it was wise not to use the mimeograph machine in the store anymore.

"I was thinking," said Margot. "You'd be very welcome to come up here to run the machine. With all the noise from the cinema, no one would hear a thing."

"That's true," said Samuel. "We'd still have to be discreet. Only one person at a time. I'm afraid our comings and goings might have raised suspicions. The Germans are not fools. They might be watching the building."

"Is it a good idea to keep going then?" asked Lucie. "Maybe it's getting too dangerous."

"Everything in Paris is dangerous now," said Aline.

"And you know, Lucie," said Samuel, "I learned a long time ago that giving up never solves anything." He clasped his hands together and spoke slowly, his tone suddenly more solemn. "Giving up means the absence of hope. And if we don't hold on to hope, we become complicit, we enable them." He gazed through the window at a pigeon struggling to grip the metal railing of the balcony. "Their soldiers can occupy our city and our country, but only we can decide if we'll let them occupy our minds."

As she walked home that evening, Lucie thought back to when she'd first returned to Paris after the exodus south. Faced with the reality of living in this occupied and controlled city, she'd sometimes imagined herself back in Australia, at the beach, walking in the bush, free to do whatever she wanted. But each time she did, it became more painful to be brought back to the reality of her life in Paris. So eventually she'd stopped imagining.

Now, walking through the darkened streets of the blacked-out capital, she thought about Samuel and Aline. With all the hardships they faced, they still found the energy and optimism to fight on—performing these little acts that might mean nothing in the end. How did they find the will to continue, to not give up on hope?

***

As May arrived the weather remained unseasonably cold and the rays of sun over the rooftops carried no warmth at all. Lucie left home at eleven o'clock one morning to go to Margot's store. She walked quickly, her chin pulled into her collar, a scarf wrapped over her nose. As she passed the Saint-Paul Métro station on the rue Saint-Antoine, she saw Samuel hurrying towards her. His eyes were down, and he didn't seem to recognize her until she stepped into his path and said his name.

"Oh, Lucie dear," he said, out of breath. "I'm glad to see you."

"Is everything all right? Where are you going?"

"I'm not sure," he said. "There's something happening. I didn't want to stay home."

"What is it?" she asked.

He took her arm and pulled her to one side, under the large awning of a pharmacy.

"A few days ago I received a green ticket from the police telling me to attend an appointment at the gymnasium on the rue Japy at seven o'clock this morning. All the Polish Jewish men in my area did. Apparently there were thousands of these tickets sent out. We were all asked to come with our identity papers and bring a family member or friend."

"Did they say what for?" asked Lucie.

"To have our situation examined, they said. I suppose to check that we had all the necessary papers. And they said those who didn't attend would be liable to the severest sanctions."

"Did you go?" Lucie asked.

"I was going to," said Samuel. "To show them that I'm still a naturalized French citizen. But I had a bad feeling. I've seen things like this too many times. So I didn't go, but many of my friends and neighbors did. They went and then a little while later their family members returned and said they'd been instructed to fetch clothes and food for them. All the men were put onto buses and no one knows where they've been taken. As soon as I heard, I left my apartment and I've been walking around the streets ever since. I don't dare return home. They have my address. I'm afraid they'll come looking for me."

Samuel asked Lucie to let Aline know what was happening and reassure her that he was safe. She headed for the university and managed to catch Aline in a break between classes. A group of Jewish students there were telling similar stories. They'd seen their fathers leave early that morning for their appointment and when the students went home at midday to see what had happened, their fathers were gone. Some were Polish, others Austrian or Czech. All had received a green ticket and obeyed the instructions of the French police.

"Apparently there were thousands taken to the Austerlitz train station," said Aline. "No one knows where they're being sent."

***

That evening while Lucie and Yvonne were setting the table for dinner, Lucie told her mother what had happened that morning.

"That's terrible," said Yvonne.

"And the men hadn't even done anything. They were just living with their families, going about their business, harming no one. Their families have no idea where they are."

"Your concern is misplaced," said Gérard, looking up from his newspaper.

Lucie put down the pitcher she was carrying and turned to face him. She hadn't wanted to discuss the matter in front of him, but it was too hard to keep the news in; it had been troubling her all day.

"They are hardly innocent men," her uncle continued. "I've heard there were large numbers of criminals among them." He folded his paper and picked up his glass from the table beside his armchair. "In any case, it was no doubt a necessary measure by our government to remove excessive numbers of foreigners. The economy can't support the burden of these people. We must look to protect our own in these difficult times."

"But I'm a foreigner too," said Lucie. "And I've been here less time than they have. Does that mean I'm a burden on the economy too?"

Gérard took a sip of cider before responding. "That's where you're wrong," he said. "There's a fundamental difference between you and those foreign Jews." He wiped the corner of his mouth with the side of his thumb. "You have French blood flowing in your veins."

15

TOWARDS THE END of June, the weather turned unbearably hot and remained that way for days on end. One stifling Saturday afternoon, Lucie decided to cool down at the floating Piscine Deligny, a swimming pool moored on the Seine that had just reopened. She asked Aline to join her. Her friend said she couldn't, but she would meet Lucie later at the Square du Vert-Galant at the tip of the Île de la Cité.

When Lucie arrived at the pool, she dropped her towel onto the hot wooden deck and slipped into the water among the multitude of oiled and slippery bodies. After her swim, she lay under the scorching sun and closed her eyes, trying to pretend she was at the beach back home. The constant burble of French voices, however, brought her back to reality. From time to time there was a hush as the mass of sweaty, pink-skinned Parisians paused their conversations and craned their necks to watch in silence as a steamboat full of German soldiers passed by on a leisure cruise.

Later, Lucie walked along the river to the small square where she and Aline were to meet. Aline arrived just after four and sat down next to Lucie on the cool stone edge in the speckled shade of a weeping willow, their feet dangling above the water. They watched the swans drifting serenely by, their necks held stiff and proud. Lucie couldn't help but feel a little jealous of the birds. They could spend time in the beauty of this city, but were free to come and go as they pleased. When the reality of occupied Paris became too much for them, they could leave, find another city just as beautiful, one without the underlying ugliness. She leaned her head against the trunk of the willow.

"If I was them, I'd fly away. Go down south to the free zone. Or all the way to Australia."

"Even they can't do that at the moment," remarked Aline. "They lose their wing feathers in summer, so they're forced to stay on the ground and look after their young."

"Really?" asked Lucie. "I had no idea."

"So no one is truly free in this city," said Aline, leaning back against the tree and closing her eyes. "Not even the swans."

Lucie looked out towards the Pont des Arts. It was crowded with Parisians strolling arm in arm. Some leaned on the metal railings or stood behind artists with their easels, looking over their shoulders as they painted. It was easy to forget sometimes that this was a city under occupation. She turned to face Aline, keeping an eye out for the guard on his slow, looping patrol along the dusty gravel path above.

"Why couldn't you come to the pool?" she asked.

"I had to meet Robert and some other students. There's been big news."

"What?" asked Lucie.

"Germany has invaded the Soviet Union. They've broken the non-aggression pact."

"What does that mean for us?"

"The Germans will be fighting in the east now. They'll have fewer men to hold their position against England. It could mean a breakthrough soon."

"That's good," said Lucie. "But what does that have to do with Robert and the other students?"

"Some of them are communists," said Aline. "They've been reluctant to take action while the Soviets were aligned with the Nazis. Now they're free. They said they're starting to make plans."

"What type of plans?" asked Lucie.

"I'm not sure," said Aline. "Robert likes to talk a lot, but I don't think he and the others in his group have the capacity to do much." She reached up and pulled a leaf from an overhanging branch. "They're excited by the thought of action more than anything. They're really just playing at being resistance fighters. I think he wants me to help by passing messages between members of the group."

"Are you going to do it?"

"I don't know." She tore the leaf apart, leaving just the veins. "I have other things on my mind at the moment."

"Like what?" asked Lucie.

"They've just passed new laws. They're limiting the admission of Jewish students in universities to no more than three percent of the total. I'm not even sure I'll be allowed to re-enroll for the new school year."

"How can they do that?" Lucie demanded. "You're French, aren't you?"

"Yes," said Aline, throwing the scraps of leaf into the river. "But to the government, I'm Jewish before anything else."

***

A few days later, Lucie had arranged to meet Aline in a cafe near Odéon. Her friend arrived late, hot and sweaty, but also visibly worried. She told Lucie that another new law had just been passed, forbidding Jewish people from being in possession of a radio.

"My mother hid our wireless set. When the police came to con-fiscate it, she told them we didn't have one. We were lucky they didn't ask to search the apartment." She leaned her face close to Lucie's and whispered, "My mother was hoping you might consider taking it and keeping it in your apartment. She's scared they'll be back to look for it."

"I wish I could," said Lucie, "but what would happen if my uncle found it?"

Aline stared at the table, saying nothing for several seconds. It was the first time Lucie had seen her so worried.

"That's all right," she said, raising her head. "We'll find somewhere else to keep it."

***

On her way home, it occurred to Lucie that there might be a way of avoiding her uncle. The couple to whom Gérard had been renting the maid's room on the sixth floor of the building on the rue de Sévigné were leaving at the end of the month and Gérard hadn't said any-thing about finding new tenants. If Lucie were to move into the room herself, she could hide the Hirschs' radio and Aline would be able to visit her there.

That evening after dinner, while she was doing the dishes with Yvonne, she decided to raise the idea with her mother.

"Do you think he'd let me use it?" she asked as she rinsed the plates. "It'd be less crowded in here."

Yvonne finished wiping a cup and placed it back on its hook.

"Is that the only reason?" she asked.

Lucie pulled her hands out of the water and wiped them on her skirt. She turned her face towards Yvonne, but didn't raise her eyes.

"And for a bit more privacy."

Yvonne paused, waiting for Lucie to look up.

"And you want me to ask him?"

"If you could," Lucie replied.

Yvonne considered her daughter for a moment, pulling at a piece of dry skin on her bottom lip. "All right," she said finally. "But promise me you won't do anything up there that might . . ." She didn't finish her sentence.

"I'll try," said Lucie. She could see that Yvonne wasn't pleased with her answer, but also knew it would be a lie to promise more.

***

In the first days of July, Lucie felt the mood in Paris changing. The Germans were clearly nervous about public insurrection, especially in the lead-up to Bastille Day on the fourteenth of July. Aline said they were worried about possible celebrations, shows of patriotism and unity. French police were everywhere, questioning people in the streets, conducting searches of apartments. The curfew was tightened even further. Cinemas and theaters were to close by eight each evening.

Then, as expected, in the second week of July, the authorities announced that all celebrations for Bastille Day were banned. It should instead be a day of quiet and solemn remembrance. On the evening of the thirteenth, Aline was with Lucie in the maid's room that Gérard had agreed to let her use. The day had been hot and the air in the cramped space beneath the roof was stifling. Lucie left the small window wide open. The streets were so silent without cars that all the other sounds of the city rose to fill the void. They echoed across the stillness between buildings and entered through the open window. Music, conversations, laughter. Babies' cries and shouts of anger. Children playing with their cap guns, and airplanes far overhead whose rumbling sent a shiver through her scalp.

They tuned Simone's wireless to the BBC. Lucie knew it was risky, that the sound of radios carried far and might be overheard by people who'd gladly report the infringement to the police, so she turned the volume down as low as she could and they leaned close to the set, their ears almost touching the speaker. After the evening news, a call was broadcast. It was addressed to all inhabitants of France, asking everyone to assemble peacefully in public on the fourteenth of July and sing "La Marseillaise."

"I'm going," said Aline. "And I'll take tracts to give out." She grasped Lucie's arm. "Will you come?"

Lucie knew how hard all the new restrictions had been on Aline, how controlled she felt. She knew this would help her friend to stay positive, to believe that the fight was worth continuing.

"Of course I will," she said.

***

The next afternoon they met by Pont Marie and made their way on foot towards the Louvre. In the main courtyard, there were dozens of men and women, working as though it was just an ordinary Monday, tending a huge field of leeks that had been planted there at the start of summer.

They headed north with the growing crowds along the broad avenue towards the Place de l'Opéra. On the street, several sellers appeared with baskets of tricolored flags and rosettes. Aline bought two rosettes and they pinned them on their collars. Lucie was nervous but felt a tremor of excitement in her chest at the sight of these first timid signs of national pride. By the time they reached the opera house, a procession of several hundred people had formed. Vélo-taxis decorated with streamers arrived with still more people. Aline took Lucie's hand, pulling her into the thick of the crowd. She gave Lucie a bundle of tracts and together they handed them out to anyone who would take them.

As those around them began to sing "La Marseillaise," the two girls joined in, yelling, "*Vive la France*," their voices fused with hundreds of others, as if they were one united body.

Suddenly, Lucie felt Aline tugging on her arm. When she turned to face her, Aline pointed to a large group of policemen on foot. They were making their way methodically through the crowd, picking off people one by one and arresting them. Lucie didn't understand why they were reacting that way. They were French too. It was just a celebration.

As Aline and Lucie pushed their way towards the Métro station, Lucie could see fighting breaking out here and there between the police and some of the more determined protesters. As they reached the stairs leading down into the station, a German truck arrived. A dozen soldiers jumped out and ran towards the crowd, guns drawn. Lucie froze. She dropped the remaining tracts as Aline grabbed her arm and pulled her down the steps into the station. They ran along the endless corridors to the platform and managed to clamber into a crowded train carriage just before it pulled away. Lucie stood panting next to Aline, her wet palm slipping on the metal pole, the skin on the backs of her knees prickling with sweat.

"I can't believe the French police were there doing the dirty work of the Germans today of all days," said Aline. "Hopefully it'll make people even more determined to speak out and this'll be the start of something bigger."

Lucie nodded, but her legs were trembling and her stomach felt like it was filled with lead.

***

As they walked home from the Bastille station, the pavement along the rue Saint-Antoine was covered with dozens of "butterflies." Lucie had seen them before—tissue-thin pieces of paper, scribbled with handwritten messages of resistance that often fluttered down into the streets, dropped from rooftops by invisible hands. Today, though, there were so many more. Maybe Aline's hopes weren't so improbable after all. Maybe there was a change taking place in the minds and hearts of her fellow Parisians.

16

THE HEAT THAT had stifled Paris all summer continued for the next few weeks and showed no sign of ending. One Saturday, as the long afternoon slipped slowly towards evening, Lucie and Aline strolled together through the Saint-Germain district. The terraces of cafes gradually filled till there wasn't a single spot to be had. At some, French women sat smoking cigarettes and laughing with German soldiers, their crimson fingernails splayed on the sleeves of the well-cut uniforms. They held their chins high, knees touching under the small round tables. Lucie wondered if all their flirting and teasing was their private way of regaining some measure of power over the occupier. She looked at them as she walked past, not hurrying, letting her gaze linger. Sometimes they glanced up but then quickly turned their eyes away and back to the men in front of them, their red lips strained in smiles, their jaws held tight. She didn't want to judge them, trying instead to understand their situation; the deprivation, both material and emotional, that pulled them towards these handsome men with their clinical correctness and their access to abundant food and wine.

Then, in mid-August, as if to challenge the languor of late summer, groups of communist youth began organizing demonstrations around Paris. Near the Place de la République, a scuffle with police turned into a brawl and students were arrested. New notices appeared in the Métro and on the walls of buildings. Any acts deemed communist activity would be considered abetting the enemy, punishable by death.

When Lucie met Aline in the Square du Vert-Galant one Friday afternoon, she told her friend she was worried about her involvement with Robert's group.

"Don't be," said Aline. "He knows what he's doing. What he has in mind isn't dangerous."

"What does he have in mind?" asked Lucie. "Did he tell you what they're planning?"

"Not in any detail."

"But he asked you to be part of it?"

Aline took Lucie's hands in hers and squeezed them tight.

"I'm sorry," she said. "I really can't tell you. You don't want to be involved and it would be dangerous for you to know too much."

"I thought you said they were just playing at being resistance fighters. What's he pulling you into, Aline? You're Jewish; he's not. Does he understand the danger he's putting you in?"

"No more danger than he's putting himself in. You've seen the warnings for communists."

"But he's reckless. I'm not sure I trust his judgment."

"Well, you can trust mine," said Aline. "I won't do anything stupid. I don't think violence is the way to go, and I've told Robert that. He'll listen to me." She paused. When she spoke again, her voice was lower, fainter. "Look, they're only planning demonstrations. I'm just passing a few messages for them. We smuggle notes to students who've been taken prisoner to try to get them out. Some of them are allowed to receive parcels and we hide messages inside the shirt collars. That's all. It's not harming anyone."

Lucie wasn't completely convinced by Aline's attempt to reassure her.

"I'm just not sure if anything Robert or any of us does makes a difference anymore. I've started to wonder whether all our little actions are worth it."

"Maybe they're not," said Aline. "No one can know for sure. But they make a difference to me. They're my rampart against indifference." She took off her glasses and wiped the lenses with the sleeve of her shirt. "Look, Lucie, maybe I am crazy to get involved in Robert's actions. But maybe that's what we need to be. In the face of futility, only the crazy persist."

Lucie leaned forward till her face was close to Aline's. "I'm just afraid," she said. "Printing and giving out tracts is one thing, but openly challenging the Germans is another. Things are changing. It's not like when we first started." She looked up, shading her eyes against the throbbing glare of the afternoon sun. "It's like this heatwave. The pressure's been building for weeks. It's bound to end in a storm. And there's the same tension in the streets, in the Métro, everywhere. One day soon, it'll burst and unleash its fury."

* * *

A few days later, a new notice appeared on walls all over the city. It was written in German and French, informing the population that two young men had been condemned to death and executed for participating in a communist demonstration against the occupying forces. Lucie hoped Aline would realize how close to home this was, that it would wake her up to the danger of supporting Robert in his activities. These two young men were students like her, in a group just like Robert's, doing nothing more than demonstrating. Aline had to understand that in the eyes of the Germans, that made no difference. They were the enemy—to be killed without mercy.

***

One Wednesday morning towards the end of August, Lucie woke early to go out and buy sugar. The weekly ration had run out and Gérard refused to drink his coffee without it or to buy saccharine from the pharmacy to use as a substitute, even though his breakfast consisted of his daily dose of peaches in sickly sweet syrup. He said it was bad enough that there was no longer any pure coffee, just the "National Coffee" mix, which was three-quarters chicory.

"You have your British friends to thank for all these food shortages," he said. "All their damned blockades mean nothing can get through to us."

Lucie knew he was hoping to provoke a reaction from her. Without bothering to answer, she slipped on her sandals and headed out the door.

The line at the grocery store wasn't as long as usual and the sun was just appearing over the tops of the buildings, so once she'd bought the sugar, she decided that rather than going straight home, she'd drop by Samuel's apartment to say hello. She was more than happy to make Gérard wait for his cup of coffee.

As she made her way through the eleventh arrondissement, she noticed that every Métro station she passed was closed. When she arrived on the Place de la Bastille, police accompanied by German soldiers started converging from all directions, stopping all the men they encountered, demanding to see their papers. She joined a small group of people huddled on a street corner, silently watching on. Next to her was a woman with a young child. Lucie asked if she knew what was happening.

"They're arresting all the Jewish men," she said.

"Did they get a letter?" asked Lucie.

"How would I know?" replied the woman, frowning at her, her mouth tight with suspicion. "I'm Catholic. It's got nothing to do with me."

Along the Boulevard Richard-Lenoir, where the ham and scrap metal market was usually held, half a dozen buses were lined up, hundreds of men being loaded onto them. At the entrance to an apartment building Lucie saw police officers guarding a large group of men they'd just arrested. More police herded another group along the footpath. She backed up tight against a cafe window, standing on tiptoes on the narrow wooden step, peering into the lines of heads, checking to see if Samuel was among them. From the entrance to an apartment building a few doors away, a young woman emerged, a small child on her hip, a hunk of bread clasped in her free hand. She was crying, running to give the bread to her husband before he was taken away. As the woman passed, Lucie stepped out and called after her. The woman paused briefly and Lucie slid the package of sugar between her arm and the child's chest.

"Take it, please," she said.

The woman opened her mouth to speak, but then turned and ran after her husband. Over her shoulder, the child looked back at Lucie, its eyes wide with confusion, its hair flapping up and down with each jarring step.

Lucie knew she had to warn Samuel about what was happening. As she turned the corner onto his street, she saw Aline hurrying towards her. Before Lucie could speak, her friend took her by the hand and pulled her in the direction of a small square enclosed by a low metal fence. Aline yanked the gate open and let it bang closed behind them, leading Lucie to a bench on the far side of the square lawn.

"We heard about the roundup from a neighbor," she said. "We're not sure who's on their list this time, but my grandfather's gone into hiding just in case."

"Where is he?" asked Lucie.

"It's better for you not to know," said Aline. "There's no point putting you at risk as well."

Lucie looked out towards the line of green and yellow buses. "I think we're all at risk nowadays," she said. "It feels like no one's safe."

17

THE DAY OF Lucie's eighteenth birthday was unusually hot for September. Early in the afternoon, she was sitting by the open window in her room, fanning herself with a book, when Aline arrived.

"Happy birthday," she said, kissing Lucie and handing her a small parcel. "It's from my grandfather, my mother, and me. I hope you'll like it."

Lucie sat down and opened the wrapping. Inside was a silver inkwell, an image of a hand holding a pencil engraved on its side. Around the base was a quote. Lucie held it up to the light and turned it to read the words curled around the shining metal:

> *Drawing is not what one sees,*
> *but what one can make others see.*
> *—Edgar Degas*

"It's beautiful," she said, setting it down on the desk.

"There's a message as well," said Aline, handing her a small blue card. She stood behind Lucie as she read the note.

Dear Lucie,
My son, Aline's father, made this inkwell. We think he would be
very happy to see it used by a fellow artist. Our wish for you and
for all of us is that this war will soon be over and we'll be reunited
with those we love.

Warmest thoughts,
Samuel, Simone, and Aline

As Lucie read the words, she thought of Samuel's son, Simone's husband, languishing in a prisoner-of-war camp. And his granddaughters, Aline's two sisters, hundreds of miles away, cut off on the other side of the demarcation line, so far from their family. She felt ashamed that she'd hardly thought of how difficult it must be every day for them all to be apart. She picked up the inkwell and traced the lines of the engraving with her index finger.

"It's such a kind gift," she said. "I feel bad about accepting something that must mean so much to the three of you. I hope you won't regret parting with it."

"We wouldn't have given it to you if we did. My grandfather appreciates you very much," said Aline. "We all do."

Lucie put the inkwell back into the tissue paper and nestled it in her lap. "This really means a lot to me. I'd like to find some way to thank you."

She thought back to the water-stained photograph of Aline's two sisters that she'd seen in their apartment. She mentioned it to Aline.

"Maybe I could copy it."

"That's a beautiful idea," said Aline. "My mother will be at the hospital all day tomorrow. You could come over and work on it if you want."

***

When Lucie arrived at the Hirschs' apartment at nine the next morning, Simone had already left. Aline pulled her small desk close to the bedroom window and cleared it so Lucie would have somewhere to work. Then she fetched the framed photograph of her sisters and sat down on the bed to watch.

Lucie had decided to use pastels for her drawing of the twins. She hadn't had much practice with them, and was a little unsure that she'd be able to accomplish what she had in mind. Although she found it a little distracting to have Aline staring over her shoulder at every mark she made, she didn't have the heart to tell her. Instead, she sent her off to the kitchen several times to make cups of tea or pour her a glass of water. She worked all morning and afternoon, stopping only to share a light lunch of bread and cheese with Aline. When she'd almost finished, she stood up from the chair and looked down on the drawing to consider it from a distance. The effect she'd managed to create with the pastels was better than she could have hoped. The girls' faces glowed, their cheeks full and pink, their eyes shining. She remembered Simone mentioning that Danielle's eyes were hazel, while Rachel's were slightly green. She added touches of color, blending them till she was sure they were just right.

When she was done, she held the drawing up to show Aline. She didn't have to ask what she thought of it. The light in her friend's eyes was enough to tell Lucie that she'd captured what she wanted.

Lucie sprayed the image with fixative and waited for it to dry, then wrapped it in a sheet of tissue paper. Aline made another pot of tea and they waited for Simone to come home.

***

"You didn't need to get us a present, my dear," she said when Lucie handed her the package.

"Your gift meant a lot to me," Lucie said to her. "I wanted to show my appreciation. It's just a small thing."

Simone sat down on the couch next to Aline. When she unfolded the tissue paper and saw the drawing, she took a sharp breath in and raised her hand to her throat. Lucie watched in silence as Simone slowly ran her fingers over the surface of the image, as though expecting the girls' faces to be warm beneath her touch. Lucie held her breath. She hoped that she hadn't been wrong to intrude into something as personal as a mother's love for her children. Finally Simone looked up, her lips squeezed tight together in a smile that was part joy, part sorrow. "Thank you," she whispered. "It's the most precious gift I've ever received."

***

As Lucie walked along the rue Rambuteau the next day, she tried to focus on the warmth of the sun on her scalp, the delicate seed pods twirling past her face, anything to take her mind off the aching in her heels and the uneven edges of the cobblestones pushing up through the worn-out soles of her sandals. She didn't have enough points on her ration card to buy a new pair, and her winter shoes were just as bad.

With the shortage of leather, wooden and cork soles had become a necessary substitute. Simone had told her of a cobbler in the ninth arrondissement who repaired shoes for a reasonable price so Lucie had decided to go and see.

Turning onto the Boulevard des Italiens, she saw a massive poster hung above the entrance of the Palais Berlitz across the road. The image was as shocking as it was enormous: a sinister and rapacious caricature of a Jew, his claw-like hands clutching the Earth. Lucie read the huge black letters above the image—*Le Juif et la France*, The Jew and France—advertising an exhibition that had just opened. She stood on the pavement opposite, watching as passersby glanced up, then lowered their eyes and hurried away. Many others queued calmly beneath the poster to visit the exhibition. She stared at them, finding it hard to believe that these were her fellow Parisians, trying to imagine how Aline, Simone, or Samuel would feel about them. As she moved away, she caught sight of Madame Maurel's son, Émile, in the line. She wasn't sure if he'd seen her, but he quickly turned away and looked down at his feet. She thought back to all the times she'd seen him on the stairs or skulking around the entry hall. He would have seen Aline coming and going. She wondered if he knew she was Jewish.

In the Métro on the way home she noticed posters advertising the exhibition plastered up on all the walls. In the carriage, the usual babble of the passengers around her was replaced by an eerie and uncharacteristic silence.

* * *

When Aline came to see her the following afternoon, Lucie told her what she'd seen.

"Yes," she said. "I know all about it. In fact, I went to see it this morning."

Lucie shook her head. "Why would you give your support to such a repulsive event?"

"I want to be informed," said Aline. "To see what they're saying about us."

"Don't you see enough of that already in newspapers and in the streets?" replied Lucie, her voice rising in disbelief.

"That's precisely why it's important to go and see it." Aline removed her glasses, closed her eyes, and pushed her index fingers against her eyelids. When she looked up, her eyes seemed darker than before. "They're calling us the Jewish peril," she said. "They say we're taking over, that France is a victim of her generosity and hospitality."

Lucie replied, but more softly than before. "Doesn't it disgust you to hear all that?"

"Of course, it does," said Aline. "But it worries me more. Their plans worry me more."

***

Lucie too was worried by what she saw around her. The atmosphere in Paris was becoming notably more hostile. In the streets, the timid solidarity that had existed between strangers was giving way to suspicion and self-preservation. The routine that the population had begun to settle into since the armistice was disrupted by stark reminders that many were continuing the battle. Violent attacks against the occupying forces were becoming more frequent across the capital. Just a day after her conversation with Aline, a German soldier was shot at the Gare de l'Est. The consequences were swift and drastic. Thirteen hostages were taken to the Mont-Valérien prison and executed by firing squad.

Despite the killings, communist youth groups seemed determined to show the enemy that they wouldn't be intimidated. Another soldier was shot that same day and another a few days later. The Germans responded by executing more hostages, another twelve in the weeks that followed. There was a real sense of fear among the population that they'd all be punished for the attacks. While she waited in food queues and on crowded Métro platforms, Lucie heard rumors, whispered frantically and passed along, that the Germans were planning to cut off the electricity and water, even poison wells.

***

Lucie met with Aline and Margot to talk about whether they should continue using the mimeograph machine in Margot's apartment. They all agreed it was becoming too risky. Lucie said she could continue to draw the tracts by hand, as they had at first. They all hoped it would soon be safe enough to start distributing them again.

One afternoon, Lucie was taking a break from her work in her small maid's room and was boiling the kettle to make herself a pot of tea when Aline arrived. Lucie poured them both a cup and sat down next to her friend on the bed. Aline sat in silence, blowing on the surface of the hot tea, the steam fogging up her glasses.

Over the previous weeks, Lucie had felt a reluctance in Aline to discuss the attacks on Germans and the subsequent executions of hostages. She didn't think Aline was implicated in any way, but she suspected that Robert might be.

"Has he told you anything?" she asked. "Do you know what he's doing?"

Aline took off her glasses and wiped them on her sleeve. "I'm not free to tell you," she replied.

Lucie wasn't surprised by her answer. "I just think it's terrible that those innocent hostages have to pay," she said. "What's the point of killing one German soldier if it means the loss of a dozen innocent lives?"

"I told you I don't know anything about the attacks. Stop questioning me, Lucie," Aline answered, her tone more defensive than Lucie would have expected. "You're not part of this. Let the people who understand the situation do what they have to."

In Aline's words Lucie heard an echo of Gérard's. It hurt that even Aline thought of her as uninformed, her opinions not worth listening to. They sat in silence for the next few minutes. When she'd finished her tea, Aline got up, mumbled something about needing to run an errand for her mother, and left.

***

Lucie didn't hear from Aline the next morning. At midday she went for a walk to the Jardin du Luxembourg, deciding it would be better than the confines of her room, even though the gardens were popular with German soldiers. Whenever she went there, she felt a little on edge, waiting for a pack of gray-green uniforms to invade the space. They were impossible to miss, moving through the tree-lined alleys noisily, taking possession with the thudding of their boots, the loudness of their voices, their unapologetic air of ownership. A section of the park had been fenced off to create a "German Garden" where they'd planted vegetables and installed sheds to store huge quantities of commandeered potatoes.

Lucie found a quiet spot to sit and closed her eyes, the dappled sunlight through the branches of a chestnut tree warm against her skin. She slipped her feet out of her shoes and brushed her soles against the fallen autumn leaves. As she breathed in the leaves' dusty, musk-sweet odor, she heard loud notes of music start up in the bandstand fifty meters away. It was a German military concert, one of the performances that were regular occurrences all over Paris. Lucie wasn't in the mood for the strident, overwhelming brashness of their polished, gleaming instruments. She stood up and walked away down the shaded alley of plane trees. She tried to find another place to sit, but wherever she went, the booming, brassy notes followed her. They weren't played so much as smashed out with fervor and aggression.

She left the gardens and wandered around the neighboring streets, discreetly observing the people she encountered. Although she'd never owned a camera, now she would have loved to photograph those she saw around her, capture their fleeting expressions, try to see into their minds. Even if she had a camera, though, she wouldn't be able to use it. The only people allowed to take photographs in occupied Paris were the Germans themselves, or the officially appointed photographers working for their glossy propaganda magazine, *Signal*. Despite the lack of cameras on the streets, though, photographed faces were everywhere. Lucie saw them every day: in identity photos, in the omnipresent portraits of Pétain, the posters of executed resistants. To counter this, she took pleasure in capturing other sorts of faces in her pencil sketches. She drew the people she saw in the streets, on the Métro, in cafes. She had to make the drawings small, on just a quarter of a sheet of paper, small enough to hide in the palm of her hand. She learned that if she was careful, she could sit right opposite someone without them realizing she was drawing them. If she didn't have her notepad with her, she sketched on the backs of Métro tickets she found on the ground.

She drew often, whenever she was alone. She would leave a bit of blank space on either side of her sketch, then, when it was done, fold the sides over her portrait as if closing it in behind shutters. Each time she finished one, she hid it in a different place—in the knothole of a tree trunk, between the pages of a dictionary on the shelf of the municipal library, in the pocket of a jacket hanging in the entry of a cafe. She imagined them being found by strangers, discovered like secret messages. She didn't know exactly what she was hoping to accomplish. She'd noticed that more and more, people looked at one another with suspicion; no one looked a stranger in the eye. Maybe her sketches would help in a small way to break down the divisions that were being created. She hoped the people who found them would take the time to look at these portraits of their fellow Parisians, not with distrust and suspicion, but with curiosity and compassion, wondering who this stranger was, imagining their life, hopefully feeling a faint connection.

It was late in the afternoon when she arrived home to find Aline waiting for her.

"I'm sorry I was short with you yesterday," her friend said, pushing a strand of hair behind her ear. "I've had a lot on my mind."

"Is it anything I can help with?"

Aline took a letter from her bag and read it out loud. As they'd feared, the new restrictions on the percentage of Jewish students admitted to the university meant Aline would no longer have a place when the new academic year began the following week.

"There must be something you can do," said Lucie.

"I don't think so," said Aline. "And I'm not sure I want to. I have no desire to spend the whole year feeling different, barely tolerated by my peers. Every day I'd imagine people thinking, *All right, you can stay, but we don't want too many of your sort.*"

***

That evening, they stayed in Lucie's room listening to Radio Londres. As he did every day, the announcer acknowledged the relentlessly climbing tally—"Today is the four hundred and eighty-sixth day of the battle of the French people for their liberation." Lucie had followed the ever mounting number as the seasons came around a second time, focusing on the one thing that gave her hope: the "personal messages" that were broadcast every evening. They were secret codes destined for resistance fighters; strange, slightly absurd phrases. *The gardener's dog is howling. The leg of lamb is cooked. Pauline likes carrot soup.* She tried to imagine the people for whom these messages were intended. She pictured groups of men and women gathered around a table in the corner of a cafe or meeting in darkened side streets. She saw them like drops of ink on paper, each small to begin with, but bleeding at the edges, expanding little by little to become one large mass.

As the news broadcast ended, there was a knock on the door. Lucie quickly turned the volume down and waited. After a few seconds, she heard Yvonne whisper, "It's just me."

She opened the door and let her mother in.

"I thought you might like something sweet with your coffee," Yvonne said, placing two barley sugars on the small bedside table.

"Thank you," said Aline.

Yvonne put her hand on the door, ready to leave.

"I won't disturb you any longer," she said. "But you might want to be a bit more careful. There are people in the building who wouldn't be particularly pleased if they overheard what the two of you are listening to up here."

Aline picked up one of the sweets from the little table and started to remove a corner of the waxed paper wrapping.

Yvonne looked at Lucie. "And some of them are under the impression that you're alone up here."

"I'm sorry," said Aline, placing the sweet back on the table. "I feel like I'm putting you in a difficult situation."

"The situation may be difficult," replied Yvonne, "but that's hardly your fault. I just don't want you to run any risks."

"Of course," said Aline. "I understand."

When Yvonne left, Lucie turned off the radio. She sat on the bed next to Aline and they ate the barley sugars, listening to the tangle of conversations rising up through the open window from the apartments below; the laughter and arguments, the daily domesticity. Lucie wondered if she'd ever get used to the inescapable closeness of this multitude of strangers.

"We should go to the Jardin du Luxembourg tomorrow," said Lucie. "It's good to get out in the open air, away from all these people."

"No thanks," said Aline. "You go if you want, but I don't like it there anymore. Too many soldiers."

"We shouldn't let them scare us out of enjoying our own city."

"It's not fear that keeps me away," said Aline. "I just refuse to be in the same space as them. We can't let this become a peaceful cohabitation." She moved closer to Lucie. "This is more than a foreign power occupying our land. This is a foreign ideology, foreign values. They've thrown out humanity. There's an ugly new truth being imposed on us—that's what you have to understand. And that's what you accept if you choose to go on living like before."

"I'm not living like before," said Lucie, taken aback by Aline's tone of accusation. The expressions she was using were unfamiliar, etched with a starkness that hadn't been there before. Lucie guessed the words were probably not her own.

After Aline left, Lucie thought about the activities that Robert and his group were engaged in. Although Aline had been guarded about what they were up to, she suspected they involved attacks against the occupying forces. She wondered if they'd reached a point where that was what was needed. Were acts of passive resistance completely futile? Was Aline right that they needed to be willing to take bigger risks? She didn't know the answer to those questions, but even thinking about the possibility made her fearful.

18

THE SECOND WINTER under occupation arrived early and was even colder than the first. Lucie spent the short, icy days in her room, her feet wrapped in blankets, drinking chickpea coffee that she heated on her one-burner kerosene stove. Despite the difficult conditions, both she and Aline felt a glimmer of hope now that the United States had entered the war. Lucie thought she'd detected a slight shift in the mood of her fellow Parisians too. Those who'd been hedging their bets now seemed a little more inclined towards the Allies. Of course, she knew there were also many who remained fiercely loyal to Pétain.

One Friday afternoon, Lucie set off to meet Aline in a cafe near the university. As she walked across the river, the sun was already low, sitting just above the tops of the lampposts on the Pont Neuf. It was a few minutes before three when she arrived and took a seat near the front of the cafe. Despite a ray of sunshine through the window, it was barely warmer inside than it had been outside. Lucie buttoned her cardigan and laid her coat across her knees to guard against the ribbon of cold air seeping in under the door.

At three-thirty, Aline still hadn't arrived. Outside, the sky had clouded over and a soft, light snow began to fall. Lucie finished the cup of dandelion tea she'd ordered, then decided to go to the Hirschs' apartment to see if Aline was at home.

As soon as her friend opened the door, Lucie knew by her expression that something was wrong. Simone was seated at the dining table, her head in her hands, her fingers pressed against her temples. Aline sat down next to her mother, and Lucie took a seat on the other side of the table.

"They came for Papy this morning," Aline said. "He dropped over to pick up a winter coat. He was only here for a few minutes, but someone must have seen him and reported it. The police knew where to find him."

Lucie leaned back, too shocked to respond, her eyes fixed on the snow melting on the back of her hands. "But he's French," she said, her voice weak with disbelief.

Simone lifted her head. Her cheeks were wet with tears. "That's what he told them," she said. "They didn't want to hear it. He even told them his son was a soldier, a prisoner of war. It made no difference. They said they had their orders and he was on their list."

"What list?" asked Lucie.

"I don't know. I heard from my colleagues that they were arresting notable Jews. Lawyers, journalists, intellectuals. I imagine it's because he was a professor."

"Is there anything you can do?" asked Lucie. "Do you know where he was taken?"

"We've just been at the police station," said Simone. "They claimed they didn't know anything."

Aline shook her head. "This isn't a good sign. It was bad enough when they were arresting foreign Jews, but this is something new."

"I don't understand how they can just arrest French citizens for no reason," said Lucie.

"Who's going to stop them?" asked Aline, removing her glasses and wiping the back of her hand across her eyes. "Who even gives a damn?"

"I think lots of people would if they knew," said Lucie.

"Who? The same people who lined up to see the exhibition of "The Jew and France"? Ask them if they care what happens to us."

Aline crossed her arms on the table and rested her head on them. Lucie laid her hand gently on the back of her friend's neck. The light from the bulb above them caught in a drop of water on Lucie's wrist. She watched it tremble with each beat of her pulse.

Half a minute passed before Simone took a handkerchief from her pocket and wiped the tears from her cheeks. She blew her nose and put the handkerchief away.

"It doesn't matter what those people think, Aline. We can't let them defeat us." Simone sat up straight and smoothed down the hairs that had come loose from her bun. "I'm going back to work. A lot of my colleagues have husbands and fathers who were arrested. They might have received news."

Lucie watched Simone as she put on her coat and scarf. Though her eyes were still rimmed with red, her gaze was perfectly still, unwavering. Lucie had never known anyone who could summon such strength and resolve.

*＊＊

When she was sure Aline would be all right on her own, Lucie went to Margot's store to tell her what had happened, then headed home. Gérard was seated at the dining table with a cup of coffee, listening to the radio. Lucie asked Yvonne to help her in the kitchen.

"One of my friends was arrested," she whispered when they were alone.

"Who?" asked Yvonne. "Not Aline?"

"No, it was her grandfather, Samuel. He's a professor at the National School of Fine Arts. At least he was, until they made it illegal for Jews to work there. Simone and Aline have no idea where he's been taken or why he's been arrested."

"I can tell you why," said Gérard appearing in the doorway, holding his cup of coffee. "He's probably a Jewish agitator. Yvonne, doesn't it worry you at all that your daughter claims he's a friend of hers?"

"He's not an agitator," said Lucie. "He's someone who's lived here for decades and can no longer work because of his religion."

Gérard scoffed. "The Jewish race has been slowly building up their influence for years now. You have no idea what they're capable of. What would you know about the international Jewry and their plans? You're so naive. You know nothing about what's really going on in France."

"I know that innocent people shouldn't be arrested and sent away to God knows where. I know that it's wrong to hate people for their religion. I know that it's wrong to be an anti-Semite."

Before Gérard could respond, Yvonne grasped Lucie's upper arm and turned to face her brother. "I won't allow you to attack my daughter. She's not a child. She knows what she's talking about." She pushed a lock of hair behind her ear and took a deep breath in before she spoke again. "I see the letters your dear compatriots write. They come through the post office every day, addressed to the police and even to the Gestapo, denouncing their neighbors, innocent people just trying to live their lives."

Gérard walked to the sink, poured his half-drunk cup of coffee down the drain, and left the kitchen without responding.

Once he had closed his bedroom door, Yvonne pulled Lucie closer and spoke in a whisper. "How well do you know Samuel? Why have you never mentioned him before?"

"I didn't want to involve you in things you might not approve of."

"What things? What have you been doing?"

"I was doing drawings for pro–de Gaulle tracts that we printed at Margot's store. Aline gave them out at university."

Yvonne took hold of Lucie's wrists. "You can't be serious, Lucie. People are being arrested just for speaking out against the occupation. They're being tortured, sent away to prison."

"That's because the Germans know it's making a difference. Aline says every little thing we do to defy them is important, even small things like this."

"Even small acts can have serious consequences, Lucie. It's too big a risk to take for something so insignificant."

"No act of defiance is insignificant," said Lucie.

Yvonne clasped Lucie's hands in hers. "Neither is what the Germans can do to you for disobeying them."

"I know that," said Lucie. "But they can also punish you for no reason at all. Look at Samuel. Obeying would have made no difference. They decided to arrest him and they did."

"That's why it's even more important to avoid attracting their attention, to be as invisible as possible," said Yvonne.

"I don't want to be invisible, Maman," Lucie whispered. "I want to *do* something."

"I know you do, Lucie—but you're risking your life! I think you should leave Paris. I've heard it's possible to pay people to smuggle you across the demarcation line to the free zone. I can ask Gérard for money. I'm sure he'd help to get you away from here. He told me he has a new furniture removal contract. The government is moving people who've lost their homes in the bombings into vacant apartments. Gérard says he's being well paid."

Lucie saw the fear in her mother's eyes, heard the pleading in her voice. And yet she knew she had to make this decision herself. She brought her lips close to Yvonne's hands, still wrapped around her own.

"I want to stay in Paris," she said. "This is where I need to be."

1942

19

THE NEW YEAR brought freezing temperatures and heavy snow that stuck to the pavements and turned them slick with ice. Despite her regular visits to the police in the weeks since his arrest, Simone had received no further news of Samuel. Through his former colleagues, she learned that over seven hundred men had been arrested. They'd been taken to the École Militaire, not far from the Eiffel Tower, at the end of the Champ de Mars. They'd spent only a short time there before being put onto trains heading north.

In the first days of January, news finally arrived in the form of a printed card stating that Samuel was being held in a camp called Royallieu, just outside of Compiègne, about eighty kilometers from Paris. There was no indication of how long he'd be detained. The director at the Rothschild Hospital had heard that many of the men were ill and some had died. Cases of typhus were widespread and the older men especially were not coping with the cold and filth, the lack of adequate food. Several of Simone's colleagues were in the same situation as her. Their husbands, fathers, brothers—doctors, professors, lawyers, intellectuals, journalists—had been rounded up on the same day. When Simone and her colleagues found themselves together in an empty corridor of the hospital or in the silence of a stairwell, their whispered exchanges were almost always the same.

"Any news?"

"None. And you?"

In the absence of facts, they traded in rumors, fears, unfounded optimism. Those who were unaffected personally by the disappearances did their best to support their colleagues in any way they could. At lunch, a fellow doctor gave Simone the small quantity of coffee she'd managed to buy and insisted she keep it for herself. A nurse gave her honey from her parents' beehives. When Simone spoke with Aline and Lucie she admitted that though she was grateful for their gestures, her colleagues' pity only made her fear the worst for Samuel.

***

Despite the cold, Lucie tried to get out for a walk most afternoons, but spent the rest of her days in her room illustrating tracts. She only went downstairs to the main apartment when it was time to help Yvonne prepare dinner.

On the first Saturday of February, when she returned from queuing at the bakery for their daily ration of bread, Aline was waiting outside the door to her room. Once they were inside, she asked Lucie if she'd heard the latest news.

"No," Lucie replied. "What's happened?"

"The curfew for Jewish people has been tightened. We're not allowed out between eight at night and six in the morning."

"You can't keep coming here in the evening then," said Lucie. "It's too dangerous for you."

"It's no more dangerous now than it's always been," said Aline. "Why would I stop?"

"Because they could arrest you."

"They can arrest me whenever they want," Aline replied.

Lucie knew her friend was right, yet she worried about the risks she was taking. "I'm just scared for you," she said. "Especially given your involvement with Robert. Don't you think Samuel would want you to be safe? He wouldn't want you to be detained like him."

"I don't know what my grandfather would want me to do, and neither do you, Lucie. Listen, I know you don't like everything Robert's doing, and to be honest, neither do I, but there's one thing he's taught me: they can only control us if we let ourselves be intimidated." She bit her lip and shook her head. "I refuse to give them that power."

***

Despite the shock of Samuel's arrest and Lucie's concerns, Margot and Aline decided to resume distributing the tracts. Within a few weeks, however, their supplies of paper and ink were running low. One Friday towards the end of February, Margot told the girls she'd managed to get in touch with a network that had access to stocks of ink that the British were parachuting into the occupied zone. "I have to leave Paris for the weekend to pick it up."

"That's great," said Aline. "But what about paper?"

"Good news on that front too," said Margot. "One of my very old and trustworthy customers has a brother-in-law who's a butcher. He can help us out."

"A butcher?" echoed Aline. "How can he help?"

Margot tapped the side of her nose with her index finger. "What do butchers wrap meat in?" she replied. "It's not good quality, but he says he can cut the paper to size and it'll do the job."

"That's wonderful," said Lucie.

"But," said Margot, "it needs to be picked up on Saturday evening and I won't be here to do it. Do you think the two of you could?"

Aline looked at Lucie. "What do you think?"

Lucie hesitated, recalling her mother's fear for her. But then she thought about Aline's and Margot's determination to carry on despite Samuel's arrest. She knew that for Aline, especially, the risks were significant. This was a way to show her friends that she too had the courage to continue. Maybe it was also a way to prove it to herself.

"All right," she said. "I'll help."

***

The paper was being stored in a shop on a narrow street that ran between the Jardin du Luxembourg and the Saint-Sulpice church. Aline was to go there first to collect the paper and then meet Lucie nearby. Margot had told Lucie to take a large basket filled with something innocuous. The only thing she'd found in the apartment were some pine cones Gérard had brought back from Normandy to use as fuel if the coal ran out.

Lucie arrived early Saturday evening and waited by the fountain in front of the Palais du Luxembourg, the old Senate building, now occupied by the Luftwaffe. The day had been overcast and the air held a wintry chill. She sat on the cold stone edge of the basin and watched a few hardy children still playing with their sailboats. One little boy was leaning so far over that his chin almost touched the water. He waited patiently for the breeze to bring his boat towards the edge, then pushed it out again with his bamboo stick.

As the clock on the palace struck six, Lucie got up, walked to the exit near the back of the building, and turned onto the rue Servandoni. Halfway along she saw Aline emerge from the shadowed portico of an ornate building on the other side of the street. As she passed Lucie she whispered, "Keep walking. I'll meet you on the far side of the church."

Without acknowledging her, Lucie continued towards the massive stone edifice at the end of the narrow street. She tried not to look up at the darkened windows above, behind which she imagined eyes peering suspiciously, observing these two women on a deserted street, slowing as they passed each other, trying a little too hard to look like strangers.

She loitered in the street behind the church, pretending to examine the religious items displayed in the windows of the nearby shops. Five minutes later, Aline arrived carrying a large bag, a bundle tied with string wedged under her arm. She stopped briefly in front of Lucie.

"Hide this in your basket," Aline whispered, handing her the bundle. "I'll meet you at Margot's apartment." She continued along the footpath and disappeared around the corner of the church.

Lucie stayed where she was, trying to arrange the pine cones. There were too many now that the parcel of paper was taking up so much room in the basket. She positioned them as best she could, then held the basket tight against her side as she started walking. She'd only covered half the length of the church, when two pine cones toppled out and bounced along the pavement. She hesitated, but decided to leave them where they lay and keep walking. She was almost at the corner when she heard the sound of feet approaching behind her. She didn't quicken her pace and didn't turn her head.

"Mademoiselle!" called a German-accented voice.

Lucie continued as if she hadn't heard.

"Mademoiselle!" called the voice again. "*Halt. Bitte.*"

Lucie stopped and turned, her heart racing, her forearm resting on the pine cones.

The soldier was right behind her. He was young, with smooth cheeks and blond hair that looked metallic in the early evening light. He held out his hands, a pine cone in each, and smiled. "I believe these are yours."

"No," she said, then realized how ludicrous her denial was. "That's all right. I have too many. You can keep them."

The soldier laughed. "*Merci,* Mademoiselle," he said. "They're just what I need." He put them into the pockets of his coat. "Why do you gather pine cones?"

"To burn them in the fireplace at home," she replied. "We don't have much coal left."

"Ah yes," said the soldier. He seemed embarrassed, perhaps aware that the winter had been hard on the population he and his army were ruling over. "But it will start to be warmer in a few weeks," he added almost joyfully, as though this were a favor the occupying forces had decided to bestow. "Spring will be here soon. The season of love. *Here then are the long days, light, love, madness!*" He smiled, his lips red despite the cold. "Do you know this poem?" he asked. "'Springtime' by Victor Hugo."

Lucie shook her head, wondering if this was a trap. Was Hugo on the Otto List—another of their banned authors? She had no idea.

"Excuse me," she said, pulling the basket close into her ribs. "I must get home. My mother will be worried."

"I'll accompany you. Give me your basket. It looks heavy."

"No, it's fine," she said, taking a step away.

Another pine cone toppled off and landed at the soldier's feet. He bent to pick it up and placed it back in the basket.

"I have to go," said Lucie, placing her arm over the pine cones. She started walking, holding her breath, listening for the soldier's footsteps.

To her relief he didn't follow.

"You are very pretty, Mademoiselle," he called after her, laughing. "I have to try. The season of love is coming soon." Lucie heard his laughter fading as he turned and walked away.

When she arrived at Margot's store, Aline was already there. As they put the paper away, Lucie described her encounter with the German soldier.

"You did well," said Aline. "Nerves of steel."

Lucie nodded but could feel her fingers trembling. She tried to convince herself it was because of the cold, but she knew that wasn't true. She'd been terrified out there on her own, doubting she had the courage that was needed. She wondered if Aline and Margot had the same doubts, but hid them away. Maybe courage wasn't something you felt yourself, she thought. Maybe it was something others saw in you.

***

On her birthday in the first week of March, Aline invited Lucie to meet her for a celebratory drink in a bar on the rue des Martyrs. When Lucie arrived, Aline was already waiting at a table near the door. They'd only been talking for a few minutes when Aline looked over her shoulder at a group of young people seated at the table behind them. They were laughing, looking at a newspaper.

"Let's go somewhere else," she said.

"Why?" asked Lucie. "Can't we have a drink first?"

"Not here," said Aline. She glanced again at the neighboring table. "There are certain people it's better not to be around."

Lucie turned her head and saw the name of the newspaper: *Je Suis Partout*, a right-wing rag full of Vichy propaganda.

"They're just young people like us," she whispered.

"I'm not sure what that means nowadays," said Aline. She buttoned her coat and wrapped her scarf tight around her throat.

As soon as they left the bar, Aline's mood seemed to lift. She took Lucie by the arm. "There's a band I know playing in a small club in Montmartre. Shall we go see them?"

"Will you make it home before curfew?" asked Lucie. "It's already after seven."

"We can be back by ten if we take the Métro."

"But your curfew's eight o'clock," said Lucie.

"I know that," said Aline. Lucie heard an edge of frustration in her voice. "But it's my birthday and I want to have a good time. Is that too much to ask?"

Lucie moved closer to Aline and lowered her voice. "What if you get asked for your papers?"

"I don't know. I'll worry about it then," her friend replied with a shrug. "I'm not about to let their ridiculous rules spoil my birthday."

As they walked up the hill and crossed the Boulevard de Clichy, Lucie saw a small crowd of people gathered around a street performer. Aline pulled her towards them. At the center of the circle was a strongman draped in a fake leopard-skin tunic. He lifted a barbell loaded with huge weights like cannonballs. Among the crowd, Lucie noticed two German soldiers looking on, unimpressed. To her right was a man in a wheelchair, one leg draped over the hand crank. He rested his head on a tea towel and softly strummed a banjo. A handwritten sign above his head read: *Paraplegic. War wounded. I rely on your kind heart.* Lucie bent down and put a coin in the tin can attached to the armrest of the man's chair.

He smiled and clasped her hand. "*Merci, ma belle,*" he said.

As she straightened, she saw one of the German soldiers staring at the man. She thought she saw a hint of pity in his eye. When he realized she was looking at him, however, he rolled his eyes and turned away.

Lucie and Aline continued walking up towards Montmartre. They arrived at the club at seven-thirty, just as the band was starting their set. There were four musicians—a trumpet, a clarinet, a piano, and a singer. They played a mix of popular songs and jazz tunes Lucie had never heard before. When the performance ended at nine o'clock, Aline suggested they go for a walk around Montmartre before taking the Métro home. Lucie felt nervous about being out after Aline's curfew, but her friend seemed completely relaxed, even defiant. Outside, the full moon was just rising above the rooftops, its silver glow like a spotlight following their movements through the narrow streets.

On the Place du Tertre, a large crowd spilled out onto the terrace of La Mère Catherine restaurant. Through the open door Lucie could hear a group of German soldiers. Their voices were raised not in anger, but in drunken good humor. Aline took hold of Lucie's arm and pulled her away, giving the restaurant a wide berth. As they reached the far side of the square, they were almost knocked over by three young men running around the corner, exchanging urgent half sentences, clearly excited about something.

Aline caught one of them by the sleeve. "What's happening?" she asked.

The young man leaned in and whispered, "The Brits are bombing the Renault factory at Boulogne-Billancourt. You can see it from Sacré-Cœur."

Aline took Lucie's hand and they ran towards the basilica. Arriving at the top of the flight of wide stone steps, they were surprised to see a young German soldier. He was clearly drunk, haggling with a North African man over the price of the pornographic postcards he was selling. As the sound of the bombs reached them, he looked up, bewildered, as if struggling to understand what he was hearing. He pushed the postcard seller away and staggered past Lucie and Aline, running back in the direction of the Place du Tertre, no doubt to alert his comrades. Lucie and Aline stood at the top of the steps, watching as the sky to the west was lit up by explosion after explosion. Before long, people started to converge from all sides. They gathered on the stairs, crowding around Lucie and Aline, cheering, clapping, calling out.

Despite the mood of celebration, Lucie couldn't bring herself to join in. She thought of the people on the ground, so close to the edge of Paris. Many of them would be asleep in their beds at this hour on a Tuesday night. Certainly the children would be. Were all the bombs falling on the Renault factory they were destined for? She knew that air strikes were rarely so precise.

She turned to Aline. "Do you think there'll be many civilians hit?"

"I'd imagine so," said Aline. "It's an inevitable trade-off unfortunately." She turned to face Lucie. "We can't expect to win our freedom back if we don't fight for it."

"I know," said Lucie, "but it's still not fair that innocent people have to die."

"That's the price of freedom, Lucie. It's a necessary evil." She turned away, looking back towards the glowing orange sky. "Whether you want to think about it or not," she said, "the truth is they're doing this to save your skin."

Aline's words made Lucie nauseous. She'd never thought of the link between the killings of innocent civilians and her own survival. Since the start of the war, she'd shuddered at the posters plastered in the Métro and in the streets of Paris—images of French towns reduced to rubble, women and children lying dead and injured, silhouettes of airplanes against bloodred skies. And across it all, slogans in stark black letters: *The English did this!* and *Cowards. France will not forget.* Faced with this propaganda, she could understand why so many French people saw the Allies as ruthless and uncaring. This latest raid would no doubt further stoke their anger. And she was starting to realize that, like Gérard, many of her fellow Parisians preferred to live a relatively peaceful life under German occupation than fight for an illusory freedom whose price was death and destruction.

20

FINALLY, TOWARDS THE end of March, news arrived from Samuel. Simone received a letter sent from a place called Drancy, a suburb a few kilometers from Paris. When Aline came to visit Lucie in her room, she showed it to her. It was packed tight with his tiny, shaky handwriting. He wrote that he had recently been transferred and was now being held with hundreds of other Jewish men in a housing development that had been transformed into an internment camp. While the conditions were extremely difficult, they had been worse at the camp in Compiègne. There, throughout winter, with no electricity, no heat, no furniture, they'd been in total darkness and bitter cold for sixteen hours a day. He said here the latrines were one of the rare places they were allowed to visit unescorted in groups of four. They made the most of this relative freedom to communicate with detainees from the other blocks, whispering rumors of their impending release as they crouched side by side over the putrid trench. He hadn't lost his sense of humor, baptizing the place "Radio Shithouse." Towards the end of the letter, though, his tone became more somber. He said the situation inside the camp was alarming. Cases of tuberculosis were becoming more frequent and there was so little food that several prisoners had died of starvation. And then Lucie read the final sentence: *If I'm not freed soon, I don't know how much longer I'll survive.*

Lucie sat in silence, struck by the hopelessness of Samuel's thoughts. She saw the distress in Aline's eyes, but could find no words to comfort her, knowing she was powerless to help.

***

April came and went with no further news from Samuel. Lucie sensed Aline's frustration growing day by day.

"I can't sit around and do nothing," Aline said one afternoon in Lucie's room.

"We're not doing nothing," said Lucie. "We have the tracts."

"Little actions like that are no longer enough. More needs to be done."

Lucie knew she was talking about the type of actions Robert and his group were involved in.

"And you're convinced it needs to be done by you?" she replied, not sure if it was a question or a statement.

"It needs to be done by someone," replied Aline. "And it can't always be someone else." She leaned forward. "I've joined a group of students—the Volunteers of Liberty."

"What do they do?" asked Lucie. "It sounds dangerous."

"It's not," said Aline. "Whenever there's an Allied bombing raid, we take it in turns to station ourselves in the Clovis Tower in the Lycée Henri IV. From there we can see where the bombs strike. Some of our members are signed up as Red Cross volunteers. They go out to the bomb sites to help out with the wounded. Then they report back to the group to confirm the exact location of the strikes, and we relay the information back to England."

"That sounds useful," said Lucie, relieved to hear that Aline wasn't involved in attacks on German soldiers.

Aline leaned her back against the wall. "I'm glad you think so," she said, biting her lip, "because we were hoping you could help us."

"Me?" replied Lucie. "How could I be of any help?"

"As a live drop for the group."

"A what?" asked Lucie.

"It's like a human letterbox. Someone drops a message off to you and then someone else comes by later to pick it up."

"But why me? Couldn't you do it? Or someone else from the group?"

"No. It's important that no one's involved in more than one part of the plan. That way each person only has a small amount of information about how the network operates, so if any one person is captured, there's only so much they can reveal."

Lucie was alarmed at the mention of being captured, but Aline reassured her. "They know what they're doing. There's very little risk."

"But where will they drop the messages? In my room?"

"No, that's much too risky." She sat on the bed next to Lucie and lowered her voice. "Do you know the cinema next to Margot's store?"

Lucie nodded.

"Margot knows the manager, Philippe. He's helped her out in the past when she was hiding English pilots. We're using his cinema as the drop-off. You'd need to work there selling tickets a few afternoons a week as a cover."

"But how would I get the messages?"

"Philippe will explain all that. For the moment, we just need to know if you'll do it."

Lucie gazed at Aline's face. The look of powerlessness and frustration she'd seen after Samuel's arrest had disappeared. She didn't need to think before she answered.

"Of course, I will," she said.

***

Aline had arranged for Lucie to start at the cinema the following week. When she arrived, Philippe met her in the foyer and took her up to the projection room. He closed the door behind them.

"It's crucial that you pay attention to what I'm telling you. If you slip up, it's people's lives that are on the line."

Lucie felt her throat turning red, the heat creeping up towards her cheeks.

Philippe noticed and smiled at her. "Relax. You'll be fine. It's not that complicated. When there's a message to be passed, someone will come to buy a ticket at your booth. They'll have a smudge of charcoal on the back of their hand. They won't say anything else. You'll just need to look out for that mark."

Lucie nodded.

"When they pay, there'll be a slip of paper hidden between two notes. Take the money, hide the paper up your sleeve, and give them a ticket. Fifteen minutes after the start of the session, you'll close the curtains on your booth and go inside to watch the film. You'll sit in the back row, to the right of the door, the seat on the aisle. Just before the end of the film, you'll slide the message down between the seat cushion and the right armrest and go back to your booth. After you leave, someone else will come and retrieve the paper. That's all you need to do. Any questions?"

Lucie shook her head.

"All right, then. You're ready for your first day on the job."

Philippe took Lucie down to the foyer and introduced her to Josette, the other woman who worked in the ticket booth. She was quite a few years older than Lucie. Her face wore a look of exhausted resignation that she'd tried to hide beneath bright red lipstick and a cluster of artificial daisies pinned to the top of her long blond hair. Apart from saying hello when Philippe introduced her, she didn't say another word.

Philippe gave Lucie a quick explanation of what she needed to know about the ticket sales, then left her alone with Josette as the first customers of the day started arriving for the midday session. Lucie sat next to Josette in the rectangular booth, each selling their tickets through a separate glass window draped in faded purple velvet curtains. As each customer passed her the money for their ticket, she paid close attention to the back of their hands, trying not to be too conspicuous. None of them had a charcoal mark.

Fifteen minutes after the session started, Lucie pulled her curtain across and went inside to watch the film. She thought Josette would come in too, but she stayed in her booth, drawing her curtain and shutting herself inside, no doubt to have a nap between films.

The short documentary was just finishing when Lucie went in. Even though she had no message to hide, she sat in the seat that Philippe had indicated so she could duck back out as soon as the film ended and return to the booth in time to sell tickets for the following session. When the newsreel began, the lights in the cinema were turned up, a new order from the authorities, an attempt to stamp out the hissing and whistling that had begun to accompany the propaganda-filled reports. As the lights came on, Lucie noticed a young German soldier sitting in the back row, on the other side of the aisle. He stood up and exited through the door just next to her. As it swung slowly shut, she had time to see him cross the foyer, open the door on Josette's side of the ticket booth, and slip in.

Lucie thought about the women she'd seen with German soldiers—those who seemed in love and those who slept with them for food or money. If selling cinema tickets was Josette's only job, Lucie imagined she'd be struggling to survive. In any case, Lucie didn't know enough about the other woman's circumstances to judge her. Whatever her reasons, she figured there were worse forms of collaboration by people who were much better off.

Lucie stayed in her seat until the movie ended, then returned to her side of the booth. Josette had opened the curtains and was sitting on her stool, touching up her makeup. The air in the booth was warm and smelled of cigarettes. Josette glanced at Lucie as she sat down but said nothing.

***

The arrangement was for Lucie to work at the cinema three afternoons a week. In the first fortnight, the charcoal marks appeared just twice, and each time she managed to hide the scrap of paper up her sleeve and slip it into the seat as Philippe had instructed her. She had no idea who came in to retrieve the messages.

Throughout the spring, between her shifts, Lucie worked on making tracts. One Saturday evening towards the end of May, she and Aline went out to see a movie and took a few tracts with them to paste on lampposts on the way home, even though Aline was increasingly doubtful of their impact. It was a warm evening and Aline suggested they have a drink before going home. It was just after eight, already past Aline's curfew, when they left the bar on the rue Guénégaud to head back across the river. The sun had disappeared, but the western sky still glowed. Above the Seine on the Île de la Cité, they watched its colors change from dusky mauve to violet.

They were halfway across the Pont Neuf when they spotted a German officer a little further along the bridge. He was leaning on the parapet, gazing at the Eiffel Tower, its silhouette just visible against the darkening sky. Aline pulled Lucie back towards the Square du Vert-Galant. As they started down the steps, they heard the man call out, though not loudly or aggressively. They couldn't be sure he was calling to them, so they pretended not to hear and hurried down the stairs. The park was dark and deserted. They took the paved path that ran along the water's edge, and hid beneath the curtain of the weeping willow's trailing leaves, their backs against its trunk. From behind they heard the click of the German's heels on the stone steps and the creak and clang of the low metal gate as it opened and swung shut behind him. As he made his way along the perimeter of the park, his footsteps on the gravel path sounded like the crushing of thousands of tiny bones. Aline slipped her fingers through Lucie's and they both curled their heads in towards their chests, hoping they were hidden in the shadows. The sound of the soldier's footsteps approached the railing above, slowed, then stopped. Lucie held her breath and closed her eyes, knowing full well how ridiculous her gesture was, like a child believing it would make her invisible.

"What are you doing down there?" said the German. "Come out." He paused, then added, "*Bitte*."

They stood up. Aline was still holding Lucie's hand and she felt it trembling.

"It's dangerous to be out after dark," said the man. His French was perfect, his accent slight. Although his words could have been menacing, Lucie thought she heard a note of concern in his tone. She looked up at him. He was middle-aged, with soft full jowls and glasses slipping down his nose. The effect was almost comical. It contrasted oddly with the crisp lines of his officer's jacket and stiff visored cap. But there was nothing funny about the situation. She knew that he could arrest them for being out after curfew. And if he asked for their identity cards and saw that Aline was Jewish, the consequences could be dire. From the corner of her eye Lucie saw Aline's face. Her expression was one of fearful defiance. Lucie knew she had to be the one to speak.

"I'm sorry," she said. "We didn't mean to be out so late. We missed our bus."

"Do you live far from here?" he asked.

Lucie didn't want to give him their real addresses, so she told him they both lived in the eighteenth arrondissement.

"You're a long way from home," he said. "It's not wise to walk all that way after curfew. I have a hotel room, quite a large suite. You can sleep there and go home tomorrow morning."

Lucie felt Aline's fingers tighten around hers. She knew her friend was counting on her to find a way out of this situation, but she couldn't think how.

The German officer must have sensed her hesitation.

"Please don't worry, I am only concerned for your safety. My own children are just a little older than you and I miss the stimulation of their company. I would welcome the chance to converse in French."

Lucie turned to Aline. Her face was still tense but now seemed resigned.

"Thank you," said Lucie, turning back to the officer. "That's very kind of you."

They walked in silence along the river to the German's hotel not far from the Palais-Royal. At the front desk, he asked for extra bedding to be sent up, along with a light supper. The suite had a large sitting room with an open fire. The man excused himself and retreated to the bedroom to change from his uniform into more comfortable civilian clothes. He emerged a few minutes later wearing dark green corduroy trousers and a pale blue cardigan. His long black boots had been replaced by plaid wool-lined slippers. Lucie had never seen a German soldier in anything but his uniform. The effect was unsettling.

Although the evening had been mild, the temperature had started to drop. He arranged paper and a few small logs in the fireplace and struck a match to light them. When the food and wine arrived, he moved the low table and armchairs closer to the fireplace and gestured to Lucie and Aline to be seated, taking a high-backed chair from the corner and sitting opposite them. On the silver tray that had been set down on the table was a selection of cured meats, five different cheeses, and a basket filled with a mixture of French and German breads. Lucie hadn't seen so much good food in years.

"Don't be shy, please," said the officer, laying a slice of pale pink ham on a piece of bread and handing it to Lucie. Aline said nothing, her eyes cast down. He poured them each a glass of wine and held his out across the table towards Lucie.

"To good food, fine wine, and stimulating conversation," he said, looking her in the eye as his glass touched hers. He drank and smiled as Lucie nodded and took a sip. He then reached his glass out towards Aline. Lucie turned towards her too, willing her to return the German's gaze. Her eyes remained lowered.

The soldier clinked his glass against Aline's all the same, offering another toast. "Always enjoy life! You're dead longer than you're alive!"

He watched Aline, waiting for her to taste the wine. She raised the glass to her lips, but paused and put it down on the table without drinking from it.

He tilted his head and frowned. "You don't like wine?"

Aline shrugged and pushed a lock of hair out of her eyes. "I'm not thirsty."

He laughed. "You're not thirsty? I thought the French were always thirsty for good wine." He picked up the platter of cheeses and held it out. "And you're not hungry either, I imagine."

Aline didn't answer.

The German looked at her, still holding the platter mid-air, then put it slowly back down on the table. He smiled. "It's all right," he said. "I understand that this must all seem a little unexpected." He wiped his hands on a napkin and folded it across his knees. "I know you may have had less pleasant encounters with some of my compatriots. I regret if that's been the case." He leaned forward, looking over the top of his glasses, his eyes moving between Aline's face and Lucie's. "We're not all the same. You can believe me."

Lucie sat still, not knowing whether she should respond. The German continued.

"That's why I invited you to spend the night here. I know that many of my fellow countrymen are not interested in getting to know the locals, learning about your culture, speaking your language. But that's not the case with me. I'm a great admirer of all things French, and I'd always dreamed of spending time in Paris. As we say, *Jeder einmal nach Paris*. Everyone should see Paris once."

Lucie glanced at Aline. It was obvious she was struggling to contain her fury at these words. The German, though, went on, seemingly oblivious.

"I love your artists especially. Monet. His *Water Lilies*. I have visited the Orangerie so many times. I can spend hours there contemplating the beauty, the translucence, the stillness. Have you seen them?"

Lucie nodded. "Yes, they're magnificent."

She wondered if he knew that the only reason he could admire them was that, unlike many other significant works of art that had been removed from Paris to prevent the Germans stealing them, these canvases could not be moved, glued according to Monet's wishes to the curved walls of the gallery. Like her, they were stuck in place, unable to avoid coming face-to-face with these strange new visitors.

From the corner of her eye Lucie saw Aline looking at the German, her lips tight, battling to contain her hostility. Lucie pushed the platter of cheeses towards her. "Try the brie," she said. "It's delicious."

Aline looked at her, holding her breath. She cut a piece of cheese and took a slice of bread from the basket. She turned to face the fire, her back towards the German, and took a bite. The sound of her chewing and the popping of the burning log were the only sounds in the silence of the room. Lucie took a sip of wine, hoping that the German would put an end to the conversation and go to bed. Instead, he picked up the bottle and topped off both their glasses.

"Are you also a lover of art?" he asked.

Lucie sat upright, hoping to draw his attention away from Aline.

"Yes," she said. "I don't know as much as I'd like to, but I hope to learn more. I like to draw."

"I am also a bit of an artist," said the German, leaning forward with an air of genuine enthusiasm. "I've been making small sketches of the sights of Paris while I've been here. Would you like to see them? They're just amateurish. Nothing remarkable."

"If you like," she said. "I'd be glad to."

The German beamed at her. "One moment, please," he said, standing up. "I'll fetch them."

When he left the room, Aline turned to Lucie. Her face was flushed, whether with the heat of the fire or anger, Lucie couldn't be sure.

"What the hell are you doing?" she whispered.

"What am I doing?" replied Lucie. "What are *you* doing? Sitting there scowling in silence. I was just waiting for you to explode. Do you realize how much danger you could put us in? I had to do something."

"I just want to go to sleep and get out of here first thing in the morning," said Aline.

"So do I, but for the moment, we have to be civil."

The German returned carrying a canvas satchel bound with a leather strap. He opened it and spread several small pencil sketches on the tabletop. Lucie was expecting to see the sites that all tourists visit in Paris, those she'd visited herself in the first weeks: the Louvre, the Arc de Triomphe, the Eiffel Tower, Sacré-Cœur. But the drawings were of none of those. They captured the city's back streets: merchants opening their shops; children crouched in a circle playing marbles; abattoir workers leaning against a wall smoking; an old woman knitting on a bench. The sketches were hurried, messy, with ragged lines and smudges. Lucie found it difficult to imagine this German officer in his perfect, pressed uniform standing on a street corner making such spontaneous, raw, unconstrained drawings. She genuinely admired the vitality and honesty of his vision. Aline too was looking at the drawings, also seemingly captivated by them. But Lucie sensed that her reaction was not one of admiration.

"They're very good," Lucie said, careful not to convey too much appreciation in her tone. "Very original."

"I'm getting better. Unfortunately, I don't have much free time for my artistic pursuits." His smile faded and Lucie thought she saw a blush of embarrassment on his cheeks. "But it's inconsiderate of me to keep you up so late. You must be tired."

The German picked up one of the drawings.

"Please," he said. "A gift for you."

It was a sketch of a young woman, eyes closed and head tipped back, sunning herself on the riverbank.

"Thank you," said Lucie, placing it on the small table next to her.

The German gathered the rest of the drawings and put them back into the satchel. "I trust you'll be comfortable enough on the couches."

"I'm sure we will be," said Lucie.

Aline didn't reply, but nodded and picked up one of the blankets that had been brought up by the hotel staff.

"I'll be leaving quite early in the morning, so I'm not sure I'll see you. If I don't, I want to thank you for a pleasant evening." He looked from Lucie to Aline. "And I hope our paths may cross again one day."

After he took his leave of them, Aline picked up the drawing from the side table. She looked at it, then leaned forward and laid it on a half-burnt log in the fireplace. Lucie had to stop herself from reaching out to snatch it back. The fire had died down and the small flames that remained blackened the edges of the paper, then slowly ate into it. Aline and Lucie sat side by side, not speaking as the flames flared yellow and blue, consuming the gray pencil lines. When the final corner of the sheet had curled and crumbled, they took the blankets and pillows and made up their beds on the couches. Lucie lay awake in the dark for a long time, staring at the last embers in the fireplace and listening to Aline's breathing, not sure if she was asleep or not. She understood why her friend had burned the German's drawing. She imagined she found his intimate portrayal of her compatriots an invasion of their privacy, a further stripping away of their rights to live their lives in peace, away from the constant scrutiny of their new masters. And even though Lucie believed that this man's gaze was one of attentiveness and sensitivity, she knew that wouldn't change the way Aline felt.

***

The sky was still deep gray when Aline woke Lucie at six the next morning. They dressed and left the blankets folded on the couches. They didn't know if the German had already gone. There was no sign of life from the bedroom or bathroom.

As they left the hotel, the air was cool and still. Two cats jumped down from a windowsill and ran across the street. Lucie walked close to Aline, their shoulders almost touching. She wanted to talk to her about the previous evening's events, the confusion she felt about her interaction with the German officer. She'd always struggled to understand how some of them could be so cultured, so courteous, while others could be so cold-blooded in their cruelty. She thought back to the attacks by the Stukas on the columns of fleeing civilians during the exodus from Paris. They'd known they were firing on old people, children, women. How could these men wear the same uniform and yet be so different? Or maybe, she realized, they were the same men, capable of both politeness and brutality.

When they reached the river, Lucie stopped and touched Aline's arm. She felt she needed to say something. Before she could speak, though, Aline turned to her and whispered, "Don't ever tell anyone."

21

THE SEVENTH OF June was a day Aline and Simone had been dreading—the day all Jewish people had to start wearing a yellow star on their clothes. They'd been informed a week earlier that they were to pick them up from their local police station and had gone to get theirs that morning, handing over one of their fabric ration points in exchange. Lucie had promised to visit them in the afternoon.

When she arrived, Simone was sitting at the dining table, a sewing basket open and several pieces of clothing draped over the back of the chair next to her. Two of the palm-sized pieces of yellow fabric were on the table. The third was already fixed to a green cardigan folded on her knee. Lucie saw the four black letters stamped in the middle of the six-pointed star: *JUIF.* Jew.

When Simone lifted her face, her jaw was clenched, her forehead damp with perspiration. "With this star they want to divide us from our compatriots. They want to set us apart from our community," she said, her eyes filled with tears. "But when I walk out onto the streets of Paris, I won't lower my gaze. And if those who see me do, then it's they who should be ashamed, not me."

Aline stood behind Simone and placed a hand on her shoulder.

"I'm not sure I can do this, Maman," she said. "They want to brand us like cattle."

"They can treat us like cattle, Lina, but only we can decide how we react. They hope this star will humiliate us, but it won't if we wear it with pride."

"I understand what you're saying," said Aline, "but I still think wearing it makes us look compliant. It's the opposite of everything I've been working for over the last two years."

Simone took a dress from the back of the chair and picked up a second star. She laid it on the left breast of the dress and smoothed the fabric flat with her thumb, then turned her head and looked up at Aline. "It's your choice, Lina," she said. "I can't decide something as important as this for you." She paused and took a deep breath. "What I ask is that you consider all those who will be wearing it and whether, by refusing, you're in some way disrespecting the courage they're showing."

"I know," said Aline. She leaned down and kissed her mother on the forehead. "I realize there are many ways to be courageous and many ways to be a coward."

That evening, Lucie walked with Aline through the streets of the Latin Quarter. The heat of the day had started to evaporate and the cafe terraces were filled with couples and groups of friends. Many others strolled along the pavements. Lucie saw several people wearing the yellow star on their clothes. Most kept their eyes down, hurrying towards their destination. One or two held a bag or a book against their chest to hide their new mark of difference. An old man walked towards them. Despite the warmth of the evening, he wore a full three-piece suit. On the right side of his jacket was a set of military medals; on the left was the yellow star. He held his head high, looking each person in the eye as he passed. Lucie noticed that some of them turned away. One man stopped in front of him and raised his hand to the side of his head in a formal military salute. Lucie looked at Aline. Her face was flushed. She knew her friend was affected by the sight of this proud former soldier, obliged to wear this symbol intended as a stigma. She passed her arm through Aline's, pulling her forward as she stepped towards the old man. Lucie held out her hand, smiling, and he clasped it tightly.

"*Bonsoir*, Monsieur," she said.

"*Bonsoir*, Mademoiselle," he replied, his voice shaking with emotion.

From the terrace of a cafe, a middle-aged man stood up and approached. He too held out his hand and the old man shook it firmly. A mother with a pram stopped in front of him and smiled. He nodded in reply.

The small group gathered on the pavement drew the attention of a young French policeman. He pushed forward until he was face-to-face with the elderly man.

"*Monsieur*," he said, touching a finger to the brim of his cap. "The rules relating to the wearing of the Jewish star state that it's forbidden to wear military medals alongside it. I would ask you to remove them, please."

The old man raised his eyes to the policeman's face. The officer looked away, glancing at the others in the group before fixing his gaze on a lamppost behind them. The old man moved around until his eyes met those of the policeman. He held the man's gaze as if to say, *See the courage it takes to wear this star? Have the courage to look me in the eye.* He took a breath before he spoke. "You know that I will not remove these medals. Arrest me if you feel it's your duty. I'll remain proud of my actions." He paused and smiled. "Will you be proud of yours?"

The middle-aged man cleared his throat and also addressed the police officer. "See here," he said. "Leave this gentleman alone. Where's your sense of decency?"

"Yes," said the mother with the pram. "Aren't you ashamed?"

The policeman took a step backwards and bumped into Aline. She straightened her back and stood her ground. He clenched his jaw, pulled his shoulders back, and stepped away to the side of the group. As the eyes of the people gathered around the old man followed him, he turned without saying another word and walked slowly away, disappearing into the crowd.

"Do you think I should wear the star?" asked Aline once they found themselves alone a little further down the street. "My mother isn't happy that I don't want to. She thinks I'm ashamed of being Jewish."

"Are you?" asked Lucie.

"Of course not," said Aline. "That's not why I refused. I'm not ashamed of who my family is. But I feel like I'm being branded."

"I understand," said Lucie. "I don't blame you for not wearing it. But you also have to consider the risks. Simone's only thinking of your safety."

"I know," said Aline. "I don't want her to be scared for me."

***

One hot Saturday afternoon, Lucie suggested they go to the Piscine Deligny. Aline had been wearing the yellow star for almost two weeks but had hardly left the apartment in that time, so Lucie was surprised when she agreed to join her.

"At least once I'm there I can take off my clothes and be rid of this damned thing," she said, pointing to the star sewn onto her blouse. "I'd happily wear my bathing costume in the streets if I could."

"That would hardly be more discreet," said Lucie.

Aline laughed, the first time she had in weeks.

At the pool, she was in equally good spirits. The woman at the ticket booth didn't seem to notice her star, or at least didn't make a show of it. They spent almost all their time in the water, swimming and floating, ignoring the young men trying to impress them by wrestling or diving from the board. They dried off on the scorching, crowded deck, squinting up at the sun-bleached sky. Above them, the clouds raced right to left, their perfect fluffy forms intact, like the backdrop of a theater set being dragged on stage. Even when they got dressed to leave and Aline had to wear the star once more, she carried with her the lightness of the swimming pool. On the way home, they bought cones of shaved ice with mint syrup from a vendor on the riverbank and giggled at each other's green-tinged tongues.

When they arrived at the entrance to Lucie's building, they heard a motor start up in the courtyard. Seconds later, Gérard's van pulled out and drove slowly past them. Gérard was at the wheel with Émile beside him. As they passed, Lucie saw them both looking at Aline, staring at the yellow star on her blouse. Lucie was sure they'd seen her before. She'd been in the building so many times. They must have seen her on the stairs or in the courtyard. But she realized now they probably hadn't known she was Jewish. Why would they? It wasn't tattooed on her forehead. She looked just like any other young Parisian woman. There was nothing to set her apart. Until now.

***

A few weeks later, Aline arrived out of breath at Lucie's room.

"Have you seen the new anti-Jewish laws?" she asked as soon as Lucie opened her door.

"How many new laws are they going to pass? What more can they possibly inflict?"

"Quite a lot, it would seem, if they put their minds to it," Aline said, throwing a printed notice on the bed. "They've posted them all over the place as usual. No saying we weren't warned."

Lucie read the list of new restrictions. Jews were now banned from public places—cinemas, swimming pools, theaters, cafes, libraries. They were not even permitted to use public telephone booths.

"They're going to disconnect our phone at home too. And we can only shop between three and four in the afternoon."

"But there's nothing left by then," said Lucie. "How are you supposed to buy food?"

"I think that's part of their intention."

"What? To starve you to death?"

"Perhaps."

"That's crazy. Not even the Germans would actually do that."

"How can you be sure? We don't know what they're capable of. What have they done with all the men they've sent away? We've had no news at all. They could be dead for all we know."

"You shouldn't assume the worst. I'm sure Samuel is all right. He'll be back when all this is over."

"When all this is over," repeated Aline, her eyes filling with tears. "If we're even here to see that day."

Lucie said nothing. She knew there was a chance Aline was right—that there would be no Jews left in Paris by the time the war ended. They'd heard on the BBC a week earlier that countless thousands of Polish Jews were missing, taken away and never seen again. There had even been reports of a "massacre." Lucie was taken aback by the brutality and scale of the word. It was a phenomenon she'd never contemplated and that, just a few years earlier, she didn't think she'd ever have to.

"I can do the shopping for you," she said. "My mother will help too. And we can make phone calls for Simone." She was aware of the insignificance of her offer, given the scale of the problem.

Aline sat on the edge of the bed, her neck bent, her head hanging low. Her eyes were fixed on the yellow star on the left breast of her shirt.

"I'm done with this," she said. "What's the point of complying with their rules when they respond by shutting us in a cage that becomes smaller by the day?"

She slipped her forefinger under the edge of the fabric and tore the star away from her shirt.

"The only freedom we still have is what we claw back for ourselves." She looked up at Lucie. "I want to be able to go out. I want to see movies, go swimming, sit in a park, drink in a cafe." Her eyes were now hard and focused. "I'd rather take the risk of freedom than live safely as a prisoner."

22

THE FOLLOWING THURSDAY, Lucie was lying on her bed, the blackout drapes still drawn across the window, trying to keep the heat of the July sun out of the room as long as possible. Gérard was spending a few days in Normandy to harvest fruit. Lucie was excited by the thought of fresh plums and peaches, and grateful for her uncle's absence.

Suddenly she heard the sound of running feet along the corridor, then a heavy knock on her door. When she opened it, Yvonne was standing there, strands of hair stuck to her sweating forehead, her eyes filled with tears. She pushed past Lucie into the room and closed the door behind her. She was out of breath, her chest heaving. Before Lucie could ask what was wrong, Yvonne began to speak.

"I was waiting in line at the bakery. There are policemen everywhere. Banging on doors, escorting people out of buildings—they're rounding up all the Jewish people. The streets are full. They're taking everyone. Loading them onto buses. There are children screaming, clinging to their mothers, babies crying. Old people, sick people." Yvonne ran her hands across her cheeks, wiping away the tears that had started flowing. "I can't believe this is happening in France."

Lucie pulled her dress on and slipped her feet into a pair of sandals.

"I have to warn Aline and Simone," she said, pushing past Yvonne into the corridor. As she arrived on the landing, she saw the two women climbing the stairs, their faces red and shining.

"Have you heard?" asked Simone.

"Yes. Maman was out this morning. She saw what's happening."

They went down to the main apartment, where Yvonne fixed them all cold drinks.

"Do you know what you're going to do?" Lucie asked Simone. "Is it safe to return to your apartment?"

"I'm not sure. I'm going to the hospital now. I've already spoken to my colleagues. None of them has been arrested. I think the authorities realize they'll need us to treat the people they're holding."

"You can both stay with us until you know what's going on," said Yvonne. "My brother is away in Normandy for a week."

"That's very kind of you," said Simone, "but I don't want to arouse the suspicions of your neighbors. It might be dangerous to have the two of us here."

"Madame Maurel wouldn't say anything," said Yvonne. "She's always been good to us. I'm sure she's just as upset about what's happening as we are."

"Perhaps," said Aline. "I wish I had as much faith in our compatriots as you do."

Lucie thought about Émile, the many times she'd suspected he was watching from behind the curtain in the concierge's lodge as she walked past. And he knew Aline was Jewish. Who knew what he and Gérard discussed when they were together?

Aline turned to Simone. "Maman, you stay here," she urged. "I'll be fine at home. If they come, I can escape out a window and onto the roof."

Simone looked at Yvonne. "Are you sure it would be all right?"

"Of course," Yvonne replied.

When Simone finished her drink, she stood up to leave. Yvonne rose too and accompanied her to the front door.

"I'm so sorry this is happening," she said. "I wish I could do something to stop it."

Simone kissed Yvonne's cheeks. "I know you do," she said.

* * *

Late that evening, Simone telephoned from the hospital to say she was staying on to work through the night. She called again the next day, explaining she wouldn't be coming back yet, there were too many patients to treat. She finally returned at eight on Saturday evening. The stories she told were horrifying. Thousands of people were being held in atrocious conditions at the Vel d'Hiv, the Winter Velodrome near the Eiffel Tower. Some were already sick when they were arrested, and many more were suffering from the heat, the lack of water, the stench and filth from overflowing toilets. They were brought to the hospital and treated, but more arrived by the hour. The patients had told her stories of babies dying of dehydration in their mothers' arms, women who'd tried to kill themselves, others who'd been shot attempting to escape.

Yvonne and Lucie sat opposite Simone on the couch. Yvonne's fingers fluttered like moths, pulling at the hem of her dress. Neither of them was able to find words to match the horror of what Simone had told them.

* * *

On Sunday afternoon, Gérard returned from Normandy a few hours earlier than expected. He brought a dozen bottles of cider, his drink of preference now that wine had become too hard to come by. He, Yvonne, and Lucie sat at the dining table and ate a few of the fresh plums and blackberries he'd picked.

"I thought you could make some jam," he said.

"There's no sugar," said Yvonne.

"You can use apple juice," her brother replied. "It works just as well. And stew some of the plums too."

They sat in silence for the next few minutes, sipping their glasses of cider.

"How was your week? Was it very hot here?" asked Gérard.

"Yes," said Yvonne.

She glanced at her daughter. Lucie knew Yvonne was hoping she wouldn't speak, but she couldn't remain silent. "They rounded up thousands of Jewish people."

"Yes, I heard," said Gérard. "Apparently they'll be sent east to work in industry and agriculture."

"There were babies, children, old people," said Lucie. "How can they work?"

"Those are just unfounded rumors."

"They're not," she replied, her voice cracking with anger. "It's all true. I know a doctor who works in a hospital. She's treated them herself. She knows all about the terrible conditions they're being held in."

Gérard stared at her. The sun through the window lit up his face, tiny beads of sweat glistening on his temples. He cleared his throat and turned to address Yvonne. "I think you and Lucie need to get out of Paris. Go and spend some time in Normandy. It'll do you good to have a break from all this unpleasantness."

Lucie shook her head, struggling to contain her rage. "This unpleasantness won't go away just because we refuse to look at it."

"This problem is bigger than you or your friends," said Gérard, setting his glass of cider down on the table. "Staying here will change nothing for them or anyone else."

"I don't care," she said. "I'm not leaving."

He didn't respond, but got up and went to his room, closing the door behind him.

Once he was gone, Yvonne took Lucie by the arm and pulled her into the kitchen. "We need to be careful what we say to Gérard," she whispered.

"Why should we have to be?" replied Lucie.

"I wish it wasn't necessary, but we need to face up to the reality of where we are and what the situation is. There are some things we have to keep to ourselves. For Simone's sake and for Aline's."

***

Simone had let Yvonne and Lucie know that it was safe for her to return to her own apartment. The police had ceased their two-day spree of roundups on Friday evening and, in any case, it seemed that Simone and her medical colleagues were not being targeted. At six o'clock, when she came back from the hospital to pick up the belongings she'd left in Yvonne's bedroom, Gérard was sitting in the living room. Yvonne had no choice but to introduce her.

"This is Dr. Hirsch. She treated Lucie when she was unwell."

"Madame," said Gérard, standing to shake her hand. Lucie watched his face, unable to tell if he'd noticed the yellow star on the cardigan draped over Simone's arm.

"Your sister has been kind enough to mend a few clothes that I left with her. Unfortunately, I'm so busy these days at the hospital, I don't have time to sew on a button."

"We're all busy in these difficult times," said Gérard, smiling. "We each have to do our bit to contribute."

"Of course," she said, without returning the smile.

Yvonne took Simone to her room and gave her the clothes she'd left behind. When Simone came back into the living room, she paused and looked at Lucie.

"Is that sore knee you had last week still bothering you? I'd be happy to take a look at it, if you'd like."

"Thank you," said Lucie. She didn't know why Simone was lying, but she followed her lead. "If you wouldn't mind."

"Fine," said Simone. "Let's go upstairs so that you can lie down on your bed."

When they were alone in Lucie's room, Simone locked the door behind her. Lucie sat on the bed and waited for her to speak.

"I'm sorry for the subterfuge, but I had to talk to you as soon as possible."

"Is everything all right?" asked Lucie. "Have you received news of Samuel?"

"No, nothing, I'm afraid. It's another matter I need to speak to you about."

She told Lucie about the patients who were being brought to the hospital. How the police had put barbed wire up and posted armed guards at the entrance. Once the patients were well enough to travel, they were removing them and taking them to Drancy. She, along with many other members of the medical staff, had protested, but to no avail. So they'd started doing whatever they could to keep the patients in the hospital as long as possible. False diagnoses. Ordering tests and treatments. Whatever would delay their return to the camp and buy them time to find another solution.

"There are women who are brought to the hospital to give birth and then they're sent back with their babies—sent back to that putrid place and put on the trains going east. Newborns. Why are they sending mothers and newborn babies to labor camps? What work could they possibly do?"

Lucie didn't know what to say. She imagined Simone had also heard the rumors of the massacre of Polish Jews.

When Simone spoke again, it was quickly, in a whisper. "We've decided to save the newborns. As many as we can. We try to convince the mothers to leave their babies behind. We write false death certificates, say that the babies were stillborn, then smuggle them out through the morgue. There are safe houses, people who take them. Good people. A Catholic priest gives us false baptism certificates. They're sent away to families, given new identities."

"Aren't you afraid you'll be caught?" asked Lucie.

"What choice do we have? If we don't do this, what will happen to these babies?"

Simone sat down on the bed beside Lucie. "One of the women who was helping us was arrested yesterday. She was the one who transported the babies to the safe houses. It's so dangerous for Jews to be out after curfew now that we have this star for everyone to see. It would be easier for a non-Jew."

Lucie felt her heart rate quicken. "And you want me to do it?" she replied.

Simone nodded. "It should only be this one time. One of my colleagues has someone who can help us, but she's not available tomorrow. I know it's asking a lot, but there are so few people we can trust."

Lucie lifted her head towards the window. In its frame, the thin crescent moon was emerging from behind a cloud. The cool air on the dampness of her scalp was soothing. She felt a sense of calm certainty. It came not from a conscious decision to act, but from the realization that it would be impossible not to.

"I'll help you," she said.

23

IT WAS EASY to spot the Rothschild Hospital, even at night. Its redbrick facade stood out among the cream and gray of the other buildings in the street. All the windows were covered in heavy blackout drapes. Simone had sent a message through Aline earlier that day with the details of what time Lucie was to come and where she was to wait.

She walked alongside a high brick wall topped with long metal spikes and coils of razor wire until she came to a metal door with a discreet sign to one side indicating that this was the morgue. Aline had told her not to knock and not to stand too close to the door, that Simone would meet her at nine o'clock precisely.

When the bells of the nearby Saint-Esprit church drifted up and echoed off the building, the door opened slowly and Simone's face appeared. She looked different, her hair beneath a white scarf, her face more gaunt, less alive. She didn't smile, but looked right and left, then whispered instructions, telling Lucie to wait further along the street. She shut the door again and Lucie moved away, lingering near the shuttered windows of a cafe, acutely aware she had no good reason to be there.

A few moments later the door opened again and Simone emerged carrying a bundle. She walked quickly towards Lucie. "There's a pram behind the rubbish bins further up the street," she whispered, then told Lucie the address of the safe house she was to deliver the baby to and handed her the bundle. "Don't take the main streets," she said before returning to the morgue and closing the door behind her.

Lucie started walking immediately without opening the bundle. It was the first time she had held a newborn baby. She was surprised at how light it was, how insubstantial. She held it tight against her chest, as if it might otherwise float away. When she found the pram, she placed the baby in it and unwrapped a corner of the sheet to expose a pale face framed by thin black curls. The baby's skin was hot and dry despite the warmth of the evening and she was terrified it had suffocated in its heavy shroud. She unwrapped more of the sheet and, in the dim blue glow of the streetlamp, tried to detect the rise and fall of its chest. She saw no movement. She licked her index finger and held it below the baby's tiny nostrils. Nothing. As her finger brushed its cheek, she finally heard a soft wet sound as its lips started moving in a sucking motion, turning towards her finger as if seeking its mother's nipple. She let it grip her finger between its smooth, hard gums until it sank back into sleep, then covered its face with the sheet in case it started crying.

She took the side streets, as Simone had advised, avoiding the boulevards around the Place de la Nation and the police headquarters of the twelfth arrondissement on the avenue Daumesnil. She headed south towards the address Simone had given her. With the cool of the evening beginning to descend, warm moist air seeped up from the Seine, sweating on the cobblestones and sliding along the urine-soaked gutters.

As she approached the wooden entry door to a large apartment building, it opened. A French policeman emerged, blocking the footpath, leaving her no room to pass. She stopped and waited, her gaze lowered, hoping he'd step down onto the road. Instead he took a step towards her, his thighs inches from the front of the pram.

"*Bonsoir,* Madame," he said.

Lucie nodded, her throat too tight for sound to pass.

"It's a lovely evening for a walk, but quite late to be out. Curfew starts in less than an hour."

Lucie smiled and let her breath out slowly. "I'm on my way home," she said. "I'm taking my sister's baby for a walk to help it sleep. It's so hot in the apartment."

The officer didn't respond. He leaned over the pram and looked in.

"It's quite warm to keep a baby covered up like that," he said, lifting his eyes and staring at Lucie. When she didn't react, he looked down at the bundle again. "May I?" he asked. Without waiting for permission, he reached in and pulled the sheet open to expose the baby's face. It didn't wake, but took a small, sharp breath in, its lips pursed, a tiny line between its thin black brows.

The policeman seemed taken aback, as if he'd been expecting to find contraband—a leg of ham, perhaps, a bag of potatoes, a kilo or two of sugar.

"Is it a boy or a girl?" he asked.

Lucie's heart started pounding. Why hadn't she thought to ask Simone, or even check herself? She knew that the toss of the coin she was about to make—boy or girl—might be one of life or death.

"A girl," she said. "Her name is Jeanne."

"Really?" replied the policeman. "My youngest daughter's name is Jeanne." He looked more closely at the sleeping baby's face, then up at Lucie's. "You should get her home. It feels like there's a storm coming."

"Thank you," she said, pushing the pram forward.

The policeman stepped off the footpath to let her pass.

"Do you want me to accompany you?" he asked.

Lucie continued pushing the pram, her palms slipping wet against the handle. "No," she called without turning her head. "Thank you all the same."

She arrived at the address that Simone had given her without further incident. The heavy green door groaned as she pushed it open. She left the pram at the bottom of the stairs and carried the baby up to the third floor. Seconds after she knocked, an elderly woman opened, glanced at her, took the baby from her arms, and closed the door without a word. Lucie stood on the landing for a few seconds, not knowing what to do, then went back down the stairs. She waited for another minute at the bottom, her palms resting on the handle of the pram, thinking about the baby. She didn't even know if it really was a girl. She didn't know what its name was, or if it even had one. In any case, that made no difference now. The baby would become someone else, be given another name, another life. Still, Lucie hoped that someone knew the name it had been given by its mother; the mother who would be sent back to Drancy and disappear from there in one of the mysterious convoys headed east. Her one wish for the baby was that someone would remember who it had once been, why it'd been wrapped in a stiff white sheet and rushed through the nighttime streets to be handed to a stranger behind a hastily closed door.

Later, in her room, after returning the empty pram, she took out her sketchpad and pencils and drew the baby's face. The next morning, when she went out to buy bread, she hid the drawing among the leaves of a flowering bush in a little square not far from the river.

***

One evening later that week, Lucie and Aline sat on Lucie's narrow bed, their backs against the wall, waiting for the BBC broadcast to begin. As Lucie leaned forward to adjust the volume on the radio, there was a knock on the door.

"It's me," said Yvonne. "I need to talk to you."

Aline stood up as Yvonne entered. "I can leave you two alone, if you want."

"No," said Yvonne. "I want to talk to both of you." She sat down at Lucie's desk, her hands folded in her lap. "I've been thinking a lot about what happened recently, all those poor people who were rounded up and taken away. It's made me understand why you say it's important to do something."

Lucie reached out and touched the back of Yvonne's hand. "I'm glad, Maman."

Yvonne looked from Lucie to Aline. She leaned forward and lowered her voice. "At work, some of the women have been intercepting letters addressed to the police and the Gestapo. Just a few a day. They told me how they do it. They slip them into the sleeves of their cardigans, then, when they go to the bathroom, they hide them under the waistband of their skirts." She paused, then reached into the pocket of her housecoat and took out a small bundle of envelopes.

Lucie gasped. "Maman, I can't believe you . . ." She stopped and smiled. "I'm so proud of you."

She took one of the envelopes and carefully opened it. Inside was a single sheet of lined paper. She read aloud the neatly handwritten opening lines.

"*As a good Frenchman and a practicing Catholic, I have the honor of informing you that my neighbor, an Israelite, is in possession of a wireless despite this being in direct violation of the law.*"

Aline opened another envelope and read aloud.

"*I have the honor of signaling to you a Jewess, Mademoiselle Fanny Ariel, employed as a seamstress by the boutique Landeau on the rue Montorgueil where she is in regular contact with clients, thereby contravening the German ordinance of 26 April 1941.*"

As they read through the letters, Lucie was struck by their authors' use of the word *honor*. They used it almost every time, along with other hypocrisy-laden words: *good*, *proud*, *patriotic*, *loyal*. The irony of it made her sick. Whenever she read those words, she heard Gérard, his red-faced, hard-eyed smallness. She knew these letters could so easily have been written by him.

Aline sat back down on the bed. "Thank you," she said. "What you did was very brave."

Yvonne lowered her eyes and shook her head. "I'm sorry it's too late for your grandfather and all those poor people who were taken. But at least I can do my small part to stop more people from being arrested."

"What are you going to do with the letters?" asked Lucie.

"Destroy them," said Yvonne. "I can't save everyone, but if I can stop at least some of these hateful messages from getting to their destination, I will."

Although she hadn't planned to reveal to Yvonne what she had done to help Simone, Lucie decided she now wanted her to know.

"I'm sorry I didn't tell you earlier, Maman. I thought you'd say it was too dangerous and try to stop me." No one was sure what happened to those who aided Jews to escape or hide, but the rumors were enough to keep most people from trying.

"I probably would have," said Yvonne. "But now I understand why you wanted to help." She paused, her fingers making slow circles on the wooden desktop. "You know, not long ago I thought young people, students, were foolhardy to show their discontent so openly. But now I see they were right. I honestly don't recognize some of my fellow countrymen and women. I don't understand what's happening to France."

"There are good people too," said Aline. "More and more are seeing that they have to act."

Yvonne shook her head. "I don't know. I wish that were true, but there's so much hatred in this country. Now it feels like those people have permission to say out loud what they've always felt."

24

IN THE FIRST days of August, the heat that had sealed the city in a heavy glaze for weeks finally ruptured in a violent thunderstorm that brought the Seine up high against the bridges. Lucie was crossing the footbridge from the Île Saint-Louis to the Île de la Cité, on her way to work at the cinema, when heavy rain began to fall. She ran into the small park at the end of the island and sheltered beneath a tree. Below, the waters of the Seine met the curved tip of the Île de la Cité as if it were the stern of a ship. The wind made the river wild, slapping waves against the stone walls, sending sprays of water up into the air. The two towers of Notre-Dame stood tall against the charcoal sky like smokestacks on a massive ocean liner.

The waters continued to rise throughout the day and the following night, flooding the banks of the river. Late in the evening, Lucie crossed the Pont des Arts, watching the water churn around the metal structure. She leaned over the railing, her arms hanging heavy in the void, the force of the wind making them sway like pendulums. She turned her face towards the surface of the river, the faint sparkle of reflected moonlight so many feet below. With each dip and rise of the waves, the fine mist sprayed up against the heavy warmth of blood pooling in her fingertips. She closed her eyes and felt the coolness creeping through all the loops and arches, like ink in the lines of the finest engraving.

Once the floodwaters receded a week later, she went for a walk along the riverbank. The cobblestones were coated in smooth, dark silt and branches. Twigs and bottles lay scattered around the bases of trees and pushed up against the benches. She looked down at the water that now lay calmly in its stone-walled bed. Just a few days earlier, it had submerged the path she stood on, surging as if from nowhere. And now it had moved on, leaving Paris behind. Lucie thought about what her life and Aline's had become in the last year or so. How it had been submerged by the surging waters they should have seen approaching. These days, she felt like they were clinging to a piece of floating wood, carried along in a river flowing so fast they'd lost all sense of direction. They could no longer see the riverbanks, were unable to swim towards them. All they could do was hold on and try to keep their heads above the swirling, silt-heavy whirlpool. She wanted to believe that, like the flooded Seine, their lives would one day soon return to a state of peace. But from where they were right at that moment, in the middle of the swollen, churning waters, it wasn't an easy future to believe in.

**

The start of September brought no relief from the heat. Lucie often spent her evenings alone doing illustrations for the tracts. She'd started to feel Aline becoming more withdrawn, less willing to help. On the evening of her birthday, Aline came to see her.

"This is for you," she said, holding out a small wrapped gift.

Lucie took it from her and removed the wrapping. Inside was a leather-bound sketchpad.

"I noticed you didn't have many pages left in your old one," said Aline. "I hope you like it."

"I love it," said Lucie.

She opened the sketchpad. Pasted inside the cover was the drawing she'd done of Aline at the student demonstration, that first November in Paris. On the page opposite, Aline had written an inscription: *Your drawings give me hope in our fight for the future of France.*

"That's beautiful," said Lucie.

"I know you really believe in the power of art and words," said Aline.

"And you don't?"

"To be honest, I'm not sure I do anymore. It's difficult to believe that they're enough."

"The Germans seem to believe in the power of images and words. You saw the poster at the Berlitz exhibition. They knew it would speak pretty loudly to some people."

"I'm not denying that. I'm just saying it's not all they use to fight. Tanks and machine guns speak loudly too."

At eight, they tuned into the BBC. De Gaulle was speaking, denouncing the violent actions in Paris backed by the Communist Party. These pointless assassinations would make no difference to the outcome of the war, he said, and too many innocent hostages were paying with their lives.

"I think he's right," said Lucie. "There's no sense answering death with death. Killing a few individual soldiers in Métro stations won't change the outcome of the war. We should put our energy into saving lives, like your mother is doing with the babies."

"Personally, I think the tracts are less futile," replied Aline. Lucie thought she heard a hint of contempt in her voice. "At least with them you might influence hundreds of people rather than taking such a huge risk to save a few individual babies." She leaned forward and turned off the radio. "If you agree with de Gaulle that killing one German soldier in the street isn't going to have an impact, then how will saving one baby change anything? It's exactly the same thing."

"It's not," said Lucie. "It's saving a life, not taking one. It's beating death, not joining in the massacre."

"It's still just a few babies. It doesn't help all the others."

"Perhaps. But it's life, at least. Otherwise what's their fate? No one knows. They'll disappear like all those other poor souls."

Lucie waited for Aline to respond but instead her friend stared at the floor, her lips pressed tight together.

"I thought you agreed with Samuel," continued Lucie. "He believes we need to spread hope and courage, not hatred and death. If not, we're just playing by the oppressor's rules."

Aline sat in silence until Lucie had finished, then slowly raised her head. "The rules are changing," she said. "Words are no longer enough. You've seen the measures they're taking against us. Where's my grandfather now? Where are his fine words?" She raised her hands, her wrists pressed together in invisible handcuffs. "Should I sit around until they come for me too?"

Lucie reached out and clasped Aline's hands. "You're not sitting around. You're taking action. You said the tracts mean something. They make a difference."

Aline shrugged. "Do they? Who knows if anyone even reads them? If my grandfather had fought with guns instead of words, he wouldn't be rotting in some hellhole in the east now. If he were here, he'd see how wrong he was."

"No, he wouldn't," said Lucie. "He'd tell you that what Robert's group is doing is wrong and that your involvement makes you a possible accomplice to murder. You can't know whether the messages you're passing will lead to arms being smuggled, or a train being derailed, or innocent people being blown up—but you can be sure it'll mean hostages being shot in reprisal. How can you feel good about that?"

Aline looked away. She didn't respond immediately, but stood with her arms crossed, taking shallow, rapid breaths. When she spoke, her voice was tight with anger. "Can you please stop with your 'the pen is mightier than the sword' bullshit? It's not true, Lucie! Not when the sword is pushing against your throat. Not when the sword is a machine gun, a Panzer tank. You don't understand! You haven't lived with war. Your country hasn't seen bloodshed on its soil."

Lucie sat forward, her face flushed. In Aline's words she heard an echo of Gérard's. "My country has lost men to war," she replied. "We've known death too."

"It's not the same," said Aline. "Even while that was happening, your life went on. Your towns weren't under siege. There were no massacres in your streets and villages. You don't know what it's like to have your home invaded, to have to take up arms and kill or be killed."

"You're right, I don't—and that's why I can see more clearly than you. Your whole vision is darkened by death and violence. You've lost sight of what really counts."

"What counts is survival," said Aline. "Nothing's more important than that."

"Are you sure? Maybe there are more important things."

"Like what?" asked Aline.

"Like principles, morals. Like not killing. Ever."

"That's exactly what they're counting on, Lucie. Good people being good. Fighting for their principles to the death. The death of all the good people. That would suit them nicely. Good, peaceful, principled lambs to the slaughter."

Lucie stood and moved closer to Aline. "I'm not saying you shouldn't fight back. Just not with the same violence that you despise them for using."

"It's not the same," said Aline. "They're the aggressors. I'm acting in self-defense."

"By bombing cafes and killing simple soldiers?" Lucie shook her head. "They're not the ones responsible for this war. They're victims, just like us."

"They're part of a machine. If they wanted to, they could sabotage it, refuse to play their part."

"They're probably just as scared as we are. Or they've been convinced they're doing the right thing. You don't know what they've been told or how they've been manipulated."

"What about your countrymen?" asked Aline. "What do you think they're doing up there in their planes? They're not dropping tracts on those German towns. Are you comfortable with that?"

"No, I'm not. But I don't know what the answer is. There's no good solution." Lucie wanted to go on, but the words caught in her throat and her eyes burned with tears.

Aline's jaw tightened. She stood and walked to the door. "I have to go. I have more important things to do than stand around here talking."

As she left, Lucie slammed the door behind her. She picked up the sketchpad Aline had given her and went to the window. When she saw her friend emerge onto the street, she leaned out and called to her. "So words and images mean nothing to you? They have no power? Fine. Take them back then. I don't want your worthless thoughts."

She threw the sketchpad down onto the pavement. It landed a few feet in front of Aline and skidded into the gutter.

Aline looked up at Lucie, then picked up the sketchpad, put it into the pocket of her jacket, and walked away.

Lucie lay down on her bed. Her tears overflowed onto her pillow even before she realized she was crying. She'd wanted to talk their disagreement through, not let it end that way. She curled herself against the wall, her forehead pressed against the flaking plaster, and tried to will herself to sleep. Though the air in the room was still warm, the temperature outside had dropped and a strong wind began to blow. Just as she was falling asleep, a flash of lightning lit up the room and rain began to fall. Soon the hammering was deafening. She got up and stood at the open window. Large hailstones were falling, bouncing off the roof and rolling down into the gutter. Below, the street was strewn with white. An old man advanced along the pavement, sheltering his head with one arm, struggling to steer the handcart he was pushing. Eventually he gave up and took shelter in a doorway, his back pushed tight against the iron gate. Lucie wondered where Aline was now. Had she gone straight home, or had she risked going out into this storm with Robert and his group? Either way, Lucie knew she was powerless to protect her friend. Aline would decide how to live her life and how to risk it too.

25

OCTOBER ARRIVED WITH a last waft of spring, but Lucie felt the walls of winter slowly closing in. Although it was still early afternoon, the sky outside her window was dark, with thick, low clouds that threatened rain. She went downstairs to the apartment to get something to eat. Gérard had gone to Normandy for the weekend and Yvonne was out queuing for food. There was bread from the morning, but no jam. She knew Gérard kept the key to the storage room in the pocket of his work jacket. Luckily he'd left the jacket on the hook behind the door. When she put her hand in to retrieve the key, she found two. She wondered why, if he had a duplicate, he didn't leave one for Yvonne and her. She took one key and went downstairs to the cellar. When she tried to open the lock on the storage room, the key wouldn't turn. She tried again, jiggling it around, pulling it out and inserting it, but still it wouldn't open. As she was leaving the cellar, Madame Maurel came out of her lodge with a bucket and mop.

"Is everything all right?" she asked. "You look a little flustered."

"I was just trying to open our storage room, but there's something wrong with the lock."

Madame Maurel looked down at the key in Lucie's hand. "Ah,

that must be the one for number twenty," she said. "It was my storage room originally, but I had no use for it. When your uncle sold half his apartment, he needed a place to store the excess furniture, so I said he could use it."

Lucie fetched the other key and went back down to the cellar to get the pot of jam, then made her way along the corridor to number twenty. Though she knew it was none of her business, she was curious to see what was in the second storage room. Maybe it would provide a glimpse into her uncle's life in happier days.

When she opened the door and turned on the light, she was disappointed to see that the space was empty apart from a trunk pushed against the far wall. She went in, closing the door behind her and leaned down to lift the lid of the trunk. It was filled with expensive-looking objects. There were two silver photo frames, an intricately engraved pill box, a brass cigarette case, and a crystal perfume bottle, as well as silverware wrapped in a piece of dark blue velvet—a cake server and forks, napkin rings, and a set of salt and pepper shakers. At the bottom of the trunk was a wooden box containing jewelry—necklaces, earrings, brooches, rings.

She thought about how hard Gérard had struggled to survive financially in the past. She wondered why, if that were so, he hadn't sold all these things. She closed the lid and left the storage room, locking the door behind her.

When Yvonne got home from work that evening, Lucie described what she'd found in the trunk.

"Do you think they were wedding gifts?" she asked.

"Possibly," said Yvonne. "Or maybe they belonged to his wife before they were married. Her family was quite well off. I can't imagine he'd have bought them himself."

"Why is he keeping them locked away in the cellar. Why hasn't he sold them?"

"I've no idea," said Yvonne. "Maybe he's attached to them. Especially if they belonged to his late wife."

"Are you going to ask him about them?"

Yvonne shook her head. "No. He's never been one to discuss his private affairs. And it's probably best not to tell him you were down there."

***

Throughout autumn, the attacks against German soldiers multiplied. Each time, greater numbers of hostages were shot in retaliation. There was also news of attacks on railway installations. Lines were cut, gates disabled. And now bombs were being planted as well, on railroad tracks and vehicles—even one in a German bookstore in the Latin Quarter. Lucie suspected that Robert's group was involved in these acts of violence, and that Aline too might be implicated.

Lucie hadn't seen her for almost a month, not since they'd fought the evening of her birthday. She missed her friend and worried about what she was doing, what danger she might be in. She wished she had the courage to go and see her, talk it through, but the thought of Aline rejecting her attempt at reconciliation paralyzed her.

One evening in early October, after eating dinner, Lucie helped Yvonne to wash the dishes as usual, then went back up to her room. She lay down on her bed without removing her clothes. The slanted ceiling trapped the heavy dampness of the day. The street outside was calm. Along the guttering at the edge of the roof came the noise of scuttling claws.

As she was starting to doze off, she heard footsteps in the corridor. They stopped outside her door. She got up and put her ear against the wood. Outside she heard breathing, but no one knocked. She hesitated several seconds, then opened the door. In the darkness, she saw Aline standing with her head bowed. She looked at Lucie over the top of her glasses. Lucie struggled to contain her joy and relief that her friend was back. She smiled timidly and moved aside to let her enter the room.

"Do you want a coffee?" she asked.

Aline nodded.

Lucie lit the stove and put a saucepan of water on, then leaned against the wall, staring at the sputtering yellow flames, waiting for her friend to offer some sort of explanation.

Aline slid one foot forward and took a breath before she spoke. "How have you been?" she asked.

Lucie looked up at her. "I've been worried about you. How could you disappear and not give me any news for a month?"

Aline rubbed her fingers back and forth across her forehead till the skin was red. "I'm sorry. I needed time to think. I've been so confused about what I should be doing. Maybe I'm a coward, but I've decided I can't do what Robert does."

Lucie sat on the bed and pulled Aline down beside her. "Not wanting to kill isn't cowardly," she said. "It's a choice. I refuse to cross that line too."

"I know," said Aline. "I thought it was a question of courage, but I've come to realize it's not. It's deciding whether killing another human is ever right."

"And have you decided?"

Aline paused. "Not yet. I'm not sure I ever can. But in the meantime, I can't bring myself to do what Robert wants me to."

"There are other ways to help," Lucie reminded her.

"Yes." Aline nodded. "And I know what my mother is doing is important. I'm sorry I was too stupid to see that before—and that it took me so long to find the courage to tell you."

"I'm sorry too." Lucie laid her hand on Aline's. "I was so afraid you'd be arrested and I wouldn't see you again."

They had just finished their coffee when the air-raid siren started up. Moments later they heard the deep thunder of exploding bombs from the west.

"Come on," said Lucie. "This one's for real. We have to get out of here."

"I can't go down to your shelter. Your uncle will be there."

"You can't stay here. They sound close this time."

"I just don't want to cause problems for you," said Aline, pulling on her coat.

"Don't worry about me. My problems are nothing compared to yours."

When they arrived in the cellar, Yvonne and Gérard were already there, seated on separate benches against the wall, not far from the entrance. Gérard didn't notice them come in; he was deep in conversation with Émile. Aline walked quickly past and continued further into the shelter, her eyes down. She sat on a bench next to a woman with a large cat curled on her lap. Lucie sat next to her mother.

"Another air-raid alert," Yvonne said. "That's three this week."

"Yes," said Lucie. "But this is the first time we've actually heard the bombs. Maybe they just sound the alarm so often to keep us anxious and turn the population against the English."

"Is that what you and Aline were talking about in your room?" Yvonne whispered.

"No," Lucie replied. She glanced over at her friend. What if Gérard had recognized Aline? What if he'd seen her wearing the star before and noticed she wasn't wearing it now? She looked towards him, but he was still talking to Émile, showing him a sheet of paper.

"It's all right," said Yvonne. "He didn't see her come in." She placed her hand on Lucie's knee. "I know it's scary," she said. "But I'm here with you."

***

The start of November was cold but dry. The streets of Paris crackled with the news that the Allies had begun an invasion of French North Africa. Lucie and Aline listened to the BBC every day, desperately hoping for reports of an Allied attack from the south. Instead, on the eleventh of November, the news they'd been dreading arrived: the Germans had invaded the free zone. The whole of France was now occupied. All those who'd fled south hoping to be safe were trapped.

Reports in the clandestine newspapers said that many Jewish people had gone into hiding in small villages wherever they could find refuge, becoming more and more convinced that deportation to the east meant they might never return. Simone was desperate for news of her daughters. Aline knew that Robert had helped other members of his group to escape to the south. She asked him if he could help her too. He said he'd try, but several days after the invasion, he received word that his contact in Bordeaux had been arrested. Aline was stuck in Paris, with little hope of being able to join her sisters.

***

A few days before Christmas, Gérard announced that he was going to spend the holiday alone in Normandy. He'd started working longer hours at his garage, coming home only when Yvonne had gone to bed. Lucie was glad he wouldn't be around for the next week or so. Since the last air raid, she was even more worried he'd see Aline on the stairs one day without her yellow star. It would be enough to have her arrested if she was denounced. That was the risk in the decision Aline had made. She might tell herself she was a French citizen like everyone else, but both she and Lucie knew there was always someone watching, thinking, *You're not one of us.*

Late in the afternoon on Christmas Eve, Aline came to visit Lucie. While they were having tea, Yvonne knocked on the door.

"Oh, Aline, I didn't know you were here, but I'm glad you are," she said when Lucie let her in. "Come with me, both of you. There's something you'll want to see."

She led them downstairs and onto the street.

"Where are we going?" asked Lucie.

"To church," said Yvonne, smiling.

"What?" replied Lucie.

"You'll understand in a minute. I walked past on my way home just now. What they've done inside is wonderful."

"Inside a church?"

"Just wait," she said. "You'll see."

Yvonne led them to a small church not far from the Hôtel de Ville. At the entrance, several parishioners were talking to the priest, nodding their heads, shaking his hand. Inside, a large group of people was gathered in front of the altar, whispering to one another, bending down to push small children forward, standing on tiptoes to see.

Yvonne led them along the aisle until they were at the back of the group. They waited until a young couple moved away, and inched forward till just a small white-haired woman remained in front of them, her hair covered by a black lace veil. Lucie craned her neck to see over the woman's shoulder. At the foot of the altar was a large nativity scene, as was traditional in all churches for the Christmas season. At first Lucie didn't understand what was so exceptional about this one, but suddenly she saw what Yvonne was so keen to show them. The plaster models of Mary and Joseph were leaning over the baby Jesus in his crib. All three of them had small yellow stars glued to their chests, the word *JUIF* handwritten on them.

Lucie turned her head to look at Aline. Her friend's eyes were fixed on the scene, unblinking. As Lucie touched her arm, her bottom lip began to tremble and her eyes filled with tears.

Yvonne noticed Aline's reaction too and put a hand on her shoulder. "You're not alone in this," she said. "There are good people willing to take a stand."

Aline nodded. "I know," she said. "It's easy to forget, but you're right."

"And we'll get through this horror," said Yvonne. "No matter how bad it gets, it will end."

As they left the church, the priest was still standing in the doorway. He smiled at Lucie and Yvonne, then turned to Aline. "Hello," he said. "I'm Father Benoît. You don't know me, but I know you. I met you when you were a young girl."

"I think you must be mistaking me for someone else," said Aline. "I don't think I've ever been in a church."

"It wasn't here. Before becoming a priest, I was a doctor. I ran a clinic for poor parishioners. Your mother used to help out there. Sometimes she'd bring you with her. You were just a small child."

"I didn't know that," said Aline.

"She's a good woman. A very good woman." He took Aline's hand in his. "You're always welcome here, my child."

Aline clasped her hand over his. "Thank you," she whispered. "I know the risk you're taking through what you've done inside."

"It's a small gesture," he said.

"But a powerful one. And your parishioners seem to approve."

He smiled. "Not all of them, unfortunately. There are some who've let me know their objections in no uncertain terms." He raised his eyebrows. "But I have better things to do than seek the approval of that type of person."

As the three of them walked back along the darkened streets in silence, a light snow began to fall. Lucie didn't know whether Father Benoît's small gesture was courageous or just foolhardy, whether it would bring him more trouble than it was worth. She looked up through the swirling flakes at the inky blackness of the sky. The moon was almost full, just the thinnest sliver missing, and it shone almost as bright as the sun. She recalled Aline's reaction when she saw the yellow stars on Mary, Joseph, and the baby Jesus. Maybe that was why he took the risk.

1943

26

SINCE CHRISTMAS, A glacial chill had taken hold of Paris, with heavy falls of snow that coated the streets in a white and icy quilt. On New Year's Day, Lucie woke early and went out alone before the sky was light. She walked along the quiet streets, stood in the middle of deserted squares. She needed this time of solitude, when she could retreat into the quiet, dark corners of the city. The stillness and invisibility helped calm her confusion. The muted sound of her shoes on the snow made it feel like she was walking in a dream, that time had stopped and only she was moving forward. Yet another year had begun. Her third new year in France, in occupied Paris. She thought about the things she used to miss, but that now she had trouble remembering. Swimming at the beach on languid summer afternoons, the smell of hot peppermint gum leaves rubbed between her palms, the salty tang of pigface squelched between her teeth.

When she arrived home, she lay on her bed and stared at the rooftops through the small window of her room. Although she tried hard to picture something other than what she saw around her, she wasn't able to. The past was no longer real and she had no sense of a future. All she saw was an interminable present.

***

Since the huge roundup of the previous July, the arrests of Jews had become more and more frequent. It was common now for women and children to be detained. They were even taking patients directly from the hospital, so Simone and her colleagues were trying to smuggle more babies out to safe houses. The Jewish members of the medical staff had been told they had nothing to fear, but they were far from reassured. The rules seemed to change from week to week and no one knew where it would end. Aline was convinced it was no longer safe to stay at home. She regretted having registered her address when the first Jewish law was put in place in 1940, even though back then no one could have suspected how things would evolve.

"When I saw them taking the children, I realized that eventually they'd take us all," she said one afternoon in Lucie's room, her neck bent low, her bangs hanging over her downcast eyes. "They won't leave any of us here. They won't leave even a trace."

Lucie wanted to tell her she didn't believe that could ever happen, that her compatriots would never allow it, but she was starting to doubt that was true.

***

As the weeks went past, the chill began to soften. By the last days of February, it was remarkably warm. Aline was in regular contact with Robert, who was still trying to organize a safe passage south. The situation had become more difficult for him too since the introduction of compulsory work service in mid-February. For months the Vichy government had run a campaign to recruit volunteers to work in Germany. There were daily speeches on the radio by Pierre Laval, the head of government, and posters in the streets. For every three French workers sent, it was promised that one French prisoner would be released. But the number of volunteers the French had managed to recruit was much lower than the Germans demanded. With the increase in troops being sent to the Eastern Front, the Reich needed more laborers at home. By the spring, they were requiring all French men born between 1920 and 1922 to register at their local town hall for two years' service in Germany. They were hunting down those who refused to register, stopping any young men they saw in the streets. Robert and the others in his group were wary of spending too much time outside.

"Two members of the group were caught a week ago," Aline told Lucie one afternoon in her room. "There's a new French militia working with the Germans now. They're absolutely ruthless. They executed the pair yesterday." She paused. "They were both Jewish. Robert thinks someone in the group denounced them."

Lucie felt the blood drain from her cheeks. "Why would they do that? We're all fighting the same enemy."

"It's more complicated than that unfortunately," said Aline. "There are old animosities, lots of conflicting loyalties. And we can't be sure the two who were arrested didn't talk. Even those we think would never break sometimes do."

"Could they come for you at home?"

"Possibly. Robert has new contacts in Bordeaux. He's still trying to source false identity papers for me. When he does, I'll go south and join my sisters in Limoges. In the meantime, he says we should all find somewhere else to stay other than our registered addresses."

***

Two days later, Robert contacted Aline to tell her he'd organized a safe place for her on the Île Saint-Louis. He said it would be safer if Lucie came to get the key. Lucie agreed to meet him in his room in the tenth arrondissement.

That afternoon, she helped Aline move in. The room was tiny and received very little sunlight. The walls were damp and smelled of mildew. Over the weeks that followed, Simone and Lucie took turns visiting Aline with food and clean clothes. Lucie worked at the cinema three times a week and continued to make tracts by hand, though no one was distributing them.

The warm spring days that should have brought hope and new life instead brought more bad news. One Sunday afternoon American planes bombed the Renault factory for a second time. Once again, bombs fell on neighboring residences as well as on the Longchamps Racecourse and Pont de Sèvres Métro station, killing hundreds of civilians.

Lucie saw images of the destroyed homes in a newsreel later that week. She shrank into her seat, gaping at the remnants of ordinary lives frozen in time, opened up and on display. An apartment cut in half, crumbling walls tilted over the street, held together by the scorched remains of striped and flowered wallpaper. Three floors up a bed balanced precariously, two of its legs dangling over the jagged concrete edge. From behind an empty window frame, a scrap of curtain shivering in the breeze, a clock still ticking on the mantelpiece. Further along, lined up on the footpath, were rows of bodies, laid out beneath sheets that had been ferried down from nearby homes to shield the dead from view.

The distress of the population quickly turned to rage against the Allies. It was fueled by the Vichy press, partly to distract the public from the continuing oppression of the Jewish population. That same week, forty-three Jewish doctors and nurses from the Rothschild Hospital were arrested and deported. Simone feared they'd been denounced by their colleagues. She wondered when her turn would come.

"But why would your colleagues turn on each other? Aren't they Jewish?" asked Lucie when she and Simone were visiting Aline that Sunday afternoon.

"Not all of them. Some are Catholic. Some aren't on our side. Not at all."

Lucie shook her head. "What kind of doctors aren't on the side of saving lives?"

"Not many," said Simone. "But unfortunately a few."

"Is it safe for you to stay at home, Maman?" asked Aline. "You could move in here with me."

Simone shook her head. "It won't make any difference. They'll find me if they want to." She paused and smoothed a hair into her bun. "I'll just keep doing what I'm doing one day at a time."

It was the first time Lucie had heard such resignation in Simone's words.

***

With the return of warm weather, Lucie sensed it was harder for Aline to accept spending her days hiding in the obscurity of her tiny, airless room. She did what she could to cheer her up, bringing flowers: lily-of-the-valley for the first of May, wild daffodils, purple lilac. When Gérard brought summer fruit back from Normandy, she took her fresh apples, apricots, peaches.

On Bastille Day Lucie went to see Aline late in the afternoon with a cool bottle of cider she'd taken from Gérard's cellar and a bag of cherries. The air in the room had been heating up since morning. Aline rose and opened the window, then remained standing with her back to Lucie.

"There's a bridge that crosses the Rhine in Strasbourg," she said. "In 1790, after the revolution, a sign was erected at the French end of the bridge. It read, *Here begins the land of freedom*." She turned and leaned back against the window frame. "Did you know that?"

"No," said Lucie, "I didn't."

"Neither did I till this morning. I read it in a resistance newspaper, *Defence of France*—in a long article on the front page."

Lucie sensed something was troubling her. "What was it about?"

Aline looked up. "Fear. It said we need to free ourselves from it. It was reminding us, especially today, of our duty to revolt."

The sun glinted off the panes of the building across the street.

"What do they mean by revolt?" asked Lucie, squinting at Aline's silhouette in the window.

"I'm not sure. But I know it isn't hiding in this room. Freeing ourselves from fear means saying no to living like this."

"Some fears are well founded," said Lucie.

"I know that," said Aline. "But allowing myself to be dominated by the fear they create means living my life by the rules of my oppressor. I'd rather die with courage than live a slave to fear."

Lucie had never heard such stark words from Aline. They scared her. Her lips felt cold despite the stagnant heat.

Aline came over and hugged her. "Don't worry," she said. "I just want to go out and celebrate Bastille Day. I'm not planning on dying tonight."

Lucie smiled, despite the unease that Aline's words created.

"What do you want to do?" she asked.

Aline pushed the hair back from her forehead. "I want to dance and drink in a bar and do everything I'm not allowed."

Lucie took a deep breath. "All right. That's what we'll do then." She gently pushed her friend down onto a chair. "But first we'll need to get you made up."

She took a cherry from the bag she'd brought and pressed it between her fingers until the juice flowed out.

"What are you doing?" asked Aline.

"Trust me. I've heard this is the latest thing. You'll look great."

She rubbed her red-stained fingertips over Aline's cheeks, then spread more juice onto her lips.

"Beautiful," she said, standing back. Aline got up from the chair and looked at her face reflected in the window.

"Oh my God!" she said. "I look like a clown."

"No, you don't. You look like a princess."

Aline pushed Lucie down onto the chair and took another cherry from the bag.

"Well, if I'm going out looking like this, you are too." She rubbed juice onto Lucie's cheeks, then painted a round smudge on the tip of her nose. She stepped back laughing.

"My lips," said Lucie, pouting.

Aline laughed, shaking her head. She wiped her tears away with her hand, leaving deep red smears across her eyes and temples. Lucie started laughing too, almost falling from the chair. She squeezed the juice from another cherry and wiped it across her lips, staining her chin and the skin around her mouth.

"Do I look like a princess too?" she asked.

Aline coughed and gasped, struggling to reply. "You look like a princess who's been ten rounds in a boxing match."

Lucie lifted her chin and raised her fists in front of her face.

"There's nothing wrong with that," she said. "All princesses should know how to look after themselves."

***

Lucie and Aline walked down to the river to stroll in the warmth of the early evening. They rested under a plane tree, leaning against its peeling trunk. Lucie ran her fingernails along the edges of the pale pink and flesh-toned bark. Up close, it resembled the sunburnt skin that peeled from her nose and shoulders when she was a young girl. She looked back on the last four summers. They stood in brutal contrast to the summers of her childhood, when the only dangers were strong currents at the ocean beach and too much sun on her freckled skin.

After a few minutes, Aline took her hand and pulled her up.

"Come on," she said. "Or this princess will be late for the ball."

They crossed the Pont de Sully and made their way through the narrow side streets towards the eleventh arrondissement, avoiding the busy Boulevard Henri IV, heading for the dance halls of the rue de Lappe. They spent the evening moving from club to club, dancing and laughing. Lucie hadn't seen Aline so carefree in a long time—certainly not since the imposition of the yellow star.

As the curfew approached, they left the club and started walking home. On the Place de la Bastille, hundreds of people were gathered. Some carried small French flags, others stood in circles of five or six, arms draped over one another's shoulders, swaying and singing. One group began to sing "La Marseillaise" and others joined in, a lone accordionist accompanying them. Passersby stopped to watch and cheer. Several young women gave out bunches of small white flowers to strangers.

Aline took Lucie's arm and pulled her towards the crowd. "Come on," she said. "One more dance."

The sky had turned from lavender to deep blue and the first stars were visible.

"Look!" said Aline, pointing at the statue on the top of the tall stone column.

Lucie looked up at the golden *Spirit of Liberty*. In his right hand he held a burning torch and in his left the broken chains of bondage. His face was turned towards the almost-full moon and he seemed to be pushing off from the globe beneath his foot, on the verge of leaping into space.

"That's how I feel tonight," said Aline, her head tipped back and a wide smile on her face.

It was after ten when Lucie said good night to Aline and watched her cross the river on her way back to her room on the Île Saint-Louis.

When she got home, she took out a piece of paper and a pencil. She sketched the golden statue of the *Spirit of Liberty*, just an outline of its moonlit silhouette against the blackness of the night sky.

***

At six the next morning, Lucie was woken by a soft but insistent knocking on her door. When she opened it, she was shocked to see Robert standing there, his chest heaving. She pulled him inside and closed the door behind him.

"What is it?" she asked.

He lifted his hand to his forehead and wiped away the sweat. Lucie saw that his fingers were trembling.

"Aline's been arrested."

27

LUCIE SAT ON the edge of her bed, her hands pressed between her thighs.

"When? How?" was all she managed to ask.

"One of my informants found out from the police," said Robert. "They told him two Gestapo officers went to her room just before one this morning." He paused and wiped his hand across his throat. "They found a sketchpad with one of your drawings in her desk. Apparently it was deemed subversive."

Lucie felt like she was going to vomit. She clasped her hand across her mouth to stifle a scream. If she hadn't thrown the sketchpad at her friend when they'd argued on her birthday, Aline wouldn't have had it in her room to incriminate her. Robert tried to reassure her, telling her he suspected someone in his own group had denounced Aline.

"It wouldn't have made any difference if she had the sketchpad or not," he said. "They knew about the other actions she'd been involved in."

Lucie covered her eyes and began to cry. Robert stood beside her, his hand on her shoulder. She tried to picture what Aline would have been doing when they arrived to get her. Was she asleep? Or was she lying on her back, looking out the window, smiling at the memory of her last moonlit evening below the *Spirit of Liberty*? She wondered if somehow Aline had known she'd be arrested. Whether she'd willed it to be Bastille Day rather than another less significant date; whether she'd decided it was the most fitting day to revolt and suffer the consequences.

"Where have they taken her?" asked Lucie, wiping her face on her sleeve.

"We can't be sure. Probably rue des Saussaies."

This street in the eighth arrondissement was well known to all Parisians, its name murmured and whispered, acknowledged with silent nods. It was a quiet, residential street in an expensive area not far from the Madeleine and the Champs-Élysées—home to the headquarters of the Gestapo. It was rumored that those who lived in the neighboring buildings slept every night with cotton crammed in their ears to keep out the screams of the tortured.

As Robert was leaving, Lucie asked him if Simone knew about Aline.

"Yes, I was just there."

"How did she take the news?"

"Not well," he said. "I think you should go see her."

When he had gone, Lucie went to the sink and looked at her face in the mirror. It was still stained with cherry juice from the night before. The deep red smears made her look gaunt, skull-like, her eyes like empty holes. She wet a facecloth and scrubbed at the stains till her skin was stinging and she'd cried out all her tears.

***

When Simone opened the door to her apartment, Lucie almost didn't recognize her. Her hair was loose, not tied back in its usual bun. It spilled messily over her shoulders, strands sticking to the wet skin of her cheeks and neck. Her eyes were swollen, rubbed raw by the hand-kerchief she held twisted around her fingers. When Lucie stepped inside and closed the door behind her, Simone fell against her, clutching her in a suffocating embrace.

"What will they do to her?" she gasped. "They'll torture her. They'll kill her."

Lucie didn't know what to say, how to comfort her. She was distressed to see her in this state, but disturbed as well. She thought of Simone as the strongest person she'd ever met. The risks she'd taken to save those babies. Her work at the hospital and all the horrors she'd witnessed. Even after the arrest of Samuel, she'd carried on fighting. But this was too much. Even Simone's strength had been shaken now.

Lucie stayed with her until she was calm, repeating what Simone already knew—that they just had to wait. Robert would try to get news through his contacts. Until then, there was nothing else to do.

***

When Lucie got home, she told her mother what had happened.

"Oh my God," Yvonne said. "Can we go to the police? Surely they can help. They should know where she is."

Lucie shook her head. "It was the Gestapo," she whispered, the word like a stone on her tongue.

Back in her room, she sat at her desk and took out a blank sheet of paper. She smoothed it with her palm and opened a bottle of ink. She picked up her pen, dipped the tip in, and formed the first three large letters: R. E. V. She dipped the nib back into the ink and traced another three letters: O. L. T.

Through the open window came the sound of angry voices rising from the street below: women yelling at a baker who'd run out of bread. Lucie paused, the nib a few inches above the poster. She stared out at the thick grayness of the sky, the squat chimney pots on the roofs opposite lined up like they too were in a queue; resigned, exhausted, fed up.

The women's voices continued to rise, though fewer in number now. Lucie's eyes remained fixed on the chimney pots, the pen held between her fingers. A drop of ink fell and hit the paper, leaving a sunburst splatter across the still-wet letters. The voices from the street below grew distant and finally were indistinguishable from the percussion of wooden heels and the muted drumming of bicycle tires across the cobblestones. When a pigeon landed on the window-sill, she blinked, slowly lowered her pen and laid it on the desk. She picked up the unfinished tract, crushed it into a ball, and dropped it onto the floor, then sank down beside it, her mind empty, her hands clutching her head.

***

A few days later, Simone telephoned from the hospital and asked Lucie to come to her house that evening.

When Lucie arrived, another woman was there with Simone. She was tall with wavy blond hair and glasses. "This is Claudette, a colleague of mine," said Simone. "She has news."

The woman explained that she was a social worker with the Red Cross and that she'd been working in the camp at Drancy where she'd seen Aline.

"I wasn't able to talk to her unfortunately," she said.

"How was she?" asked Lucie.

"She had bruises on her wrists, but other than that she seemed unharmed." Claudette explained that Aline was in a dormitory in a block on the left side of the compound, which she said was a good sign.

"Those leaving on a convoy are moved to the block closest to the gates a day or two before their departure," she said. "From there they're taken by bus in the early morning to the railway station at Bobigny." At the station they were put into cattle cars that were sealed with lead and sent east—to Germany, perhaps, or Poland. No one believed any longer that they'd be working in agriculture or in a German armaments factory; not since the convoys had started to be filled not just with men, but with women and children, old people, and those too sick to walk.

***

On Thursday afternoon, one week after Aline's arrest, Simone and Lucie took a bus out to Drancy. The road that ran alongside the camp had several shops, a garage, and a small hotel. Although it wasn't possible to visit, Simone had heard from family members of other detainees that the owner of the hotel would give them access to a room on the third floor from which you could see into the camp. It wasn't an act of compassion on his part; he charged them for their use of the room, fifteen minutes at a time. In a day, he probably made more than he would for the rest of the week.

"I don't have to spend my free time running up and down all day," he said to justify his charges. "I don't owe you anything. I'm doing you a favor."

Simone and Lucie climbed the stairs behind him. He took his time, pausing on each landing, wheezing and coughing. On the third floor he led them to the end of a short corridor, opened a door and let them in. He cleared his throat and spat a gob of phlegm into a handkerchief, then turned and left them alone.

The room was narrow and dark, furnished only with a single bed and an armchair whose springs had pierced its worn-through canvas seat. Simone pulled aside the dusty drapes and they looked out over the camp on the other side of the road. The long, high buildings of pale gray U-shaped apartment blocks with their neat black window frames were clearly visible. A barbed-wire fence surrounded the whole complex and there were wooden guard towers at each corner. Several French policemen stood at the gated entrance to the large open space between the three-sided block of buildings. Dozens of detainees moved slowly about the yard, walking aimlessly in regular curves, leaving tracks like pigeons in the brown dirt.

"They're too far away," said Lucie. "She'll never see us."

"Here—wave this," said Simone, pulling a bright red square of fabric from her bag. "The others told me this is what they do. The detainees know to look up. They know we're here."

Lucie took the fabric, not fully convinced by Simone's optimism. She stared down at the rectangular slice of yard. The detainees' faces were pale smudges, no features discernible. She couldn't tell if any were wearing glasses, if they were looking up in her direction or simply staring into space. Lucie raised the piece of red material above her head and waved it, her eyes fixed on the figures far below, waiting for a sign from one of them. She continued to stand and wave until her arm grew numb.

There was a knock at the door and the hotel owner called out, "Time's up. You'll have to pay for another fifteen minutes if you want to stay any longer."

On the bus that took them back to Paris, Lucie didn't dare admit how futile she feared the whole exercise had been. The thoughts that filled her mind were not something she'd share with Simone. The truth was, looking down onto that enclosed, barren space, all she'd felt was a loss of hope; all she'd seen was a stark and empty future.

* * *

The next morning, Lucie walked along the Seine towards the Jardin des Tuileries. She needed to spend time alone, to process what she'd seen at Drancy. As she looked out along the river, she thought about all that she and Aline had been through together over the last two and a half years. Any strength she now possessed, any passion she felt, had come from Aline, her courage, her conviction. When they were together, they could endure. But now Aline was gone, caught up in the deadly net, just as Lucie had always feared. She wished she'd tried harder to talk her out of joining in Robert's activities. If only she had, Aline might still be free.

As she neared the Pont Royal, a *bateau-mouche* passed beneath the middle arch on its way upstream. On its deck there were fewer German soldiers than the previous summer and the one before that; just a few silhouettes leaning on the railings and sprawled across the empty rows of seats. She imagined them drawn in pencil—grubby, messy scribbles on an otherwise carefully rendered background. She put her hand out in front of her, an imaginary eraser held between her thumb and forefinger and swept her hand back and forth, erasing them from the scene.

She continued on to the Jardin des Tuileries, where a crowd was gathered on the terrace outside the Jeu de Paume museum. As she approached, she saw that an area had been cordoned off, soldiers keeping everyone at bay. In the middle of the open space was a huge pile of wooden pallets, like a Hindu funeral pyre. From the museum, dozens more soldiers emerged carrying paintings. Lucie recognized several by Picasso, Léger, Klee, Ernst, Miro. She watched in horror as the artworks—labeled "degenerate art" by the Nazis—were layered on top of the pallets, then doused in kerosene and set on fire. The canvases were alight in minutes, the oil paint bubbling and blistering like skin, giving off acrid black smoke. She pushed her way further into the tightly packed crowd and stood, her arms pressed against those of the people on either side of her, all of them staring silently into the flames. She tried to tell herself that this was just one tragedy among so many others. She thought of Aline and Samuel, what they might be suffering at this very moment. She thought of the millions of lives lost, so many people bombed, so many arrested, so many sent away. And yet, as she watched the paintings burn, she was over-come with grief. As a child, she'd seen newsreel images of the book burnings in Germany. That had been bad enough, but at least books could be reprinted. These paintings were irreplaceable and now they were gone forever.

***

Two days later, Simone came to see Lucie in her room. Claudette was with her.

"Is there news of Aline?" Lucie asked anxiously.

"Possibly," said Simone.

"It's a complicated situation," explained Claudette. "I've just found out that some detainees aren't being deported with the others from Drancy. They're being kept there and not sent east by train."

"Is Aline one of them?" asked Lucie, feeling a surge of hope.

"Unfortunately it only seems to apply to certain categories of detainees," replied Claudette.

"What categories?"

"Some are Jews who have one non-Jewish parent," said Simone.

"But that's not Aline's case," said Lucie.

"No," said Simone. "But they're also selecting Jews who have an Aryan spouse. Claudette knows of several instances where husbands and wives have managed to get their spouse recategorized. You just need to take the marriage certificate to the Commissariat-General for Jewish Affairs."

Lucie frowned. "I don't understand how that helps Aline? She's not married."

Simone sat down on the bed next to Lucie. "That's what we want to talk to you about. If we can get a marriage certificate for her, we might be able to stop her from being deported. We know that some of Aline's university friends are involved in obtaining false papers. Are you able to get in touch with them?"

Lucie nodded. "I know how to contact Robert."

"Explain that it's urgent," said Claudette. "Every day Aline spends in Drancy increases the risk that she'll be sent east."

Simone's eyes suddenly filled with tears. "I have to get her out," she said. "I couldn't do anything for my husband or Samuel. I can't lose Lina too."

Lucie bowed her head. She knew the fear she felt for her friend must be nothing compared to what Simone was feeling. She wished she could say, *I understand your pain*, but it would be claiming a grief that wasn't hers to feel.

***

That evening, Lucie went to see Robert to explain what she'd learned, and the next day the two of them met in a quiet cafe near the Père Lachaise cemetery. Robert brought with him a blank marriage certificate, as well as one issued by the town hall of Vitry-le-François to use as the basis for the fake. He explained that all the records of this small town in the Marne had been destroyed in a bombing in June 1940. It was therefore impossible to check the records of anyone whose birth, marriage, or death had been recorded there.

"But it'll need to be authorized," he said, pointing to the official stamp at the bottom of the certificate.

"Can you get one?" asked Lucie.

He shook his head. "They're almost impossible to come by now. There's a lucrative trade in them on the black market."

Lucie looked closely at the tiny lettering around the edge of the stamp and the crest in the center. "I could make one," she said.

"Are you sure?" asked Robert. "It's very fine work. It has to be completely accurate."

"I'm sure," said Lucie, folding the certificates and putting them in her bag.

On the way home, Lucie called in to Margot's store to pick up the supplies she'd need to make the stamp—linoleum, etching knives, and a blue inkpad. That evening, when she went down to the apartment to help Yvonne make dinner, she took a small turnip from the kitchen and brought it back to her room. She cut the vegetable in two and rubbed it over one of the small squares of linoleum, as Robert had instructed. When she pressed the identity card onto the damp surface, the blue ink of the stamp was transferred onto it, giving her a reversed image of the lettering. She blew on the wet linoleum to dry it before tracing over the faint lettering with ink to get a clearer outline. With the help of her magnifying glass she began the delicate process of scoring and etching the linoleum to leave just the fine raised lettering of the stamp. Her first attempts to guide the tip of the etching knife were tentative, but it didn't take her long to grow accustomed to the new tool. It was the opposite of the delicate illustrations she did, removing material fine line by fine line rather than adding them in ink. It was a less forgiving technique, but the letters were simple block capitals, less complex than some of the drawings she'd executed in the past.

She worked late, pressing her fingers against her aching eyes as the air in the room grew warm and sour with exhaled breath and sweat. She was wary of opening the window and drawing the curtains aside in case she could be seen from the apartments across the street. She took her time, knowing the slightest imperfection could reveal the stamp as counterfeit and result in Aline's arrest and deportation.

When finally she finished, she pressed the stamp into the inkpad, and pushed it down on the bottom of the marriage certificate. She held it in place for several seconds, then pulled it away, exhaling with relief as she saw the result of her long night's work—a perfect replica of the official stamp of Vitry-le-François.

28

LUCIE STOOD NEXT to Simone outside the barbed-wire fence of the camp in Drancy. Simone held a copy of the official document attesting that her daughter was married to an Aryan, issued by the Commissariat-General for Jewish Affairs when she'd presented them with the marriage certificate. They'd assured her they would send the original to the camp authorities, but Simone was worried it mightn't have been received. She wanted to take a copy there in person.

Lucie gazed through the wire into the large flat yard bordered by the tall gray apartment blocks. When the housing complex was first built, it was named La Cité de la Muette—the City of the Mute Woman. The image sent a shiver across Lucie's scalp.

From ground level it looked even more vast than it had from the third floor of the hotel. Like that day, detainees walked aimlessly in the yard, their features barely more distinct; their individuality still masked by the gray uniformity of despair.

One of the French gendarmes stationed by the entrance approached and raised a finger to the visor of his hat.

"Mesdames," he said, his eyes sliding slowly from Simone's yellow star up to her face.

"We sent you an attestation regarding my daughter's marriage," Simone said, holding the paper up for the gendarme to see.

He clasped the paper between his thumb and forefinger and dislodged it from her grasp, frowning as he read the words. "And where is your daughter's Aryan husband?" he asked.

"He's been sent to Germany," replied Simone. "Compulsory work service."

Without responding, the officer folded the paper in two, turned, and walked away towards the low wooden shed that served as an on-site police station. After a few minutes, he emerged and headed across the yard to the accommodation blocks.

Lucie stood waiting beside Simone. The sun shone directly onto her back, sweat making dark circles on her dress that spread from her armpits and trickled down towards her waist. Almost half an hour passed before the gendarme returned. He walked slowly towards them and handed the paper back to Simone.

"Your daughter's no longer here," he said, his eyes narrowed against the sun, not looking at Simone.

Simone stared at him, her eyes wide. "Where is she?" she asked, her voice full of air.

Lucie took hold of Simone's hand, afraid she might faint. She was terrified that they'd arrived too late, that Aline had already been deported.

The gendarme responded without shifting his gaze. "She's been transferred," he said.

"Where?" asked Simone, squeezing Lucie's hand. "Not to Germany?"

The gendarme shrugged. "I don't know any more than that." He glanced at Simone, then removed his hat and wiped his forehead before turning and walking back to the wooden shed. As Simone began to sob, Lucie put her arm around her shoulder and slowly led her out past the barbed-wire fence.

***

By the time they got back to Paris, Simone was a little calmer. Lucie suggested she contact Claudette to see if she could get any information about Aline. She tried to convince Simone that there was no point imagining the worst. They just needed to wait for news.

That evening, Yvonne and Lucie ate dinner together and Lucie told her mother about the visit to Drancy and the news they'd received about Aline, relieved to be able to talk without worrying they'd be overheard. Gérard was so busy with his work that he was usually gone before Lucie and Yvonne were awake and rarely returned home before nine. He would eat the dinner that Yvonne left out for him, then go straight to bed.

The next morning, after Yvonne left for work, Lucie went out to buy bread and whatever else she could find in the nearby shops. She came home just before midday and began preparing lunch for Yvonne and herself. Ten minutes later, Madame Maurel knocked on the door to tell her she'd heard there was real coffee available at the grocery store at the end of the street. Lucie decided she'd try to get some for Simone. She took the book of ration tickets and hurried down the stairs, hoping the store wouldn't run out before she arrived. As she passed the first-floor landing, she saw Gérard's van parked in the courtyard. Peering over the railing into the stairwell, she saw him enter the building carrying a bundle wrapped in a blanket. After a quick glance towards the concierge's lodge, he headed for the cellar door rather than up the stairs. Lucie wondered what he was taking down there; no doubt he was doing some sort of shady dealing on the black market, trading their stores of preserved fruit for something more valuable. While he was still in the cellar, Lucie quickly continued down the stairs and headed outside.

There were about a dozen women lined up outside the grocery

store. The midday sun felt hotter than the previous days, but a slight breeze played against Lucie's legs and fluttered around the hem of her dress. In the gutter a pigeon pecked at a trampled cabbage leaf. Lucie squeezed into the narrow strip of shade beside the store, her back against the cool stone wall. She'd been waiting about five minutes when she saw Gérard's van exit the courtyard of their building and drive away down the street. She was surprised he hadn't stayed to eat lunch, but couldn't say she was disappointed.

As the next customer emerged from the store, the grocer stuck her head out and yelled, "No more coffee!" Normally this would set off a chorus of complaints among the women in the queue, but their urge to object had wilted in the heat. One by one they peeled away and trudged off home.

***

The next day, Lucie was on her way back from the bakery just before midday when she again saw Gérard's van parked in the courtyard. She hoped that, like the previous day, he was just visiting the cellar and wouldn't come up for lunch.

As she passed the van, her eye was caught by an unusual pattern in the otherwise dull layer of grime that covered the bottom half of the side panels. The angle of the sun hid the side of the van in shadow, so she bent to take a closer look. The pattern had been made by a finger rubbed through the dirt. Her eyes followed the curved lines as they swept up and branched out. She gasped as she recognized the Hirsch family symbol she'd seen on the engraved objects at Samuel's workshop—the stag's antlers. Below it was a single letter—A. It had to be a message from Aline! Gérard must have been to the place where she'd been sent and Aline must have recognized the van. Lucie had to find a way to let her friend know she'd seen her message. But she had to act quickly; Gérard might return from the cellar at any moment. Crouching behind the van she licked her index finger and traced a single letter—L—beneath the A.

Worried that she might cross paths with Gérard as he came up from the cellar, she decided to hide and wait for him to leave before going upstairs. She hurried to the doorway on the far side of the courtyard, and stood watching from the shadows until she saw her uncle emerge. He climbed into his van and drove straight off, unaware of the message hidden on the passenger-side panel.

Lucie ran to Simone's apartment to tell her the good news. Although they still didn't know where Aline was, at least they knew she hadn't been sent east, that she was somewhere in Paris. And now there was a slender thread that they could follow. Lucie knew she needed to tell Yvonne what she'd seen and ask for her help. If her mother could find out where Gérard was working, that might lead them to Aline. Lucie certainly couldn't ask Gérard herself; he was already suspicious of her behavior.

When Yvonne came home for lunch, Lucie told her about Aline's message.

"What do you know about his moving jobs, what he actually does each day?"

"Nothing. Just that he starts early and finishes late."

"Is there some way you can find out?"

"I don't know," said Yvonne. "I can't just come out and ask him. He'll suspect something."

"You have to try," Lucie said. "It's our only link to Aline."

Her mother pulled at a piece of loose skin on her lip. "I'll talk to Gérard tonight," she said. "I can't guarantee anything, but I'll do my best."

Lucie clasped her mother's hands. "Thank you, Maman."

Yvonne squeezed her daughter's fingers. "Don't worry, *chérie*. We'll find a way."

***

Late that evening, after Gérard had come home and gone to bed, Yvonne went up to Lucie's room.

"I spoke to him," she said once Lucie had closed the door behind her. "I told him I was concerned about how late he was working. I tried to get him to tell me where he was going each day, but he didn't give me many details. He just said he has a lot of jobs for the Germans and it's not his business to know what they're doing. But he was complaining about all the paperwork he needs to complete. That's why he comes home so late. He goes back to the garage after he's finished his last trip and gets started on the forms he has to submit the next day. I told him I could help out, spend an hour or so a day doing some of his paperwork."

"What did he say?"

"He seemed surprised, but he agreed. I'm not sure how useful it'll be, but I thought it might give us a bit more information about his comings and goings."

"That's good," said Lucie. She had no idea whether it would lead anywhere, but she was grateful for Yvonne's help. It felt like they were one small step closer to finding Aline.

***

The next day, Gérard dropped by the apartment at midday with a carton full of invoices and forms for Yvonne. He didn't stay to eat lunch, and once he'd left, Yvonne and Lucie sat together at the table to examine the documents. They seemed to be mainly details of moving jobs. Each page contained an address along with instructions to remove all the belongings from a specified apartment. The delivery address was always the same: Lévitan at 85–87 rue du Faubourg Saint-Martin in the tenth arrondissement.

"What's Lévitan?" asked Lucie.

"It's a department store," replied Yvonne. "Or it was. It was closed down a couple of years ago because the owners were Jewish."

"Then why is he delivering there?" asked Lucie.

Yvonne just shrugged.

*　*　*

The next morning, Lucie went to meet Simone at her apartment. She'd asked her to invite Claudette too. She told them the information she and Yvonne had gathered from the paperwork. Simone was over-joyed.

"This is more than I could have hoped for," she said. "At least we know where she is now."

Claudette drummed the nail of her index finger on the tabletop. "This could be useful," she said. "Some of my Red Cross colleagues have been delivering parcels to the old Lévitan store. The Germans have taken it over. Apparently they're using it to store furniture and other belongings they've taken from Jewish apartments. They sort the goods there before sending them to Germany." She leaned over the table. "We'd heard there were civilians working there. They must be the detainees from Drancy."

"Why would they have transferred them there?" asked Simone.

"Free labor," said Claudette. "Some of them have skills that are needed to repair things—clockmakers, tailors, silversmiths, uphol-sterers. Others sort the goods or load them into crates to be taken by truck to the Austerlitz train station and sent to Germany. That must be where they sent Aline."

Even though they had no way of contacting her yet, it was an immense comfort to know that Aline was so close. She was only a thirty-minute walk away, in the center of Paris—not in a detention camp surrounded by barbed wire and watchtowers, and not on a train headed east to God knows where.

"Do you think we'll be able to see her?" Simone asked.

"I doubt it," said Claudette. "It's a very secretive operation. All the doors and windows are covered up. Trucks come and go from the loading bay underneath, but it's impossible to visit anyone in there. The workers sleep on-site." She paused, her eyes flicking over the tabletop, as if searching for a solution. "I'll talk to my colleagues," she said finally. "Perhaps I can manage to get myself assigned there to distribute parcels."

"We could send a message in a package," said Simone.

Claudette shook her head. "That would be too risky. If it's like Drancy, the parcels are searched. They read and censor all the letters."

"But we have to do something," said Simone. "She could still be sent away at any time. Who knows how long they'll keep her there."

Lucie remembered that Aline had once mentioned hiding messages in shirt collars to communicate with imprisoned students. She told Simone and Claudette.

"We can't be sure she'll find it, but we have to try," said Lucie.

"If you put a parcel together, I can try to get it to her within the next few days," said Claudette.

Simone fetched one of Aline's blouses from her bedroom and some paper to wrap it in. Lucie turned the collar up and slid out the small flat metal stay. On a small piece of paper she wrote, *We'll get you out soon. Be brave.* She folded the paper tightly, running her nail along the crease until it formed a thin strip, then slid it into the slit under the collar. Carefully she smoothed it back into place. She took a pencil from her bag, undid the buttons, and laid the blouse flat on the table. On the inside of the fabric halfway down the back of the blouse, she sketched a small set of stag's antlers. She buttoned the blouse back up and folded it neatly, hiding the sketch from view.

***

A few days later, Lucie received a phone call from Claudette asking her to come to Simone's apartment. When Lucie arrived, she told her she had good news.

"I went to Lévitan to hand out parcels." She smiled and laid her hand on Lucie's arm. "I saw Aline."

Lucie looked at Simone, whose eyes were filled with tears.

"Did you manage to speak to her?" Lucie asked Claudette.

"No, it wasn't possible unfortunately. But I made sure she got the package."

"How did she seem?" asked Lucie.

Claudette glanced at Simone before answering. "All right," she said. "Better than in Drancy." She paused. "Better, but not good."

"What kind of work do they have her doing?"

"She was sorting the goods that arrive by truck in the loading bay."

"Is it heavily guarded?"

"Not as much as I'd expected," said Claudette. "There were soldiers watching the detainees, but only one or two in each area and many of them were invalids. According to my colleagues they're being posted to this role because all the able-bodied soldiers are needed to go and fight against the Russians."

"We have to find a way to get her out," said Simone. "For the moment, our only connection to her is your uncle. Is there some way we could smuggle her out in his van?"

"Not with him driving it," said Lucie. "That would be much too dangerous."

"Could we take the keys and go ourselves?"

Lucie shook her head. "He uses the van every day."

"What if Yvonne tells him he looks tired and suggests he take a day off to rest?"

"Not a chance," said Lucie. "He'd have to be at death's door before he'd do that."

"We'll have to find a way," said Simone. "Lina's so close. We can't let them send her away."

Lucie laid her hand on Simone's shoulder. "We won't. I promise."

***

The next morning, Simone went to see Lucie in her room. She sat on the edge of the bed and took a sip from the glass of water that Lucie handed her before leaning forward and speaking softly. "I think I've found a way we could use your uncle's van to get Aline out of Lévitan."

"How?" asked Lucie.

"You said the only way your uncle wouldn't work was if he was at death's door," said Simone. "I think I can make him believe he is."

Lucie frowned. "I don't understand."

"You'd have to find a way to give him some ipecac syrup. Once he drinks it, he'll start vomiting violently within a matter of minutes. He'll feel much too ill to go to work."

"But how would I get him to drink it?" asked Lucie.

"It has a very sweet taste, not unpleasant at all. You could hide it in his food or a drink."

Lucie leaned on the back of her chair, her eyes following the sunlight as it caught in a vase by the window, glowing golden against the wooden desk.

"Peaches," she said, looking back up at Simone. "He has them in syrup every morning. Would that work?"

"Yes, that's perfect," said Simone. "Then Yvonne can say she'll call a doctor and I'll come to the house. I'll tell him he needs to spend the day in bed."

"I'm still not convinced it'll work," said Lucie. "He'd be too worried about losing his contract. I'm not sure he'd agree."

"Would he agree to let you and Yvonne go in his place?"

"I doubt it. And anyway, we're not removalists. If the Germans saw two women in the truck, they'd know something wasn't right." She thought for a moment. "I'll ask Robert to help. Maman can tell Gérard she knows someone who can replace him for the day. She can say he's a colleague's son."

"But isn't there another man who works with him?"

Lucie sighed and closed her eyes. "Émile," she said. "The concierge's son." She'd forgotten about him. Gérard didn't seem to use him as often now, but Émile still helped out occasionally.

"What would he do if he found out?" asked Simone. "Would he denounce us?"

"I don't know," said Lucie. "Maybe. We'll have to tell him Gérard is sick and won't be working for the day."

Simone frowned. "There's so much that could go wrong," she said, her tone suddenly less hopeful. "What if someone sees her getting into the van? And even if we get her out of Lévitan, where would we hide her? She's already been denounced once. If she were caught again . . ." Simone swallowed. When she spoke, her voice was so faint Lucie could barely hear her. "This time they would surely execute her." She stood up and walked to the window. "Maybe it's too dangerous."

Lucie knew Simone was right—they would be putting Aline's life at risk. But at least if they managed to get her out of Lévitan she had a chance of survival. "We don't have a choice," she said, her words soft and slow. "Aline could be sent back to Drancy and deported at any moment. We might never get another opportunity like this." She waited till Simone turned to face her. "We'll make it work—I know we will. We just have to be careful. I'll talk to Robert today." She stood up and joined Simone by the window. "When can you get the syrup?"

Simone took a deep breath. "Tomorrow, I think. Could you give it to your uncle on Wednesday morning?"

"We'll have to," said Lucie. "We can't afford to wait."

"How will she know what to do when the van arrives?"

Lucie knew the first obstacle for Aline would be managing to get into the van without being noticed. "Do you think Claudette could get another package to her tomorrow?" she asked.

"I think so," said Simone. "She goes there every day."

"Could you get hold of a man's cap and shirt?"

"Yes, I have my husband's. Why?"

"We'll put them in the package and hide another message in the collar. If she can manage to blend in among the men, it might be easier for her to get close to the van."

Lucie tore a piece of paper from her sketchbook.

On it she wrote, *Wednesday 4 August. Wear these clothes. Hide in the back of my uncle's van.*

29

ON WEDNESDAY MORNING, Yvonne went up to Lucie's room at seven. Her face was flushed, but she looked confident.

"It worked," she said. "Gérard is sick in bed. I took the keys from his pocket. We need to tell Émile that he won't be working today."

"Can you do that?" asked Lucie. "I have to meet Robert at the garage."

"All right," said Yvonne. "And I'll keep an eye on Gérard. Simone left me some extra ipecac in case he starts feeling better."

When Lucie arrived at the garage, Robert was waiting as planned, leaning against a wall, pretending to read a newspaper. She unlocked the door and made her way inside. A few minutes later, Robert followed her in and closed the door behind him. Lucie pulled Gérard's work jacket from her basket.

"You should wear this," she said, handing it to Robert. "You need to be at an apartment in the sixteenth at eight-thirty. Here's the address." She handed him the keys to the van and the form Yvonne had given her. "When you arrive at Lévitan and unload the crates, Aline should be nearby, working on the sorting line. She knows she has to be in the back of the van before it leaves. The most difficult part for her will be getting in without being noticed. Hopefully the cap and jacket will help. Drive her straight to my apartment building. I'll hide her in my room till it's safe to move her."

After Robert left, Lucie returned home. She climbed the stairs to the top floor, but stayed out on the landing and opened the window that looked down over the courtyard. Although she knew it would be hours before Robert returned, she was too anxious to do anything else but wait. She sat down on the window ledge and breathed in the still, cool air to try to ease her doubts about whether the plan would work. There were so many things that could go wrong. Robert might be stopped and arrested. The message might have been discovered. And even if Aline had seen it, there might have been a change in her work schedule meaning she couldn't be at the loading bay when Robert got there. What if a guard saw her getting into the van? Lucie pulled her knees tight against her chest and squeezed her eyes shut to try to stop the procession of scenarios running through her head.

***

It was after eleven when she heard the sound of a motor below. She leaned out the window and saw the van entering the courtyard. It swung around and backed up into the corner closest to their stairway. Robert opened the driver's door, stepped out, and glanced up towards Lucie. He nodded once and walked towards the back of the van. As he opened the doors, Aline jumped down, still wearing the man's jacket and cap. Robert grasped her arm and hurried her into the building.

Lucie rushed down the stairs, her knees shaking with the tension she'd been holding in her legs. She met them as they arrived on the first-floor landing. She hugged Aline, tears of relief filling her eyes, afraid to speak for fear of alerting the neighbors to her presence. Robert gestured down to the courtyard. "I'll take the van back," he whispered.

Aline grasped his arm. "Thank you," she said.

He nodded and smiled, then headed back outside.

"Come with me," whispered Lucie, taking Aline's hand and climbing the stairs.

As they reached the next landing, they heard the van start up. Lucie looked down through the window and froze, her grip on Aline's hand tightening. On the far side of the courtyard she saw Émile. He was standing completely still in the shadows, watching the van as it drove away. She had no idea if he had seen Aline getting out of the van—or what he would do if he had.

Once they were in her room, Lucie explained that it wasn't safe for Aline to go back to the apartment on the Île Saint-Louis.

"We're not sure who denounced you, but it could have been a member of Robert's group."

"Do you know if he's been able to get false identity papers?"

"He's still waiting for his new contacts in Bordeaux to tell him they're ready."

"So what do I do in the meantime?"

Lucie explained that Philippe, the manager of the cinema, had a room on the top floor of the building for storing old equipment. Margot had asked him if Aline could use it until they found a more permanent solution.

"They hid a parachuted English soldier there for a week at the beginning of the war." Lucie sat down on the bed next to Aline. "If there's any suspicious activity in the building, or if there are rumors of arrests in the neighborhood, you can escape down the service stairs. The cinema toilets are in the central courtyard. If you need to, you can hide there and then slip out onto the street via the cinema."

"How will I know if I need to leave?"

"Margot has a system she used when the English soldier was hiding there. From the room, you can see the window of her apartment. If there's any danger, she'll position the left-hand shutter so that it's half closed. She'll open it again when it's safe to return." Lucie placed her hand on Aline's shoulder and looked her in the eye. "Will you remember that?"

Aline forced a smile. "As if my life depended on it."

***

Lucie took Aline to her new room, where Simone was waiting. When she saw her daughter, she wrapped her arms around her, then suddenly let go and raised her fingertips to Aline's forehead. She gently touched her eyes, her lips, ran her hands over her hair, across her shoulders, down her arms. Aline stood perfectly still, allowing her mother to take in every detail, as if she were conducting a medical examination, as though she had to feel the skin, the flesh, the bones, to be sure she was really there.

Finally, Simone spoke. "I thought you were gone forever."

Aline looked down at the floor, her gaze far away. "So did I," she whispered.

Simone heated up the stew she'd brought with her and they ate it crowded around a small wooden table. After they'd finished, Aline related what she'd gone through since her arrest.

"Drancy was horrendous," she said. "It was just like Papy's description of the camp in Compiègne. And it was even harder knowing we were so close to home. From the top floor of the building, we could see Sacré-Cœur."

She described the overcrowded dormitories, the thin, filthy mattresses on which they'd slept. They received very little to eat, mainly soup and bread. The French police who guarded them were brutal and corrupt. If someone received a package, they confiscated the food and cigarettes and sold them back to the detainees at exorbitant prices— many times higher than the black market in Paris.

"But the worst thing was not knowing what was going to happen to us. I'd see people being taken away and know they were being sent east, but not where or why. I was always worried I'd be next in line."

Simone wrapped her arm around Aline and pulled her close. "I wish we could have let you know we were trying to get you out."

Aline ran a finger across Simone's cheek, wiping away a tear, before continuing. "They separated us into categories. Those with one Jewish parent were classified as 'half-Jews' and given a green card. One day they gave me a blue card and told me it was because I was the spouse of an Aryan. I didn't know that you'd organized a false marriage certificate, so I thought it was an error. But I'd heard that detainees with blue cards were treated better, so I didn't argue.

"Then, about ten days ago, a whole group of those with blue and green cards were separated from the others. We were loaded onto buses and driven back to Paris. They didn't tell us where we were going, so I was sure they were taking us to the train station to send us to Germany."

Simone placed her hand on Aline's head and gently stroked her hair. Aline closed her eyes for a moment and took a few deep breaths before continuing her story.

"When we arrived at Lévitan, they took us up to the fourth floor and told us that's where we'd be sleeping. To begin with there was nothing up there. No beds, no mattresses. Just bare floorboards. Straightaway we were divided into groups of ten. Mine was work team seven. Each group was assigned to a different area of the building. I was stationed in the basement where the removalist vans came in loaded with goods taken from vacated apartments. We had to sort everything into separate crates—pans, crockery, cutlery, lamps, curtains, linen, books, ornaments, even toys. There were photographs and letters too—so many of them, you can't imagine. But we didn't pack them. They were just thrown onto piles to be burned.

"Some things were sent to other areas of the building to be cleaned or repaired. For a few days, my team was sent to work in a different part of the building, packing the goods that were ready to be sent to Germany. Once the crates were full, we nailed the tops in place and stenciled a message on the lid—*Gift from the French for German Refugees*. They made us write our identification number on them too, to try to stop us sabotaging the shipments. It didn't work, though. Whenever there were no guards around, we used the hammers to break whatever we could—teapot handles, clock mechanisms, mirrors. Then we'd carefully hide them under the straw and seal the crates."

Aline explained that among the loads of household belongings were the gasmasks that had been distributed at the start of the war. These too were recovered to be sent to Germany.

"But they wanted to test them to be sure we hadn't sabotaged them. One morning after roll call, they told my group to stay behind. A soldier ordered us down to a small room in the basement and we were each given a gasmask and told to put it on. Then they left the room and closed the doors behind them. After a few seconds, I heard the sound of a truck motor starting up and exhaust gas was pumped into the room through a hole in one of the walls."

Lucie stared at Aline. Even imagining the fear her friend must have felt made the skin of her cheeks go cold.

"We stood in a circle looking at each other," Aline continued. "We had no idea whether any of the other detainees had sabotaged the masks. All we could do was wait to see if they leaked."

"Oh, my poor Lina," said Simone, her hand over her mouth.

"After a few minutes the soldiers opened up the doors and let us out. They took the masks from us and told us to go back to our posts and continue sorting."

When Aline finished telling the story, she took off her glasses, closed her eyes, and leaned back against the wall. No one spoke. After a few seconds, Simone reached over and wiped a drop of sweat from the small red mark on the bridge of her daughter's nose.

30

SINCE THE START of the summer, Lucie had felt a change in the Germans' presence. In the interminable stretch of scorching days that had lasted most of July and August, they'd begun to look uncharacteristically hot and bothered. Some of them shed their uniforms and joined the throngs of bathers at the Piscine Deligny on the Seine, mostly managing to go unnoticed in their swimming trunks.

Even when the weather began to cool in the final days of August, they still seemed on edge, as if they no longer took for granted their solid hold on Paris. Aline had told Lucie she thought they might be getting nervous about the defeat in North Africa and the increase in Allied bombings in France. The massive destruction of cities in Germany must also have been taking its toll, making them anxious about their families back home.

***

Lucie's twentieth birthday dawned gray and cool. She left home early and walked aimlessly through the streets of the sixth arrondissement. The absence of color muddied her thoughts. It felt like the world had been painted over with a wash of ink, soaking into its surface and dimming the light forever. She met Margot midmorning in the cool damp shade by the Medici Fountain in the Jardin du Luxembourg. As they strolled afterwards, cafe terraces in the area were filled with German soldiers, though there were fewer women sitting alongside them now.

Lucie spent the rest of the morning with Aline in her room, eating a cake that Margot had made for them and drinking dandelion tea.

***

Early that afternoon, Lucie was still in her room when Simone arrived out of breath and visibly shaken. Before Lucie could ask what was wrong, the older woman pushed past her and closed the door.

"They're removing patients from the hospital by force," she said. "They're taking them back to Drancy. Women who've just given birth. People who've just been operated on. No matter what state they're in. If they can't walk, they carry them out on stretchers. One woman with a newborn baby threw herself from a window of the maternity ward on the second floor rather than be taken."

"How can they do such things?" exclaimed Lucie.

Simone shook her head and leaned against the door, waiting till her breathing returned to normal. "We need to get as many babies out as we can." She paused and pushed a stray hair out of her eyes. "Is your uncle out of town this weekend?"

"Yes," said Lucie. "Why?"

"Has he taken his van?"

"No. He only has enough gas coupons for work. He takes the train to Normandy."

"That's what I was hoping," said Simone, straightening her back. "Do you think we could use his van to transport the babies?"

"When?"

"Tonight. They've already started taking adults. We don't know when they'll take the children. This might be the last chance we have."

"You take care of things at your end," said Lucie. "I'll organize the van." She scribbled the address of the garage on a slip of paper. "Meet me there at eight tonight."

After Simone left, Lucie went downstairs to the apartment. She found her mother in the living room, mending a blouse.

Lucie explained how urgent the situation with the babies had become and told her about Simone's request to use the van. Yvonne didn't hesitate. She went into Gérard's bedroom and returned with the key.

"I'll go to the hospital with Simone tonight," said Lucie. "She'll need help."

"Are you sure?" whispered Yvonne. Lucie saw the fear in her mother's eyes.

"I'll be all right, Maman," she said. "I'm already part of this. I'm not going to stop now."

Yvonne nodded, her cheeks drained of color. "All right," she whispered. "I understand."

***

When Lucie arrived at the garage that evening, Simone was waiting. They didn't speak until they were inside.

"I'm happy to do this on my own," said Simone. "You can wait here for me."

"No, I'll come with you," Lucie said. "It'll be faster with two of us to carry the babies."

"I'm worried that you'll be out after curfew."

Lucie frowned. "It's already past yours."

Simone looked down at the yellow star on her chest. She forced a finger under the edge, between the small black stitches she'd sewn in place fifteen months earlier. She tore at the rough fabric, pulling it free from the coat. She folded the star in two, put it into her pocket, then picked out the threads left behind. The star shape was still faintly visible, a slightly darker shade of blue. Lucie didn't say anything. She didn't need to. Simone knew it was there.

Opening the back of the van they found two crates filled with straw.

"Perfect, we can hide the babies in there," said Simone. "It'll be safer than having them in the front seat."

Simone reversed the van out of the garage, and Lucie closed the door behind them, then climbed into the passenger seat.

They drove slowly through the dark streets, the covers over the headlights allowing just a strip of light to shine through onto the bitumen.

They parked in a street near the hospital, then hurried to the morgue where two women were waiting, each holding a baby. They passed one to Simone and one to Lucie.

"There are two more. Can you take them now or will you come back for them?"

"We'll take them now," said Simone. "I don't want to be out any later than we have to be."

Once they'd laid the babies in the crates, they returned to the hospital to fetch the other two. Lucie crouched in the back of the van beside the crates while Simone slid into the driver's seat. One of the babies woke and started crying, a high-pitched feeble mewling. Simone turned her head.

"Make it stop," she whispered urgently.

Lucie pulled the wrap away from the tiny face and stroked the baby's head with her fingertips, cooing softly and clicking her tongue. Simone started the engine and the van advanced, rocking gently from side to side. Almost immediately the baby stopped crying. A few minutes later it was asleep.

As they drove through the empty streets, Lucie craned her neck to peer out through the windshield, fearing that at any moment a policeman would wave them down and make Simone open the van. After a few minutes, they arrived at the address of the safe house. Simone drove past the building and parked the van a little further down the street. When she opened the back doors, Lucie handed her two of the babies.

"Stay here and wait till you see me come out of the building," Simone whispered. "I'll walk past the van and around the block. When I'm out of view, you take the others up. Second floor, the door on the right."

Through the windshield, Lucie watched her walk quickly along the deserted street, the two bundles tight against her chest, then disappear through an open doorway. She waited, humming a lullaby and tapping her sweaty palm on the edge of the wooden crate, even though both babies were asleep.

At first, all Lucie heard was a faint sound resonating along the darkened street, almost imperceptible, yet she recognized it immediately. She'd heard it often enough over the past three years. It started as a ticking, as regular as a clock. As Simone exited the building, she must have heard it too, because Lucie saw her turn her head. She hesitated, took several steps towards the van, then looked away, her eyes searching for the obscurity of a side street.

The ticking grew louder until, at the far end of the street, helmets and gleaming boots appeared, reflecting the streetlights in twinkling points like stars, forming their familiar constellation. The silver-blue cast of the lamplights made it feel like a scene from a movie was playing out in front of Lucie as she crouched beside the crate, trembling.

As the patrol approached, Simone crossed the street, taking care not to look in the direction of the van. Then came the cry so often heard: "*Halt!*"

Simone didn't break her stride as she headed towards a small street to her left.

A few seconds later, two of the soldiers broke away and started running along the street towards her. "*Halt!*" they yelled again.

Oh God, please stop, Lucie urged silently, but Simone carried on.

The rest of the patrol was advancing towards the van now. Lucie felt the thump of her pulse drumming in her ears. All she could think was that she had to draw the soldiers away so they wouldn't find the babies. She climbed out, quietly closing the doors behind her. As she moved to the side of the van, one of the soldiers spotted her.

"*Halt!*" he called, firing a shot in the air.

Lucie ran, her legs like ice water, following in Simone's steps. Before her was the Port de l'Arsenal, the masts of boats rocking in unison like giant metronomes. She gained on Simone, the wooden soles of their shoes loud on the cobblestones, echoing off the facades on either side of the street. As they reached the port, Lucie turned and saw the soldiers only thirty meters or so behind. They ran with their guns drawn, barrels pointed downwards. Lucie's heart thumped so hard it squeezed her throat and choked off her breath. Her mind was filled with just one thought. *This can't be it. This can't be how I die.* She grabbed Simone's sleeve and pulled her towards a gangplank leading to a houseboat. On the slippery deck, they crouched and hid behind a rusted metal trunk. As the footsteps of the soldiers came to a stop, the light of a flashlight swept along the riverbank and across the boats moored side by side. Dark shadows turned and twisted, lengthening, then shortening. The white light fell on the blue of Simone's coat and stayed there.

"Come out! Hands in the air! Or we shoot!" yelled a soldier.

Lucie knew that obeying might still mean a death sentence for them both as well as for the babies. They had to try to escape. She clutched Simone's arm and brought her lips up to her ear. "Follow me," she whispered, sliding across to the edge of the boat. She removed her coat and silently lowered herself into the dark, oil-slicked water.

On the deck above, Simone watched her but didn't move.

"Hurry!" whispered Lucie, her voice strangled by the cold pressing on her chest.

Simone slipped out of her coat, leaving it like a chrysalis on the deck behind her, the white light of the soldier's flashlight still sweeping over it. She slid over the side of the boat, making a splash as she broke the surface. The soldiers shouted once again and fired a shot over the deck. Lucie flinched and held her breath, then silently wrapped her tingling hand around Simone's arm and pulled her close to the boat, hidden from the soldiers' view.

Further upstream, Lucie knew, the waters of the Canal Saint-Martin ended their two-kilometer journey beneath the Boulevard Richard-Lenoir, and emerged into the port from under the Place de la Bastille. The end of the covered waterway formed a wide black mouth. There was a gap of at least thirty meters of open water from the shelter of the last boat. She thought about the babies alone in the van and what would happen to them if she and Simone didn't make it back. They had no choice but to swim for cover. She reached for Simone's hand and pulled her towards the tunnel entrance. She knew that if the soldiers were looking in that direction, they'd easily spot them. Their only hope was that the soldiers might presume they were hiding among the boats, making their way towards the lock where the port entered the Seine.

Lucie looked out across the stretch of open water, then took a deep breath and ducked below the surface, pushing away from the boat with her legs. Thirty seconds later, she emerged almost halfway to the tunnel entrance. Her cheeks were numb, her hair sharp and stiff, like needles scraped along her scalp. She turned and saw Simone still waiting by the boat, her face a pale blue oval. With one hand she broke the surface, signaling silently for Simone to follow. Simone pushed herself off from the boat and thrust her arms clumsily through the thick water. Lucie turned away, the other woman's slow, arduous progress too painful to watch. She took another breath and pulled her body back down into the stifling blackness. As she surfaced a second time, she saw the stone vault of the covered canal above her. With three more strokes, she was at the bottom, where the curved wall met the water. She reached up and gripped a large metal ring fixed to the wall, pulling herself against the side of the stone steps that rose from the water to the quay above.

She turned and waited for Simone to reappear, watching for bubbles, for a wave of displaced water. A few seconds passed before her head surfaced, small and smooth, still twenty meters away. She'd swum in a diagonal line, heading for the other side of the port instead of towards the cover of the canal. She turned onto her back and let her body float. Lucie could see her jaw opening and closing as she gasped for air. Suddenly, a buzzing started in Lucie's ears, punctured by metallic clacks that resonated through her skull. She looked up and saw two soldiers running along the quay towards where Simone was still immobile in the water.

"*Halt!*" they yelled.

Simone looked towards them, then rolled onto her front and started swimming for the far bank, towards a flight of stone steps leading out of the water. Her arms made small ineffectual arcs, her head above the water. As she pulled herself onto the bottom step, one of the soldiers fired a shot. It ricocheted off a stone just inches above her. She ducked her head, but then hauled her body up another step, her feet flailing, sending ragged blades of water left and right.

A second shot was fired. Lucie gasped as Simone's back arched, her left arm thrown up into the air. She slumped forward, her right arm reaching up, one knee bent up out of the water, trying to pull herself up the stairs.

The other soldiers had run along the port and crossed the footbridge above the lock. Now they ran back along the bank towards Simone, their guns held low in front of them as though charging towards enemy troops. Lucie's hand was frozen in its grip on the metal ring, her legs dangling limp beneath her, her chin sinking below the surface. Her lips quivered and she spat out the bitter water that filled her mouth. She watched, unable to move, as the soldiers seized Simone by the arms and pulled her up onto the quay, her knees and feet banging on each step. They laid her on her back, pistols pointed at her chest, talking among themselves, loudly but calmly, as if this was a mere inconvenience, an interruption to their plans. Then one of them stooped and pulled her up. Simone sat, slumped but alive, her head down, her shoulders heaving.

Lucie's mind raced as she tried to work out what to do, even while a voice inside her head told her that nothing she did would help Simone now. She was struck by the sudden realization she was still in danger herself. She strained her neck, trying to see the two soldiers who had been on the quay on this side of the port. She spotted them further away now, searching the decks of the boats. They must have assumed she'd climbed aboard one of them. Finally, they moved away, crossing the footbridge to the far side to join the others.

Two soldiers were holding Simone up now, one on either side. Lucie watched as they forced her along the quay, then dragged her up the steps to the road above. A military truck pulled up on the quay. When it departed, it took Simone and the soldiers with it.

Lucie waited several minutes, listening till she was sure they'd gone, then pulled herself to the bottom of the stairs and crawled up on her hands and knees. The air against her skin was even colder than the water had been. The muscles in her legs and arms were quaking, and the palms of her hands felt shredded. She stumbled back along the quay to the street she'd run down with Simone, her eyes burning with the fuel from the canal. She gasped for air, the water that she'd swallowed churning in her stomach. She stopped on the corner and grasped a lamppost, vomiting it up. As she ran on, she tried to remember how long ago she'd left the van, how long the babies had been alone. She must only have been in the water for ten or so minutes, and yet it seemed as if hours had passed.

The van was still where she'd left it. She opened the doors and climbed into the back. In the crates the two babies were still asleep, their breath warm and slightly sour. Her hands were shaking violently as she folded an old blanket, stiff with dirt and smears of paint, and wrapped it around her body so that the babies wouldn't be startled awake by her cold, wet clothes. She picked up the sleeping babies one by one, then slid from the back of the van, locked the doors, and walked quickly along the street to the doorway she'd seen Simone enter earlier. She climbed the stairs to the second floor and tapped lightly on the door to the right of the landing.

She waited, her clothes dripping onto the scuffed brown tiles, her arms and legs trembling. At first she heard no movement inside. They'd obviously been expecting her to arrive straight after Simone. Perhaps they suspected something had gone wrong and were afraid to open the door. Or maybe they'd left the apartment and gone somewhere else to hide. Lucie started to panic. What would she do with the babies? How would she get home? Just as she was about to turn and go back down the stairs, the door opened slightly and a woman's face appeared in the crack, a candle in her hand.

"What happened?" she whispered once she'd pulled Lucie inside and closed the door behind them.

"Germans," said Lucie. "They captured Simone. They shot her." As the words left her mouth, her jaw trembled uncontrollably and the tears began to flow.

"Did they kill her?" asked the woman.

Lucie shook her head. She had to take a deep breath in before she could speak. "She's badly injured. They took her away in a truck." The woman nodded, then put the candle down on a small console and took the babies from Lucie's arms. She showed her to the bathroom and told her to remove her wet clothes, gesturing to a towel and dressing gown she could use. While Lucie dried herself, the woman made a telephone call. Lucie overheard a few phrases that didn't seem to bear any relation to Simone or the babies. She assumed the woman had to use some sort of code to communicate with others in the network. When Lucie came back out into the living room, the woman had laid the four babies side by side on a low divan. One of them had woken but lay quietly in its swaddling, its eyes gazing unfocused at the tasseled lampshade above its head.

"You should stay here tonight," said the woman. "That patrol might still be searching for you."

Lucie nodded. "Can I call my mother?"

"All right," said the woman, "but be careful what you say. Don't give her this address."

When Yvonne answered the telephone, Lucie spoke slowly, pausing after each careful phrase. "I've been studying with my friend and we lost track of time. I've missed the curfew. I'll have to stay here for the night." She could hear the tremble in her own voice, all the swallowed tears.

Yvonne was silent for a moment, then responded with a simple, "I understand."

Lucie cleared her throat. "Can you meet me at the Place des Vosges tomorrow morning at eight?"

"Yes," Yvonne said in a voice barely louder than a whisper. "I'll be there."

31

WHEN YVONNE HUGGED her in the chill of the Place des Vosges the following morning, all Lucie wanted was to lay her head against her mother's chest and let her grief and fear flow out. But she knew she had to hold it in. She couldn't be sure who might be watching from a window or from behind a shadowed doorway. She linked her arm through Yvonne's as they walked in silence to the van. Her clothes were still damp from the previous night. Over the top she wore an old coat the woman had given her. She waited until they were seated side by side and driving slowly through the empty streets before she spoke. She recounted the events of the previous evening, struggling for breath as if she were once again in the icy waters of the canal. Yvonne's hands gripped the steering wheel, the skin pulled tight over her knuckles. She let Lucie speak without interrupting or asking questions.

Despite the tragedy of Simone's arrest, Lucie knew there were things that had to be done. The first was to get the van back to the garage.

When they had parked it and locked the door behind them, Yvonne wrapped her arms around her daughter and pressed her lips to Lucie's temple. Her breath was hot and moist, and Lucie closed her eyes and let the warmth work itself under her skin.

"I'm sorry," whispered Yvonne.

"For what?" asked Lucie.

Yvonne let her head fall, the corners of her mouth pulled down in pain. "For not being there," she said. "This isn't the life I'd planned for you." She raised her eyes to meet Lucie's. "I feel as though I've failed you."

Lucie took her mother's head between her hands. "Plans change," she said softly. "And we do too. It's no one's fault."

***

They arrived back at the apartment just after nine o'clock. When they opened the front door, Gérard was standing in the entrance hall, his cap in his hand. Lucie froze, sliding her body behind her mother's.

"I wasn't expecting you home so early," said Yvonne, pulling her scarf from around her throat.

Gérard shrugged, but didn't offer an explanation. "You're both out early on a chilly morning," he observed.

Yvonne handed Lucie her scarf and Lucie hung it on a peg behind the door. She didn't remove her coat for fear that Gérard would see the dampness in her clothes and question her.

"We heard there were potatoes at the market," said Yvonne.

"And were there?" asked Gérard.

"Well, we don't have any potatoes with us, so obviously there weren't."

"Obviously," said Gérard, taking a step forward to hang his cap on a peg. "And you didn't find anything else to buy?"

"No," said Yvonne. "Everything was gone by the time we got there."

"That's strange," said Gérard. "Because I came home and, seeing there was no food in the house, I went to the market myself. I arrived home just two minutes before you and it certainly wasn't all gone when I was there. In fact, you'll find your shopping basket full on the kitchen table." He paused and crossed his arms. "I'm surprised you didn't think of taking the basket yourself. It would've been hard to carry those potatoes home from the Place de la Bastille in your hands."

Lucie started to shiver. She pulled the coat tighter around her shoulders and looked down at the floor.

"We didn't go to the Bastille market," said Yvonne, her gaze fixed on Gérard. "Madame Maurel said the town hall market had potatoes so we tried there."

Gérard's eyes narrowed, but he didn't say anything more. He nodded as Yvonne pushed past him and went down the hallway to the kitchen. Lucie stood in the entry, not moving until Gérard walked away towards the living room. Then she slipped through the front door and went up to her room to change.

A few minutes later Yvonne came up to her room carrying a cup of strong sweet tea.

"How are you feeling?" she asked.

As Lucie tried to take hold of the cup, her hands began to tremble. Yvonne set it down on her desk.

"All I could think as they were dragging her away was, *This is all a big mistake.*" She looked at Yvonne, her eyes filled with tears. "I wanted to yell, *What the hell are you doing? She's a doctor, for Christ's sake!*"

Yvonne wrapped her arms around Lucie and drew her head down onto her shoulder. "You need to rest, *chérie.* After what you've been through—"

"I can't," said Lucie, cutting her off. "I have to see Aline. She needs to know what's happened." Lucie didn't know what she was going to tell her friend. She didn't know whether Simone was alive or dead, where she'd been taken, what they'd done with her. She took in deep breath after deep breath to stop herself from crying.

"I'll come with you," said Yvonne, rubbing her hands up and down Lucie's arms to warm them.

Lucie shook her head. "It's better if I go alone. Gérard's already suspicious about where we were this morning."

* * *

Lucie crossed the river and wound her way through the narrow streets till she arrived at Margot's store. The shutters of the apartment on the third floor were open, meaning all was clear. The matinee show at the cinema was about to start. A small crowd waited outside; others packed into the small smoke-filled foyer. She walked past them and headed to the stairs. When she arrived on the fifth floor, she leaned against the balustrade, waiting for her breathing to return to normal, knowing that she'd have difficulty enough speaking as it was. She'd barely knocked once on Aline's door when it opened. The smile faded from Aline's lips as she registered the distress in Lucie's eyes.

Once they were inside, Lucie clasped Aline's arms and brought her mouth close to her friend's ear.

"I'm so sorry," she whispered. "It's your mother. Last night. With the babies. They shot her, took her away."

Aline pulled back, her eyes half closed, her lips pale. "What happened? Tell me everything. I want to know."

She listened to Lucie's account of what they'd been through, their attempt to flee, the shooting, Simone's arrest. She took in every word, showing no sign of anger or distress. Instead, she stood completely immobile in the center of the room, arms by her sides, a look of quiet resignation on her face.

When she eventually spoke, she didn't ask for any further details. She simply said, "I need to get down to Limoges. I have to get my sisters out of France."

* * *

The next day, Lucie took Aline food and clean clothes. Her friend sat on the floor beneath the window, her back pushed against the wall. When she spoke, her voice was almost swallowed by the sounds rising from the street below.

"Do you think it's cowardly of me to leave Paris?"

Lucie went and sat beside her and held out her hands. "I never told you the whole truth about how I got these scars." She took a breath in. "It was my father who set our house on fire. He killed himself." She looked at Aline. "I've often asked myself if his decision was cowardly. Now, I think it was his way to escape the horror. I did what was needed to escape that night. We each find our own way."

A few minutes later, Robert arrived. Lucie asked if he had any news of the false papers.

He shook his head. "All my contacts are out of action. We've got no one at the moment." He turned to Aline. "But we have to get you away from Paris as soon as possible. We can't wait." He took her hands in his and spoke softly. "The Gestapo might be interrogating your mother."

"But she's a woman—a doctor," Lucie protested. "Surely they're not that inhumane."

Robert turned to look at Lucie. In his eyes she saw how naive her statement was.

He turned back to Aline. "If they are questioning her," he said, "it won't be long before they track you down."

"What can we do?" asked Aline.

"We'll have to get an identity card from somewhere else," replied Robert. "There's no shortage of them in Paris. The hard part is finding good-quality fakes—and trusting that the seller won't take your money, then denounce you in exchange for a second payment."

Lucie looked at Robert, the tip of her tongue finding an ulcer on the inside of her cheek. She realized there was only one way to ensure

Aline's safety. "I'll make it," she said. "I can use the stamp I made for the marriage certificate. Can you get a blank identity card?"

Robert nodded. "You'll need a photo too."

"I'll go to a Photomaton first thing tomorrow," Aline said, looking at Lucie. "That way you'll have spares just in case."

"Great. I'll come here to pick them up midmorning."

"No," said Aline. "I don't think you should come here anymore." Lucie knew what she was thinking: her hideout might not be safe much longer.

"There's a bookstall down on the Seine," said Robert. "I know the owner. We use his stall to pass messages between members of my group."

He explained the process to Lucie. Whenever they had a message to send, one of them would go to the stall and ask for a specific book. The owner would pull it out from a back shelf and the "customer" would pretend to flip through it, then discreetly slip the message between two pages. They'd hand the book back to the owner who'd return it to the shelf, hidden behind other obscure books. Later that day or the next, the intended recipient would come to the stall, inquire after the same book, and retrieve the message.

"I'll drop the card and photographs there sometime before midday," said Robert. "You'll know I've been if the bookseller is wearing his cap with the peak facing backwards."

"Which book should I ask for?"

"Rimbaud's *A Season in Hell*," said Robert.

Lucie knew she wouldn't forget that title.

"I'll need money for the train and to pay the smugglers," said Aline. "Maman has some back at the apartment. Can you get it?"

"Of course," said Lucie.

"Ask the concierge to let you in. She knows you're a friend. She'll help. There's a roll of notes hidden in a jar of dried lentils on the top shelf of the pantry."

"Will it be enough?" asked Lucie.

Aline shrugged. "It'll have to be."

"How will I get the identity card and money back to you?"

"The same way," said Aline. "Go back to the stall, ask to see the book, and slip the card and money between the pages."

***

The next day Lucie waited till early afternoon to go down to the bookseller's stall. She walked across the Seine and followed the street along the riverbank. Opposite the Monnaie de Paris, she spotted the bookseller, the peak of his cap turned backwards as Robert had said it would be. She approached the stall and started looking through the books, running her fingers across their spines, pulling one out from time to time. After a minute, she looked up at the bookseller and cleared her throat.

"Do you have a copy of Rimbaud's *A Season in Hell*?" she asked him, keeping her voice low, wary of passersby.

"Yes," replied the bookseller. "I think I might." He hesitated, then pulled a copy of the book from the back shelf of the display and handed it to her. She opened it and lifted it to her nose. The paper gave off a sweet, sharp odor like sliced onions. She turned the pages until she found the card and long, thin strip of photographs tucked tight into the binding. She dislodged them with her fingernail, slid them into her palm and from there into the pocket of her jacket. She closed the book and handed it back.

"Thank you, but I'm after an earlier edition," she said, repeating the coded phrase Robert had taught her.

The man nodded and placed the book back on the shelf. As Lucie walked away, she glanced back to see the bookseller raise his hand to his cap and pull it around till the peak faced forward.

When she got back to her room, Lucie locked the door and placed the card and photographs on the small desk below the window. Robert had helped Aline create a new appearance for her new identity. The new Aline looked completely different. She wasn't wearing glasses and her long bangs were pulled back from her face, pinned into a tight roll on the top of her head. Her lips were darkened with lipstick and she wore pearl earrings and a cardigan with a lace collar. This new feminine version of her friend was almost unrecognizable, and of course that was the aim. Lucie brought the images close to her face. Without her glasses, Aline's eyes were even more serious, more focused.

Lucie dipped her pen into the bottle of ink and filled in the blank identity card:

Family name: ROUSSEL
First name: Edith
Born: 1 October 1921
Place: Vitry-le-François, Department of la Marne

She cut one of the photographs from the strip and turned it over, then took a clove of garlic and crushed it on a plate. She spread a thin layer of the sticky juice carefully over the back of the photograph, positioned it over the top right-hand corner of the stiff piece of card, and pressed it down, her fingertips on either side of Aline's new face. The photo held perfectly, just as Robert had said, but would be easy to remove if Aline needed to change it in the future. From the back of the drawer Lucie took an inkpad and the linoleum stamp she'd made a few weeks earlier. She looked at it again, trying to detect any imperfection in the tiny letters. She knew the authorities were desperate to stop the flow of false papers. One small mistake could result in

Aline's arrest. If that happened, there'd be no chance of rescuing her. She was a marked woman, a Jewish detainee who'd escaped. And she knew the Germans didn't tolerate being made fools of in this way. If Aline were recaptured, they'd show no mercy.

Lucie pressed the stamp into the inkpad, positioned it above the edge of the photo, and pushed it down evenly. Once the ink dried, she folded the identity card in two and slid it into an inside pocket of her satchel. She was to drop it at the bookstall the next day.

***

Later that afternoon, she went to the Hirschs' apartment building to retrieve the hidden money. When the concierge opened the door of her lodge and recognized Lucie, she ushered her inside and closed the door before speaking.

"Those poor people," she said. "I heard what happened to Dr. Hirsch. Do you know if she's all right?"

Lucie shook her head. "I'm afraid not," she said. "But Aline is safe."

"Thank God for that," said the concierge. "I was so worried when they arrived to seal up the apartment."

"Who?" asked Lucie.

"The Germans. They came yesterday and put a seal on the door, and then later in the afternoon the apartment was emptied. Everything was removed. *Everything.* They left the key with me once they'd finished. I went and looked inside. There's not a scrap left."

"What about in the kitchen?" asked Lucie, hoping desperately they wouldn't have bothered to take a jar of lentils.

"Everything's gone," repeated the concierge. "The plates, cups, dishcloths. They even took the lightbulbs from the ceiling and the food from the pantry."

32

ONCE ALINE HAD the identity card, she was to wait for Robert to tell her it was safe, then leave immediately. But Lucie didn't know how she would manage without money. Now that the free zone no longer existed, it was even more dangerous and expensive to travel south. There was so much occupied territory to cross, so many chances she'd be stopped and checked, or denounced. And if all went to plan Aline would have her sisters with her too. Robert had said people smugglers were charging higher and higher rates, or taking money from people only to hand them over to the French militia for a supplementary payment. He'd advised her to try to get to Spain. Who knew how much she'd need to pay someone to guide her and her two sisters over the Pyrenees? How many bribes would she have to pay the people she'd be relying on to house and transport them throughout their journey? Aline would need money—but with the Germans having stripped her family of anything of value, there was no way to raise it. Lucie would gladly give her any money she had, but what she earned was hardly enough. Then Lucie recalled the trunk in her uncle's cellar. The money Aline could make from selling just a few of the items might be the difference between freedom and capture.

* * *

The next morning, Lucie woke at five and crept down to the apartment. From Gérard's room came the sound of his snoring. On the hook behind the front door hung his work jacket. Her heart thumped as she slid her hand into the pocket and removed the two keys.

In the cellar, she tried first one and then the other in the lock of her uncle's second storage room. When she opened the trunk, it seemed to her that there were fewer objects than there had been previously. She hurried to choose the items she thought looked most expensive but were small enough for Aline to carry easily. From the jewelry box at the bottom of the trunk, she took three gold necklaces, a pair of sapphire earrings, and a gold signet ring.

Once she'd returned the keys to the pocket of Gérard's jacket, she went up to her room, laid everything on a handkerchief, and tied the corners together into a small, tight bundle. She scribbled a quick note to Aline telling her about the emptied apartment and asking her to be in the cinema at four o'clock that afternoon. Although she knew it was risky to meet in a public place, it was the only way she could think to give her friend the jewelry.

* * *

That afternoon, Lucie walked to the cinema, hoping Aline had received the message she'd left along with the identity card at the bookstall and that she'd come despite the possible risk of meeting face-to-face. After Simone's arrest, Lucie had told Philippe she would no longer work selling tickets. It was too dangerous for the Volunteers of Liberty to continue passing messages in any case. All ties to Aline were potential risks.

In the foyer, the curtains of the ticket booth were drawn. Lucie imagined Josette was busy in there with today's visitor. She entered the cinema through the left-hand door and found Aline seated in the back row, her eyes fixed on the screen. Aline didn't make the slightest movement to acknowledge her when Lucie sat beside her.

Lucie silently took the bundle from her satchel and tucked it between the armrest and the outside of Aline's thigh, then slowly slid her hand away over the warm leather.

On the screen the new Clouzot film, *The Raven*, was playing. Lucie stared straight ahead, watching as a letter of denunciation fell from a funeral wreath and an angry mob pursued a nurse through the streets of a small village, her cape flapping out like huge black wings. The air in the cinema was bitter with smoke and perspiration. Lucie was exhausted. The ache that had started at the top of her skull earlier that afternoon had seeped down behind her eyes. She wanted to sink down into the leather chair, rest her head on Aline's shoulder, close her eyes, and sleep away the dread of the previous days and nights. But she knew it wasn't wise to stay too long. She could sense her friend's unease in her stiff-backed posture. Lucie wished she could look Aline in the face, smile at her, tell her everything would be all right. But she knew it was impossible. She kept her eyes on the screen, seeing only blurred and shifting forms. She let a minute pass, then slowly stood and slid past her friend into the aisle, the back of her calves brushing against Aline's knees. She walked quickly towards the exit, biting her tongue to hold in her tears, and left without a glance in her friend's direction. She knew this might be the last time she ever saw her.

***

When she got home, Lucie told Yvonne she wasn't feeling well and that she wouldn't be coming down for dinner that evening. She sat at her desk, holding the stamp that she'd spent so many hours perfecting. She studied the letters, each one less than a quarter of an inch high. How close would someone have to bring those letters to their eyes to see the tiny imperfections? Would anyone be determined enough to look for them? She took the spare photographs of Aline from the desk drawer and gazed at them, trying to see beyond the serious expression to the earnest young student she'd first met just three years before. Aline's features seemed to have aged a decade in the last few months. There were darkened smudges beneath her eyes like brushstrokes of Indian ink. Lucie closed her eyes and saw her friend's face at the Sorbonne that day in November of the first year of occupation, excited about the student demonstration, full of optimistic fervor.

She lay down on her bed, trying to hold that image in her mind, as if it might somehow keep Aline safe. Through the open window she heard the pigeons coming and going from the roof, their hard, dry claws clicking against the zinc gutters. The church bells struck six. Aline must have left for the south by now, bound for a vague elsewhere, an uncertain, elusive safety.

* * *

She was woken an hour later by the sound of her name, a soft but urgent whispering. She sat up and listened, unsure if it was simply the echo of a dream. But the voice was real, whispered through the keyhole of her bedroom door. As soon as she heard it again, she knew it was Aline. She hurried to let her in and shut the door quickly behind her, hoping no one had seen her on the stairs. She closed the curtains before turning on the small desk lamp and draping a blue scarf over it to dim its light. Aline sat on the bed, her face crisp with agitation.

"I thought you'd already left," said Lucie, sitting down beside her. "Has something happened?"

Aline put her hand into the pocket of her jacket and pulled out the signet ring Lucie had wrapped in the handkerchief that morning.

"Where did you get this?" she asked, holding it up to her friend's face. Lucie looked at it—a beautiful gold ring, engraved with oak leaves on the band, the initials G.H. at its center.

"I took it from a trunk my uncle has down in the cellar," said Lucie. "It's his. They're his initials—Gérard Hébert."

"It's not his," said Aline. "It belonged to my father. My grandfather engraved it."

"Are you sure? It could have been done by someone else."

"No. I know this ring. My grandfather gave it to Papa for his thirtieth birthday. He engraved his initials on it. My father's name is Gabriel. Gabriel Hirsch."

She pulled Lucie over to the desk, held the ring beneath the lamp, and angled it so that the light shone on the inside surface. Lucie leaned down and looked closely at the image engraved on the underside of the ring. It was a pair of stag's antlers.

"I don't understand," said Lucie. "How did my uncle get it?"

"He stole it," said Aline, her voice cracking with anger. "He must have been the one who emptied our apartment."

"What?" exclaimed Lucie. "How could he do such a thing?"

"He's not the only one. I heard all about it at Lévitan. The people from the moving companies steal, the French police steal, the Germans steal. Even concierges and neighbors do. As soon as the Jewish occupants of an apartment are arrested, the scavengers are everywhere."

"He has a lot more things in the cellar," Lucie said. "I thought they belonged to his dead wife. They must all be stolen." She shook her head, the air escaping from her lungs. "I can't believe it. People like your mother are risking their lives, smuggling babies out of a hospital to keep them from being sent away, while he steals from these same people, enriches himself with the property of deported Jews." She clenched her fists. "God, I hate him."

Lucie froze as they heard a shuffling noise outside the door. Aline raised her index finger to her lips. She waited until they heard footsteps moving away along the corridor.

"Do you know the people in the rooms next door?" she whispered.

"Most of them are empty," said Lucie. "There's a young mother and her child at the end of the hall. I haven't seen anyone else."

Aline put her ear to the door, then knelt and peered through the keyhole. She turned towards Lucie. "I can't see anyone."

They sat back down together on the bed.

"What are you going to do?" asked Aline.

"What can I do?"

"Confront him. Tell him you know everything."

"What good will that do?"

"You could denounce him to the Gestapo."

"I can't," said Lucie. "There are some people you can't deal with, no matter what."

Aline looked into her eyes and nodded. "I understand," she said. She held Lucie's arms and kissed her on both cheeks. "I have to go. My train's leaving at eight."

"How will I know if you've made it to Spain?"

"I'll find a way to get a message to you."

Lucie followed her to the landing and watched as she descended into the darkness of the stairwell.

When she heard the latch on the wooden entry doors click shut, she returned to her room and looked out the window to the street below. As Aline crossed to the other side of the street, Lucie saw a man standing a little further along, watching as she walked away. He then headed for the cafe directly across the road. As he passed under the dim light cast by the veiled streetlamp, she saw that he was wearing a mustard-and-black-checked cap.

33

"IS GÉRARD HERE?" Lucie asked, rushing into the apartment down-stairs.

"No. He went down to the cellar about ten minutes ago to fetch some apples. He said he was going to take some up to you as well."

"He didn't bring me any apples," said Lucie. Then she remembered the noise they'd heard outside her door a few minutes earlier. It must have been her uncle.

"Aline was in my room," she said, her thoughts racing. "Those things Gérard has in the trunk in the cellar didn't belong to his wife—he stole them from the Jewish people whose apartments he's been emptying."

"How do you know?" asked Yvonne.

"There was a ring that belonged to Aline's father. She recognized it. I think Gérard heard us talking in my room. When Aline left just now, I saw him in the street. He watched her leave and then went into the cafe over the road."

"Why?" she asked. "You don't think he'd denounce her?"

Lucie gazed out of the window towards the empty street. "I don't know," she said, "but I can't wait to find out. I've got to warn her."

As Lucie opened the front door, she gasped and stumbled back. Gérard was standing on the landing. He looked just as shocked to see her.

Yvonne linked her arm through Lucie's. "We know what you've been doing," she said. "We know you've been stealing from the apartments you empty."

Gérard's face froze. "For Christ's sake, be quiet," he whispered. "Are you crazy?" He pushed past them into the apartment, pulling the door closed behind him.

"It's disgusting," said Lucie. "Those things belonged to Jewish families. Do you have any idea what's happening to those people? Do you care at all?"

"You make it sound like I'm the one deporting them," said Gérard. "It's not my fault they're being sent away. The Germans are responsible. What the hell do you think I can do about it?"

"So you might as well profit from it?" replied Yvonne. "You can't stand the thought of others being more successful than you. That's what this is really about. You've always wanted to be the big, important man. But you're not—you're a pitiful little rat who's incapable of thinking of anyone but himself."

Gérard pointed his index finger at Yvonne's throat. "For your information, I was stealing from the Germans to show them that they're not as clever as they think. And the money wasn't for me; it was to pay to get you two down to Gibraltar and from there to England. That's what you wanted, wasn't it? That's why I took those things. To save the two of you."

"I don't want you to save me," Lucie hissed. "I don't want anything to do with you. My place is here. You've been spying on Aline, haven't you? Is that why you went to the cafe just now? Telephoning your militia friends to tell them about the Jewish girl who's not wearing her star?"

Gérard glared at her. "That girl is a danger to us all. I know you've been meeting her in secret. I denounced her because she's an enemy of France. They're all dupes of foreign powers working against the greater good. And they're drawing innocent people into their net."

"Innocent people?" shouted Lucie. "Where was your concern for innocent people when children and babies were being rounded up and sent away with the help of your precious Pétain and his cronies?"

"Why should I care about those people's children?" snapped Gérard. "Did anyone care about my child?"

"What the hell are you talking about?" replied Yvonne. "What does the death of your daughter have to do with this? Why should these poor children pay?"

"Someone has to," said Gérard. "I fought for my country and look at the situation I was left in when my wife died. Having to care for a baby on my own. No family to help me. No money. A miserable apartment. Now it's their turn to suffer. All those Jews who took our jobs and our money. It's not going to help them now, is it?"

"You're a sick man," said Yvonne. "If you can't see how monstrous your thoughts are, there's nothing I can say that will make any difference."

Gérard looked down at Lucie, the bare bulb above his head throwing dark shadows beneath his eyes. "Is it sick to want to protect my family?" he asked, his jaw suddenly slack. "I couldn't save my own daughter, but I can save you."

Lucie took a step forward. "Shut up!" she screamed. "I never asked to be saved. I'm not your daughter. You're nothing to me. Now, get out of my way!"

She pushed past Gérard, flung open the door, and rushed down the stairs. As she ran along the footpath, the beat of her wooden soles echoed like gunshots in the empty street. She stopped, pulled her shoes off, and grasped them in her hands as she continued running, the pavement damp and slick against the soles of her bare feet.

As she turned the last corner and headed towards the cinema, someone seized her arm, clasped a hand over her mouth, and pulled her into a doorway. Against her ear, she felt hot breath and heard Margot's urgent whisper. "It's me." She took her hand from Lucie's mouth and signaled to her to follow. They silently made their way to the entrance of Margot's building a few doors away, skimming the walls, hidden in the shadows.

Once inside, Lucie grasped Margot's arms and asked her what had happened.

"They got her," the older woman said, her words stifled by tears.

"Who?"

"A Gestapo officer. He had two militia with him. They were waiting down the street. I spotted them from my window and ran down to try to warn her. They grabbed her before she saw me. There was nothing I could do. It all happened so fast. I'm so sorry. I tried . . ."

Lucie wanted to tell her it was all right, that she wasn't to blame, but the pain deep inside her chest radiated upwards and tightened like a belt around her throat. All she could do was look into Margot's eyes and hope she understood.

***

When Lucie arrived home, her mother was waiting outside her room. Once they were inside, Lucie told her about Aline's arrest. When Yvonne took her in her arms, Lucie slumped as if all the air had been sucked from her body.

"I'm so sorry," whispered Yvonne.

The tears that Lucie had been holding in began to flow. She sobbed until her head felt filled with mud. Suddenly, she remembered something she'd said to Aline when they were in her room.

"Maman, I think Gérard might have heard me talking about the baby smuggling at the hospital. He'll inform the Gestapo, I'm sure. We have to stop him."

Yvonne nodded slowly, took Lucie's face between her hands and looked her in the eye. "He's been stealing from the Germans," she whispered. "I'll denounce him."

***

They decided to go to the central police headquarters on the Île de la Cité. Lucie knew it was risky. They didn't know if the police could be trusted. And what would Gérard do once he was cornered? Did he know about the tracts, about the forged papers? He might use that information against her if he did. She didn't care. She wasn't turning back.

It was after nine when they walked out onto the street and made their way towards the river. A soft drizzle was falling and the crescent moon gave off little light. All the same, they decided it was safer to go down to the quay, where the high walls cast thick shadows. They walked quickly and without speaking until they passed the towers of Notre-Dame. As they prepared to climb back up to the street to cross the river, Lucie looked up and saw Gérard standing at the top of the steps. He started down towards them, clasping the thin metal handrail. Yvonne took Lucie's arm and they hurried towards the next flight of stairs, a hundred meters further along. Gérard's footsteps thudded behind them. He was walking quickly, his lopsided gait beating a rhythm like a heartbeat on the slippery paving stones.

As they reached the bottom of the stairs, Yvonne stopped. She pushed Lucie away and turned to wait for Gérard.

"So, this is what it's come to," he said, panting. "You'd denounce your own brother to the Germans. After what they did to me in the last war. After all my sacrifices."

Yvonne shook her head. "You're no longer my brother. You're a stranger to me now."

Gérard's neck stiffened. "Well, I call your bluff, Yvonne. You're not capable of carrying out your threats. You'd never stoop so low. It's beneath you and your fine principles."

"Just watch me," she replied. She turned to go. Lucie could see that she was shaken.

"Come on, Maman," she said, taking Yvonne by the hand and pulling her away. They had only gone ten meters or so when she heard Gérard running to catch up with them. He grabbed Yvonne by the shoulders, turning her to face him.

"You don't know what you're doing," he said, shaking her forcefully with each word. "You're crazy."

Yvonne struggled to free herself. "I'm not a little girl anymore, Gérard. You can't control me."

He released her shoulders and breathed in slowly. For one brief moment Lucie thought he'd given up, but instead he clasped his hand over Yvonne's mouth and nose, his other hand on the back of her head. Lucie screamed, terrified, as she watched Yvonne twist, her back arched, her eyes wide with fear. Without stopping to think, Lucie charged towards Gérard, a low growl rising from her gut. Gérard turned his head at the sound, just as Lucie rammed her shoulder into his chest. He staggered backwards, his ankle turning on a crooked cobblestone. He reached out and grabbed Lucie's arm as he fell, his legs giving way, pulling Lucie down with him. As his head hit the ground, she heard the cracking of his skull like a tremor through the cobblestones. She pushed herself up and stumbled back. She looked down at his face, clearly visible against the dark ground in the pale blue lamplight. His eyes were half open, his jaw slack. Blood was starting to flow from beneath his head, spreading across the wet stones and seeping into the gaps between them.

"Oh God," she said, turning to Yvonne. Her mother was standing with her arms by her side, her mouth wide open in a soundless wail. Lucie leaned down and brought her ear close to Gérard's pale lips. His breathing was fast and ragged. There was a strong smell of urine, and when she looked down at his trousers, she saw the spreading wet stain. As she stood up, Yvonne came to stand by her side and clasped her hand. Together they watched as his breathing slowed, then seemed to stop completely. Lucie felt the blood draining from her face. Her scalp pricked and her head was light. Yvonne turned to her and whispered, "Help me."

Lucie began to move as if in a dream. They took one of Gérard's arms each and dragged him towards the river. A flight of stone steps led into the water, moss-covered and smooth. They carefully descended, tugging Gérard behind them, his shoes making a muffled thud on each narrow step. Once they were at the bottom, they twisted his body around, and pushed him over the edge. As his legs touched the cold water, he gasped, his eyes opening wide, the reflection of the moon superimposed on the pale gray irises. Yvonne screamed as Gérard's hand closed around her elbow, pulling her down as his body slipped further into the water. Lucie tried to pry his fingers away, but his grip was too tight. Yvonne threw herself backwards, struggling to stay on the step. Before her thoughts could form, Lucie leaned over and placed both hands on Gérard's throat, pushing downwards until his staring face was all that remained above the water. As she pushed harder, it sank below the surface. His grip on Yvonne's arm loosened and his body convulsed, sending water splashing against the side of the steps. When he finally stopped moving, she took her hands from his throat, then pushed his body away from the bank. She watched as it floated out towards the middle of the river and was sucked down below the surface. She put her arm around Yvonne's waist and pulled her up the steps. Together they stumbled towards the high wall. Lucie fell back against the cold damp stones, shivering and gulping down mouthfuls of sweaty river air. The skin of her scalp pulled tight and cold. A voice in her head screamed over and over, *What have you done? What have you done?*

***

Back in the apartment, neither of them spoke. Yvonne took off her damp clothes and got into bed. Lucie went to the bathroom and filled the tub. She took the red bar of carbolic soap, lowered herself into the tepid water, and scrubbed every inch of her skin. She lifted her hands, pressed her wrinkled palms against her face. She closed her eyes and breathed in. Through the stinging, tarry odor of the soap, she still smelled the urine. She took her hands from her face, but kept her eyes shut tight. She pressed her palms over her ears, but it made no difference. She could still hear the crack of Gérard's skull, still see his bulging eyes as they sank below the surface of the Seine.

34

THE NEXT MORNING, Lucie sat at the dining table staring out the window, her eyes fixed above the rooftops on the pale gray autumn sky. She hadn't eaten breakfast, but her stomach was full, heavy with bile. She wondered how long it would take for Gérard's body to be found, how long it would take for the police to discover what she and Yvonne had done. She tried not to think about what her life would become then; destroyed like so many others by this war.

She heard Yvonne get out of bed and go to the bathroom. When she came out, she'd washed, but was still in her nightdress. She lay on the couch, pulled a blanket up to her chin, and closed her eyes.

Lucie went to the kitchen and made a pot of tea. She poured two cups and brought them to the living room. Putting them on the side table, she sat on the floor next to the couch. Yvonne turned towards her, but didn't speak. Lucie placed her hand on Yvonne's forehead. It was hot and her eyes shone with fever. She went to the bathroom and wet a facecloth. As she placed it on Yvonne's forehead, the doorbell rang. Yvonne pushed herself up and stared at the front door.

"Should I answer?" whispered Lucie.

Yvonne hesitated for a few seconds, then nodded.

When Lucie opened the door, Émile was standing there, his hands behind his back. He didn't say hello.

Questions clattered through Lucie's mind. Why was he here? Was he supposed to work with Gérard today? What did he know?

He spoke, not looking at her face. "Is your uncle here?" he asked.

"No, he's not," she replied, then turned away, looking back at Yvonne in alarm. They hadn't yet discussed how they'd explain Gérard's absence. Lucie struggled to calm the trembling that had begun in the base of her skull and was seeping through her bottom jaw.

Yvonne pushed herself up against the arm of the couch, her face somber, but calm. "He's missing," she said.

Émile's eyes shifted past Lucie to her mother.

"We think he might have been in Rouen picking something up on the day of the last bombing," continued Yvonne. "We haven't heard from him since. The police are trying to help, but they have no news for the moment."

Émile frowned. "I'm sorry to hear that." He shifted his weight from one foot to the other. "I hope they find him soon."

Yvonne nodded and smoothed the blanket over her thighs.

"I came to say I won't be able to work for Monsieur Hébert anymore. I'm leaving for Germany. Compulsory work service."

"Oh, I see," said Yvonne.

"I came to drop this off." He took a step forward and handed Lucie a work jacket with the name of Gérard's company on the breast pocket.

"Thank you," she said as she took it from him. She hesitated, then hung it on a hook in the entry. She took hold of the edge of the door, pushing it forward an inch or two, hoping he would leave. Instead he remained where he was, sucking on his bottom lip, turning the skin below it red. After several seconds, he took his other hand from behind his back and held out a mustard-and-black-checked cap.

"I found this down on the riverbank," he said. "I think your uncle might have lost it."

Lucie stared at it, speechless. It must have fallen from Gérard's head when he fell. Why hadn't she realized? Why hadn't she thought to look for it?

From the corner of her eye, she saw Yvonne push the blanket from her knees, stand up, and take a few steps towards Émile. "That's not his cap," she said. "He was wearing his when he left for Rouen."

"Oh," said Émile. He turned the cap over in his hand, kneading the brim between his fingers, his eyes wandering across the satin lining. From where she stood, Lucie could see the label that was sewn there. Beneath an image of a ram were the words *100% Merino Wool*. In capital letters along the top were three small words: *HANDMADE IN AUSTRALIA.*

Émile lifted his gaze from the label and looked at Lucie. She stared back, trying to repress the tremor in her jaw. Surely he knew they were lying. Surely he knew what they'd done—knew about Gérard, about Aline, about everything. He'd betray them, she realized, and there was nothing she could say that would change his mind.

Émile glanced back down at the cap. "Well, you can have it," he said. He reached up and hung it on a hook on the wall inches from Lucie's head. Clearing his throat, he looked from Lucie to Yvonne. "I'm sorry for your loss," he said, then turned and left.

As she closed the door behind him, Lucie's head began to spin and her vision filled with black. She leaned against the wall and slid down to the floor. "Why did he give it back?" she asked, as the blackness started to retreat. "He knew it was Gérard's. Why didn't he turn us in?"

Yvonne shook her head. "I don't know," she said. "I no longer try to understand why people do the things they do."

***

When Lucie went to see Margot later that morning to tell her what had happened, she told Lucie they needed to declare Gérard missing straightaway. She offered to accompany Yvonne and Lucie to the police station to make a statement.

It was another three days before a police officer arrived at their door to inform Yvonne that they'd found Gérard's body washed up a kilometer or so downstream of the Eiffel Tower.

"I'm sorry to have to give you this tragic news, Madame."

Yvonne nodded. Lucie could see the characteristic red blotches appearing on her throat.

"The coroner will conduct an autopsy, but at first glance it appears that your brother was struck on the back of the head."

Lucie took hold of Yvonne's hand and squeezed it tight.

"And I'm afraid I have some more news that might come as a shock to you and your daughter." He paused and clasped his hands behind his back. "We discovered that Monsieur Hébert had been selling stolen goods on the black market, items he was supposed to be transporting for the Germans. We believe he was selling them in Normandy so that there was less chance of them being traced. In any case, we can be fairly sure he would have been dealing with some very dangerous characters. I'm afraid that's most likely what brought him undone."

Yvonne took a deep breath in before speaking. "What will happen now?"

"There'll be a formal investigation to try to find the culprit, but I have to warn you: there are so many cases of this type these days and there is so little evidence. It's highly likely the perpetrator won't be found, I'm afraid."

***

When the tribunal sat a fortnight later to determine the circumstances of Gérard's death, in the absence of sufficient evidence they found it to be death by misadventure.

The following Monday, Yvonne was contacted by a notary with whom Gérard had lodged his will. He confirmed that her brother had left all his worldly goods to her.

1944

35

THE FOURTH WINTER under occupation crept quietly in. Lucie moved out of her room and back into the apartment with Yvonne. On New Year's Day they went out together and walked along the Seine. The streets were almost empty, all the shops closed. After so many years of hoping and waiting, it felt like Paris was exhausted; like she'd lain down and said, *I'm tired, I need to rest.* Lucie tried to recall Samuel's plea about the need for hope, but his words were no longer clear in her mind, their urgency blurred and faded. How was she expected to hold on to hope when so many of those who'd given her hope were gone? Hope couldn't stand up to so much sorrow, so many secrets, the principles she'd compromised, the dark and terrible thing she'd done.

As they crossed the Pont du Carrousel opposite the Louvre, Lucie saw a German soldier on the riverbank below. A small group of ragged children hung back at a distance, watching him as he advanced. His gait was unsteady, as if he might be drunk. Lucie had seen several soldiers starting to show signs of distress in the last few weeks. More and more of them were being transferred east in the desperate fight to stem the advance of Russian troops. It wasn't difficult to imagine how the prospect of an interminable winter on the Eastern Front would drive them to despair. The reports of German losses on the BBC made it clear that a transfer there was as good as a death sentence for these men.

The soldier slumped down by the edge of the quay, his legs dangling over the water. One of the children, a boy of about eleven or twelve, ventured a little closer. The soldier noticed him and yelled out something in German. The boy stopped and picked up a small bare branch lying at the foot of a tree. He dragged the tip along the cobblestones, tracing a circle around his feet. The German muttered to himself and took off his cap. He folded it and rested his head on it as he lay down. He removed his pistol from its holster and waved it in the air above him. The young boy crouched at the base of the tree and watched, his arms around the trunk, the other children huddled together at the foot of the bridge.

Overhead, a group of swans was coming in to land on the river, their necks extended. The soldier turned his head to follow them as they passed, then rolled onto his side and watched them as they tucked their feet away, ducking their heads beneath the surface and raising their beaks to drink. One of the swans drifted towards the bank just below the soldier and began preening its feathers. The soldier propped himself on one elbow, swung his other arm above his body in an arc, pointed his gun at the swan, and shot. Lucie gasped as Yvonne grabbed her, her nails digging into her shoulders. The detonation sent the other swans scuttling across the surface of the water, floundering as they tried to flee. By the river's edge white feathers fluttered down onto the water and danced along the cobblestones. The bloody corpse of the swan floated upside down, bumping against the bank, its black feet splayed left and right, one of them still twitching. The soldier rolled onto his back and fumbled his gun back into its holster.

After a few seconds, the boy emerged from behind the tree, his hands covering his ears. He waited till the soldier closed his eyes, then ran towards the riverbank. He whistled to another boy, a smaller version of himself, who ran to join him. The older boy lay on his stomach and held the other by his ankles as he lowered him over the edge of the quay. As the body of the swan floated within the boy's reach, he wrapped his hands around its scaly legs. The older boy pulled his brother up until, between the two of them, they managed to hoist the whole bird out of the water. The rest of the children came running and formed a circle around them. They watched in silence as the older boy grasped the swan's neck and held it up, its head dangling backwards, its beak open. He carried it back along the riverbank, the other children following him.

As they passed below her, Lucie called out to the older boy, "What are you going to do with it?"

He looked up and grinned. "What do you think?" he called back. "We're going to have it for dinner." He hoisted it higher, its head hanging over one arm, its beak knocking against his thigh as he walked. The other children clapped and chatted excitedly, marching in time in a strange and spontaneous funeral procession. Lucie watched them go, a weary sadness in her chest. Was this what children played at now? Was this what they'd become?

***

Day after day throughout the winter, the clouds were so thick that Lucie could barely tell when the sun came up. Like the previous year, however, they were spared the heavy falls of snow. As the days lengthened, Lucie spent hours alone walking the streets she'd walked so often with Aline, her friend's absence like a shadow always in her peripheral vision, disappearing each time she turned her head to see her. In the Square du Vert-Galant, beneath the weeping willow, she closed her eyes and tried to feel her presence, but all she saw was black.

She continued to do her drawings of Paris and its people, and hid them as she walked. But she no longer knew if they served a purpose.

What message would they convey to whoever found them? *You are not alone. I see your face, your suffering.* Did people want to hear that message now? Or had the time for compassion and connection passed?

At the start of March, thousands of huge red posters appeared all over the city. Everyone saw them, talked about them. People called it *l'Affiche Rouge*—the Red Poster. It portrayed members of the "Manouchian Group." Towards the middle of the previous November, the newspapers had been filled with reports of their arrest. The police claimed they were responsible for nearly every violent act of resistance in Paris over the past six months. They were almost all of foreign origin—Polish, Italian, Hungarian, Armenian, Romanian—and most of them were said to be Jewish. At the end of February, after three months of interrogation and torture, all twenty-three were condemned to death and executed at Mont-Valérien.

Lucie knew the poster was designed to evoke fear and disgust, its deep red background like a bloodstain on the walls. At the top, in large white capitals, were the words *DES LIBÉRATEURS?* Below, dark, threatening photos of ten members of the Manouchian Group stared blankly out, unshaven and disheveled, their nationality, their hard-to-pronounce foreign surnames, their religion, and the gruesome details of their crimes stamped below.

The Germans handed out flyers in the streets, determined that their message would not go unheeded. Lucie found one lying on the footpath.

Here is the proof, the flyer stated. *If some French pillage, steal, sabotage, and kill, it's always foreigners who command them. It's always the unemployed and professional criminals who carry out the acts. It's always Jews who inspire them. It's the army of crime against France.*

When she finished reading, she tore up the flyer and threw the pieces in the gutter. She thought about how Aline would have responded. She decided she had to do something. She couldn't give up. Despite everything, she'd started to detect a tiny reawakening of hope with the big Soviet offensive in the east and the news of the German retreat. There was increasing talk of an Allied landing in France, either in the south or west.

That evening just before curfew, Lucie went out. On the corner of the rue de Rivoli, she'd noticed one of the huge red posters. She looked along the street. There was no one around. She took a black pastel from her pocket. For the first time since Aline's arrest, she felt a sense of purpose. This was the first action she'd taken since that day, the first where she was completely on her own. Under the names of the men, she hastily scribbled four words—*Morts pour la France*—the words engraved on the monument that stood in every town and village in the country to honor the memory of fallen French soldiers. The authorities might want to portray these men as criminals, but she saw the true value of their actions.

36

ONE FRIDAY IN late April, Lucie and Yvonne woke to the news of a bombing in the eighteenth arrondissement. It had started before midnight and continued for almost three hours. The Allied bombers had apparently been targeting the rail yards at La Chapelle, but as was so often the case, residential areas nearby had also been destroyed. The radio bulletin spoke of over six hundred dead. Lucie tried to summon the sorrow she knew she should be feeling. But there'd been so many deaths to mourn. Though she was ashamed to acknowledge it, this felt like just another bombing, another inevitable tragedy. What made her angry was the realization that it was always the people in the poorer areas who suffered most—those who had no choice but to live next to the factories and train yards that were the targets of the Allied bombing raids. She knew the attacks were necessary, that each one was preparing for the Allied arrival in the north, but that didn't stop her from wishing for them to end, for the long-promised invasion to begin.

In the hot dry days of May, the atmosphere in the capital vacillated between anger at the deaths caused by the Allies and excitement at the prospect of their impending arrival. When the news finally came in the first days of June that they had landed in Normandy, it felt like the entire population released the breath it had been holding for the last four years.

Yvonne and Lucie spent the long summer days with Margot, the three of them drinking the iced tea that Margot made with leftover tea leaves and eating preserved fruit from the cellar. In the evenings, they opened the windows wide to capture the cool dampness that rose up from the river. They sat by the radio to follow the slow advance of Allied troops from the west, reciting the names of the towns as they were retaken one by one. Cherbourg, Caen, Saint-Lô.

And then August came with deadly battles in Brittany—Brest, Saint-Nazaire, Saint-Malo, Lorient. More towns were liberated. Rennes, Chartres, Orléans, Le Mans. On the western edge of Paris, explosions lit up the night sky. The stifling August air was thickened by the smoke that drifted in and settled on the city.

In the streets, life continued in slow motion. Train drivers, police officers, and postmen went on strike. The Métro was no longer running. Supplies in the shops ran low with food supply routes cut off. No official newspapers were published and Radio Paris was off the air. Lucie and Yvonne listened to the coded messages broadcast by Radio Londres and the rumors winding through the food lines. They watched the skies, waiting for a sign. The streets were tense, with more and more German patrols, armored vehicles covered in branches for camouflage, posters threatening execution for any act of resistance or support for the Allies. No one knew whether the occupying forces were planning to retreat or fight to keep the capital.

New posters appeared on the walls: a call to arms by the FFI—the French Forces of the Interior—proclaiming it was time for the entire population to rise up. They implored police, gendarmes, and prison guards to join the fight for liberation. The first French flags were hoisted above the police headquarters and the town hall. Before long Lucie saw them appear on balconies and shopfronts.

In the final days of August, as the Allied troops approached the western outskirts of the city, Paris was transformed into a battleground. Early one morning, Lucie and Yvonne were woken by the sound of gunshots. They ran to the window and saw people running through the streets with pistols, solitary German soldiers scurrying for cover. Civilians crouched behind walls of sandbags and fired from windows, pointing rifles and handguns, reclaiming Paris street by street from the German soldiers who were holding on, refusing to believe in the crumbling of their empire. Lucie imagined Robert was among them. She wondered if Aline would have been there too, fighting at his side.

Many German troops were fleeing, taking any means of transport they could find. They crowded onto jeeps and other military vehicles. When there were none left to take, they stole bicycles or fled on foot. Burnt-out trucks hit by grenades stood black and smoking in the streets. Captured German tanks were marked in white paint with the Cross of Lorraine, the symbol of the Free French Forces. Barricades of cobblestones, felled trees, and metal grates blocked the streets. Lucie sheltered with Yvonne in the apartment, watching armed men and women running through the streets. Dead bodies lay where they fell. Red Cross nurses ran with white flags held high to retrieve the injured.

At midnight on the twenty-fourth of August, the bells of Notre-Dame rang out for the first time since the beginning of the German occupation. As day broke, Margot arrived at the apartment on the rue de Sévigné. Together, the three women joined thousands of Parisians heading for the Champs-Élysées. Convoys of military vehicles rumbled through the streets again as they had four years earlier. This time, though, they were greeted with tears of joy. Barricades were torn apart and the German signs were pulled down and burned in the street or carried away as trophies.

As Lucie watched the French and Allied soldiers parading through the streets, she wept for joy at the liberation of this beautiful city. The love she had for it was more than for the beauty of its monuments. She loved Paris as if it were a living being. And the city's liberation gave her hope that she'd be reunited with Aline. In the optimism of this August day, she wanted to believe it would be soon, but her gut ached with fear. Even though Paris was free, it might be many months before the Allies managed to push through the resistance of the remaining German troops and liberate the rest of the occupied territory. And it would only be then that Aline and all those others who'd been sent away might be freed and finally return home.

At seven in the evening, Lucie, Yvonne, and Margot joined the huge crowd gathered in front of the Hôtel de Ville to hear General de Gaulle speak. He was surrounded by reporters holding microphones and hundreds of others who'd pushed through the throng to be near him. He towered above them all, his face clearly visible above a sea of heads as he began to speak.

"Why do you wish us to hide the emotion which seizes us all, men and women, who are here, at home, in Paris that stood up to liberate itself and that succeeded in doing so with its own hands? No! We will not hide this deep and sacred emotion. These are minutes which go beyond each of our poor lives. Paris! Paris outraged! Paris broken! Paris martyred! But Paris liberated! Liberated by itself, liberated by its people with the help of the French armies, with the support and the help of all France, of the France that fights, of the only France, of the real France, of the eternal France!"

As Lucie listened to him so proudly asserting that Paris had been liberated by the whole of France, she found it difficult to share in his sense of pride. She knew why he needed to make that claim, understood that it was necessary to rebuild a sense of French unity, but she felt it was dishonest to do so. She'd seen so much in the last four years, been so disillusioned, come to understand so many sides of human nature. She couldn't help but think that, in order to heal the nation and focus on the future, the truth that he was turning away from, the shame of collaboration, was too big a truth to remain hidden in the shadows.

* * *

After the first days of jubilation at their reclaimed freedom, the mood in Paris began to turn. Anger and a desire for revenge took hold. Those known to have collaborated were arrested or even summarily executed. Women deemed guilty of "horizontal collaboration" with German soldiers were dragged from their apartments and out into the streets, crowds assembling in squares to see them punished.

Lucie was on her way to visit Margot when she saw her former colleague from the cinema, Josette, being pulled along the street by two men. They had stripped her, leaving her wearing just a thin cotton slip. Swastikas had been daubed in black paint on her forehead and cheeks, the word *pute*—whore—scrawled across her chest. Lucie followed from a distance, horrified, as they led Josette towards the Place Saint-Michel, more and more people joining to view the sickening show. When they arrived, they pushed her down onto a wooden crate, a group of men standing tall around her, smiling, some brandishing rifles. Lucie wanted to yell out, to ask them where they'd been all these years, when they'd become so morally upright. Had they been resistants all along, or had they been just as guilty as Josette, just as compromised, just as opportunistic? Why were they so intent on punishing a woman? What were they trying to divert attention from?

One man in a white coat pulled on Josette's hair till it came loose from the pins that were holding it in place. He held it up above her head and hacked away with a large pair of scissors. The crowd that had gathered cheered as he brandished a long thick lock of blond hair high in the air like a severed head, then threw it to the ground. Another man handed him a pair of barber's shears and he ran them across her scalp. As the locks of hair tumbled over her bare shoulders and onto the ground, women cheered and children stared, fingering the corners of their open mouths. When the barber finished, Josette was pulled back to her feet. Ragged tufts remained here and there on her bare scalp. Three men held her by the arms and pushed her forward through the crowd. There were so many people lurching, jeering, spitting, laughing. Lucie wished she could call out to her, to tell her she was sorry for what was happening, but she was too afraid to acknowledge that she knew her. As Josette passed closer, she caught Lucie's eye. She raised her hand to wipe away a tear, then averted her gaze. As she was swallowed by the crowd, Lucie hoped that Josette had recognized her, that she'd seen one compassionate face amid so much contempt and spite. Lucie desperately wanted to hold out hope that a nobler France would re-emerge in time. She couldn't help but fear, though, that the mob she saw around her was a sign of things to come.

1945

37

AS NEWS CAME through from the east that victory was close, Yvonne started talking about leaving France, going to England or maybe even returning to Australia, trying to erase the memories of what this country had become, what its people had done to one another.

"I can't leave," said Lucie. "I have to stay till the war's over and Aline comes home."

Yvonne held her hand and told her she'd wait with her as long as she needed.

They stayed on in Gérard's apartment but emptied it of all that had belonged to him. The wild boar and deer heads from his bedroom were thrown into a corner of the cellar, covered by a pile of his clothes and shoes. They traded the heavy dark furniture for just a few cheap new pieces—a small table and two chairs, a narrow settee, a slender wooden bookshelf. The apartment felt empty, purged, with room to breathe. They stripped the somber paper from the walls and painted them in white.

***

On the first warm day of spring, Yvonne opened the tall windows and sat on the narrow balcony. She lined up three powdered milk tins on a wooden apple crate and filled them with soil that she'd filched from a building site on the Quai de l'Hôtel de Ville.

"What are you planting?" asked Lucie, pulling a chair out and sitting next to her.

"Heather," said Yvonne. "Here, you do one." She handed her a small plant, its roots wrapped in damp newspaper.

"It's pretty," said Lucie.

"The florist told me it symbolizes independence." She turned to Lucie and smiled, her eyes half closed against the morning sun.

Lucie scooped up a handful of soil and packed it into the bottom of one of the milk tins. She removed the paper from the plant's roots and placed it on top. She took another handful of soil, but held it in her hand, hesitating before she spoke.

"Have you forgiven Dad for what he did?"

Yvonne paused for a moment before replying. "I didn't live through everything that he experienced. I can't judge him for not wanting to live through it again." She picked up another plant, her eyes fixed on the delicate purple flowers. "But I can't forgive him for wanting to kill us too."

They both sat in silence for a moment. It was the first time either of them had acknowledged this truth out loud.

Lucie let the handful of soil fall into the pot. "I think maybe he wanted to save us," she said. She pressed her palms against the plant's roots. "Perhaps he knew what was coming. Perhaps he'd understood the warnings."

Yvonne lifted her head and looked out into the street. "Maybe you're right," she whispered.

***

At the end of April, the newsreels in the cinemas began to show scenes of the camps in Germany and Poland that had been liberated by the Allies. Lucie sat alone in the back row of the cinema and watched General Eisenhower visit the camp of Ohrdruf in Germany. She stared, numb with horror, as the images flickered on the screen—survivors dressed in striped outfits, heads shaved, so thin they moved like articulated puppets as they were led to ambulances, the sharp edges of their jaws and cheekbones straining beneath their skin.

Then they showed the bodies. Piled up or laid out in long rows. Naked or still dressed, mouths frozen open in silent screams, hands curled in towards rib cages. In the cinema, people turned their faces from the screen. Some got up and left. Lucie sat paralyzed in her seat, hardly able to take in what she saw.

That same week, news came that the first deportees would be returning home. They arrived by train at the Gare de l'Est and the Gare du Nord and were taken by bus to the Hôtel Lutetia in the sixth arrondissement. Margot and Yvonne accompanied Lucie and they waited alongside hundreds of family members. As the first bus arrived at the front of the hotel, Lucie saw the survivors through the windows, gray-skinned and angular, many with shaved heads or hair that had just started to regrow. Some still wore the striped uniforms of the camps. People rushed towards them, encircled them, crying, imploring, holding photos out, their arms stiff, desperation in their faces.

"Where have you come from?" they called out. "Did you see my husband there? My daughter? My son? Here's his photo. Look, please. This is him."

As the deportees shuffled through the crowd, they gazed from face to face, opening their mouths to speak, but then simply shook their heads. Lucie stood among the crowd of hopeful people trying to pick out features that resembled Aline's, but none of them looked anything like her. None of them looked like anyone she'd ever seen. The huge eyes in emaciated faces bore no resemblance to the people she saw around her in Paris. They seemed to be from another world, to have lived through something she couldn't begin to imagine. She waited as busload after busload of people arrived and were ushered into the hall to be processed by officials.

Hours later, a few of them began to reappear, washed and fed, wearing fresh clothes, holding a travel pass, a wad of francs in their hands. They stumbled out into the bright sun and made their way to the Métro station or to Le Bon Marché department store on the other side of the Boulevard Raspail. Some went no further than the small park that faced the hotel. There they sat on benches under the trees or on the cool stone base of the monumental statue. They closed their eyes and turned their faces to the sun.

***

Every day Lucie returned to the Hôtel Lutetia and every day the same parade of people was repeated. There were municipal elections happening that week and someone had commandeered the wooden boards on which information about the candidates was usually posted, setting them up in the corridor that led from the hotel entrance to the restaurant. People searching for their loved ones had covered the boards in photos and notes with any information that might help to identify their family members. All Lucie had was one of the small photos of Aline that she'd used to make her false identity card. She pinned it up among the thousands of others along with her name and address in the hope that someone who'd been in Aline's convoy or in a camp with her would recognize her from the image. Quietly she spoke her name to the people who passed in front of her, hesitant to ask anything of them. One after another they shook their heads, lowered their eyes. Sometimes they mouthed a single word: *No*, or, *Sorry.* And with each response, Lucie felt the despair taking hold, the unwilling acceptance that Aline might not return.

***

When the news came through that the papers of surrender had been signed in Reims, the bells of every church in Paris rang out. They were accompanied in their chorus by the blare of automobile horns and the cheers and singing of people gathered in the streets.

Lucie went down to the cellar and found a bottle of champagne that Gérard had put away in anticipation of this day. She and Yvonne dragged the settee in front of the open window and sat together, sipping the champagne and listening to the sounds of rejoicing that rose up from the street. Though Lucie had so often imagined celebrating this day, now that it was here, she struggled to swallow each mouthful. How could she be thankful for peace and freedom when so many people she cared about were not here to share it? She went to bed early, but couldn't sleep.

38

THROUGHOUT THE SUMMER, the numbers of people returning from the east diminished week by week. By the end of August, they'd dropped to just a handful a day. The new government reported that about seventy-six thousand Jewish men, women, and children had been deported. As far as they were able to ascertain, only about two and a half thousand were still alive when the camps were liberated.

The photo-covered boards at the Hôtel Lutetia had been removed and the family members no longer called out their loved ones' names. They stood silently in the foyer, their backs bent with the weight of dwindling hope, chins dropped down towards their chests.

On the last day of the month, Lucie returned home knowing she wouldn't go back to the hotel. She knew she had to accept what she'd so long refused to face. It was over. There was nothing more to do. Yvonne had already gone ahead to England to complete the paperwork for their return to Australia. She'd booked their passages on a ship leaving London the following Friday.

Early on Monday afternoon, Margot dropped in to say goodbye. She too was packing up and returning to England to be with her parents. She gave Lucie a full set of Winsor and Newton sable paintbrushes.

"Use them well, my dear," she said.

Lucie hugged her, sobbing against her shoulder. "I feel so guilty. I was safe here while so many millions of innocent people were murdered. I should have done more. I should have been more courageous, like Simone and Aline. And now I'm leaving them behind, without even knowing what became of them."

"You did everything you could," Margot assured her. "It's not you who's to blame. It's so many others, but certainly not you."

***

That evening, Lucie packed the last of her belongings into her suitcase. Yvonne had found someone to buy the van and he arrived at six o'clock to pick it up. After he'd left, she went down to the cellar and brought up the last two jars of preserved fruit, which she gave to Madame Maurel. They were leaving the key to the apartment with the concierge until the real estate agent they'd engaged found someone to rent it. As Lucie was turning to go, she saw Émile standing in the doorway that led from the lodge to the living area. She raised her hand in farewell. He looked at her without smiling, then turned and disappeared into the darkened room.

Back in the apartment, Lucie knelt on the floor beside her suitcase and buckled the two leather straps. She sat down on her heels and laid her hands flat on her thighs. She knew she should be feeling relief that she was finally able to leave the pain of this nation and this continent behind and return to the peace and isolation of life in Australia. She tried not to ask herself if her former countrymen would have acted the same way as the French if they too had lived for the last four and a half years under German occupation. Would they have resisted? Would they have denounced Jews? Would they have been complicit in their capture and detention? These were questions she dared not contemplate.

She was carrying her suitcase to the entrance hall when the doorbell rang. Three short impatient rings. When she opened the door, she was stunned to see Robert, out of breath after running up the stairs. He gulped in one big breath before he spoke.

"Aline's back."

For a second Lucie was sure she'd misunderstood. She took him by the shoulders. "What? Are you sure? Where is she?"

"She's here," he said. "I left her down in the entrance hall. She's very weak. I didn't want to make her climb the stairs until I was sure you were home. I thought you might have left."

Lucie ran down the stairs, not knowing what to think, what she should be preparing herself for. As she descended the final flight, she saw a woman seated on the bottom step, dressed in a navy skirt and pale blue blouse. At the sound of Lucie's footsteps, she turned her head. It was really her. It was Aline.

Lucie sank down beside her and took her friend's hand in her own before leaning forward and kissing her gently on both cheeks. She leaned back and studied the once-familiar face, now changed in so many ways.

Aline smiled, her skin—pale and blotched like curdled milk—stretching tight across her cheeks. Behind her new glasses, her eyes looked even deeper in their sockets. When she spoke, her voice was soft and weak. "I went back to my apartment. There are strangers living in it." She tried to go on, but her words caught in her throat. Lucie wrapped her arm gently around her friend's shoulder.

When Aline was finally able to speak again, Lucie was overcome by the horror of the news she shared. Samuel and Simone were both dead. After Compiègne, and then Drancy, Samuel had been sent to Auschwitz, where he'd been gassed immediately on arrival. Simone had survived the injuries she'd sustained that night in the canal, but had died on the train that was transporting her to Auschwitz.

"I don't know where my father is. I don't know if he was still being held prisoner or if he was sent to a camp too. And I haven't been able to find out where my sisters are. They were separated from my aunt and uncle, but I don't know what happened to them after that." As Lucie pulled her close, Aline began to cry. "I feel like I'm dead," she said. "I'm just waiting for my body to realize it's all over."

Neither of them spoke. They stayed there as the moon rose over the courtyard and cast a rippled bluish glow through the window and over their bodies. Lucie's mind was blank and her scalp was cold and tight. She felt like she was floating in a dark and endless sea.

Eventually, Lucie and Robert helped Aline climb the stairs to the apartment. They sat her on the settee and brought a blanket to cover her legs.

"We don't have any food here," said Lucie. "I'll go down and get something from Madame Maurel."

"It's all right," said Aline. "I'm really not hungry. They gave us a meal at the hotel this evening."

Lucie sat on the settee and put her arm around Aline's shoulder. "I'm supposed to be leaving France in two days' time," she whispered. "If you hadn't arrived today, we might never have found each other."

"Where are you going?" asked Aline.

Lucie was about to say *home*, but couldn't. The word had lost its warmth, its sense of solace.

"Back to Australia," she said instead. She cupped Aline's cheeks and looked into her eyes. "Come with us. You can apply to emigrate. Start a new life. Leave all this behind."

Aline placed her hands over Lucie's and gently pulled them away from her face. "I can't leave," she said. "They've started sending the soldiers back. My father might be home soon. And my sisters. I have to wait for them." She paused and looked down, her fingers picking at the calluses on her palms. "And if they don't return, I have to stay here to find out what happened. I have to find out where they were taken, where they died, how they died."

She glanced out the window to the darkened street. In the building opposite, lights were on in several apartments, their windows open to let the warmth of the day escape. Muffled sounds drifted into the room, carried on the cooling eddies of evening air—dishes being washed, music playing on a radio, a newborn baby crying.

"I need to stay here and believe this country is better than what it showed itself to be. That the last five years are not what France truly is."

"I'm not sure I share your belief in the goodness of this country," said Lucie. "Not anymore. I don't think I can feel good about living here." She frowned. "How can you live among these people not knowing which of them betrayed you, which of them was willing to see you, your family, every one of your people annihilated?"

Aline shook her head. "I don't know," she said. "But I'm going to do it anyway. I've got to. Someone has to stay and try."

***

The next morning, Lucie woke early. It was the fourth of September; almost exactly six years since war was declared; her twenty-second birthday. For the first time in months, she thought about her father, about the gift he'd given her before he died—the sketchpad and pencils. Although his problems had prevented him from expressing any love for her, Lucie knew it was a special gift, a meaningful gesture, despite everything.

While Aline slept, Lucie got up and walked to the living room windows. Outside, the street was still dark, the yellow glow of the streetlamp warm and reassuring. She looked at her reflection in the pane. She tried hard to see the traces of the last six years in the lines of her face, the look in her eyes. The changes were only lightly sketched on the surface of her body, far from an accurate depiction of the changes she felt inside. She fetched her sketchpad from her bag and drew a portrait of herself, not as she saw it in the window, but as she pictured her true self. She tore it out, folded it in four, and put it in the pocket of her dress.

She went out to the post office and sent a telegram to Yvonne, telling her of Aline's return and her decision to stay in Paris to help her. She hoped her mother would understand. She finished the message with two short phrases: *She has no one. Only me.*

Afterwards, she walked along the river and crossed the Pont Neuf to the Île de la Cité.

In the Square du Vert-Galant there were only a few people. She walked to the far end and sat beneath the weeping willow tree. She looked out over the Seine to the Pont des Arts, the Louvre on her right. The sun glinted off the surface of the languid river, coating the vista in a golden haze. It had rained overnight and the leaves around her shimmered in the early morning light. She reached up and ran her fingers through their glistening trails. She pulled a few together, weaving a fragile net of their thin, thread-like sprigs, then took the drawing of herself from her pocket and placed it in the cradle of leaves. She stood up and walked away, happy to leave this version of herself behind to disintegrate among the dewy leaves or be dislodged and blown into the river.

On the way home, she stopped at a bakery and bought two croissants for breakfast. When she arrived at the apartment, Aline was awake. She smiled at Lucie, her eyes not quite as empty as the night before. After they ate, Aline said she wanted to go out to get some fresh air and sunshine. She was still too weak to walk very far, so they took a vélo-taxi to the Tuileries.

When they arrived in the gardens, the sun was rising over the tops of the buildings, its rays already warm against the back of Lucie's neck. She sat with Aline by the large octagonal pond, their chairs pulled close together. Their two thin shadows stretched out before them on the pale dusty gravel.

After several minutes, Lucie turned to Aline. "I saw," she whispered. "I saw the photos, the newsreels of the camps." She looked down, her eyes heavy with shame. "If I'd known, I would have done more," she said. "I realize now that principles mean nothing in the face of such barbarity."

Aline leaned forward and looked into Lucie's eyes. "That's not true," she said. "It's precisely because we're faced with such acts that we mustn't compromise our principles."

Lucie didn't reply. She knew she'd have to tell Aline about Gérard one day, but today was not the day for such a conversation.

In the quiet heart of Paris, its millions of residents just waking up, Lucie thought about Aline's belief that her compatriots were capable of building a better future for this tortured continent. She tried to visualize the sense of hope that her friend had managed to retain despite all she'd endured, despite all she'd lost. In Lucie's mind, this faint hope took the form of a fragile thread, the finest of lines that held the past and the future together.

As they sat with the sun on their backs, the clock on the Orsay Station clicked to eight o'clock. Aline closed her eyes and leaned her head on Lucie's shoulder. Her cheek felt cool through Lucie's cotton shirt, her breath a feather on her collarbone. Lucie sat without moving, watching as the Eiffel Tower emerged slowly from the haze, its outline etched in silver by the pale morning sun.

ACKNOWLEDGMENTS

TO EMMA, MY first reader and editor of dodgy drafts, my sounding board, my always constructive critic—I can't thank you enough for your love, support, and words of wisdom. You've had to share a house with both me and this novel for the past three years . . . and all three of us survived!

To my precious family—Mum, George, Sacha, Philippe, Janine, Camille, and Sean—thank you for your patience, support, and caring. You've been hearing about this novel since it was just three lines scribbled in a notebook. Your belief in me has helped me more than you can know.

To my dear friend Fred, who bravely agreed to read the manuscript when I was full of self-doubt, thank you for your enthusiasm, your insightful comments, and endless confidence-boosting.

Thank you to my incredible friends, who are always ready to listen, console, affirm, and cheer on—Kaz, Maria, Lisa, Jules, Jess, Fred D., Steph S., Gerry. And my special thanks to Kaydo and Kaye for being an oasis of love, nurturing, and mind-restoring beauty. Thank you also to Rachel who shared her home with me and gave me a beautiful space to write in.

ACKNOWLEDGMENTS

Thank you to my fabulous writing groups and writer friends for your support and inspiration—Myf, Keren, Catherine, Glenys, Danni, Jenaya, Steph, Sophie, Sofie, Mel, Steve, Toni, Paddy, Jane, Jim, and the Class of 2016.

Much of the research for this novel was completed during a six-month residency at the Cité Internationale des Arts in Paris. I am forever grateful to the Australia Council for the Arts for this incredible opportunity. Thank you to all the artists I spent time with there—especially Mel, Lydia, and Inga. To my long-time Parisian friends—Dominique, Martine, and Chantal—thank you for your support, advice, and catch-ups.

For all their invaluable help and commitment in bringing this book to publication, I would like to thank my wonderful agent Clare Forster at Curtis Brown and the dedicated and expert team at HarperCollins—especially May Chen and Alivia Lopez.

I am grateful to Creative Victoria for a grant that allowed me to take time off to complete the final-stage development of the novel.

This novel honors the lives, loss, courage, and heroism of those whose existence was forever marked by the horrors of Nazism, especially the six million Jewish men, women, and children murdered in the Holocaust. I acknowledge those who survived and who have generously shared their memories, as well as those who helped them to avoid capture, and those who took a stand against their persecutors.

Finally, I pay tribute to all those who, today, continue to fight extremism, oppression, and injustice through their courageous acts of defiance, both large and small.

Michelle Wright is an award-winning writer who brings to life a remarkable range of characters, winning many honors, including *The Age* Short Story Award. Her collection of short stories, *Fine*, was shortlisted for the Victorian Premier's Literary Award for an Unpublished Manuscript and published in 2016.

Michelle's debut novel, *Small Acts of Defiance*, is the fruit of her deep love for Paris—her home for twelve years—as well as her decades of passion for French language, culture, and history.

In 2017, Michelle was awarded a six-month Australia Council for the Arts residency at the Cité Internationale des Arts in Paris to carry out the extensive research needed to create her vivid portrayal of life in occupied France.